LIGHT SPIRITS

LIGHT SPIRITS

Horrific Specters, Comedic Shades, and Criminous Phantasms in Vintage Periodical Ghost Stories

Edited by Chad Arment

COACHWHIP PUBLICATIONS
Greenville, Ohio

CONTENTS

AUNT ANN'S GHOST STORY
LAURENCE OLIPHANT

Blackwood's Edinburgh Magazine, 1864

On the 1st of December, fifteen years ago, I made my first appearance in a county ball-room. That I should choose the 1st of December, fifteen years later, to make my first appearance in print, is probably due to the fact that I have spent the interval in Russia. Considering how extremely fond I have always been of putting my impressions upon paper, and the voluminous correspondence with which the friends of my youth have been favoured during my long absence from England, I can only suppose that it never occurred to me to publish, because I never met a lady in my adopted home who had ventured upon so bold a measure. Moreover I feel certain that, had I hinted at the possibility of so unfeminine a proceeding to my husband—who was then an officer in the Imperial Guard—I should have increased instead of dissipated certain prejudices against the English nation, which, however, had not prevented his asking me to go with him to his own country. That I did so at the age of seventeen, is the best proof I can give that I am not constitutionally timid—a fact which I will ask my readers to bear in mind in the course of the narrative I am about to relate. I am encouraged to believe it to be worth telling from the circumstance, that no sooner did I reach my old home in England, than a cluster of children who had not existed when I left it, invaded the sanctity of my bedroom when I was lying down to rest before dinner on the day of my arrival, and insisted upon my telling them myself the ghost story, by virtue of which the name of their near relation was kept ever fresh in their memories. Those thrilling

details which I had communicated in my letters at full length
at the time had been repeated by my sister to each succeeding
nephew and niece as he or she had arrived at years of sufficient
discretion to enable his or her hair to stand on end when terrified; but the luxury of horror which Aunt Ann's story invariably
inspired was religiously kept as a great Christmas treat, and was
looked upon as quite unrivalled in its line—partly because it was
true, and partly because no other aunt in any neighbouring family
had ever had any such thing happen to her; a circumstance which
was always dwelt upon with great triumph and satisfaction when
any other children ventured either to praise their aunts or to discuss ghosts in the abstract. So in the darkening hours of a gloomy
autumn afternoon I told my own story, for I saw it would be
impossible to put it off until Christmas; and when my little audi-
ence, whose thorough knowledge of every incident did not in the
least prevent them listening with the same rapt interest each time
the story was told them, had trotted off, I thought that if they
could bear to hear it so many times, some older children might
bear to read it once. So now, as the clocks are striking midnight,
I stir the fire with a chuckle, for I have not seen a fireplace for
fifteen years, and I pull near it my comfortable arm-chair—I have
not seen what I call an arm-chair for the same time; with a fervent
blessing on "the stately homes of England," I shall proceed to give
my first experience of my dreary home in Russia.

I had been little more than a year in St Petersburg when my
husband was ordered on special service to a distant part of the
empire. As the duty he was sent to perform would, in all probability, involve a prolonged absence, it was decided that I should
be sent to a chateau which belonged to him in the Ukraine, and
there wait his return; as, however, I was utterly inexperienced in
the manners and customs of Russian country life, I was furnished
with a guide, philosopher, and friend, in the person of his sister
Olga, then a very charming *debutante,* now a very distinguished
member of the Russian *corps diplomatique.* It was no wonder, after
having turned so many heads during the winter, that her own began to swim, and that she should look forward with pleasure to the
repose of a country life, and the novel task of initiating a stranger

into its mysteries. Nor was it without a flutter of excitement that
I found myself packed into a roomy travelling carriage, contain-
ing my friend, my baby, and the nurse, and followed by two other
curiously constructed vehicles, covered with as many goods and
chattels as if we were going finally to settle in some newly inhabited colony. When I looked at the servants, bedding, and provisions
that were stowed away in and over our three cumbrous equipages,
I felt as if I was leading an exploring party, and responsible to the
Geographical Society for the results of my observations; indeed,
so vivid were the impressions which the incidents of this my first
journey through the heart of the country made upon my mind,
that I feel sure I should have produced a very good paper for an
evening meeting. But now, how monotonous does that well-known
way—with its sign-posts over dreary wastes of snow in winter,
its bottomless sloughs in spring and autumn, its clouds of dust
in summer, its tracts of deep sand, its gloomy pine forests, and
its rolling grass steppes—seem to me! How distinctly do I recall
the deserted post-stations where the horses are never forthcoming,
and how well I seem to know even the individual horses when
they do come, and can distinguish between the yamchiks who are
my friends, and those for whom I have an antipathy. As for night
quarters, there is not an inn on the whole line of road the rooms
of which I have not, at some time or other, furnished with all that
portable material which I carry with me on such occasions, and
which, if it goes on increasing, will ultimately include a pier-glass
and a piano.

How I wondered then at the rapidity with which the servants
made things comfortable, and still more at the singular ideas which
both they and Olga entertained of what comfort was!

At length, after many days, and now and then a night or two,
of travel, we came upon the steppe country, where the forests were
more scattered and the population sparser, until at last the whole
landscape was a boundless expanse of grass, except in one direction,
where a dark mass, like the shadow of a cloud, marked a distant
wood. No sooner was it visible than my companion clapped her
hands with delight, the horses were urged into a gallop, the carriage bounded more wildly than usual over the deep ruts formed by

the winter rains, now baked into troughs that would have smashed ordinary springs, and I needed no other evidence to prove to me that our destination was at hand. I confess my heart sank within me, for there was something inexpressibly dreary in the prospect. My baby, who had undergone the trials of the journey with a fortitude and a power of endurance truly Sclavonic, set up a loud wail, which it seemed to me could only arise from instinctive dread and dismay. I looked round in every direction, and though the range of vision was most extensive, not the vestige of a cottage was visible, not a human being enlivened the scene; so I sank gently back and in silence, and added my tears to baby's. Fortunately, Olga was too much excited to notice me, and after violently hugging my firstborn in a paroxysm of delight, she performed the same operation upon me. Thanks to the moisture she had acquired from the cheeks of that little cherub, she did not discover the tears on mine; so we plunged into the gloomy recesses of the wood, and I was cheered by seeing a road branch off to the right, which she informed me led to the village. While wondering whether it would be possible to do a little "parish" in it, and secretly making up my mind to open a Sunday school, I was startled by the hollow sound of the horses' hoofs upon a wooden bridge, and looking out, saw that we were crossing a dry moat, and entering an old moss-grown castle, through a somewhat dilapidated archway.

Immense trees overhung the building, which I had only time to observe was very ancient, but still apparently substantial, and very quaint and irregular in form.

We pulled up at a low door in a grass-grown quadrangle, where stood an old white-headed servitor, into whose arms Olga precipitated herself with the most ardent expressions of joy: behind him a row of domestics evidently gazed with no little awe and respect upon the retinue of town servants we had brought from St Petersburg. Notwithstanding the bustle and the high state of preparation of everybody for our arrival, I felt chilled by a sensation of solitude and desolation I had not experienced since leaving England: the whirl and gaiety of the capital, the constant attendance at court which fell to my lot—the excitement and novelty of a life altogether which never allowed a moment for serious thought—

had kept me, as I supposed, contented and happy. Too young to discover cares in life which did not exist, too giddy to seek out occupation I did not desire, I had lived like a butterfly in a beautiful garden, and now suddenly found myself without the flowers, and the sunshine, and the other butterflies that used to pay me court. It was a moment of terrible reaction—even my companion's high spirits failed to make me take a cheerful view of things. When I followed the old white-headed man under the low doorway, and Olga linked her arm in mine, I felt as if he was the jailer, and she was escorting me to a dungeon in which I was to be confined for life. It was very wrong, I know, and I concealed my feelings as much as I could, but she felt me shudder as I leant upon her arm, and stopped suddenly. "Why," she said, "do you tremble so much? are you frightened? Who told you the castle was haunted?" I had never heard anything about the castle, except that my husband used to make there what he called his "economies," by which he meant that he had a bailiff who lived in it and farmed his property for him; and as for its being haunted, it was a positive relief to my mind to hear anything about it half so interesting. So I laughed at the notion of an Englishwoman either believing in or being afraid of ghosts, and said I shivered because a cold draught came down the passage along which we were passing. "Yes," observed my companion, "since the bailiff refused to live in it, the castle has been quite uninhabited, so that the air feels chilly; but we will have the stoves lighted and make ourselves comfortable. There is not the least danger in the daytime, and at night we will sleep in the cottage, which papa built just before his death, when the ghosts made it impossible to sleep any longer in the castle." As she said this we were standing in a fine old hall, round which were ranged some figures in armour; the walls were decorated with tapestry, and where the wood paneling appeared, it was in many places painted so as to form a picture with the edge of the panel for the frame. Very uncouth men and women indeed the worthy progenitors of my husband appeared, as depicted upon these ancestral walls—capable of any deed of darkness, and just the sort of people who would continue to live in the castle when they ought to have been reposing like respectable members of the Greek Church in the number of square feet of soil allotted to them. Unfortunately, instead of being buried, some had been put into a family vault, and were perhaps more restless on that account. Whatever be the reason, the current superstition was, that the originals of some of the portraits which adorned the walls of this large hall continued to inhabit the castle, to the exclusion of its present lawful possessors; and an extremely savage-looking Sclavonian warrior, with a battle axe in his hand, and what seemed to be some sort of drum at his feet, was the most generally acknowledged spectre. Why he was chosen, I know not, except that the favourite sound of the ghostly occupant was said to be the rattle of a drum, or rather a thing like a tom-tom, which in those early days was one of the musical instruments of these barbarians. I confess, at the moment I was thinking very little about my husband's restless ancestors; my thoughts were back in my own dear little room at home—that room in which I am now writing this; and I would have embraced the knees of the most disreputable of spectres who should at that moment have pounced upon me from any of the surrounding pictures, and in the twinkling of an eye have landed me on the doorsteps of the paternal mansion. So I turned a deaf ear to Olga's patter about goblins, and gazed vacantly at the gaunt figures in armour, and the gloomy groined roof overhead, and the faded tapestry and ill-drawn portraits. I saw that a massive staircase led to regions overhead, as yet unexplored, and I perceived that it was really true that we were not going to sleep in the castle. Still we seemed to be going partially to inhabit it, for a rather dark passage led from the hall into a really charming drawing-room, where the air had been warmed, and the temperature was agreeable. It was furnished in the most modern Parisian style, and from one window a view was obtained of a straggling cottage or two of the village, the greater part of which was concealed by the wood. That window was quite a consolation to me for the moment, and altogether the room looked habitable and light, and I felt my spirits rising again. A small dining-room opened off the drawing room, but on festive occasions the large hall I have already described was used. Beyond the small dining-room there was a billiard-room. A passage led from the drawing-room to a glass door, upon opening which we emerged upon a bridge which crossed the moat, but which was covered in partly with glass and partly with planking. This led into a detached cottage, consisting of nothing but bedrooms. The fact that the castle itself was of immense dimensions, and contained any amount of accommodation, and that the family had nevertheless been positively driven out of it by ghosts, and obliged to build a cottage to sleep in, was the most practical evidence I could have desired that, whatever might be the foundation of the belief, it existed pretty strongly. I have been obliged, for reasons which will presently appear, to be thus particular in describing the plan of the castle, and of the principal rooms in it.

The cottage was decidedly an improvement on the gloomy structure we had left. Whereas the castle was surrounded on three sides by dense black pine forest, the trees of which overhung the moat, and almost shot their branches into the upper windows, the view from the cottage windows presented the strangest contrast from my bedroom window: not a tree bigger than a rose-bush was visible anywhere; a neglected flower-garden was bounded by a sunk fence, to which it descended in a gentle slope, and beyond that nothing but grass, with here and there a field of Indian-corn or wheat stubble; still, with the bright sun setting upon it, there was something comforting in its very grandeur and expanse. I seemed to breathe again after having been nearly stifled in the castle. The dungeon-feeling was going off, and a momentary sensation of butterfly seemed to thrill through me. Two peasant women were returning from work to the village, and as I opened the window I heard them sing. Decidedly I should visit the poor of the parish to-morrow. I would find out an old serf "bad with the rheumatiz, my lady," and take him "Rhus." Then I looked at the women as they walked away, and wondered if I wanted to sell them how I should have to set about it—whether they were fixtures on the land, or if I could let them; and then I thought it would be more philanthropic to hire anybody I saw belonging to a neighbour that seemed unhappy, and that led me to think of neighbours, and I asked Olga who our neighbours were, and how far off they lived. She told me the nearest lived seventeen miles off, but that he was a horrid man, who had ill-treated his wife till she died, and he now lived there alone; and the next nearest was a lady, who had been married and divorced a great many times, and finally got tired of going through the ceremony, but who did not the less prefer the society of gentlemen to that of ladies. Then there was an old lady who lived by herself, twenty-four miles off; and a charming family thirty miles off, whose acquaintance I made some years after. All this was discouraging, and I ceased to be a butterfly again. The growling and grumbling of my English maid, who ever since her arrival in Russia had, for some reason known only to herself, pertinaciously refused to have her tea made in a samovar, and who now said that when I engaged her to accompany me to Russia I should have mentioned that "the family was inhabited with ghosts," did not improve my frame of mind; and when she gave me warning, and announced her intention to go, and I thought how difficult it had been to come, I told her with a malicious satisfaction that I should be the least obstacle she would have to encounter in carrying out her design of returning to her native land; on which, feeling the impossibility of putting her threat into execution, she retorted that it was my fault if I had made her "an Elisabeth, or Exile in Siberia," and burst into a violent paroxysm of tears.

Fortunately the ills of life do not assume large dimensions at eighteen, and in a few days I had quite recovered my wonted spirits. I had explored every nook and corner of the old castle in the boldest and most sacrilegious way. I had opened rooms supposed to be exclusively inhabited by ghosts. I had been stifled with clouds of dust in the course of my investigations. I had taken the skin off my fingers trying to turn gigantic keys in impossible locks, and Olga had kept at a respectable distance behind me, and uttered a little scream every time I had broken into a new room. As to the old steward, he was as much scandalised at the exploratory tendencies of the mistress as at the fine airs of the maid: while I was scrambling up rickety ladders in spite of all warning about the dangers of their breaking, she was insisting upon hot-water bottles for her feet. To my intense delight, I discovered two very sociable greyhounds at the bailiff's; and as horse-breeding was part of the farm operations, I had no difficulty in getting a new mount every day until I was satisfied; and then how Olga and I used to fly across the country after hares, and how fond the dogs and the horses and the riders all got of each other at last! Then I made acquaintance with the whole population of the village, and though I could not exchange an idea with one of them, I found plenty to do; and I was beginning to forget all about the ghosts, when one night, just as I was going to sleep, in flounces "Elisabeth, or the Exile," gives two violent gasps, and faints dead away by the side of my bed. Not being at all of a nervous temperament myself, I don't generally make allowances for persons addicted to hysteria; but there was not the slightest doubt about the genuineness of Elisabeth's present condition, and at least half an hour elapsed before, by dint of violent remedies, I succeeded in restoring consciousness. Not that I gained much, for no sooner did she "come to"—to use her own expression—than she shut her eyes and "went off" again. This she did three times, and then her anxiety to tell me the story overcame every other consideration, and she sat up, took rather a long sip of sal-volatile and commenced. I should premise that I had allowed Elisabeth—who, by the way, never permitted either me or anybody else to call her anything but Phillips, and whose Christian name was Jane—to sit and work in a sort of little boudoir that opened off the billiard-room, in order that she might not mix with the other servants, who, she said, were not "sympatica" to her—she had spent a winter in Rome with a lady before coming to me. "So," says Phillips, "knowing, my lady, that you would want your riding-'abit the first thing in the morning, and that I should have to let a whole new bit in, in consequence of your ladyship's always tearing your 'abit exactly in the same place—leastways three mornings running—I hanticipated rather a long job, and so I determined to set about it at once; and your ladyship may imagine the 'orror I conceived when I found, on reaching my apartment after undressing of your ladyship, that I had left my needle-book and thimble, and hother working materials, in my morning boodwar. Well, my lady, I was in a great many minds before I could summing up courage to go into that dreadful castle at this time of night; and it was not without awful trembling—and I may say even haspen-like shakings—that I 'urried along the glass passage across the moat, a-shading of the candle with my 'and. When I opened the door into the billiard-room there come a gust of wind that almost extinguished my light; and I got so frightened that I turned back again as far as the passage, and there I stopped to take breath, and that gave me time to think of your ladyship's displeasure if I did not get the 'abit ready, and so I gently opened the door again and listened,—but, as Mr. Munckting Mills beautifully observes, 'the beating of my own 'art was the honly sound I 'eard,' leastways at that moment, my lady. A moment after, I tripped over a billiard-cue which was prostrated,—and, oh! what another start that give me. I felt as if I was made up of electrical wires and was keeping on having shocks from everything I touched—being continually and perpetually expecting of ghosts made me almost feel as if I was somebody else, especially when the light made my own 'orrid shadow stand up on the wall all of a sudding, right opposite to me. Well, my lady, I was shaking so when I got 'old of my working materials that I run the needles into my fingers without caring, and was running away, feeling always that somebody might be close behind me in the dark for all I knew to the contrairy, when of a sudden, as I got into the passage leading from the great hall to the billiard-room—oh, my lady!—" Here Phillips began again to tremble so violently that I poured out some more sal-volatile; and, in order to encourage her, as I administered it, said, "Well, my good Phillips, what did you see?" "Oh, nothing, my lady; nothing visible could ever make such awful sounds; and it was right in my ear, not an inch off, as I am a living woman. Just as I come out of the billiard-room off it went with a bang, exactly like the militia."

"Well, but off what went? could you see nothing?"

"Why, first, I never looked; and, second, it was too dark if I had; it was just at the corner where the passage turns to the glass door; but, oh, it was so loud, I wonder you did not hear it here; it were like a number of little pistols going off quick as light, one after the other. Coming on me of a sudding, and me feeling as I was, and being wound up to the 'ighest pitch at any rate, I gave a scream and a jump, my lady, as I shall never know how many feet in the air; and I never stopped screaming and running with occasional jumps, and once I fell down, till I came to your

ladyship's bedside, where here I shall remain and never again to
move. O dear, O dear!" and Phillips went off into a fit of inco-
herent lamentation and much sobbing, in the course of which I
induced her to get upon the couch, where she finally cried herself
to sleep. I was excessively annoyed. In the first place, Phillips was
full enough of fancies without silly practical jokes being played
upon her to increase them; and, in the second, she was sufficiently
difficult to please without making Russia more intolerable to her
than it already was. So spake the sensible, practical Englishwoman;
but in so speaking I am bound to say she was not telling the real
truth. I felt I was deceiving myself. I knew well enough it was
no trick of the servants to frighten my maid. There was not a
servant in the place who would venture into the castle after we
had left the drawing-room. Moreover, had not the very owner, to
say nothing of the bailiff, been frightened out of the place years
ago, and gone to the expense of building bedrooms! Again, what
Phillips said about the nature of the sounds was consistent with
general report; it was said they were so loud sometimes that there
was not a servant in the place who had not heard them. So much
so, that on certain nights of the week the villagers used timidly to
approach the castle, and listen; and then, the moment the noises
broke out, would run away terrified. The day most patronised by
the ghosts, I had heard, was Saturday; but whether our presence
had kept them unusually quiet, or whether I was always too sound
asleep at the interesting moment to hear them, I know not; but
my curiosity was at last violently excited, and my temper somewhat roused: so I determined, *coute qui coute*, to get to the bottom
of the mystery, and having arrived at this decision irrevocably in
my own mind, I turned round, and went peaceably to sleep. My
first injunction to Phillips on the following morning was, that she
should not breathe a word of her experience—which I affected to
treat lightly—to the Countess Olga or any other soul; my second,
that she should bring my riding-habit torn as it was, as I thought
a day with the greyhounds would not be a bad preparation for a
night with the ghosts. Fortune favoured my plans, for it so happened that Olga went to bed early with a headache, and left me
reading alone in the drawing-room. When the servants came to

take away the tea, I told them they might go to bed; and, putting a small reading-lamp by my side, I determined to meet the ghost single-handed. Although I attempted to read while awaiting his arrival, I must confess that I found it impossible to fix my attention—my hearing seemed to have become preternaturally acute, and I had strung my nerves up to a pitch which was perhaps a little beyond what they could bear. It must be admitted, that for a girl to sit quite alone in a castle so notoriously haunted that no man had ventured into it at night, either alone or in company, for years, for the express purpose of waiting for the ghosts to appear, was a very fair test of courage; and I do not think that I incur the charge of timidity because my heart did beat more rapidly than usual on this occasion, and I was aware of a dampness on the forehead, accompanied by that description of chill known as gooseskin, although the room was uncomfortably warm. At last, after a silence of two hours, so oppressive that I almost longed for the ghost, I thought I had done enough for one night, and had fairly earned my bed. It was not to be expected by the most exigeant spectre that I should sit up for him till daylight; and I took up the lamp to go. At the very last moment, however, I was irresistibly impelled to take a look into the Great Hall. I felt I was shrinking from a conscientious discharge of my duty if I left this part of it unfulfilled. So, very much in the same frame of mind as Phillips when she went to her "boodwar," I marched towards the door of the hall. I opened it very silently, partly because I was afraid of the sounds I made myself, and partly because I wanted, if there was a ghost, to see him without his seeing me, though, as I had the light, a moment's reflection would have shown me that would be impossible. I walked straight into the middle of the hall, and turned the light boldly upon all the pictures and tapestry. Everything was still and silent as the grave. I then kept the light fixed upon the other entrance, so that nobody should come in without my seeing it, and walked towards some of the figures in armour to look if anybody was concealed behind them. I had just satisfactorily settled this point when I suddenly heard a deep sigh. My heart seemed to jump at once into my mouth, and I felt as if I should choke; but I put my back against the wall, so as not to be taken unawares, and listened, but not for long. In another moment a long, deep, heavy sigh—so long, so deep, so full of misery, that it almost amounted to a moan; but there was no intonation in it. It was like a stage whisper—so clear, and yet without any other kind of sound than that made by wind.

It seemed very near me, almost at my ear; so near that I turned suddenly round. I found myself actually leaning against the Sclavonian warrior with the battle-axe and the drum. My flesh was now beginning to creep, I felt my hair positively rising, and I wanted to run away, but was afraid to leave the wall against which I had placed my back, for it seemed a sort of protection. Again a long deep sigh, then another. There is something abominable in sighs. They seem a sort of sound that it does not require a regular body to make. A pair of lungs is all that is necessary to sigh with; a mouth is quite superfluous. One might sigh through a hole in one's throat, or without a head at all for the matter of that. Then there was a sort of catch in one of the sighs that was particularly disagreeable, as if the ghost had been interrupted in his misery, and then it had been suddenly very much increased. I was still hesitating what to do, when the stillness which had succeeded the last sigh was followed by a muffled sound of beating or thumping, very low and regular, and seeming to echo all round the room, but to come from no particular part of it. As it grew louder my fears rose to such a pitch that all my resolution vanished. I rushed at the door leading to the drawing-room, which I banged after me, but failed to shut out the sound which seemed to pursue me through the drawing-room and along the glass passage, with its increasing volume still ringing in my ears. Into bed, dressed, and just as I was, and with my head under the bed-clothes, I was still unable to shut it out. A pressure on my shoulder made me start with a scream of terror—overtaken at last, my bed not even a refuge! it was too horrible!

The thought had hardly flashed across me when Olga's gentle voice reassured me. She was shaking from head to foot; the sounds from the castle had been loud enough to wake her up, and now as we tremblingly clasped each other we could hear them dying away. The loud drum roll was subsiding into the muffled murmur I had heard at first, and by degrees it ceased altogether.

The next morning Phillips came to me with the triumphant intelligence that all the servants had been roused by the noises in the castle, and that her story, which I had affected to disbelieve, had thus received the most satisfactory confirmation. Poor Phillips! I felt I owed her some apology for the apparent scepticism with which I had treated her story, and admitted to her that I had also heard the sounds—in fact, had passed a very uneasy night in consequence. This seemed to afford her great comfort and consolation, though she relapsed into disappointment when she found that I steadily refused to admit that the sounds in question could possibly be caused by supernatural agency. Notwithstanding all which very brave language, my nerves were so much shaken by the incidents of this dreadful night, that I could scarcely bring myself to enter the Great Hall even by day, and our evening sittings in the drawing-room were by no means protracted to so late an hour as they had formerly been. Having unlimited confidence in the salutary effects of a great deal of exercise in the open air upon the nervous system, I devoted myself to the destruction of hares, and for some days coursed so vehemently, that a new couple of greyhounds, which the bailiff had bought to relieve his own, were fairly worked off their legs. Still I was as perpetually haunted by the desire of discovering something more about the ghosts as the castle was by those uncanny beings. For some nights I lay awake, listening in vain for sounds, until, at last, one night as I lay wondering whether they would ever come again, the distant roll gradually swelling and as gradually falling broke the midnight stillness. It was not nearly so loud as upon the former occasion, and so far from frightening me, seemed this time rather to inspire me with courage. It was on a Saturday, just a fortnight after my last adventure, and I listened and calmly speculated upon the mysterious sound. I had been reading rather a heavy book, in which, nevertheless, I had been deeply interested; for, although young and giddy, I was excessively fond of study, and the repose of country life had suggested to me the expediency of beginning a course of serious reading and following it up. My lamp was burning brightly, every corner of the room was lighted, Olga and all the servants slept between me and the castle,—altogether, my

nerves felt so strong and steady, that I quite wondered why I had
experienced such terror on the previous occasion; so I once again
resolved to fathom the mystery, and this time I determined that
not the whole misery of the universe concentrated into one sigh,
nor the tattoo roll of all the armies of Europe concentrated into
one drum, should drive me from the Great Hall. Having, as upon
the first night of Phillips's adventure, arrived at this irrevocable
decision, I turned round and went peaceably to sleep.

The first thing which my sister-in-law asked me next morning
was whether I had heard the sounds in the night. On my admitting
that I had, she said that she had not felt so frightened as upon the
last occasion, and remarked that she supposed in time we should
get quite accustomed to them. I told her I had already so far overcome my original dread, that I had determined in my own mind to
make another nocturnal experience, and proposed to her to join
me. However brave one may be individually, a companion on such
occasions is always an immense support. To my great delight she
readily consented to my proposal. I suggested that we should not
wait until the next Saturday night, but try at once, and keep on
making experiments every night during the week; by these means,
if nothing was seen or heard, we should have become accustomed
to the loneliness of the Great Hall, and be better able to face the
dangers of the fatal Saturday. I am bound to say that we passed
the whole of this day in a fever of excitement and anticipation. I
went half-a-dozen times into the Great Hall, impelled thither by
a fascination which was quite irresistible. I gazed at all the pictures, examined all the paneling, ascended the massive staircase,
which nevertheless creaked even with my light weight, and became
familiar with every object which a heated imagination could possibly turn into a ghost. Gaunt figures in armour, with a dim light
upon them, are especially ghost-like and supernatural. The bars
of their visors always look like long teeth, and they make a nasty
rattle when you touch them, extremely disagreeable in the dark. I
determined that I should allow my mind to rest on none of these
things when I came at night with Olga. Indeed, I tried to take one
warrior to pieces, on purpose to feel on intimate terms with him,
and succeeded so far that I got his helmet off, and could not get

it on again; so, as a piece of bravado, I put it under his arm, and made him look more ghastly than ever. Then I went back to the drawing-room, and by the time ten o'clock struck I had worked myself up into such a recklessly defiant mood, that I felt almost intoxicated with excitement. Olga caught the infection. We could scarcely restrain our impatience till the moment came to dismiss the servants: then we jumped up and waltzed round the room, a sort of war-dance of triumph and defiance. Then we lighted every candle, and went into the billiard-room and lighted it up too, careless of what the servants would suppose,—laughing, indeed, at the terror which the unusual illumination would inspire, and which would certainly be attributed to a posse of debauched ghosts; then we played a noisy game of billiards,—all which, be it remembered, was merely a form of Dutch courage. We were both by this time in our secret souls excessively terrified. Both would willingly have danced off to bed instead of round the billiard-table; but our honour was at stake, and we kept up appearances magnificently. At last the midnight hour struck, and, arming ourselves each with a cue in one hand and a candle in the other, we marched defiantly towards the Great Hall.

The first thing I saw was my friend the warrior whom I had left with his head under his arm, glaring at me with his black, ghastly cavern of a mouth and hollow eye-sockets; but, to my horror and dismay, his head was back again upon his shoulders. As none of the servants would have ventured into the Hall since the comparatively late hour that I had last visited it, I was driven to the unpleasant conclusion that this mailed knight had either put on his own head, or had got an equally unearthly friend to put it on for him. I felt my courage already giving way, so I laughed and talked boisterously, and rapped his helmet soundly with my cue, as I told the story in a loud tone to Olga. She was at the other end of the room, tapping the paneling with her cue, as she laughingly said, loud enough to drown the sound of the ghost's drum. We seemed both penetrated with the conviction that our only chance of safety lay in making as much noise as possible, so I began to tap the panels on my side of the room also. At that moment, the most piercing scream I ever heard issue from mortal throat burst from

Olga; her candle dropped with a crash, and before I could look round she tore wildly past me, screaming, "Fly! fly! save yourself!" I needed no further admonition. Never turning my head, I rushed after her to the passage leading to the drawing-room, my candle also going out, and in we both burst to the brilliantly lighted room, pale, panting, and exhausted. Our first care was to double-lock the door by which we had just entered; and as, in order to regain our bedrooms, it was necessary to traverse the glass passage, now dark, we rested for a minute while I lighted my candle, and Olga took another out of the candelabra. This gave me time to think that a retreat to the cottage, after all my resolutions, without even knowing what had happened, would be ignominious, so I implored Olga to sit down and calm herself, and give me some reason for her extravagant alarm. I had taken the precaution to provide sundry restoratives in case of our needing them, and in a few moments she had comparatively regained her tranquility. All she could say was, that as she was tapping the panel on which was painted the Sclavonian warrior, the cue was suddenly drawn out of her hand by some invisible influence. She had not let it drop, nor had she brought it back with her. There was no denying the fact; the cue had vanished—but how, remained a mystery. When she felt it being pulled from her hand she screamed, dropped the light, turned and fled, and she could give me no further information upon the subject. Meantime we sat and listened. Not a sound could we hear except the murmur of the wind and the rustling of the pine branches which overhung the window. Feeling that this silence would unnerve us, and reluctant to yield to Olga's entreaties to go to the cottage, I proposed that we should return to the billiard-room, lock both the doors, and play a game of billiards. A ghost would scarcely be bold enough to enter a room in which there were fifteen candles burning; and if the sounds were as loud as usual, we would sit there and listen to them safely. After some hesitation, my companion consented to this arrangement, and we went through the form of knocking the balls about, without, however, being able to get rid for an instant of the one thought uppermost in both our minds. Every now and then, by mutual consent, we stopped and listened, but not a sound was audible. I was on

the point of proposing another visit to the Hall, when the bang of
a distant door checked the words as they rose to my lips, and made
us both start and tremble. Then again profound stillness. It was
now nearly two o'clock, but as I had quite made up my mind not
to go to bed without one more attempt at unravelling the mystery,
I determined first quietly to go over in my mind the events which
had occurred up to this point, hoping that somehow I might hit
upon the clue. As I did so, it flashed across me that upon the
occasion of my first visit I heard the sighs when I was standing on
the side of the room near the picture of the Sclavonian warrior,
and that as I leant my back against it they seemed nearer and
louder. This then might be the haunted spot, if any one place in
this "possessed" old building was more haunted than another, for
exactly here it was that Olga had lost her cue. It was a sort of comfort getting some definite locality to fix upon for investigation,
and a comfort to have a distinct reason for revisiting the Hall—
my distinct reason being that I wanted to see whether the cue was
lying upon the floor, or had really, as Olga maintained, been spir-
ited away altogether. My curiosity on this point was so great that
I firmly resisted all her endeavours to dissuade me from going
back. I finally promised, however, that we should only go as far as
the Hall door, this time on tiptoe; that we should open it gently
and look in, and be satisfied, if we saw the cue lying on the floor,
to leave it there without venturing further; if not, to rest content
with our experiences for the night, and put off our investigations
as to what had become of the cue to some future occasion. This
being decided upon, we once more screwed up our courage to the
sticking point, and returned to the drawing-room, where everything was still lighted, and stayed for a moment to listen. To my
dismay and regret, for I saw my companion's resolution would
fail her, we distinctly heard a sort of shuffling sound, as of some
one crossing the Hall in slippers. At this time I felt such intense
anxiety to know what had become of the cue that I was resolved to
go on alone if Olga would not come with me; and when I saw her
sink back almost fainting into a chair, I felt it would be cruel of
me to urge her further. Indeed, at the moment she was so frightened that she was unable even, to go back to the cottage, much

less to the Hall. I therefore crept cautiously on by myself, and, before opening the door into the Hall, leant my ear against it and listened. All silent. I put my hand gently on the old-fashioned latch, which, fortunately, I could turn without noise, and pushed the door softly open. The Sclavonian warrior hung on the wall to the left as I entered, and as the door also opened back into the Hall on the same side, I found I should be obliged either to fling it well back or advance into the room in order to have a view of the floor at the foot of the picture, where I expected to find the cue lying. I should remark that, on passing through the drawing room, it occurred to me to take, instead of a candle, a read-ing-lamp with a very strong reflector, which, though somewhat heavy, could be made to throw a bright light. Before pushing the door wide open I gave my lamp an extra twist; then, with every fibre strung, I took one bold step into the room, and turned the lamp full on the left-hand wall. What I then saw fairly rooted me to the spot with amazement and dismay. The Sclavonian warrior had utterly vanished, and in his room, or I should rather say in a room, there appeared a bed, a table with a loaf of bread upon it, a chair, a pair of jack-boots, and a sword hanging above them. For an instant I felt dizzy with bewilderment, then turned and fled. I was more thoroughly frightened than if a legion of drumming ghosts had marched into the Hall. The denouement was so utterly unexpected, so terribly real, so exactly the reverse of supernatural, that the very contrast was a shock. Spectral figures in white robes, or even the Sclavonian warrior beating his own drum, I could have borne; but a bed which had evidently just been occupied, for the clothes were all tumbled, a pair of jack-boots probably just pulled off, and a half-eaten loaf of bread, were sights infinitely more alarming. I felt that the occupant of the mysterious chamber must be the sort of person who would murder me if he caught me; and my tell-tale face as I rushed through the drawing-room required no explanation. Olga was sufficiently recovered to fly after me, and once more, breathless and exhausted, we reached my bed-room. Here I explained to my sister-in-law what I had seen, and we spent the remaining hours till daylight in accounting for the ghostly sounds, and in vague conjectures as to the identity of the

individual who produced them. The servants were somewhat
astonished not only to find us up at the earliest hour in the morning, but to receive an order to send the white-headed steward to
us. Meantime Mrs. Phillips had been made acquainted with our
discovery, which she communicated in a tongue of her own inven-
tion to the rest of the household, so that when the steward came
we were followed by the whole establishment to the Great Hall. To
my astonishment another change had taken place since my last
visit. The Sclavonian warrior was no longer there, it is true, but
no more were the bed, or the table, or the chair, or the big boots,
or the loaf of bread, or the sword. Everything had disappeared
except the room, and into that we entered. It was built into the
solid wall, here nine feet thick. The panel occupied by the warrior
had been five feet by seven, and this was the size of the entrance
to the room. The dimensions of it were as follows:—eight feet in
breadth, twelve feet in length, seven in height—the floor was one
foot higher than that of the hall. It was now quite empty, though
the stains of liquid spilt on the floor showed it to have been recently occupied. After some difficulty we succeeded in drawing
out the panel, which slided noiselessly along its grove, and the
warrior gradually emerged once more to the light of day. We
examined the edge of it carefully, and did not close it completely
for fear of not understanding the trick of the spring. When we
discovered the right spot to touch outside the panel, we found it
acted almost like a hair-trigger. It was in the crevice of a rock,
against which the warrior was leaning. The effect of a very gentle
pressure here made the panel roll softly back of its own accord
about an inch. As the carving of the panel projected, this opening
was generally in shade, so that it might very well be a little open
without being visible. There was no difficulty, supposing I had
been leaning within a foot of this apartment, in accounting for
the sighs which the occupant had probably resorted to as the eas-
iest mode of frightening me away, before he began to beat his
drum. In the same way the point of Olga's cue must have slipped
into this opening, and been dexterously snatched out of her hand.
We never saw the cue again. The unfortunate part of it all is "that
here my story ends." Who the man who lived in this room was,

why he lived there, whether more than one lived there, are all questions which we went on asking until we gave it up in despair. I used often to suspect that the old steward knew something about it; but he pretended to be as much surprised as any of us at the discovery. The most likely hypothesis is that some political refugee had made it his abode, preferring it to Siberia, or something still more summary. Whoever he was, he had enjoyed free lodging for twenty years, as during all that period the castle had been haunted. Judging by the specimen I saw of it, his fare had been of the simplest description; indeed, not the least difficult part of the problem is how he managed to get supplied with provisions at all. Nor is it easy to explain why he left the panel open for us to discover his room, unless we suppose that he did not give us credit for sufficient courage to revisit the hall after he had taken Olga's cue. Again, he must have seen me standing in the hall, or he could not have known that I had found out his secret, and have decided on utterly abandoning his home for ever and taking all his property with him. Where he took his table and his chair and his bed to is another mystery that will never be solved, more especially as the old steward is dead, who, as I have already said, I have always felt firmly convinced could have thrown some light on the subject.

I need scarcely say that no sounds have ever been heard in the castle since that eventful night. Some of the trees have been cut down, and some of the bedrooms are refurnished, and made habitable and cheerful. The recess itself always stands open, and contains a whist-table; but the Sclavonian warrior often sees the light, for the story is still often told, and without him it would be a ghost story with the ghost left out.

GUY NEVILLE'S GHOST
PERCY GREG

Blackwood's Edinburgh Magazine, 1865

No: I have met plenty of ghost-seers, and have heard them tell their stories with a sincerity of awe and a shuddering recollection of the terror past that left no sort of doubt as to their belief. And history assures me that, ever since the days of Homer, and perhaps before then, ghosts have from time to time been seen of men, and have made the hair of the seers stand on end, and their blood curdle with fear. But I never saw a ghost myself, except once. And then? Yes; then I must do the ghost the justice to say that I was horribly frightened.

I was very glad to accept Charlie Neville's invitation to pass a few days with him in the cottage which he inhabits in one of the pleasantest valleys in Westmoreland—right through which valley runs the road from Lancashire to Scotland. I was very tired of being chained to my desk in one of the dirtiest, gloomiest, dampest towns in England—a town that for six months in the year alternates between fog and sleet, and for the rest between fog and rain—a town where nobody lives except to make a fortune, where nobody does anything or thinks of anything but his fortune till he has made it, and whence, the fortune made, every one goes as far away as possible to spend it. I had been a prisoner, or a slave, all summer, and it was now September. All the more did I delight in my journey, knowing that September is the pleasantest of months in Westmoreland, where May is cold, the summer mostly wet, and August dense and oppressive. Charlie was a pleasant member of a pleasant family, and the idea of once more enjoying the society

of young ladies—a species unknown in the neighbourhood of my
prison-house—was enough to excite my spirits to the uttermost.
Even a long railway journey, in a carriage from which the presence
of an asthmatic director-looking old gentleman banished alike the
breath of fresh air and the hope of tobacco, failed to subdue them.
It was in a joyous mood that I sprang upon the platform at Wind-
ermere, valise in hand, and looked out for Charlie.

A big dog made his appearance first, who, after suspiciously
glancing and snuffing at a travelling suit which retained an atmosphere of the printing-office about it, rubbed his nose against the
hand that held my valise just as my friend came up and shook me
heartily by the other.

"Is that monster yours?" I said, as we walked to the phaeton.
"He was more friendly than I expected, and more formidable than
I liked."

"Ah," said his master, "Cæsar was puzzled by the smell of facto-
ry-smoke and cotton-fluff about you. If it had been tobacco-smoke
and cigar-ashes he would have recognised it. But Cæsar always
finds out a gentleman. There is a baronet of my acquaintance who
goes about in such rags that the servants offer him a penny when
he calls for the first time on a friend; but Cæsar recognised his
title at first sight, and made him the humblest obeisance. And the
best dressed of burnt-out tailors or shipwrecked sailors, in whom
I might expect a visitor, cannot take in Cæsar. He never lets them
open the gate. Dogs are the most aristocratic of living creatures."

And this commenced a discussion, in which Charlie, who quartered the Kingmaker's Bear and Ragged Staff, and could recite his
whole pedigree since the battle of Barnet, bore his part with great
spirit and vivacity. This occupied our tongues while the pony traversed many miles of the loveliest scenery in England. This, and
the speculations with which it branched off, wholly irrelevant to
the subject of my tale, were interrupted only when we reached the
valley, at the other end of which the windows of Neville Grange
flashed back the golden light of the sun that was sinking behind
the western mountains.

"That is my home," said Charlie, as I gazed in silent admiration at the beautiful sight. "It is small, as you see: it has been

very much larger. The ruins of what in the olden days was Neville Grange lie on the other side of the cottage, which my great-grandfather built on part of the old site. Our present abode is so small that, with our large family, it requires some close packing to take in the few guests whom we can persuade to relieve our solitude. Relief it is, for there is no other gentleman within a dozen miles, except the curate."

"Is that the curate?" I asked, pointing to an elegant figure which, in a sporting costume, and with his back turned to us, was climbing at some little distance a steep path which led to a little farmhouse, the residence of one of the poorer of those "statesmen" who are the pride of the English Highlands. "I think even your fastidious eyes will admit him to have the air of a gentleman."

"No; that is not the curate. That is Crosthwaite's house. His family have held that farm longer than history runs back—probably in the days of Alfred. I don't know who the man is—some tourist, I suppose. It has a look of Guy Monthermer, my cousin; but Monthermer is with his regiment in India, and, if he were not, he would hardly come so near us."

I remembered that there had been a fierce quarrel between Guy Monthermer and Charlie's father, who was Monthermer's guardian. Guy was a few years senior to Charlie, but very young at the time of the quarrel. He had been foolish enough to make the feud public by challenging his relative, but had, of course, been met with a contemptuous refusal. Thus much I knew; but I did not know then, nor do I know now, the exact merits of the quarrel, or the demerits of Guy Monthermer. I can only tell my readers that he distinguished himself in India alike by his courage and his insubordination; that, some years after the date of my visit to Neville Grange, he engaged in the Garibaldian expedition; and that—but the rest they will learn from my story, and I will not spoil it by anticipation. I knew then only enough to let my companion's remark pass unanswered. He looked for some time after the stranger, who, however, was too distant for recognition.

We reached Neville Grange, and were greeted with hearty welcome by two boys and three little girls, the junior branches of the house, who had rushed out to meet their brother at the door.

Without going into the drawing-room, Charles undertook to show me up stairs; and for this, remembering Cæsar's opinion of my travelling suit, I was not ungrateful. The part of the cottage into which I was introduced was clearly of old date. The oak flooring was perfectly black; it had become irregular in its level from the gradual "settling" of the walls, and it was broken at uncertain intervals by capricious steps. The walls were paneled with dark old oak; the doors were of the same material, with old-fashioned latches in place of hidden locks and rounded handles. One of these Charles opened. Two downward steps led into a small room, oak-floored, with scanty carpet and oak-paneled walls, on which hung two or three modem sketches and one ancient portrait in oils. One window gave a view over the valley; the other, in a strange situation, just beside the fireplace, reaching to the ground, without sill or sash, apparently a mere hole in the wall, looked out upon a network of broken walls, mouldering and moss-covered, in which it was possible to trace the ruins of a larger house than the present cottage which had renewed the name of Neville Grange.

My toilet made, I left my room, without bestowing much attention on the details of its appearance. I was joined by Charles; and when we reached the drawing-room he introduced me to his mother, a lady still beautiful and elegant, in middle age and widow's weeds, and to her elder daughters, girls between sixteen and twenty. Annie, the younger, resembled her mother. Her beauty was of the best Saxon type; that which, in spite of fair hair, blue eyes, and clear, soft complexion, is redeemed by something of refined elegance about the features, and of intellectual expression in eye and brow, from the painfully close resemblance to a wax doll, which is so generally characteristic of Teutonic loveliness. Flora was thoroughly Norman—such as might have been the heiress of Warwick ere her marriage with the last hereditary chief of the house of Neville—with slender form, a hand which every sculptor must have admired in perfect despair of imitation; a head small, gracefully set on, and of exquisite shape, with ringlets of raven blackness and—the only instance I ever saw of true black hair that was not coarse—as soft and fine as her sister's. Her eyes were dark; of their exact colour I never could satisfy myself, but of their brilliancy there could be no doubt or forgetfulness, nor yet of that exquisite softness which belongs only to dark eyes when earnest emotion finds unconscious expression in their upturned gaze. Why I did not fall in love with Flora is not now to the purpose. But so penetrated was I with interest in her and admiration for her beauty, that during the evening I could not help observing her with a close attention which made me aware—certain beyond the possibility of doubt—that some painful anxiety was preying upon her mind. A jest from her brother, a sudden appeal to her notice from the children, would bring colour to her cheek in warm, fast-fading flushes; when unnoticed she seemed absorbed, not so much in reverie as in calculation. I am not a close observer of countenances, but I can tell the difference between the face of a dreamer and a thinker—can even discriminate between meditative thought and that kind of consideration which is preparing for the future, planning the achievement of a plot or the avoidance of a misfortune. The closer my observation, the clearer became my comprehension of the nature of the thoughts which disturbed that transparent countenance. Always, as she seemed to despair for a moment, and intermit her calculation, a shadow that spoke of fear, and of something that seemed like shame, passed over her face. If it had been possible to associate with that face and form, so evidently belonging to the highest "aristocracy of nature," so lofty and so pure, any thought of dishonour or untruth, or if Flora had been young enough for the innocent scrapes of childhood, I should have said that she anticipated some fatal discovery—was scheming to avoid being *"found out."* Most men, perhaps most women, are subject to such alarms from time to time; but men do not like to believe that there can be anything to be "found out" in the mind of a young and beautiful girl.

We talked pleasantly and frankly, all of us. Flora spoke unfrequently; but when she did speak, the clear tones of a voice that "like a silver clarion rang," though only like the clarion's notes subdued by distance, and something noble as well as novel in what she said, gave our conversation its chief zest and charm. I had fallen into the bachelor habit of smoking a cigar immediately after the evening meal, and that digestive had become to me as necessary as the meal itself; and Charlie was fully of my mind. But after tea that evening—for the Nevilles dined early, and Charles was too true a gentleman not to know that nothing so annoys a guest as household changes made for him—I was pleased that there was no excuse for the accustomed departure of the ladies, and deaf to his hints, that pointed towards sunset clouds and meant tobacco-smoke. And when bedtime came—their hours were early—my regrets were more sincere than Annie believed them.

"You will get your cigar with Charlie, and 'thank us much for going.' I know he has been watching for ten o'clock a full hour and a half."

"I plead guilty to the cigar, Miss Neville; but I, who have that every night of my life, and enjoy ladies' society only by such rare chances as this, would readily go to bed cigarless if you would postpone your retirement but half an hour."

"Take care lest they take you at your word," said Charlie, in horror; and his sister, smiling, followed Mrs. Neville and Flora from the room. Charlie and I turned out. The wind blew hard; it generally blows in Westmoreland throughout the autumn, and to smoke, save under shelter, had been impossible. We wrapped railway rugs round us, and sought shelter in an angle of the ruins. A wall, some eight feet high, joined that of the cottage just beneath the second window in my room. Cæsar's kennel, where he lay unchained, stood at a little distance by what had once been the opposite wall of a small room or closet, apparently enclosed in the centre of the old house. Here it was possible to light a match; here we found seats upon the fallen fragments of the wall, and smoked in peace.

"This place," said Charlie, "or rather some ten feet above our heads, was the scene of the family tragedy from which our house dates its decay, and the doom—if your modern principles will let me call it so—that hangs over us."

"And what is that doom?" I inquired, in perhaps a sceptical tone.

"Do you not know," my friend asked, "that in no generation does more than one male of the house live to reach the full maturity of manhood, and that he never dies in his bed? Ah, you may smile. But so truly have we believed in the doom, that every chief of my line has married before he reached my age, lest his race should end with him; and yet never since Sir Guy's time have two brothers of our blood been men together. And never has any head of the family died save by a violent or a sudden death. My great-grandfather fell at Yorktown; his father had been drowned while bathing in Grasmere; my grandfather was killed at Bada-jos—"

I knew why he paused. I remembered the riot unquelled; the blame of civilian imbecility laid on the soldier; the forbearance slandered as cowardice, the sentence of the court-martial avoided by suicide, four months before Charlie's youngest sister was born. I remembered for what cause his mother wore the widow's weeds she had never abandoned. The superstition of my friend began to touch me. I could not turn to indifferent matters, as I might have done had any other man spoken to me of his family misfortunes; for Charlie was my intimate friend. So I asked him,

"And what is the story of the crime by which this doom has been entailed on all Sir Guy's posterity!"

"What, have you never heard the legend of our house? Well, it is not so strange, for it is not one of which we care to talk to strangers; and even to you, I should hardly have cared to speak of it anywhere but here. Elsewhere you might have doubted it or smiled at it; here, where it occurred, though you have no better reason to believe it, you are more likely to do so."

I felt that there was some truth in this. My companion proceeded.

"Sir Guy's picture hangs over your fireplace. It is worth a careful scrutiny, for much of his strange and wayward character is to be traced in those lineaments. He quitted his house at an early age for the Court of King Charles I., leaving behind him his aged father and a brother, a mere child, to whom he was tenderly attached. This boy had been Sir Guy's constant companion in boyish pranks, while yet so little that his brother would carry him on his shoulder; he rode out for miles perched before Guy on the saddle, went with him up the hills or on the lake, followed him like a dog, and was cherished by him as if he had been not a brother but an only son. Ere the elder went from home, the old man called him to his chamber and earnestly commended the child to his brotherly affection. 'You love him now, Guy; but you are wayward of mood, ambitious of heart, unforgiving of temper. Many things may change you; many clouds may come between you and your youth before you return home. You will not see him again for many years, and time changes affection and wears out memory. Swear to me that you will never wrong him or neglect him; that he shall never have reason bitterly to feel the difference between a father's and a brother's love.' 'May God forget me; may good fortune desert me and my house,' answered Guy, 'if by fault or default of mine my brother come to harm.' And with these words Sir Guy left his father and went forth into the world.

"News came of him now and anon. At first he was in favour with the King, and rose to rank and influence in the royal service. His father died, believing that all was well, and more hopeful for his son than he had ever been. Then he was expected at home. But he wrote, arranging for his brother's education under the care of the venerable clergyman of the parish, and came not. He had ties at Court; the wife of a great nobleman, one of the loveliest in Henrietta's train, had fixed his fancy, and, as he thought, had smiled upon him. He was a man of ungoverned passions and fearless temper; he pursued the lady with a fierce fervour which terrified herself, and with a reckless vehemence which endangered both. Whether she yielded or not was never known; enough was said to excite suspicion, and her husband, a man of calm and generous disposition, but of unflinching determination, resolved to save his wife, if there were yet time. He obtained from the King a foreign appointment for young Neville. It was peremptorily and not very respectfully refused. Lord — then withdrew his wife from the Court, and sent her to his country seat. Sir Guy suspected his purpose, and was infuriated. In those days it was easy to force a quarrel, even on so eminent a man. Guy Neville contrived publicly to insult his enemy; a duel followed, and Lord — was mortally wounded. Ere his enemy had quitted the ground, Lord —'s mother, who had suspected the nature of his engagement, came to the spot in time to see her son expire. Beside his bleeding corpse she cursed his assassin, and prayed that, as he had brought desolation on a happy home, so his own might be desolate; that as he had cut short an honourable and useful life, so might his own life, and the lives of his descendants, be cut short in their prime. Sir Guy cowered beneath her curse, and it was with difficulty that his second hurried him from the field. He had to hide himself for the time, of course. Presently he learned that there was no such chance of pardon for his crime as he had hoped. The childless dowager had thrown herself at the King's feet, and Charles, greatly moved, had promised her justice in the emphatic words of David, 'As the Lord liveth, before whom I stand, the man that hath done this thing shall surely die.' Sir Guy fled his country and took refuge in Holland, tormented alike by the bitterness of remorse and the fury of vindictive hatred towards the sovereign who had refused to treat his quarrel as a fair use of the chivalric practice of private combat, and dealt with him not as a duellist but as a murderer. In Holland he fell in with Puritan exiles, who, while not pretending to palliate his crime, encouraged and fostered his lust for vengeance against the King who had sought to punish it. Sir Guy became the associate of Puritans; married a daughter of one of their chiefs; and, while refusing to lead the life of an ascetic, joined heart and soul in the wildest and most wicked of their conspiracies.

"The rebellion broke out, and Sir Guy Neville returned to England, and joined the armies of the Parliament. He held a command in a force which was operating in the north of Lancashire. One day information was received through a spy that a messenger had been sent, with a mounted escort, to convey despatches from the royal partisans in the same quarter to the Marquess of Montrose, and Sir Guy, with his troop, was detached to intercept him.

"They came up in sight of the escort a few miles from hence, and gave chase. Seeing themselves completely outnumbered, the Cavaliers set spurs to their horses, and, being admirably mounted, contrived to distance the majority of their pursuers. Neville, with a few of his troopers, outstripped the rest, and pressed the fugitives hard. Suddenly the latter drew bridle, turned round, and rode full upon this vanguard, evidently intending to overpower it before the remainder of the troop could come up. The leader of the Royalists was a very young man, without a beard, and with a mustache almost silken in softness, with slender form and very youthful air and figure, but with the same stern expression, the same dark deep-set eyes and black eyebrows that you will recognise in the portrait of Sir Guy. His long lovelocks, which escaped from his steel cap and fell over his shoulders, were of raven black. In a word, we have his portrait; to-morrow you shall see it. Flora resembles it as much as a girl may resemble a man. The Cavalier rode straight at Neville, who was a yard or so in advance of his foremost troopers, and swords were crossed. Sir Guy was a first-rate swordsman, but in the young Royalist he had met his match in skill and courage. It was to sheer strength that the Round-head owed the advantage which enabled him twice to overpower his opponent's guard, and inflict two fearful wounds, one on the head, and one on the left shoulder. The Cavaliers, meanwhile, had beaten back the rebels; two of them rode to the rescue of their young chief, and it was only by a desperate exertion of his own swordsmanship and his horse's power that Sir Guy evaded their swords, and made good his retreat. The remainder of his troopers were now fast approaching, and the Cavaliers resumed their flight, carrying off with them the victim of the Puritan's sword.

"The rebels continued the chase; and though they were distanced, and the turns and windings of the mountain-road concealed their enemy, Neville was confident of success. He knew the road—he knew that it led directly to his ancestral home, and that the fugitives could not go much farther without halting, especially as they had to carry with them a man, in all likelihood mortally wounded. There, or at the neighbouring residence of the clergyman, they would probably leave him. The troopers rode on rapidly. They reached the rectory; it was deserted, and they searched it in vain. With difficulty their captain restrained their savage wish to fire the home of the man who had been the friend and teacher of his youth, the guardian of his brother—now, as Guy had learned from rumour, serving with the King in the south. It was that rumour which had determined Guy to seek service in Lancashire. The band rode up to Neville Grange. The Cavaliers were not there: they had passed by, said the one domestic who was

visible, at full gallop, and without drawing bridle. Guy looked at
the man hard and sternly, and he trembled and turned pale beneath that gaze.

"'Ride on in pursuit,' said the captain to his lieutenant; 'I,
with four men, stay here to search the house.' And he dismounted
and entered the house. The servant followed him, with voluble
protests that no one had crossed the threshold except the aged
clergyman, who had consented to take charge of it, since Master
Philip had quitted it to join the King. Guy cast a hasty glance over
the lower rooms and then passed on up-stairs. The servant accompanied him in ever-increasing terror, which might, however, be
attributed to the fact that two troopers followed him with loaded
carbines, and two others held theirs at full-cock pointed at either
side of his shaking head. Passing through room after room Neville
paused at the door of that you are to sleep in to-night. It looked
then much as it looks now, save that where this window is was then
a panel of the oak which lines the rest of the wall. The door was
half-open, and Guy entered. A stain on the bare floor caught his
eye. He stooped and touched it with his hand.

"'Blood!' he said, sharply; but he said no more. He asked no
question. He strode straight to the fireplace; and, putting forth
his right hand, touched a part of the panel where that window is
now placed. The troopers stared. He pressed it hard; still harder
did they stare, while the servant stood with his eyes almost starting from his head, gazing in mute and motionless terror on the
proceedings of the unknown intruder.

"'Bring your carbines here, three of you!' said Sir Guy, in a
low tone. 'One of you keep his at that rascal's ear, and blow out
his brains if he speaks. Now, bring the butts to bear one above the
other in a line with my hand; knock me this panel in.' The sol-
diers looked at each other, clearly thinking their leader mad. Why
should he choose to try to knock to pieces this part of the wall
rather than another! Nevertheless they obeyed. The carbine-butts
went with full force against the oak paneling; a hollow sound was
returned. They struck again with all the strength they could mus-
ter. A sound of crashing wood followed; the panel was broken.
Still it held its place, until Sir Guy thrust his arm through the

hole broken in by a carbine blow, and drew a bolt. A shot was fired
from the other side; and, as he drew back his broken wrist, the
panel gave way and fell before the renewed blows of the troopers.

"A secret room, or rather closet, stood open, just above our
heads. Opposite the door was a pallet, by the side of which a light
was burning. Beside this pallet knelt an aged man in the robes of
a priest, his back to the intruders; upon it lay a youth, his head
bandaged, his shirt blood-stained, his face livid with the hue of
approaching death, and yet grasping a smoking pistol in his right
hand. Guy Neville recognised the adversary with whom he had
crossed swords an hour before. He recognised more. He grew suddenly pale, and staggered back: he strove an instant for utterance.
A look of surprise, anguish, and horror, but also of recognition,
crossed the face of the dying man. An exclamation rose to his parted lips; but ere it was uttered, ere Guy could recover breath, a ball
from one of the carbines crashed through the bandaged head, and
the Cavalier, without a word or a groan, fell back—dead.

"Paralysed with horror, the fratricide stood on the threshold
of the death-chamber. His staring eyes were fixed upon the corpse,
his hand had fallen by his side, the pain of his wound unfelt, his
very senses frozen with the terror that had stricken him to the
soul. He was wakened to consciousness by a voice that he knew
well, speaking in tones of prophetic denunciation that pierced the
conscience of the assassin. The aged priest—his tutor—had risen,
and confronted the startled troopers and their cowering chief.

"'So, Guy Neville, rebel to thy King, recreant to thy God, murderer of thy brother! is it thus we meet for the last time? Go hence:
the curse of Cain is upon thee, and the measure of thy crimes is
not yet full.'

"He passed out, untouched by the troopers, holding his robes
together lest the murderer's touch should pollute them. Guy Neville stood rooted to the spot till the old man was gone. Then he
turned—fled from the chamber and from the house, mounted his
horse, and rode none knew whither.

"Fifteen years later, an old and worn man, a young woman,
and an infant, arrived late one night, and took possession of the
Grange. They were all dressed in deep mourning; the father, wife,

and child of a second Philip Neville, the heir of the race, who had
just perished in a drunken brawl. The widow and orphan were
lodged in the most distant quarter of the house; the old man, aged
in middle life, occupied the chamber that opened into the secret
room. They sought him the next day; his chamber was vacant. One
old servant of the house, who alone knew the secret of the panel,
entered the hiding-place whither a brother had led his brother's
murderers. There lay Sir Guy, on the bed on which that corpse had
lain, still spotted with blood. There was no sign of violence on his
person, but he was dead. Nothing to account for his death, but
the expression of mortal terror on a countenance that had never
blanched in the face of battle; the features convulsed with such an
agony of fear as might well suffice to kill. The dead body lay in
state, and the trembling peasantry and the horror-struck yeomen,
who looked upon it, whispered one another that only some fearful visitant from another world could have wrought on those iron
nerves the terror which had driven the blood-stained soul from a
frame still erect and vigorous. And it is an accepted creed among
their descendants to this day, that either his brother's spirit, or
some yet more terrible apparition, had come to summon the fratricide to his last account."

I listened in silence. Charles told the story with a faith that
imposed upon and awed me, and I have since satisfied myself that
it is as true as documentary history can make it; that Sir Guy really caused his brother's death, and really died in that chamber of
terror—the terror of a guilty conscience or a ghostly vision.

I once spoke with a young Crimean soldier of his feelings
under fire; a man of whose physical courage no one who looks in
his face could doubt. Speaking lightly of musketry and of round
shot, he confessed his horror of shells in the naive expression: "I
never became so used to them but that I let my cigar out when
they passed over my head." So did my extinct Cabana bear witness
to the effect of the Neville legend. It was a minute or two before I
could shake off the spell sufficiently to light a second.

"Some unbeliever in ghosts remarks," I observed, "that whenever a man really believes that he sees a visitor from another world,
either his life or his reason gives way. If this be so, it is nowise

wonderful that the vision of his brother's ghost should frighten to death your amiable ancestor."

"Don't jest with my tale," said Charlie, somewhat displeased. "If you don't believe it, I do; and on ample evidence."

"One sometimes jests with things that are too terrible to be seriously contemplated, just by force of reaction," I replied. "Hence it is that the two most awful ideas known to man—Death and Satan—are most frequently the themes of jest, even to those who believe in the one as heartily as when they realise it they dread the other."

After a pause, Charles said:

"I have never thought that the sight of a ghost, apart from the horror which may environ an evil spirit or a bad conscience, would be terrible. On the contrary, I have often longed to see one—one that I knew—as a proof that would set at rest for ever all doubts concerning the future. I have great sympathy with those bargains between friends of which we hear in legend, that the soul of the one first deceased should return to warn the survivor."

"I doubt," I answered, "whether a ghost would serve your purpose. From the days of Homer down to these, men have seen ghosts from time to time. But they have all been alike. What are Homer's inhabitants of Hades but ghosts, as they are seen of ghost-seers—empty phantoms without sense or speech, rather the shadows than the spirits of the departed, whose form they assume? And who that should collect his idea of a future existence from the ghosts that have been seen of men—wandering about churchyards, gibbering over buried treasures, haunting the scenes of crimes done or suffered—to say nothing of those which rap out bad verses and bad grammar by the aid of ill-educated tables—but would echo with sad foreboding the wish of the dead Achilles:—

> "Make not light of death, I beseech
>   thee, gallant Odysseus.
> Fain would I, still living on earth, be
>   slave to another,
> Slave to a landless master with scanty
>   store of subsistence,

Rather than reign below, a prince of
the dead that are perished."

"You ought not to confound the seen ghosts with the table-rapping phenomena. Whether human or not, the agency of the latter is certainly not *super*human. Now, the ghosts that are seen may be all that we could wish to be as spirits, wanting nothing but the power of communicating with us, and that through our deficiency, not through theirs. As to their occupations, do they not agree exactly with what philosophy would suggest as the future fate of those who, while on earth, had no ideas above or beyond the best of earth's pursuits?"

"Well," said I, "I won't debate the philosophy of Mr. Owen, or the evidences of Mrs. Crowe, after sunset. If you would like to see a ghost, I would not; and he who falls asleep talking of them may well meet one in his dreams. We will talk politics till our cigars go out, and then I shall go to bed."

But I did not. My nerves were too much excited for sleep. I had not spent an evening of pleasant talk for a long time, nor heard a family legend before, as told by a firm believer in its horrors, and the effect of the double stimulus was to render me thoroughly wakeful. As I took off my coat, and looked for a peg to hang or a chair to lay it on, my eye was caught by a garment hung in one corner—it was a lady's shawl. Then one of the drawers which I opened, in order to deposit the contents of my valise, was full of those pretty feminine trifles which seem to a bachelor so mysterious and so charming—sleeves and collars, and needlework that did not seem intended for either. It shows strongly the innate grace of woman that she should spend so much art and labour in rendering ornamental what is never to be seen; and this trait alone should dispose of the slander that women dress only to fascinate men. A pincushion here, an unfinished fragment of work there, a general prettiness and tasteful arrangement of the whole, proved to me that I occupied a lady's room. "Whose? If any of the family have sole possession of this room, it must be the eldest daughter. I have, therefore, ousted Flora from her apartment. I hope she does not dislike a change as much as I do. I think I should be glad, however, to escape the gloom of these paneled walls and oaken ceiling, and the eyes of that portrait, which follow one everywhere." And here my observations brought me face to face with the picture of Sir Guy Neville. Painted in his youth, it nevertheless betrayed, or I fancied in its expression, the passions which blasted his life. The dark, deep-set eyes spoke at once of fiery spirit and of iron will; the mouth, despite the mustache which half-hid it, betrayed in the fulness of the under lip the vehemence of passion, and in the curved upper lip the scornful impatience of control which made that passion his master. In a word, the face was one in which a glance could detect a nature which would hardly be held within the bounds of law, either by conscience or by fear; which would never know how to forego a purpose or forgive an injury. I gazed long upon the portrait, and then turned away. I have said that it hung over the fireplace, and, therefore, beside the strange window that had once been the secret door. I took up a book, wrapped a dressing-gown about me, and sat down in a rocking-chair by the grate, to read. I sat on one side, so as to have the window on my right hand, and my eyes directed away from it. I read for some few minutes before I began to feel uncomfortable. An impression that I was not alone—a nervous horror, as of the presence of some unseen evil—gained so powerful a hold of my senses, that for some time I could not resolve to move or look around. Some at least of my readers will recognise the sensation. When I did move by a strong effort, I turned my eyes full upon the window, smiling at my own folly, while I avoided the fixed look with which the portrait seemed to haunt me. My reason contemptuously assured my shrinking nerves that there was nothing there; that I should turn only to look upon vacant darkness.

Wrong! what are these eyes fixed on mine with no painted stare? what is this face, on a level with my own, and almost within reach of my hand, between which and me is nothing but a thin sheet of glass? There, at the window, rose the head and bust of Sir Guy Neville, each feature the exact semblance of the portrait, with pale, terror-stricken countenance, and dark piercing eyes gazing in horror upon me, as they had gazed on that vision which scared his soul from her habitation! For a time, which could not be counted by moments, I sat fascinated, paralysed, my sight fixed upon those spectral eyes that glared into mine. For an instant I regained will enough to hide my face with my hand. When I looked again the spectre had vanished. At that moment a sound which broke the dead silence of night startled me, and made me spring to my feet, trembling in every limb. It was the stroke of the clock, which, from the neighbouring church, rang out the signal of midnight I heard that, and for a long time I saw and heard no more.

When I woke from that trance, or swoon—for I have no idea of the nature of the insensibility that had fallen upon me—my candle was flickering in the socket, and my teeth chattered, and my limbs shook with cold. Happily for me there was a nightlight in the room; I lighted that, mechanically undressed, and crept beneath the blankets. I looked at my watch as I took it off: it was two in the morning. Strange as it may seem, I was scarcely in bed before I fell asleep.

I was wakened from a dreamless rest by Charlie's emphatic summons, and had to dress myself with a haste which left no time for reflection over the horror of the night. I was startled, however, when I looked in the glass, by the ghastly pallor of my face, and was conscious of sensations of mental exhaustion and bodily pain such as often follow a day of severe toil and exposure, but rarely trouble us when we wake from a rest however short. When I joined the family at breakfast, Mrs. Neville almost started as she greeted me, and Charlie exclaimed, "Why, old fellow, you look like a ghost!" I could not repress a shudder at the word, and Annie asked, laughingly, "Did you meet one in the ruins last night?" "Not in the ruins," I answered, half unconsciously. By this time the attention of the whole party was fixed upon me, and I made a desperate effort to rouse myself, and shake off my absence of mind and the sense of gloom and terror that hung over me. Annie had ventured another question, but was silenced by her mother, and Charles, to relieve himself from the general feeling of curiosity and embarrassment, took up the newspaper of the previous day, which the post had brought in time for their breakfast. I forced myself to look up, and attend to what was going on. Flora was tea-maker, and I held out my hand to take a cup from hers. In doing so I felt that her wrist trembled so that she could hardly hold it; and, looking in her face, I saw an expression of alarm and dismay, where yesterday there had been only uneasiness and perplexity. Certainly she feared something, and the danger had come nearer. The ghost could have nothing to do with it. It was a very earthly fear that troubled that sweet face. Suddenly Charlie uttered an exclamation, and read the following paragraph from the newspaper:—

"Captain Monthermer, —th Hussars, was tried on the 10th July by court-martial, for disobedience to orders and insulting his superior officer on parade. The court assembled at Meerut, under the presidency of Colonel —. Captain Monthermer was found guilty, and sentenced to be dismissed her Majesty's service. The sentence has been confirmed by the Commander-in-Chief."

I noticed the deep colour that came over Flora's face as this was read, and comments were made upon it by Annie, Mrs. Neville, and Charles. Certainly, I thought, this is no news to Flora, and it has some painful interest for her. Does she know this scapegrace? Surely not; she was a mere infant when he quarreled with her father.

After breakfast, Charlie summoned me to join him in a cigar. I could not repress a shudder as we came to the very spot where we had sat the night before, just under the haunted window.

"What's the matter?" said he, in surprise. "It is not cold. And you look as pale as a ghost, or as if you had seen one. Did my story spoil your night's rest?"

"Its hero did," said I, trying to smile. "Don't laugh at me, Charlie, and don't be in a hurry to attribute what I tell you to my own fancy. Hundreds of times have I sat at night recalling much more horrible stories, and expecting when I looked up to see some frightful spectre with its eyes glaring into mine: and yet never has my imagination painted a visible form upon the darkness. But last night I saw at that window the ghost of Sir Guy, the exact semblance of the picture over the mantelpiece; ay, saw it as distinctly as I see you now; and that with a light burning by my side, bright enough to read a penny newspaper by."

"The deuce you did! Are you sure you were not dreaming?"

"I had a book in my hand, and had just looked up from it. I was as wide awake as you were when you told me the story."

"Sir Guy's ghost was never seen by a stranger before, and but once or twice by the men of our own family. Are you certain it was that face, and that your imagination did not lead you to attribute to some intending robber the features of Sir Guy, whose image just then filled your mind?"

"I am as certain of the face as that I saw the—thing at all. Feature for feature, it was the face of the portrait, save that it lacked the long flowing hair, and seemed somewhat older. I cannot say that I observed it attentively, but it burnt itself into my memory in that moment; and if I were a painter I could draw it line for line, with the very expression of horror, or of consternation, that it wore. I may, though I feel assured that I was not, have been deceived altogether. It may have been a spectral illusion, the vision of a diseased brain. But if I saw anything I saw what I have described. Besides, who could have climbed to that window and not have been torn down by your dog? Cæsar was loose."

"Strange—very strange," observed Charles, musingly. "How was he dressed?"

"In black; at least perfect blackness surrounded the face. That was all I observed. It is folly to talk of the dress of a ghost." I said this a little angrily. I was quite certain that I had seen, and not fancied the apparition—that it had really been there, and that it was no ordinary denizen of this world.

Charlie did not answer, and we smoked on in silence. After some ten minutes he threw away his cigar and rose.

"I am going over to Crosthwaite's. I should like to know who was the guest we saw yesterday. My mind misgives me, now that I know that Guy Monthermer is in England. Will you come with me?"

"Gladly," I answered, as we went off together. "But what should bring Monthermer here? The place has few attractions for one excluded from Neville Grange."

"I may as well tell you, for if he is here you may render assistance in getting rid of him, or in keeping the watch on him, which I must maintain. Guy has inherited, apparently, the romantic temper and ungovernable passions of our ancestor—whom, by the way, he resembles exceedingly in personal appearance. His mother and great-grandmother were both Nevilles, descendants of Sir Guy, and members of our own house. Early left an orphan, my father brought him up, till he was about eighteen. Flora, then a little girl in short frocks, was his especial favourite, and was warmly attached to him; and the quarrel which separated him from our family affected her so much, child as she was, that she became seriously ill. About three years and a half ago she was staying with a relative in Liverpool, and Monthermer's regiment was quartered there. He, being unknown except by name to my aunt, met Flora more than once at the houses of friends, and I fear in her walks; and both of them persuaded themselves that the love they had felt for each other in their childhood had ripened into passionate attachment. Before they were separated, some rash pledge had passed between them. Flora was brought home, and gradually seemed to forget this bit of romance, as we forbore to allude to it, and took it for granted that nothing of a serious kind had occurred. But she has seen no one comparable to Guy in personal beauty, intellectual brilliancy, or romantic humour, since her return home: her quiet life in this secluded place has been but too likely to leave her time to dwell on the one interesting episode in her life. If she and Monthermer were to meet again, one interview would fix his hold on her imagination as strongly as ever. I hope to God that my fancy deceives me, and that my fear that Guy Monthermer was the man you saw yesterday evening just by Crosthwaite's house, is as unfounded as it seems improbable."

We reached the farm, and questioned the stout old yeoman. He was very uncommunicative, and evidently suspected that our questions had some unfriendly purpose. Thus put on his guard, the spirit of hospitality made him vigilant in his guest's behalf; and we could only gather that a young gentleman had been there some days, and had left very early this morning—whether suddenly or not, we could not ascertain. Charles felt satisfied at finding that the stranger was gone. If he had been Guy Monthermer, he would hardly have departed without seeing Flora. I pondered and debated, but came to no conclusion.

My visit was a pleasant one. Flora grew cheerful and at ease; she and her sister were charming, frank, amusing companions, as free from affected shyness as from that fast and forward manner which is the more popular and fashionable affectation of to-day. The children were pleasant and well-behaved; their mother kind and hospitable; Charles as agreeable a companion as ever. Many were our pleasant excursions; incessant our conversation on all subjects, grave and gay, that did not partake of a political flavour; and I never left a friend's house more reluctantly than when an editorial summons warned me that I had overstayed my leave at Neville Grange. I certainly slept more soundly at home; but, though expected with fear and trembling, the ghost never again appeared at the window, or entered the haunted chamber.

Next May I ran up to London, to visit theatres and exhibitions, and enjoy three days of dissipation. On the morning before my return, I entered the rooms of the Royal Academy. I had looked at a dozen of the most bepraised and best-abused pictures, when, hanging just above the line, a striking portrait caught my eye. I staggered against an elderly gentleman, whose gouty foot was unhappily next to me; his lusty curses restored me to myself, and I gazed again at the picture with more self-possession. Above the collar of a cavalry uniform, one sleeve whereof—of course with the arm in it—rested on the saddle of a fine bay charger, looked out right into my eyes the face I had seen at the window of Neville Grange. But not as I should have painted it. The features were the same; but they were calm and stern, save that the upper lip seemed to curl slightly, as with the expression of habitual pride. The same eyes gazed into mine; but the expression was no longer that which they had borne on that terrible night. Then, they were full of a terror which overspread the whole countenance; now, they looked forth with a glance of scornful fire. The picture was that of a soldier on the instant before battle; it bore no other title than "An Officer," and the catalogue gave the name of an artist just deceased. I had no clue to the individuality of the figure; was it perchance a fancy sketch by one who had seen the portrait of Sir Guy Neville? I could not tell.

I visited Chester on my way back, having business with the editor of a county paper. On returning to the station I had some

half an hour to wait, and I strolled up and down the platform. A
train came up from Liverpool, and out of it flowed a stream of
passengers. A young lady was left standing by the carriage, whence
her companion had gone in quest of their luggage. As she turned
her face towards me I recognised Flora Neville.

She saw me, and coloured and trembled violently. I was greatly
surprised, but advanced to speak to her. She gave me her hand
mechanically, and strove to answer my greeting, but in vain.

"How comes it that I meet you here, Miss Neville?" I asked. " I
understood from Charlie that you had been in Liverpool, but were
to return to the north to-day. Are you paying a visit to Chester, or
going on elsewhere?"

My questions seemed to trouble Flora extremely. But I had
not time for surprise or conjecture. A figure was coming towards
us, with a large portmanteau in one hand and a carpet-bag in the
other. It was my turn to tremble, and, if not to colour, to turn very
faint and very pale. Unspiritual as his present occupation was,
I saw there not only the original of the Academic portrait, but
the very face that had gazed in upon me through the window of
Neville Grange. Again an expression of dismay, though far less
intense than then, overspread that face as its owner recognised me.
But his approach restored to Flora the self-possession which had
deserted both of us. Turning round, and fairly looking me in the
face, with a blush and a smile, she said:

"Allow me to introduce my husband, Guy Monthermer!"

It flashed across me at once. I had heard from Charles three
days before, and not a word of this marriage; nay, words which
distinctly implied that Flora was returning home. Instead of doing so, she had turned off, by appointment, at some point on her
route; met Monthermer, and married him, having gained in this
manner a full day's start of all pursuit. I looked gravely at Monthermer.

"Come, sir," he said, in answer to my look, "be just to us both.
I was a hot-headed youngster when I quarreled with her father;
on that account I knew it was hopeless to ask the consent of her
family: on that and others, if you will. I have done many foolish
things, but never anything that should make a gentleman blush for

himself, or a woman weep for him. I have loved her since she was a child; she has loved me for nearly five years." Flora pressed his arm. Her face was turned from me, and her eyes were looking up into his. He went on:

"I met her again last autumn, at great risk, in her own home. We should then have concerted our marriage but for you. I had only ventured to see her at night, for there were too many about who knew my person, and would have recognised me instantly had they seen me by day. Several nights in succession had I climbed the wall and spoken with Flora through the single pane of that window which opens with a rustic latch. One day, when I had ventured down into the valley, I saw at a distance young Neville returning from a drive; I hastened home, but was still in sight as he drove by. That night I postponed my visit to Flora's window later than usual: it was midnight when I climbed to my accustomed place—the dog, who had been civil to me from the first, evidently understanding that I did not belong to the usual order of trespassers, remaining silent—and was about to tap at the window, when I recognised a stranger—a man—in Flora's usual seat. The blood rushed back to my heart, and I nearly fell; he shrank as if he had seen a spectre, and covered his eyes with his hand. I recovered my presence of mind, dropped instantly to the ground, ran home, and left at daylight. Some days afterwards I received a letter from Flora, in which she gave me a graphic account—derived from her brother—of your ghostly vision. Heartily I laughed over our mutual terror, mine of a spy, and yours of a spectre."

"Then it was no visitant from another world I saw that night? it was—you were—"

"I was Guy Neville's Ghost."

A GHOST IN A STATE-ROOM
A STORY BETTER SUITED TO A CHRISTMAS NUMBER
SAMUEL BLOTTER

The Galaxy, 1868

I was always greatly taken by those ghost stories, which Mr. Washington Irving and Mr. Dickens relate, with an uncle as the hero. There is a certain air of mystery enveloping an elderly uncle in knee-breeches, a cocked hat, and powdered hair, which gives a delightful probability to the tales of their entertaining supernatural visitors and undergoing all kinds of uncanny nocturnal experiences. I wish with all my heart that this adventure, which I am about to describe, had happened to my uncle, because I know the reader would have been much more entertained by it; besides, it is much pleasanter to have one's uncle see a ghost than to have such an experience one's self.

To be sure, on second thoughts, an uncle is at the bottom of this story, because I am dictating at this moment to my nephew, who scribbles a little for the magazines, and who thinks he can see in it material which can be well worked up. But the fellow is conceited, and I don't believe he will print it as I tell it, and I don't believe, moreover, that he will make out of it anything worth reading.

I like to trace the relation between cause and effect; and to begin, I think my ghost arose indirectly from a lobster salad.

"Oho!" cries out the experienced and acute reader. "I see. This fellow had a bad dream."

I beg your pardon, but allow me to say you are in error. I think I have been enough annoyed, not to say disgusted, in my day, by ghost stories, which, after describing the most impossible apparitions, ended with—

"—when he suddenly awoke and found himself safe in his own room."

I can safely promise that my story, however stupid it may be, will not end with my waking up. I woke up before I saw the ghost. I beg to point out that I said that my ghost rose *indirectly* from a lobster salad.

I saw *it*—I like that word *it* used for a ghost: there is something delightfully weird about it—I saw it in state-room No. 72, on the steamer *John Halifax,* which runs on Long Island Sound in connection with one of the New York and Boston lines. You do not believe there ever was a Sound steamer with that name? Neither do I; if I did I should choose some other. I get passes over this same line now, in consideration of the quantity of freight shipped to our house in Boston, and, of course, I am not going to have the directors coming to me and complaining that I have given their boats the name of being haunted. The *John Halifax* was laid up some years ago, to be sure, but it might become necessary, for aught I know, to put her on some night, in an emergency. The number of the state-room, however, was 72, and it was pretty well aft; there can be no manner of doubt about that.

I had been to New York on business and was returning home. The month was May, and the boat left at 5 o'clock, p. m. As I like to be punctual, I reached the pier precisely at ten minutes before five, with my bag in my hand, having walked down from the Astor House. I declined, with suavity, seven invitations to have my boots polished, and I bought only one newspaper out of the large editions offered me. I got my ticket and the key of my state-room, which had been previously engaged—without much delay. I put my small bag in my stateroom, and finding a vacant seat on the after-promenade deck—if that is what they call it; I am not a nautical man—I sat down quietly to read my paper. At the same time, I kept my weather eye open, to use a seafaring term, now that we were fairly off, and I found no body on board I knew, which was with me rather an unusual circumstance. Next me, sat a man with red face and rather a stupid look, whom I took to be a bar-keeper in search of actuation. He used tobacco offensively, and when he volunteered some remark about the weather, I answered civilly indeed, but in such a way that he did not attempt to continue the conversation.

There are few more inspiring sights than the rivers and harbor of New York on a pleasant day, and I have no doubt that my nephew will insert something of his own here about "the small craft darting hither and thither," and the "majestic steamers sailing out of their docks, freighted with the world's merchandise," etc., etc. If he does, I dare say it will all be very nice, but he cannot, if he tries, describe that quiet feeling of contented interest which steals over a man, when being for the moment quite free from every duty and care, he surveys such a busy scene. All this is not much to the purpose, since this day was not at all pleasant. It was cloudy, and rain was threatened so clearly that everything looked dull and gloomy. I should hardly have returned by the boat, if I had not already engaged my state-room; and the condition of the weather was, perhaps, the reason why there were so few passengers on board.

Castle Garden, Governor's Island, Brooklyn, Williamsburg, Green Point, Blackwell's Island, Jones's Wood, Ward's Island, Hurl Gate, in sight. I went below to supper. I had dined at two o'clock—I always dine at two, in fact—and, having taken some exercise since then, I was rather hungry. All the dishes which should have been hot, had been spread out on the table so long that they had grown quite cold. They manage things better now-a-days, but then there was a melancholy array of black waiters, red paper flowers, frizzled butter, and nothing good to eat. I ordered some lobster, however, and made a salad. I flatter myself I can make a good salad; this time I was particularly successful, and this led me to eat rather too much of it.

After supper, I smoked one cigar, "abaft the wheel," as the notice read; I watched the engine while the paddle-wheels made one hundred and twenty-five revolutions. I walked twice the length of the vessel in the upper cabins; and then I went to bed. I am very moderate in my smoking. My nephew confesses to nine or ten cigars a day, but pretends that so much tobacco does not hurt him. I don't believe it. It is just as easy to become intemperate in smoking as in drinking. I never exceed three cigars a day and make it a rule never to smoke in the morning.

I think I have hinted that I indulged too freely in lobster salad. When I reached my state-room the boat was rolling and pitching a good deal, and the door lock and the water jug were rattling like the bones of an Ethiopian serenader. It occurred to me that I needed some corrective for the sake of digestion. Now for the last ten years I have never travelled without a rather large flask, with leather outside and old cognac within. I know the brandy is good, because I bought it in '48, and knew where it came from, and although I never drink it at home, occasions do sometimes arise when I am away when it becomes useful for sanitary purposes. My wife jokes me about the size of the flask, but I do not mind that in the least; I always carry it, and I judged that one of the occasions had now arisen when it was proper to use it. I turned out what I considered a moderate dose—it is to be observed that I took it simply as a medicine—drank it off, speedily experienced a warming and comfortable sensation under the waistband, screwed the top on the flask, placed it on the wash-stand, and made preparations for retiring.

I do not know to this day, although I confess I am old enough, why they call these little boxes "state-rooms." I think that ship-builders' ideas of lying in state must be different from mine. This one had two berths, one above the other, and had no light except the rather dim rays which came in through scroll work at the top from the cabin, and a lamp near by outside. Opposite the berths, were the door in one corner and the immovable washstand in the other. One stool completed the furniture, and there was room enough left for me to take off my overcoat, and by due caution to avoid bruising my elbows. My preparations for retiring were simply to remove my boots and take off my coat and waistcoat, and hang them up. I also stuck my pocket-knife hard into the door, or rather between it and the post, and thereby stopped its rattling in some measure. I mentally concluded that the upper berth looked rather the lighter and less dismal of the two, and climbed into it, after I had examined the life-preservers on the shelf at the foot. They were like two long empty tin preserve-cans lashed together, and I was glad to see them there, although I had not the remotest idea of how they ought to be worn. The sheets of the berth suggested the influenza, but there were blankets enough, and I presently composed myself to sleep, although the motion of the boat set rattling everything which was loose.

I have found that I usually wake up at least once an hour on a steamer, and this is especially true when I am travelling on the Sound toward Boston, and feel that I shall be left by the train when the boat arrives, if I sleep too sound. The first nap I had that night, lasted about fifty minutes, as near as I could judge by consulting my watch when I awoke. I had a bad dream, and found myself lying with my arms over my head. I do not remember now what I dreamed about, but I attributed it to the salad; and turning over, with my face toward the front of the berth, I presently dropped off again into a doze. In awaking again, I became conscious of an unusually loud crash of the panels and lock, and whatever it was, which kept up the continual rattling and banging which annoyed me. The effect was to make me quite wide awake in an instant, and as I lay there, looking through the lace curtain toward the wash-stand, or, rather, the jarring pitcher on it, which was all I could see from my position, the neck and upper half of my flask slowly and noiselessly rose into my line of vision. I was sufficiently awake to see the flask very clearly as it gradually appeared, but I suppose my faculties were not quite enough aroused to reason about it. Certainly I was not in the least startled at the moment, and I lay there a few seconds arguing with myself as to whether the flask had actually risen into sight, or whether it was an optical delusion, caused in some way by the motion of the boat In the process of reasoning about this phenomenon, I rose on my elbow, and leaning forward, looked about the state-room. A glance showed me that everything was as I had left it. My flask stood bolt upright on the washstand, as if it was a sentinel in guard over the pitcher, and was in exactly the same place where I had left it. My coats and waistcoat were hanging on the hooks, my watch and money I had on my person, my knife was still sticking between the door and its post, and not even my boots—I always wear boots— had toppled over; they still leaned against the wall in an attitude suggesting mild inebriation. I even went to the length of leaning over far enough to take a good steady look into the berth underneath me, but there was nothing there, and the sheets and pillow were as near unruffled as maritime sheets and pillows ever are. I pushed back the lace curtain so as to give me an uninterrupted view of my flask, and looked at my watch. It was ten minutes past midnight. There was nobody stirring in the cabin outside, and no noise except that caused by the motion of the steamer.

I lay down again in a state of uncertainty whether I had dreamed that I saw my flask move, or was really awake, as I had supposed. I meant to keep my eyes on the flask, but I suppose I was a little restless, for when I awoke the third time, which was the next thing of which I was conscious, my face was toward the wall. I turned slowly over, speculating as to how long I had been asleep, as a man will who has only to pull out his watch to satisfy himself, and there was the flask in its place this time.

"I was asleep and dreaming," I said to myself.

And as I thought this, there came at the instant, from somewhere beneath me, a deep, low groan.

For the first moment I was startled. Then I said to myself, "Nonsense! it's only the boat creaking." Then I listened for the sound again, with my sense of hearing strained to the full to catch the slightest unusual noise.

I had only to wait half a minute. The groan was repeated, only fainter, but still the noise seemed near me. You may guess that this time there was no doubt of my being wide awake. A third groan, still fainter, but yet distinct! I rolled out of my berth, and coming to my feet, rallied against the door and stood with the knob in my hand.

It lay in the lower berth. Its eyes were wide open and staring at me. Its face was livid in the dim light, and there was an ugly red gash in its cheek.

For a second we stood staring at each other. Then he—I had forgotten to mention that *it* was a *he,* and that it was dressed in the habiliments of its sex—he stretched out his arm as he lay there, and pointing his finger at me, said, three times, slowly and distinctly,

"Murdered! Murdered! Murdered!"

I do not quite know what it is proper to do when one sees a ghost of this disagreeable species. None of my friends ever confided to me that he was haunted, and although I have seen a great number of theatrical spirits, they are very different things from the reality. I know how Hamlet is exercised both in mind and body when he sees the ghost of his father, late King of Denmark. I know how Richard III. behaves when he sees the apparition of his victims as he lies asleep in his tent. I have seen the low comedian in a certain farce go into the most ridiculous contortions at the sight of a living man whom he supposes to be quite dead. Perhaps if I had had a pistol, I should have fired it at but I very much doubt this. What I actually did was to turn the key in the lock, open the door, leaving my pocket-knife to lie when it fell, and all the time keeping my eyes steadily upon *it,* to see that *it* did not spring upon me, I backed quietly out of the state-room into the cabin, and closed the door after me.

When I got into the cabin, I began to feel as if I had better sit down very soon. Immediately opposite my state-room door was the colored stewardess of the boat, sitting bolt upright, but half asleep and uneasily nodding. When I sat down close by her, she woke up with a great start. Her astonishment was not altogether unreasonable. I suppose that the sight of a middle-aged gentleman, rather bald, without either his boots, his collar, his coat, or his waistcoat, meandering about the cabin at that hour of the night, was rather unusual.

"Lor' bless you, how you scared me!" she cried out. "Why, what on airth's de matter. You look as pale as ef you'd seen a ghost."

"Well, I have seen something a good deal like one," I answered.

"When?"

"In my state-room—72, there."

Some persons will laugh when I say that the colored stewardess turned very pale at the avowal, which the next moment I felt rather ashamed at having made. Those who are familiar with colored people, however, understand very well that pallor is quite as conspicuous on their faces as on those of the white races.

"Guess you're mistaken, sir," she returned. "I've been runnin' on this boat ever sence she was built, and I never seed no ghost."

"And never knew of any murder?"

"Never heered of no murder neither."

"Well, I just saw a man there, lying in a berth, with a gash in his face, who said he had been murdered. He may be a ghost and he may not, but I know he was not there when I went to sleep."

"Guess you've been dreamin', sir," said the stewardess; but she grew visibly paler.

"Do you think I'm a fool, woman? I tell you I saw this just as plain as I see you. I don't believe in ghosts, myself. I don't know what it was, but I saw it."

"Well! well!" said the stewardess; "I declare!" Then, after a moment—"Well, any way, de boat'll be in now in a few minutes, so you need'nt go back."

"Yes; but I can't go ashore in my shirt-sleeves."

"I'll go and get yer tings fur yer."

To my utter surprise, the stewardess rose, and without hesitation walked to the state-room door, opened it and disappeared inside, closing it after her. I watched her with some satisfaction, I confess. It seemed to me that it must still be there, and I was very willing another person should bear witness to its appearance. I waited anxiously for a scream. Some moments elapsed, and I mechanically felt for my watch and money. They were safe, and it was no robber at all events.

The door opened again and the stewardess appeared, calmly bearing my clothes, my bag, my boots, and my flask. I found my hands shaking a little as I drew on my boots; but I do not think I had been more frightened than any other man would have been under the circumstances.

"Well!" said I to the stewardess. I began to feel as if I had made a great fool of myself.

"Well," said she, "I didn't see no ghost. Guess you must have been dreamin', sir, sartin, sure."

I knew that I had not been dreaming; but what could I say? I did not wish to be laughed at, and when I had dressed myself, I put five dollars in her hand and requested her to say nothing about the ghost. Of course, she very readily assented.

Then I went to the state-room door and looked in, the stewardess following me, as if anxious I should show her the apparition. She was quite right. The berths and the room were empty; a glance around showed that very plainly. The stewardess offered to take my key; but I showed her by my watch that the boat would not be in for an hour yet, and, although I did not choose to go to bed again, I preferred to leave my bag in the state-room until we landed. The stewardess went back to her old place and appeared to drop off to sleep at once, while I walked up and down the cabin, taking its whole length. I was puzzled, annoyed, mortified, and angry, by turns.

When I reached the forward end of the cabin for the third time, there was a man there peering out of the window into the darkness. When I approached quite near him, he turned; it was the barkeeper, whom I had met the evening before. I returned his salutation rather gruffly, for I was not pleased with his looks, and I was in no mood for conversation. I was turning away, when he said:

"So you saw a ghost last night."

"How do you know?" I asked, turning back rather angrily.

"Why, I heard you say so just now. I was on the other side, right behind you, when you were talking about it You did not see me, because I was in the shadow. I slept there all night. I can sleep just as well in a chair as in a berth. It don't make no difference to me."

I was forced, in defence of my sanity to stop in my walk and explain the circumstances at some length. When I had finished, he said:

"Let's see your flask."

I was disgusted, although I was not surprised. I had related to him my adventure, and without a word of sympathy he asked for a drink—and at that time in the morning, too! However, I found the flask in an inner pocket of my overcoat, where I had seen the stewardess place it, and as I had the coat on my arm and the flask was rather large for the pocket, I held the coat while he pulled out the bottle.

"You'll find that very good liquor," said I, complacently. "Don't shake it!"

"How much was there here when you went to bed last night?" he asked, without paying much attention to what I had said.

"I suppose it was at least half full."

He unscrewed the top, and turned the mouth down. It was empty.

"A very dry ghost," he said, with a grin. "I tell you what, sir; if you can wait over one train, when the boat gets in, I guess I can show you your ghost. You will? All right. Just you go and sit down opposite your state-room, and see that nobody goes out nor in. If the stewardess tells you the train is starting, just say to her you are waiting to take your ghost along with you."

"Why not look for him now?"

"Because I had rather wait, if it's all the same to you. Just you keep a sharp look out, that's all, and I shall be around."

I went and sat down opposite No. 72 and waited for the boat to arrive at the town where passengers take the cars for Boston. Presently, certain restless people began to come out of their rooms, and bustle about, and compare notes, and wonder when we should get in. Then a colored man went about waking up the sleepers, and by-and-by they appeared, one after the other, half awake and very cross with having to rise at such an unseemly hour. Then there was a great ringing of bells below, a great bumping of the boat against the wharf, and a great trampling of feet The passengers took up their bags and bandboxes, their umbrellas and canes, and went off down stairs in a procession as melancholy as if Charon had just ferried them across the Styx, and they were about to disembark in Hades.*

I noticed the barkeeper loitering on the other side of the cabin, and he did not go down until the occupants of the state-rooms on both sides of No. 72 had come out and departed. Then he followed, and the cabin was presently very quiet. The black stewardess had, apparently, been called away by her duties; at any rate, she was not to be seen. I shall not attempt to describe my reflections

---

* This simile, I may say, was suggested by my nephew.

at this time, because, as it afterward turned out, they were worth very little. I may say, however, that I began to have some new ideas about it.

When the barkeeper came back, he was accompanied by a man in plain clothes, and a policeman. He placed one in each of the state-rooms adjoining mine, and then I unlocked my door and we entered No. 72. Just over the threshold, I trod on my knife, which I had before forgotten. I pointed out the position of things at the time of the appearance of the spectre, and showed my companion where my flask had stood. He took from his pocket a box of wax tapers, and lighting one, got down on his hands and knees and looked under the lower berth.

I suppose some wiseacres will ask why I had not done this myself, earlier in the night. In fact, my nephew goes to the length of asserting that my neglect to do this gives my story an air of improbability. But I beg to ask if a person always does in moments of excitement what he himself, looking back upon the circumstances afterward, would say ought obviously to be done. I think not. At all events, when I examined the state-room, with the stewardess looking over my shoulder, it did not occur to me to do what my companion was now doing. One reason for this, doubtless—and this seems to me important—was that the frame work of the berth appeared to one looking at it from above to come within two or three inches of the floor.

My companion's first match went out and he lighted the second one. By this time I was not much surprised to hear him exclaim:

"I see you, my friend! I'll trouble you just to come out of that!"

The lower portion of the board immediately above the space I have mentioned was lifted up, and it now appeared that the board was cracked its whole length and was held together only by certain strong fibres, which acted as hinges. Through the aperture thus left and which was still very narrow, there wriggled the slender form of a young man, who on turning over to the light and rising, showed me the features of *it*.

We came out into the cabin, and my companion called out exultingly.

"Here you are, Brown! I've got him."

So the other two men came out, and Mr. Brown, who proved to be a detective in plain clothes, slipped a pair of handcuffs on the prisoner, who looked very unhappy.

"I suppose," said Mr. Brown, "you know what you are wanted for. I've got the warrant here all right."

"I suppose I do," said the prisoner, "but I can prove that I did it in self-defence. Look here,"—and he pointed to the scar on his face. "He gave me this."

"If you can prove that you did it in self-defence," said Brown, "so much the better for you. But that is as it may be."

With this sententious remark, Mr. Brown and his prisoner were about to take up their line of march, when the black stewardess appeared in a state of tears and perturbation. My former companion took her by the arm and drew her aside.

"See here, ma'am," said he, "we don't want anything of you, now, but if you want to keep safe, you had better be uncommon quiet; do you understand?"

This advice was accepted, and the stewardess went off, swallowing her emotions as best she could.

"What has she to do with it?" asked I. "But no, first of all, be good enough to tell me who you are." And as we went along, he gave me his name, and explained to me all the facts of the case, which was really very simple, when I came to understand it.

He was not a barkeeper, at all, as I had hastily concluded, but was a New York detective officer, on his way to Boston on quite different business from that which he had just transacted. He was, however, in possession of most of the facts of this case, which had been telegraphed on to the New York police headquarters, before he started. Charles Hardy, the prisoner, was a young man of respectable family, living in this town where we now were. He had, however, "gone to the bad," as my nephew would express it, and two evenings before, in a disgraceful brawl in a low public-house, he had shot and fatally wounded a young man whose connections were still richer, and so no time had been lost in setting on foot the hue and cry. The affair took place in the evening, before the arrival of the Boston train and the departure of the boat. Favored by the darkness, young Hardy had managed, either by the aid of a skiff or from the wharf, to get on board the steamer unobserved. Here he found the stewardess, who had in former years been a servant in his father's family, and, telling her only a part of the truth, he easily persuaded her to let him conceal himself. When the boat reached New York, the stewardess made some guarded inquiries and observations which led them to believe that it would not be safe for him to venture out, so that when I went to bed in No. 72, he had remained cramped up in his place of concealment for the greater part of the time for nearly twenty-four hours, with very little food and with no stimulants, which he was accustomed to use in large quantities and which he, of course, needed just then more than ever. It may be guessed that my flask proved too great a temptation to him, and that he returned to it again and again until he reached such a pitch of indifference to his situation that he concluded to take the lower berth, in preference to his narrow quarters underneath. He had partly slept off the effects of his potations, when I woke him by getting out of my berth in the hasty manner which I have described, and he was quick-witted enough to turn my astonishment to account. Now this seems to me, I may add, the most improbable part of the story, but I can only say that it happened. My nephew insists that it is easily explained, and that the young man, having nothing else to think of in his confinement, had very carefully planned, the day before, a way of frightening the occupants of the state-room, if by accident he should be discovered. This may be so, but it seems to me very remarkable that on waking out of a heavy sleep, under such circumstances, he should have had the presence of mind to act as he did. The most surprising thing to me, however, is, after all, that he could carry off so much liquor. I am confident there was enough in that flask to have kept me intoxicated for a week.

A good deal to my disgust and somewhat to my pecuniary loss, I was compelled to be present both at the preliminary examination and at the trial, although what I knew about the alleged murder seemed to me of very little importance. The upshot of it all was that the young man was convicted of manslaughter.

It has seemed to me, since then, that his detection was entirely owing to that lobster salad, for if I had not eaten it, my flask would have remained all night in my bag, and I should probably have left my state-room in the morning without having seen any ghost. I got no sympathy from my wife, who indeed reaped a slight advantage from my adventure, for I have never since laughed at her for her habit of always looking under the bed for burglars before she retires.

THE GHOST OF A FACE
FREDERICK H. DEWEY

Ballou's Monthly Magazine, 1878

Darkness was gradually closing over the sedate little village of Edgeville, and night was drawing on apace. The subdued twilight was giving place to gloom deep and opaque: night was settling down over Edgeville and its quaint old church under the hill.

A gloom of awe seemed to pervade the village, which, remote and small, was in its liveliest days but a dull old hamlet. But to-night seemed unusually dismal and sombre, perhaps owing to the solemn tolling of the bell in the tiny belfry of the little church.

Toll! toll! Out on the heavy night air the tones sounded mournfully clear and distinct to the adjacent villagers, but vague and spectral to the farmers away over the hills, to whom they half seemed the ghosts of ringing bells. In the door of more than one farm-house far and near, whose locality was revealed by a little twinkling star of candle-light, men, women, and children, stood gazing toward the village and listening to the solemn peals. In the village itself, the inhabitants, possessing more urban indifference than their rural neighbors, were collected in knots on the corners; and it was perhaps singular that every face was turned toward the church, which was invisible, being deeply in the shadow of the hill under which it stood.

Toll! toll! The ringing had begun at sunset, and it was now quite dark; but the measured tolling continued until the number of sixty-one strokes had been sounded, when the peals were heard no more.

Near by the little church—being, in fact, only separated from it by the churchyard—was a small, neat cottage, the dwelling of the sexton, a little, withered old man, who, having been born in the village, and never having made a day's journey away from it, was a sort of pensioner of the village, who considered him a village institution, and withal looked up to him as an oracle.

Adam Hill was town-clerk, as well as sexton, and postmaster besides,—although his postal duties consisted in distributing the half-dozen or so of letters which arrived weekly by the mail-rider. As he could actually pronounce the majority of the polysyllabic words scattered through the columns of the newspaper which occasionally strayed into Edgeville from the great outside world, and as he was known to have quoted Latin once in his youth, he was considered a person of boundless sagacity and erudition, and to him all mooted questions were referred. On red-letter days, such as Fourth of July, Thanksgiving, Christmas, and so forth, he would ascend the dusty pulpit of the quiet old church,—for Edgeville was unable to maintain a parson,—and, with "words of learned length and thundering sound," would hold forth to the admiring villagers, to their intense edification and possible enlightenment.

Adam Hill was a prominent man in Edgeville.

While the bell had been tolling, Adam Hill's hale old wife had been composedly knitting, in the demure society of the smoul-dering fire, the purring cat, and snoring hound curled up on the red-brick hearth,—raising her head ever and anon to glance out of the window across the graveyard to the church where her goodman was tolling the bell in memory of Squire Lovell, who had departed from Edgeville and this world five years before, at the age of sixty-one. On the anniversary of his death, the church-bell was tolled every year. Why, no one could tell; for, though the squire had been rich, he had also been snug, if not miserly, and exacting, as many an unfortunate tenant of his—and he had owned half the village—could testify. Perhaps the reason was that as Squire Lovell had been held in awful respect by the simple villagers during life, their veneration for him resulted in keeping his anniversary by tolling the bell as it had been tolled at his funeral five years previously.

There hung a mystery over his death. He lived in the old family mansion on the skirts of the village, and, although known to possess wealth, lived entirely alone, as he had no relations. True, he had a nephew, Eugene Lovell, a harum-scarum boy of sixteen, who, having rebelled against the authority of his severe and exacting uncle, ran away, and had never since been heard of. This occurred a short time previous to the squire's death. The old man, brooding and revengeful by nature, cut his nephew off without a shilling, leaving all his accumulated wealth to the son of his old nurse. The will was drawn on the 9th of October, 184-, and the next morning the squire was found dead in his bed.

Stricken by heart disease, some said; apoplexy, suggested others. But not a few whispers floated about that, as the squire had been of robust habit, and on the day of the drawing of the will had been in excellent health, his sudden death was marvelous and suspicious. But no marks of violence were perceived on his person, and the old squire was buried, the house was closed to all saving bats, owls, rats, mice, and spiders, and the fortunate heir obtained possession of his fortune.

But although the squire was dead, he was not forgotten. On every anniversary, when Adam Hill tolled the church-bell at sunset, the villagers would think kindly of the stern

old squire, whom in life they feared, and speculate on the cause of his sudden death. Each succeeding anniversary augmented the number of those who believed the old man had met with foul play, until finally, on the present one, not a man or woman in the village had a different opinion. But suspicion attached itself to no one, and no attempt was ever made to ascertain the cause of his death.

As previously mentioned, the squire bequeathed his entire property to the son of his old nurse, Gilbert Ray. Prior to the squire's death, "Gil Ray," as he was familiarly called, had been employed by the neighboring farmers in common farm labor. He was a young man of industrious habits, but close-fisted and moody; and, being morose, vengeful, and averse to the society of his acquaintances, had acquired the name of "Dark Gil,"—though he was never addressed by that sobriquet, as he possessed a terrible temper, and visited vengeance on those who provoked it.

After the squire's death, Dark Gil went out to farm service no more, but shrewdly invested that portion of his inheritance which consisted of money, and employed himself in attending to his tenants.

The tenantry had deemed the squire an exacting landlord, but Dark Gil proved far more so. Woe to the unfortunate delinquent, for he showed him no mercy. On rent-day he regularly appeared, and coldly demanded the rent. If it was forthcoming, he received it in silence; if not, no matter how reasonable the excuse advanced by the tenant, it was of no avail,—for Dark Gil would seize household goods to its equivalent value. He was inexorable, and the villagers' dislike of him increased every rent-day.

It was a subject of occasional comment among the villagers that Dark Gil never visited the mansion-house. Indeed, he seemed to avoid it; for since the squire's death he had not visited it, and allowed it to run to decay quietly.

The sexton's wife sat knitting until the bell ceased to toll. Soon afterward the door burst open, and in came Adam Hill, excited and trembling, with a look of awe and alarm on his wrinkled face.

"Husband! husband!" cried the goodwife, as Adam sank into the nearest chair.

"Nannette, I've seen the squire's ghost!" whispered the old sexton, involuntarily looking over his shoulder in the direction of the church.

"Seen the squire's ghost!" gasped his frightened helpmeet.

"Ay! just as he used to look when he and I were young, and rivals for the favor of my Nannette. I was pulling the rope on the last stroke,—the sixty-first,—when a current of cold air swept over me from the interior of the church, and, looking up, I saw the squire's face (no more), looking as he looked at twenty-one. The blue eyes looked calmly into mine for barely a moment; then the face disappeared, and I left the church,—losing no time, I can tell you."

"Lord preserve us! And you are sure you saw his young face?"

"Sure!"

And the expression of awed conviction on the old sexton's face left no doubt in his wife's mind.

A pause ensued, during which the old couple looked at the smouldering fire. Then said Nannette:—

"What can it mean, Adam?"

"Foul play!" responded Adam gloomily.

"Mercy on us!"

"I always thought the squire didn't die a nateral death, and now I know it!" declared Adam, striking his knee with his clenched fist. "For why did his young face appear to me but to remind me of the boyish love we bore each other, and for the sake of that love to set wrong right, that an old man might rest easy in his grave? Nannette, the squire was always good to me, always,—though I did get the lovely Nannette, for whose sake he lived and died a bachelor,—and now I'll do a good turn for him if I can; and tonight to boot! Get me the lantern, Nannette, and my oak stick, and sit here by the fire until I get back,—there's a dear girl,—for I go to the squire's house tonight."

"Lord preserve us! You surely can't be so mad!" cried Nannette, as Adam rose. "To the squire's house! why, do you know they say it is haunted?"

"I know they say it is haunted, and, after what I've seen to-night, I know it *is!* It is haunted by the sperrit of an old man who can't sleep easy in his grave because foul play goes unpunished." Then he said sturdily: "Don't be skeered, Nannette; the squire's ghost won't harm old Adam Hill, his best friend."

But Nannette dung to him.

"Adam! Adam!" she implored; "don't go,—don't! You'll never come back again if you do. Promise me you won't go."

"No, Nannette," said Adam sturdily, "it is my duty to go, and go I must and will. Don't be afeerd, old lady,—the squire's ghost will never hurt the squire's best friend."

So saying, Adam bustled about, procured his lantern and oak stick, and, resisting the entreaties of his anxious spouse, set out on his expedition, leaving Nannette by the hearth, shaking like a leaf, with her face buried in her hands.

Up the quiet, grass-grown, village street Adam Hill's lantern bobbed and glimmered, casting fantastic shadows round about, and giving to his moving legs a shadow resembling a piece of machinery.

The squire's house was situated at the other side of the village, at the extremity of a long, wide lane, between two rows of lofty poplars, which threw the lane into dense obscurity. Even in vivid moonlight—and this night was dark and murky—the lane was of inky darkness, and, as it led to the old house, it was avoided by the simple villagers, who regarded it with dread. Perhaps for several years no human foot had trodden the lane after darkness had fallen, and the children feared to frolic in its shades, though its attractions to them were manifold.

But Adam Hill, though superstitious, and usually as afraid of the ghostly lane as his neighbors, neither looked to the right nor left, as, plunging into its obscurity, he strode sturdily toward the old house. His eyes were bent upon the luminous spot made on the ground by his lantern, and he was deeply pondering over the cause of the apparition which had alarmed and amazed him so in the church. He finally became abstracted, but was abruptly brought to his senses by a concussion which caused him to look up.

He had run against the crazy old gate which of yore used to exclude the cows of the villagers from the tasteful grounds; but since the squire's death the premises had gone to decay. The fences rotted and fell in many places, leaving great gapes which afforded the village animals ingress to the luxuriant herbage of the lawn. Like the fences, the gate was crazy, and, with a slight push, Adam passed through it, and strode steadily up the graveled walk toward the house.

As he walked along, he could not fail, even in the deep gloom, to observe the decay and desolation that had fallen over the grounds, and to contrast them with their former elegance. The last time he had set foot on the premises was on the day of the squire's burial, when house and surroundings were well-kept and attractive; and now, as he looked about on the decadence, old Adam felt sad at heart.

He walked up the graveled path, and soon arrived before the house. The mansion was large and rambling, of two stories, with a piazza on the ground floor extending the whole length of the house, and a corresponding one on the floor. Numerous doors and windows opened out on these piazzas, and in its former days the house was a pleasant one, facing the south, commanding a view of pretty Edgeville nestling among its groves, and of a smiling landscape beyond. The roof was square, like the house, slanting gently up to a graceful cupola, which had a window in each side. In this cupola the squire had been wont to sit in the dying day, smoking his pipe, and reading his book,—for Squire Lovell had been happy in a refined literary taste. Many a time, in passing by, Adam had seen the squire's gray head in the window of the cupola; and now, as the remembrance occurred to him, he mechanically raised his eyes to the place.

What was his alarm—ay, terror—at beholding a white face framed in the window!—the face of the squire as ho had looked when a boy of twenty. The face was plainly visible, albeit the night was dark and the atmosphere thick; and so distinctly did Adam see it that he shuddered under the dark eyes which were steadfastly regarding him with a look of deep significance.

Perhaps the sexton may have had some lurking doubts whether he indeed saw the face in the church. If he had, they were now dissipated; for in the cupola above him—where it had formerly been seen—was the squire's boyish face turned steadfastly toward him.

For a moment old Adam was terrified, notwithstanding his natural fearlessness, and his firm belief that the squire's ghost would occasion him no evil; for there is something in the apparition of a dead friend which appalls the stoutest heart. But Adam's terror was only momentary. With a strong effort he collected his senses, and regained his courage, as the face slowly faded, became a nebulous blur in the window, and finally disappeared.

Adam looked steadfastly at the window. He now could only determine its locality by distinguishing the white window-casing through the gloom. One keen look satisfied him that the face had disappeared. Then, grasping his oak stick more firmly, he sprang with youthful agility upon the piazza.

"It is a chain! a chain!" he cried. "He appeared to me in the church, and again here. Does that mean for me to follow him here?

Of course it does; and old Adam Hill will follow Squire Lovell in death as he did in life!"

With this declaration, the sexton shifted his cudgel to his left hand, and tried the ponderous front door. Adam himself had securely locked the house after the squire had been laid in his grave, and he clearly remembered securing this one with bolt and lock. He was confident that no one had entered the house since that time, for the villagers would rather have risked their lives than venture within the grounds after nightfall, and studiously kept aloof in broad daylight; and no pedestrian travelers wandered to Edgeville, for it was remote from the bustling towns of the world. Nevertheless, to his surprise, the door yielded readily to his arm, and swung back with a dismal creaking, an unusual sound, which caused a scampering of rats and mice throughout the hall and the adjoining rooms.

The weird sound of the tiny feet caused an icy shiver to traverse Adam's spine for a moment, and when all was still again, the silence was so profound, so awful, that he hesitated whether to turn, and make the best of his way back to the safety of his comfortable fireside and gentle Nannette. But the strong sense of duty engendered by the apparition outweighed bodily fear, and, drawing a long breath, Adam again grasped his cudgel in his right hand, and strode along the hall.

Throughout the quiet house his footsteps echoed noisily, reverberating dreadfully in distant rooms, and causing numberless bats to take wing, and flit erratically about the hall; invisible creatures, eldritch and uncanny, fit inhabitants of an ill-omened house when human beings avoid it, and condemn it to melancholy decay. The night-wind, soughing through the spectral firs on the lawn, swept through the house, bearing upon its wings rank smells of decay and mildew, and set doors creaking, windows rattling, and blinds banging,—all of which noises conduced not a little to increase the perturbation which was rapidly undermining Adam's hardihood. There is no sound so dismal, so creative of awe, so fraught with dread, as a night-wind moaning through a deserted house. But Adam strode sturdily down the hall, striving to repress the undefinable fear that was gradually pervading him. He essayed to whistle: although he could whistle like a flageolet, his lips refused to obey. He was well acquainted with the house, and went directly to the broad staircase at the further end of the hall, for he had determined on ascending to the cupola, where he had first seen the face. His foot was on the lower step, when he halted abruptly, and listened, while icy chills traversed his spine, and crept among the roots of his hair.

Was it the night-wind that had caused the unearthly sound at the door? Adam looked, and every particle of color forsook his face.

Standing by the door, distinctly visible in the doorway, was the youthful figure of the squire, standing with white face turned toward Adam, who shook like a leaf. One arm was extended, pointing to the floor; and Adam could not refrain from a startled outcry as he remembered that on that very spot the squire had been last seen alive.

Adam's courage departed, and, sinking on the stairs, he buried his face in his hands. He was stricken with terror. Down the hall came heavy footfalls, directly toward him. The apparition was approaching him, but he was unable to move,—even to fly. Terror had paralyzed him.

The footsteps advanced to his side, and a hand was laid upon his shoulder. Adam screamed.

"Fear not," said a calm voice, whose accents he well recognized. "Have you then quailed so soon? Have courage: no harm befalls the innocent, but justice shall overtake the guilty. Cast off your terror,—for which you have no cause,—and follow me."

The calm voice and evident friendliness of the speaker, if not dissipating Adam's terror, so far re-assured him that strength returned to his limbs, and, rising, he mechanically followed the apparition, which stalked up the stairs.

Ere they had reached the landing above, Adam became vaguely aware that the apparition was a strange spectre,—for his gait resembled that of a living person, and his footfalls equaled his own in heaviness. To Adam, the idea of a ghost was a draped vapor, in the semblance of a mortal, gliding through the air noiselessly, penetrating walls and passing through doors with the greatest facility, and speechless; whereas the squire's spirit had spoken, his footfalls sounded heavily, on the stairs, and, on arriving at the landing, he was obviously short of breath.

Without even looking to see whether the sexton was following, the spectre stalked up the long "upper-hall," as it was called, and entered an open door at the further extremity,—the squire's room, Adam saw by the dim light of his lantern. The room was precisely as it had been left after its occupant's burial. The furniture was disarranged, and the book he had been reading on the evening before his death lay on the stand by his bedside, in company with his half-smoked pipe, tobacco-box, the lamp, and match-safe. His slippers, unmolested by mice, lay on the floor by the bed, his dressing-gown was lying across a chair, and the bed itself—mildewed, and thickly covered with dust—was disordered precisely as the neighbors had disordered it when they lifted the squire from it to lay him in his shroud.

To Adam it half seemed a nightmare, and he was inclined to deem himself laboring under a delusion. The fantastic shadows cast from the furniture by his lantern, the profound silence that rested over the house, the awful spectre, and, finally, his terrified self, seemed like scenes and characters of a bad dream. But Adam Hill was never more thoroughly awake than at that moment.

A monstrous rat leaped from under the bed, and ran across the room, passing between him and his ghostly companion. The incident was trivial, but it sent Adam's heart throbbing to his throat. A bat flitted about the room, and his knees shook; and his hair fairly rose as a blind banged in a distant window, and the night-wind moaned through the corridors. Then the conviction came overwhelmingly upon him that he would never leave the haunted house alive.

The spectre had been standing by the bedside, gazing steadfastly down upon the bed; but he now stalked toward a closet across the room. As he did so, he looked significantly at Adam, who, divining his meaning, followed him.

The door of the closet was ajar, and, as he observed it, Adam remembered that in the excitement consequent upon the squire's death the closet had not been opened. Extending his arm, the spectre noiselessly opened the door, and motioned to Adam to enter.

The sexton obeyed tremblingly, and when he arrived in the door he raised his lantern, and looked around the closet. Articles of wearing apparel were hanging on the walls, which Adam passed over with a cursory glance; but on the floor were two articles which elicited a cry of surprise and anger from him. One was a peculiar handkerchief of dark-red material, flecked with sickly yellow squares: the other was a vial, whose label bore a death's-head and cross-bones, and the startling warning, "Prussic Acid: Deadly Poison!"

"Foul play! I knew it!" screamed Adam, almost dropping his lantern in his excitement. "And, O Heaven! I know the murderer."

The spectre spoke.

"Your coming to this house of dread and ill-omen, at dead of night, and in the face of hereditary superstition and simple apprehension, is laudable, and shall be rewarded. It is not strange that you quail. But listen, and know all."

The village clock had struck the hour of twelve before Adam returned to his Nannette, who, terrified by his prolonged stay, was almost frantic. Sobbing for joy, she flung herself into his arms with the ardor of a bride. Although Adam returned her caresses, he did so mechanically, for his manner was pre-occupied. The worthy old soul, not lacking in the voluble inquisitiveness of feminine old age, harassed Adam with a legion of questions, which he evaded as well as he could without giving offense; but the good dame, piqued at her master's seeming churlishness in refusing to satisfy her curiosity, finally went to bed in a pet, while Adam absently followed her example.

Nannette fidgeted all night, unable to sleep a moment until Adam should reveal the secrets of his expedition. That something strange had happened she well knew by the unusual thoughtfulness of his face; but to her persistent questions he merely returned a shrug of his shoulders. They were sitting at breakfast, when Adam suddenly struck the table a mighty blow with his fist.

"I would never have dreamed it," said he, with another blow.

"Dreamed what, Adam?" eagerly inquired Dame Nannette.

"That the moon was made of green cheese."

Nannette grew red, and her eyes sparkled; but, restraining her anger, she essayed one more question.

"Adam, tell me: What did you see last night?"

"The Evil One," replied Adam.

Thereupon, Nannette burst into tears, and flounced away from the table in high dudgeon.

Adam apparently did not observe his wife's indignation, but ate his breakfast absent-mindedly, rose from the table, got his oak stick, and left the house, leaving poor Nannette bathed in tears, and seething with curiosity.

Adam Hill walked briskly across the village toward Gilbert Ray's residence, with eyes downcast in meditation, and bringing his oak stick down with a thump. The landlord, pursuant to his close disposition, lived hermetically in a desolate cottage on the opposite side of the village from the mansion-house. Adam soon arrived at the cottage, walked up to the door, and knocked sharply.

"Well,—come in!" was growled, rather than spoken, by a voice which the sexton recognized as that of Dark Gil. He entered a small, meanly furnished room, cold and cheerless, and saw Dark Gil seated at his desk poring over his rent-roll.

"Well, what do you want, sexton?" demanded Dark Gil sharply, eying Adam savagely. "Want your cottage repaired, I suppose. I generally receive a similar petition every day. Pest! as if they couldn't live in a house as good as their landlord's. They are all better than mine," he complained, casting a glance round on the bare wall.

"Which is not saying much," thought Adam.

But he discreetly kept his own counsel, only saying, as he took a chair,—

"Since you won't invite me to sit down, Mr. Ray, I'll do so uninvited."

"What is your business?" again demanded the landlord impatiently. "Be quick, for I'm hurried this morning."

Adam cast a look out of the window. Three men were approaching the house. He turned again to Dark Gil.

"What do you suppose I saw last night?" he inquired, looking steadfastly at the other.

"Pest! How should I know?" snapped Dark Gil.

"The ghost of Squire Lovell!"

"What!" shouted Dark Gil, starting to his feet with an ashy face, and overturning his chair.

"The ghost of Squire Lovell!"

"Ha!"

Dark Gil made no other comment, but glared in fury and terror at Adam, who bore it without flinching.

"Yes," resumed the sexton, casting a second look out of the window, "and facts have come to light which prove that the squire met his death by foul play. Murder will out."

"Murder! It is false!" cried Dark Gil, with white lips. "So—he died of apoplexy."

"He died of poison!" thundered the sexton. "See, here are the accusers,—silent, but, oh, how true!"

And he took from his breast the peculiar handkerchief and the vial he had seen in the closet of the squire's room.

Dark Gil glared at Adam, and his face was terrible to see.

"Where did you get them?" he gasped.

"Where they had been dropped by the murderer. Ha! Hands off! Help!"

Dark Gil had sprung upon Adam to seize the accusing articles. The force of his attack was so great that the old man was hurled to the floor; but three men rushed into the cottage, and throwing themselves on Dark Gil, secured him after a desperate struggle, bound him with stout cords they had evidently brought for that purpose, and laid him upon his bed. Then one young man advanced,—so precisely like the spectre of the previous night that even if Adam had not formed his acquaintance he would instantly have recognized him.

"Villain," he said sternly, "your deed is discovered, and the hand of Fate brought it about. I am the nephew of Squire Lovell, returned from foreign lands to avenge murder. Listen, all," he said, addressing his coadjutors and Dark Gil, to whom he related the marvelous occurrences which had led to the detection of Squire Lovell's murderer.

Eugene Lovell, having run away from his uncle, betook himself to a seafaring life, and by diligence and ability had attained the captaincy of a New-York vessel plying between that port and Liverpool. During his last voyage a mutiny occurred among his crew, which he suppressed, mortally wounding the ringleader, an ex-convict, and a desperate man, who, accidentally discovering that Captain Lovell was nephew to the squire, made a startling dying confession. Five years before he had escaped from prison, wherein he had been confined for smuggling. He fled to Edgeville, and the officers were on his track, when Dark Gil, who had reasons of his own for assisting him, harbored him until the officers abandoned the search. Then he demanded requital, and on the day the squire's will was drawn in his favor, he prevailed upon the man, by the guaranty of a large sum, to steal into the squire's bedroom at night, stupefy the old man with chloroform, and then take his life by poison.

Brutes can be grateful, and so was the felon. He did the deed,—but, fearing the gallows, surreptitiously used for administering the chloroform one of Dark Gil's peculiar handkerchiefs, well known throughout the adjacent country, and after the deed was done threw both handkerchief and vial into the closet, in order to divert suspicion from himself. Strange to state, the closet was never opened; and had not the marvelous chain of events led to the detection of the murderer, Dark Gil might have lived and died unsuspected by the simple villagers.

By the time Captain Lovell concluded, Dark Gil was raging, and in a few hours' time was a raving maniac. He was immediately conveyed to the mad-house at the neighboring town of Ware, where he may be seen to this day (for we believe he is yet alive) raging in his cell. He is "dangerous," and his insanity consists of his laboring under the mortal terror of an imaginary enemy, who is constantly attempting to apply to his nostrils a handkerchief saturated with chloroform, in order that he may poison him while in a state of stupefaction. He lives in continual terror, starting up out of sleep, shrieking, and beating off his implacable foe; and the sight of a bottle or handkerchief will throw him into convulsions.

Captain Lovell succeeded to the property, and liberally rewarded Adam Hill for his zeal. The mansion was entirely repaired and refurnished, the grounds were rejuvenated, and the premises underwent a general and beneficial change. And now, on every anniversary of the squire's death, old Adam Hill is the lion of the day, which he spends in relating the story of The Ghost of a Face.

AN ANTIQUARY'S GHOST STORY
AUGUSTUS JESSOPP, D.D.
Frank Leslie's Popular Monthly, 1880

Little more than two months have passed since my own personal experience of mental phenomena was strikingly enlarged by the occurrence with which the following narrative deals. Yet already I find that round the original story there has gathered a surprising accumulation of the mythical element, and that I, myself, am in danger of becoming a hero of romance in more senses than one. As I object to be looked upon as a kind of medium to whom supernatural visitations are vouchsafed, and, on the other hand, do not wish to be set down as a crazy dreamer, whose disorganized nervous system renders him abnormally liable to fantastic delusions, I have yielded to the earnest request of some who have begged me to make public the following paper. I am told that there are those who busy themselves in collecting similar stories, and if it be so, it is better they should hear the facts from me than after they have passed through other channels. The narrative was written, at the request of a friend, not many days after the event, when all the circumstances were fresh in my recollection.

On the 10th of October, 1879, I drove over from Norwich to Mannington Hall, to spend the night at Lord Orford's. Though I was in perfect health and high spirits, it is fair to state that for some weeks previously I had had a great deal to think about, some little anxiety, and some considerable mental strain of one kind or another. I was not, however, conscious of anything approaching weariness, irritability or "fag." I arrived at four p.m., and was engaged in pleasant and animated conversation till it was time to dress for dinner. We dined at seven; our party numbered six persons. Of these, four at least had been great travelers. I, myself, was rather a listener; the talk was general and discursive, and amused and interested me greatly. Not for a single moment did it turn upon the supernatural; it was chiefly concerned with questions of art and the experiences of men who had seen a great deal of the world, and could describe intelligently what they had seen and comment upon it suggestively. I have very rarely been at a more pleasant party. After dinner we played a rubber. We "left off as we began," and as two of the guests had some distance to drive, we broke up at half-past ten.

The main object of my going over to Mannington was to examine and take notes upon some very rare books in Lord Orford's library, which I had been anxiously wishing to get a sight of for some years, but had never been fortunate enough to meet with up to this time. I asked leave to sit up for some hours and make transcripts. His lordship at first wished me to let his valet remain in attendance to see all lights put out, but as this would have embarrassed me, and compelled me to go to bed earlier than I wished, and as it seemed likely that I should be occupied till two or three in the morning, it was agreed that I should be left to my own devices, and the servants should be allowed to retire.

By eleven o'clock I was the only person down-stairs, and I was very soon busily at work and absorbed in my occupation.

The room in which I was writing is a large one, with a huge fireplace and a grand old chimney; and it is needless to say that it is furnished with every comfort and luxury. The library opens into this room, and I had to pass out from where I was sitting into this library and get upon a chair to reach the volumes I wanted to examine.

There were six small volumes in all. I took them down and placed them at my right hand in a little pile, and set to work—sometimes reading, sometimes writing. As I finished with a book, I placed it in front of me. There were four silver candlesticks upon the table, the candles all burning, and, as I am a chilly person, I sat myself at one corner of the table, with the fire at my left, and at intervals, as I had finished with a book, I rose, knocked the fire together, and stood up to warm my feet.

I continued in this way at my task till nearly one o'clock. I had got on better than I expected, and I had only one more book to occupy me. I rose, wound up my watch, and opened a bottle of seltzer-water, and I remember thinking to myself that I should get to bed by two, after all.

I set to work at the last little book. I had been engaged upon it about half an hour, and was just beginning to think that my work was drawing to a close, when, *as I was actually writing,* I saw a large white hand within a foot of my elbow!

Turning my head, there sat a figure of a somewhat large man, with his back to the fire, bending slightly over the table, and apparently examining the pile of books that I had been at work upon. The man's face was turned away from me, but I saw his closely cut reddish-brown hair, his ear and shaved cheek, the eyebrow, the corner of the right eye, the side of the forehead, and the large high cheekbone.

He was dressed in what I can only describe as a kind of ecclesiastical habit of thick corded silk, or some such material, close up to the throat, and a narrow rim or edging;

of about an inch broad, of satin or velvet serving as a stand-up collar, and fitting close to the chin. The right hand, which had first attracted my attention, was clasping, without any great pressure, the left hand; both hands were in perfect repose, and the large blue veins of the right hand were conspicuous. I remember thinking that the hand was like the hand of Velasquez's magnificent "Dead Knight" in the National Gallery.

I looked at my visitor for some seconds, and was perfectly sure that he was not a reality. A thousand thoughts came crowding upon me, but not the least feeling of alarm, or even uneasiness; curiosity and a strong interest were uppermost. For an instant I felt eager to make a sketch of my friend, and I looked at a tray on my right for a pencil; then I thought, "Up-stairs I have a sketch-book—shall I fetch it?"

There he sat, and I was fascinated; afraid, not of his staying, *but lest he should go.* Stopping in my writing, I lifted my left hand from the paper, stretched it out to the pile of books, and moved the top one. I cannot explain why I did this. My arm passed in front of the figure, and it vanished. I was simply disappointed, and nothing more.

I went on with my writing as if nothing had happened, perhaps for another five minutes, and I had actually got to the last few words of what I had determined to extract, when the figure appeared again, exactly in the same place and attitude as before. I saw the hands close to my own; I turned my head again, to examine him more closely, and I was framing a sentence to address to him, when I discovered that I did not dare to speak. *I was afraid of the sound of my own voice!*

There he sat, and there sat I. I turned my head again to my work, and finished writing the two or three words I still had to write. The paper and my notes are at this moment before me, and exhibit not the slightest tremor or nervousness. I could point out the words I was writing when the phantom came and when he disappeared.

Having finished my task, I shut the book and threw it on the table; it made a slight noise as it fell—the figure vanished.

Throwing myself back in my chair, I sat for some seconds looking at the fire with a curious mixture of feeling, and I remember wondering whether my friend would come again, and if he did, whether he would hide the fire from me.

Then first there stole upon me a dread and a suspicion that I was beginning to lose my nerve. I remember yawning; then I rose, lit my bedroom candle, took my books into the inner library, mounted the chair as before, and replaced five of the volumes; the sixth I brought back and laid upon the table where I had been writing when the phantom did me the honor to appear to me.

By this time I had lost all sense of uneasiness. I blew out the four candles and marched off to bed, where I slept the sleep of the just or the guilty, I know not which, but I slept very soundly.

This is a simple and unvarnished narrative of facts. Explanation, theory or inference I leave to others.

THE GHOST OF ALDRUM HALL
ANONYMOUS
The Argosy, 1880

"This will never do," I exclaimed, awaking rather suddenly to a consciousness of the fact that I was writing utter nonsense, and the fourth chapter of my second volume bid fair to become a mere mass of verbiage. With something of a groan I flung the pen down, and betook myself to the sofa, prudently determined to get rid of a tormenting headache before I attempted to write another word.

It was a blazing, brilliant July evening, and my chambers, with their shabby, dusty furniture and litter of books, looked somewhat dreary. I glanced round with a weary longing for the wooded slopes and shady lanes and meadows of my old Warwickshire home. For the past six months I had been working hard, often far into the night, at my writing-table; I needed rest, but it was useless to think of rest until my book was finished. Moreover, going into the country meant spending money, and of that I had little enough to spare. All I could do was to give up work for some twenty-four hours, and think of nothing till I sat down again to that unfinished chapter.

With this end in view, I ran over two or three places in my own mind where it might be pleasant and profitable to spend my enforced holiday—Hampton Court, Twickenham, Burnham Beeches. I had half decided in favour of the latter, when a step on the stair and a thundering knock at the door startled me. Before I could answer, the door opened, and the fair head and broad shoulders of my old school chum, Phil Wentworth, appeared, followed by a big dog.

"I suppose I'd better not let Shot in, had I, Charlie?" said he, trying to keep the dog back. "He'll be trampling on your best love scenes and lying down on the proof sheets. I know your room of old."

"Hang the love scenes!" I exclaimed. "Come in, old fellow, and bring the dog too. You don't know how glad I am to see you."

I pushed open the door, and Shot bounced in, and overturned the waste-paper basket with a sweep of his tail. Phil Wentworth followed, only a shade less actively, flung himself into a chair, and mopped his face gravely with a wonderfully-scented handkerchief.

"I've half a mind not to come to see you again, 'pon my word, you live so near the sky; it's enough to kill a delicate fellow like me to get up all these stairs. Hallo, Shot! lie down, and stop wagging your tail! I told you how it would be, Charlie—he's overturned that basket of yours."

"Never mind the basket," I returned. "I wish I knew as little about the contents of it as he does. I certainly didn't expect you to-night. I thought you were at the Isle of Wight."

"Yes; I've been yachting," answered Phil; "but I came up front Cowes yesterday. You look seedy, Charlie."

Phil put up his eye-glass (a vanity about which I chaffed him unmercifully), and stared at me with a solemn face.

"Very likely I do, through those spectacles of yours," I retorted; "but I have a headache."

"Ah! I don't wonder at that, stewing up here all day writing! I tell you what, Charlie, you shall go down to Aldrum for a week or two. You can make hay, and pull all the fish out of the river, if you like. I know it would set you up again, and I hate to see you looking so confoundedly thin and white."

"Aldrum?" I returned. "I thought the place was all tumbling to pieces, and inhabited only by bats and owls."

"So it was," said Phil; "but I have had the house done up a bit. My old bailiff and his wife live there now, and I always have a room or two kept ready for my use if I should feel inclined to run down for a night. It will be the very place for you—jolly old ru-ined chapel, moat, fish-pond, and weird towers: everything ready for the first chapter of a new novel."

"My dear fellow," I replied, gratefully, "you are very kind, but I can't spare the time. I promised to have my book ready for the publishers by the end of September."

"Hang the publishers!" cried Phil. "You can finish it when you come home again, and if it isn't done it won't matter. I'll go and punch the publishers' heads if they say anything."

"Thank you, Phil, but it's impossible. I—"

"It's no use saying any more, Charlie," interrupted Phil, putting his hands on my shoulders. "I've made up my mind for you to go, and go you shall. I only wish I could too, but the mother wants me to stay with her till we start for the moors. There's your brother Jack. Why not write and ask him if he can get a fortnight's leave? I know he likes fishing and flirting."

It was a species of enjoyment that of late had not fallen to my lot—a fortnight of my twin-brother's society; and I felt very strongly tempted to accept Phil's offer.

"I shall write to old Brown to night," continued Phil, seeing me waver, "and tell them to get ready for you. Better go on Saturday, both of you. You'll find plenty of fishing-tackle there, and a couple of horses. Besides, there's another reason why you should go down," he added, whilst a more serious look came into his face.

"What's that?" I asked, wondering.

"Well, the truth is, Charlie, I haven't felt quite the thing lately, so I consulted old Eastwood. The heart's not strong, he says; nothing wrong—nothing I need fear. I am careful, you know. I have always gone in for muscular Christianity, and that kind of thing, and I suppose I have rather overdone it in the long run. Eastwood says big men seldom have strong hearts."

"Bosh!" I interrupted. "I don't believe a word of it, Phil. I never saw a man who looked more the picture of health and strength than you do."

"Oh, I daresay I shall live out my three-score and ten," laughed Phil; "but it's best to be on the safe side. So what do you think I've done?"

"Made your will," I suggested in joke.

"Exactly," he answered to my surprise. Phil was coming out in a new character. I should have supposed him the last man in the world to think of these things. "You know," he added, "I am the last of my race. If I die unmarried and childless, I have no heir; so, Charlie—you know that you and Jack are my best and dearest friends—I have just been and gone and left Aldrum between you."

In the first moment of astonishment I could not speak; then I jumped up and endeavoured to protest. "Not a word," cried Phil, "if you love me. You don't know what a weight it has taken off my mind, and what a happy man it has made me—in case it should be needed."

"Phil," I cried, grasping his hand and almost throwing my arms round his neck, "if ever I come into Aldrum, it will be the most miserable day of my life. If I lost you, old fellow, I should never be quite happy again."

"Well, well," retorted Phil, laughing it off, "no one wishes you to come into Aldrum less than I do, Charlie. And now we will dismiss this melancholy matter. But you will go down to the old place, won't you?"

I saw he had set his heart upon it—and, indeed, I could no longer resist: so I flung all other considerations to the winds, and gave way. We arranged that I should write to my brother and ask him to join me, if his Colonel would give him leave, lock up my papers, pack my portmanteau on Saturday morning, and start.

After a little more conversation, Phil took his departure, to keep an appointment, refusing to hear a word of thanks. Ever since the first day I fagged for him at Rugby, he had been the kindest and best friend a fellow could have; and though within the last few years our circumstances had changed—he was rich, and I had to work for my daily bread—it had never made the slightest difference to him. There was something about his generosity at once so frank and delicate, that, proud and sensitive as I very well knew I was, I could never feel hurt or offended, scarcely under any obligation.

I wrote to Jack that night, and he answered my letter by appearing as I was at dinner next evening, his handsome face aglow with pleasure, and flinging his hat up to the ceiling like a schoolboy. He had a week's leave of absence.

"The Colonel's a brick, Charlie," he said. "But what's the matter with you, old fellow?" and Jack sat down with a very concerned face, and insisted on feeling my pulse, making believe he knew a great deal about it. I succeeded in persuading him that a week's rest would set me up again; adding that I was afraid he would be bored to death down in the country with only myself to speak to, and nothing to do but fish.

"Bored," he returned; "well, there isn't such a complete dearth of society there as all that. There are the Jermyns and the Davenports, and a few others. I've been to Aldrum before, with Wentworth. Let's have some of the MS. to read while you finish your dinner."

We had no secrets from each other, my brother and I; but I confess I should have been a little surprised at his evident delight, had I not happened to know that he was on pretty intimate terms with the Davenports. I guessed that his appreciation of Squire Davenport's merits was not entirely due to the fact that he was a keen sportsman. Devoted as Jack was to horses, dogs, and guns, I felt pretty sure that he admired the Squire in a great measure because he was Janie Davenport's father.

More than two years before the time of which I'm speaking, my father had died rather suddenly while abroad. His property was to be divided equally between Jack and myself, but we soon discovered there was very little property to divide. I was reading for the bar; Jack had been at Sandhurst, and was already Ensign Kenyon. Several of his friends advised him to sell out and emigrate, but he wouldn't hear of it, and declared his intention of living on his pay and working hard. He did work, nobly and well, and kept out of debt too, with such efforts as only a brave heart and resolute will could have made; but he had his reward. I had been called to the bar in due time, and was getting my living by writing, waiting pretty patiently for the briefs that never came.

To return. We went down by the 4.30 train from Paddington, on Saturday. A three hours' journey by rail, and we found ourselves at W— station. The dog-cart was there to meet us, in charge of an ancient groom, and, after rattling over five miles of country

roads, we arrived at our destination. It was too dark to see much
of Aldrum or the neighbourhood, to which I was a stranger. The
house itself stood in a hollow, and was shut in on all sides by the
great, stately Warwickshire elms: I only received a general impression that it was a large, rambling old place, covered with ivy up to
the very chimneys.

We were not unexpected guests. The library and breakfast-room
adjoining had been made ready for our reception; we had a jolly
little supper, and smoked our pipe of peace in the window-seat by
the light of a glorious yellow moon. At last Jack yawned terribly
and declared his intention of going to bed: so we rang for candles.

The library door opened at the foot of the broad, polished oak
staircase. The spacious corridor in which we found ourselves was
lighted at the farther end by an oriel window, round and across
which long sprays of ivy waved and swayed in the breeze. The cold
moonlight streamed in and lay in ghostly lines of light on wall
and floor.

The spaces between the doors were hung with pictures, and
beneath each be-ruffed and be-wigged ancestor of the Wentworths
stood a huge china beaupot, round which there seemed to linger
still a faint scent of roses, though the fair hands that plucked
them must have been mouldering in the Aldrum vaults for many
a long year. There was not a vestige of curtain or carpet, and the
gloomy shadows and dark corners made the place altogether one
you would not choose to linger in.

Almost directly opposite the head of the staircase, a small archway led to a long, narrow passage, the end of which was swallowed
up in darkness, and which I did not care to explore. Just inside the
archway was my room door. There I wished Jack goodnight. He
went off to his own apartment in some remote region on the north
side. Candle in hand, I proceeded to make a survey of my quarters.
Oak paneling, an oil-painting or two on the walls, two four-post-
ers—large enough to have accommodated four people at least, and
sombre enough for a funeral—three long, narrow windows, and a
general air of antiquity and disrepair. There was, nevertheless, a
sort of dignity in the faded aspect of this solemn chamber—the
dignity of past glories and mouldering beauty.

I had just completed these observations when Jack came back, growling.

"My room is a good quarter of a mile off yours," said he. "Can't imagine what the dickens they put me there for. It's rather too bad! Suppose I were to have an attack of apoplexy in the night, and die—I shouldn't be able to make you hear."

"I don't suppose you would," I answered, laughing.

"Or I might see a ghost," continued Jack.

"You might."

"Well, I shan't stand it!" And Jack flung himself into the arm-chair and took out his cigar-case again.

"Stay here then, and we'll sleep together, as we used to do at home," I suggested.

Jack signified his approval of the proposition, and went off for his belongings. But then, instead of going to bed, we sat down opposite each other on either side the empty fireplace, and chatted on till midnight, discussing plans for the future, and memories of the past; the hopes that are so strong, the regrets so transient, with youth and strength, and the world before one. Jack threw away the end of his cigar at last, and began pulling off his boots lazily.

Just then we heard a step in the passage outside, apparently at the other end; not the deliberate heavy tread of the old bailiff, or the short trotting step of his buxom wife, but a regular, measured "tap-tap" of high-heeled shoes on the polished floor, faint but distinct, and growing nearer and nearer.

We looked at each other in surprise. There was not a soul in the house but ourselves and the Browns—so we had been told, at least. Who could this be?

"Sounds as if one of the stately dames from the pictures in the gallery was coming to pay us a domiciliary visit. Scandalous, I call it!" remarked Jack, laughing, and pulling his boot on again.

Nearer and nearer they came, those cautious, unhesitating footsteps, and we listened till they seemed to pass the door and reach the little archway. Then, suddenly, the most awful wailing shriek rang out in the dead silence, and Jack and I rose to our feet simultaneously, with a startled exclamation. There was a sound as of a slight struggle, as Jack sprang to the door with the light,

pulled it open and dashed out. I followed him through the archway into the corridor. There was nothing there; nothing but the
cold splendours of the moon, and those calm, immovable faces
high up on the wall.

"What on earth was it?" said Jack, with a puzzled air.

"I can't imagine," I replied. "Let us look down this passage."

I fetched my candle, and together we explored it. Nothing
at the extreme end but a locked door, and a tiny narrow window
looking out on to some leads. We returned to the other landing,
and tried the doors of all the rooms. All were locked, and Jack
examined every nook and cranny with soldierlike precision. In
vain: there was nothing to be seen; not a sound to be heard but the
faint sighing of the wind.

We returned to my room more puzzled than perhaps we cared
to acknowledge to each other.

"It must have been a bat flying against the window," I suggested at last, anxious in some way to account for sounds that seemed
so utterly unaccountable.

"Bats don't walk in high-heeled shoes," returned Jack. "And
what was the cry we heard?" he demanded sharply.

"It might have been an owl," I said.

"I never heard an owl hoot like that, Charlie. Ugh! it seemed
to make one's blood run cold. Anything so awfully despairing and
full of terror I couldn't have imagined. I'm certain I heard a scuffle
as well. I can't make it out."

"I'm equally puzzled," I answered. "Perhaps we may find some
clue to the mystery in the morning. It might have been a ghost—
though I have never heard Phil say the house was haunted."

Jack interrupted me with a scornful laugh; the very notion of
such a thing roused his loftiest contempt. He was a firm disbeliev-
er in ghosts.

"If I thought you were speaking seriously, I'd pound those ideas
out of your too lively imagination," he added, severely. "However,
we're not likely to be disturbed again; so let us to bed."

And down he knelt to his prayers—unlike most young fellows
now-a-days, he didn't think himself too old for that. I followed his
example, and we were both very soon soundly asleep.

Gloomy passages and oak-paneled rooms flooded with brilliant July sunshine wore a totally different aspect next morning; and Jack and I felt a little inclined to chaff each other about our midnight alarm, as we sat down to an eight o'clock breakfast. Jack was given to early rising, and, although it was Sunday morning, insisted on my turning out when he did. Mrs. Brown was evidently not a little dismayed at our untimely appearance, so we left the good lady to broom and duster, and went off to explore the garden and grounds.

It was like a Paradise to me, after six months of my musty chambers, and the noise and glare of the London streets; and Jack's enjoyment of the change seemed scarcely less than my own. How we laughed and joked, sang snatches of songs, and quoted poetry as we sauntered up and down the grass-grown terraces, whistling to the surly old pointer on the doorstep, as he lay basking in the sun! How we shied pebbles into the weedy fishpond like a couple of mischievous schoolboys, frightening a pair or two of ancient sheldrakes out of their remaining wits! The memory of that summer morning comes back to me often with wonderful freshness, though years have since rolled over our heads.

Mrs. Brown came in to wait upon us at breakfast. At Jack's suggestion, I told her of the disturbance of the previous night, and cross-questioned her a little as to its cause. It did not appear to puzzle her very greatly. We had been dreamin' most likely. When folks sat up so late o' nights they were bound to have bad dreams; it was one of the ways o' Providence a-showin' them as they were wrong. Evidently Mrs. Brown had a bad opinion of us, as a couple of dissipated men about town. We assured her that we had not been asleep, and that it was no dream.

"Then it was howls."

("It certainly was a howl," Jack muttered between his mouthfuls of toast.)

There was numbers of howls in the old tower, and their screechin' was that unearthly, Brown had often said it was like somebody bein' murdered. No, she had never heard of no ghostes; didn't believe in 'em.

It was apparent that Mrs. Brown was sceptical in regard to ghosts. We dismissed her and the subject accordingly, and Jack lighted a cigarette, and dragged me out into the stable, to have a look at the beauties in the loose boxes. He couldn't be satisfied without an early inspection.

"Wentworth sent those horses down from Catheron for us," Jack observed, as we started towards the park. "What a good fellow he is! This place seems to be a kind of Chelsea Hospital: old men, old horses and old dogs, sent here to end their days in clover."

We strolled back to the house, and then started for church, Jack with a white rosebud in his buttonhole. We arrived at the church door about the middle of the psalms, and were, I fear, the occasion of no little commotion among the less devout, by our untimely appearance. Of course they put us in the Hall pew, and I caught many furtive glances of Jack's dark eyes at the dainty muslins and laces behind the red curtains of the Davenport seat.

After service he lingered in the churchyard to exchange greetings, and introduce me. Davenport père made rather a fuss of him, talked of calling on us next day, and hoped we should spend a night at the Grange. Jack seemed to like the idea, and promised to do so, and the fact of his having parted with the white rosebud did not escape my fraternal vigilance when we reached home.

All the afternoon we lounged about the library, and smoked, varying the proceedings with an occasional skirmish over the bookshelves. Finding the library unbearably hot, after dinner we went out into the garden, and Jack grew confidential as we sauntered up and down the moonlit walk, and treated me to a lengthy account of the rise and progress of his affection for Janie Davenport. He was hopeful, as indeed he well might be. There were few girls, I should imagine, who would have refused him, and I had a conviction that Janie Davenport was not one of those few. Nevertheless, I felt it my duty to suggest that her father might have some remarks to make upon the subject, and Jack looked serious. His income was confined almost wholly to his pay, and the prospect of matrimony upon that very modest sum was not a lively one.

"Never mind," he said at last, with hopeful audacity: "perhaps old Davenport will give her a fortune, and then it will be all right. If he doesn't, I can work for her. Hallo! who's this?"

We had turned into the laurel walk, and were going away from the house and towards the gate into the park. Looking down the long dark vista of overgrown, untrained shrubs, lighted here and there by a stray moonbeam, I saw a figure coming towards us from the direction of the park gate. As it drew nearer, I could perceive that it was that of a girl apparently quite young, scarcely more than a child. She had on a white dress and a long dark cloak over it, but no hat or bonnet, and her fair curly hair fell in a mass of bright disorder down her shoulders. I noticed that the cloak was of a quaint, old-fashioned shape and make, but there was nothing peculiar about the dress: and a white dress was not unusual in the summer, even among the village girls.

"Who on earth can she be?" said Jack, in a puzzled tone. "Out alone at this time of night, too."

"Someone going to see Madam Brown, likely enough," I said.

"Nonsense, Charlie, Mrs. Brown wouldn't have a very cordial welcome for so late a visitor. I fancy it's the old story, and she is on her way to the trysting tree. Depend upon it, the expectant lover is not far off. I rather envy him, she's confoundedly good-looking."

Jack lowered his voice, for we were quite close by this time and the moonlight was shining full on the girl's face. A fair, lovely face it was, though perfectly white and colourless, and there was a half-frightened, half-resolute look in the blue eyes, and certain lines of pain about the little mouth, that would seem to indicate all was not smooth sailing for the fair truant. She passed us without turning her head, and hardly appearing to be aware of our presence, though the walk was narrow. With the slightest movement of my hand I could have touched her dress. Jack, impudent fellow, stared full at her from over my shoulder.

"We shall be in the position of eavesdroppers soon, if we don't look out," he observed in a low tone. "But it's an awful pity she should be out at this time of night with no one to look after her. Right about face, Charlie—let us follow her."

"Hardly fair, is it?" I answered, turning round nevertheless. But we were too late: the girl had reached the upper end of the walk, and disappeared in the dark shadows of one of the three winding paths that led to the lawn and terrace.

We walked back to the house slowly, keeping a sharp look-out for the white dress among the trees: there was nothing to be seen or heard. On going into the library and ringing for lights, Mrs. Brown appeared in something suspiciously like a night-cap: a delicate intimation, I suppose, that she was on the point of going to bed, and would consider our speedy retirement desirable. It was evident she had no visitor. We were not so rash as to disregard the good lady's hint, and went upstairs forthwith. Jack flung himself down on the sofa, and was fast asleep in ten minutes.

The opportunity was too good a one to be lost, and I sat down to the window with a novel and a freshly-filled pipe, but somehow I failed to get up any interest in my book. After skimming over half a dozen pages, I let it fall, moved the candle away, and leaning out of the open window into the bewitching beauty of that summer night, I began the building of my castle in Spain, as I had built it, ah, many times before.

The room we were in fronted to the west, and looked out upon the broad terrace and narrow strip of lawn sloping rather sharply down to the fish-pond. A gravel path ran half-way round the pool, and on the farther bank a belt of larch and fir trees threw a dense black shadow across the water. The moon was at the full, and shedding a cold, white, lustrous light over the silent world. There was not a breath of air, not a leaf stirring, not a sound to be heard. The cattle in the park stood dumb and motionless in the moonlight. The great black bats, wheeling and skimming in their noiseless flight in and out of the trees, were the only sign of life and movement. The distant sound of the church clock striking midnight, fell with startling distinctness on the absolute silence and stillness that reigned.

I turned to look at Jack. He was sleeping as calmly as a child, a half-smile on his handsome face. With a curious sense of expectation, a waiting for something—I knew not what—I sat still and watched the scarcely perceptible movement of his broad chest as he drew the long, soft breaths of a deep, dreamless sleep; the perfect and intense repose in every line of his magnificent limbs, and the almost faultless outline of his clear, bronzed face: a perfect type of manly beauty.

I do not know how long I sat thus, but it could not have been many minutes before I heard a footstep in the passage outside—the same light, hurried "tap-tap" of high-heeled shoes we had heard the night before. I remember now that I listened to the sound with a strange fascination, and that it was with an effort I rose and stretched out my hand for the candle.

Jack slept on quietly; I would not wake him, I thought to myself. And then, a second later, that awful, wailing shriek rose on the midnight silence, and he had sprung to his feet with a white, startled face and a smothered exclamation.

"The owls again, old fellow," I said, as he turned to me.

"I dreamt they were murdering Janie," he answered, rather hoarsely. "Why did you let me sleep like that? Let us go and have another search in the corridor; the thing is most mysterious."

We each took a candle and looked high and low, as we had done the previous night: there was nothing but absolute silence and darkness. At last we returned, perforce, to our room, and retired to bed, neither volunteering any further conjectures respecting the disturbance.

The same silence on the subject was maintained between us at the breakfast-table next morning, by tacit consent it would seem. For my own part, I felt a little uncomfortable about it, I confess; not so much in the impossibility of assigning any cause for the mysterious sounds, as in the strange sense of awe and expectation with which I had waited for them, while Jack was sleeping; the curious feeling of helplessness and oppression with which I had listened to the tapping of those high-heeled shoes as the—what?— drew nearer and nearer. I wasn't a believer in ghosts, but—well, the whole thing was so very unaccountable.

Will Davenport and his father drove over in the course of the morning, and insisted on our going back with them to luncheon. We went, and played tennis all the afternoon, spite of the heat; Jack and Janie Davenport monopolising one court, Will, his two younger sisters, and myself having to put up with the other, which was not so good. But I am under the impression that our play was of a more energetic, if less absorbing, character than that of the young couple on our right. Old Davenport sat under the trees smoking, and watching us with a half-smile lingering at the corners of his moustache. I could not help regarding this as rather a hopeful sign on Jack's account. They persuaded us to stay to dinner, and we didn't get home till late.

There was a portmanteau in the hall, and Phil Wentworth met us at the library door.

"I have been learning the experimental truth of a certain proverb," he exclaimed oracularly. "You didn't expect me, I suppose, you fellows. I'm glad I came, though; I know now in what an immoral manner you conduct yourselves under favourable circumstances. Charlie, my lad, you look better already."

We gave him an explanation of our absence over brandy-and-soda and cigars, for which Phil rang ere we were seated.

"Well, you know," he said, setting to work on the third bottle of soda with a practised hand, "I didn't think I should be able to run down and take a look at you, but as Providence would have it, my aunt from Yorkshire—you know her, Charlie—a lady who has ideas about 'woman's rights,' and one of those misguided individuals who *will* wear green silk dresses—came in last night quite 'unexpected and promiscuous,' maid and parrot to follow. Shot hates the parrot, so he and I bolted, and here we are."

Phil rattled on gaily until Jack grew silent and preoccupied, passed a resolution to retire, took up his candle to go, and then turned round abruptly to Wentworth and demanded to know if the house were haunted. Phil stared.

"Haunted by rats, owls and bats, yes; ghosts, no. Never heard of any, at least."

Jack sat down again, and proceeded to relate our nocturnal experiences in a brief matter-of-fact fashion, appealing to me occasionally for confirmation of his statements.

It struck me as rather odd that he should say anything about the girl we had met in the shrubbery; but he detailed that encounter no less carefully than his account of the mysterious sounds in the corridor.

Phil listened with wide-open eyes, and leaning forward with his elbows on his knees. I rather expected he would ridicule the whole affair as the product of a too vivid imagination, and a too liberal supply of St. Julien at dinner. On the contrary, he seemed interested and impressed with the quiet, laconic description.

"Most extraordinary!" he exclaimed at last, as Jack paused. "Have you said anything to Mrs. Brown about it?"

"She treated the subject with such lofty scorn, we felt constrained, to abandon it," I laughed.

"Well, I have never slept in the house myself. You know I have not so very long come into the property," resumed Phil. "In fact, it has been empty for the last forty years, I believe, with the exception of a succession of superannuated couples from Catheron and Yorkshire, and I've never heard a word as to its being haunted. I shouldn't have taken any notice if I had, for I don't believe in that sort of thing. But 'pon my word, this is really very extraordinary!"

Wentworth pulled the ends of his yellow moustache and put up his eye-glass in much perplexity.

"It is nearly midnight now; let us go upstairs, and wait for this unearthly visitant," I suggested.

"The very thing to be done," answered Phil, seizing on a candle and his cigar-case. "Bring that bottle of soda, Charlie, and come on. We'll overhaul this mystery before we're much older."

Upstairs we dashed with noise enough to have affrighted a score of ghosts. Phil proposed we should search the corridor and passage at once, but Jack would not agree to it.

"If we did so, we should probably not hear anything to-night," he said. "Let us sit down and wait."

We lit a fresh cigar apiece and sat down, Jack and I on either side of the fireplace, Phil in the window-seat. He was, I believe, the only one of the trio who thoroughly enjoyed the prospect of a visit from some deceased ancestor or ancestress.

We were silent till the church clock struck twelve; we compared watches, and I was about to make some irrelevant remark, when Jack turned his head towards the door quickly, and at the same moment I distinctly heard the light footfall outside, and the soft sweep of a dress on the floor; Phil heard it too, and was on his feet as soon as I was.

"Hush," said Jack under his breath. "Put the candle out of the draught, and we'll go into the passage." He opened the door noiselessly and stood there for a second in the doorway; then he went outside, and Phil and I followed. There was nothing to be seen save one ray of moonlight—one soft, brilliant ray falling through the little window at the end of the passage—and a length of shadowy space between us and that weird, cold light; but still the quick, cautious footsteps came on and on.

I cannot describe the feeling of horror and dismay with which I listened to the gentle tap-tap of those high-heeled shoes, coming from out of the darkness, or the strange desire that I had to laugh when Phil put up his eye-glass and stared blankly at that window opposite and its little slit of light; conscious all the time that to save my life I couldn't have spoken a word. I scarcely know what I expected to see emerge from those black shadows to pass through the square of faint yellow light that streamed from out our open door.

The footsteps came on, but nothing else. I heard one little heel set down on the very same polished oak board on which my own foot was planted; I could have sworn I felt a slight vibration, and I heard the soft rustle of a dress, but I saw nothing.

"Hallo!" called out Jack. "Who's that!"

His voice sounded hoarse with suppressed excitement, and, ere the sound had died away, an awful, despairing shriek rang out, it seemed at our very feet. Phil started and half muttered an exclamation. Jack turned to him.

"You see," he said hurriedly, "it is as I told you."

Phil did not hear him. He had sprung out through the archway and into the corridor beyond, and in another moment Jack and I followed with the light. We searched as we had done the two previous evenings, high and low; we tried doors and windows, peered behind brackets and vases; we went downstairs and explored the hall and library, but with the same result. Silence and darkness reigned, save where the cold moonlight fell through the uncurtained windows, on paneled walls and polished floor. At last, even Phil was satisfied as to the fruitlessness of further search, and we returned to my room to hold a council of war. "In the multitude of the counsellors there is wisdom." Nevertheless, we failed in getting at the bottom of the mystery, and Wentworth got up at last and took up his candle. "Well," he said, meditatively, "it couldn't have been an optical delusion, because there was nothing to see; it must have been a—what d'ye call it?—an acoustic illusion. I'll go and sleep it off."

He departed; and Jack and I went to bed, rather bewildered if the truth be known.

We were not very early next morning. In came Mrs. Brown with the coffee and cutlets, and a punctuality-is-a-virtue expression of countenance, the moment she heard us in the breakfast-room. Phil followed her in, in his slippers, caressing his moustache sleepily.

"Mrs. Brown," he began, over her shoulder. "This house is haunted."

Mrs. Brown set the dish down on the table with a bang, and turned round to look at her master with respectful but unmeasured contempt.

"It's not houses that is haunted, sir, it's folks themselves, with their own wicked thoughts," she said, severely giving me at the same time a stern glance round the corner of her cap border—a fortification in white muslin that would have done honour to Vauban. I was a maker of books, and therefore a wicked and abandoned member of society in the good lady's eyes; and Jack, as one of "those wicked hofficers," was only a shade less guilty.

"Oh yes, I know all that," rejoined Phil in a conciliatory tone, and sitting down at the head of the table. "But thoughts don't walk about the passages at night, and shriek loud enough to wake the dead. Mr. Kenyon and his brother have heard this row for three nights, and I heard it myself last night. Don't you know what it is?"

"No, Master Phil, I do not know what it is. I've lived here for six months now, and I've heard nothing o' nights but the howls and rats, and I never expect to hear nothing as long as I live a sober and a godly life." Jack was the victim of a withering glance from out the cap border, which I fancy rather spoiled his appetite for breakfast.

"Brown—I suppose he has heard nothing?"

"That I will answer for, he hasn't, sir; he's as deaf as a post since he came here; it ain't any use my readin' prayers to him even; he says Amen at the wrong place and puts me out continual."

"It's very strange," said Phil dreamily, helping himself to more sugar.

"What you heard, sir, was howls and nothing else, if you'd only believe it; but folks is so fond of making tales and mysteries now-adays, it's no wonder, I'm sure, the Almighty lets 'em be caught in their own net."

With a little contemptuous sniff, Mrs. Brown took up her tray and marched out, in the comfortable consciousness of having no net of wickedness spread wherein her own well-shod feet might be caught by special permission of Providence. We all laughed, and, after another "very extraordinary" from Phil, the subject was dropped, and we fell to discussing plans for the redemption of time during our brief holiday.

The Davenports had asked us for a day's fishing, and Went-worth expressing himself as ready and willing to accompany us, we had the dog-cart out after breakfast and drove off; carried away the post going through the lodge gates; ascended a heap of stones by the road-side about a hundred yards farther on, were whirled round and taken in every direction but the right one, four times in as many consecutive minutes; till finally the mare planted her fore-feet in the hedge, and gazed tranquilly into the field on the other side. "I've had enough of this, old lady," observed Phil calm-ly at this juncture. "Besides, I want to get on: we'll have the whip brought into action."

I gave myself up for lost, and began to think seriously of the unfinished second volume. Phil's style of punishment was the re-verse of soothing, and once we were clear of the hedge, the rest of the journey was performed in shorter time than I should like to tell. I fancy Jack enjoyed that day's fishing: he caught nothing—a fact which was not surprising, since he found it necessary to resign his rod to Miss Janie at a very early hour; and, after luncheon, old Davenport got hold of him, and treated him to a disquisition on the gentle craft, angling past and present, and the speaker's achievements in almost every known trout-stream in the United

Kingdom. Very soon afterwards I felt a hand on my shoulder, and turned to see Jack standing beside me with a radiant face.

"I've done it, Charlie," he said in a low tone.

"Well?"

"It's all right, she has promised to wait for me. I hardly dared to hope she would."

"I'm awfully glad, Jack," I said, as he returned my brotherly squeeze of his hand. "But, 'pon my word, I don't know whether you ought to have done it yet."

"Oh, I've been to head-quarters—Janie insisted upon that. Old Davenport was inclined to be a little bit snappish at first; talked about my engaging his daughter's affections without her parents' consent, and all that sort of thing; he has given his consent though, and he's going to set us up in trade. I mean, Janie will have a fortune, so money matters are not to stand in the way. A perfect old brick he is," concluded Jack, with affectionate disrespect.

Twelve o'clock that same night we were all three pacing up and down the shrubbery by the light of our cigars and the moon; Jack in a beatific silence that disdained to answer or even listen to the running fire of chaff kept up on either side of him.

"Hallo!" exclaimed Phil at last, as we wheeled round for another turn down the walk. "Here she is."

True enough, there was the white dress and golden head gleaming in the moonlight, not thirty yards in front of us.

We went forward slowly, and in another moment the girl was close to us, looking straight before her as if she saw nothing but the long, dark vista of the walk, and the moonlit lawn at the end. Her face was perfectly white and colourless, and there seemed to me a certain indistinctness, a something shadowy about it—and indeed her whole figure—that I had not noticed on the former occasion of our meeting her. Wentworth stepped in front of her and raised his hat: "I beg your pardon," he began, and then stopped—he was speaking to nothing! My eyes had been fixed on him and on the girl, intently; I had not taken them off for one second—no, nor one tenth part of a second—but, as the words had left his lips, I could see him only; the little white figure had disappeared, the place where it had stood was empty; and, hat in hand, Phil paused, staring in mute amazement. "Are we all mad?" he exclaimed fiercely, wheeling round on us.

"I suppose we must be," I answered. "And, in that case, we had perhaps better go to bed, and leave further investigations till tomorrow."

"I'll investigate and get at the bottom of this confounded mystery before I'm much older," Phil rejoined in a passionate tone. "I see no fun in being made a fool of night after night."

"Well, come in and wait in the gallery; there is sure to be a row of some kind to-night." Jack knocked the ashes from his cigar as he spoke, thrust his hands deep down into bis pockets, and marched on. We made the best of our way back through the shrubbery into the house, with watchful eyes bent on every turn of the walk, and opening in the trees; Wentworth questioning us both as to what we had seen, and as to the precise moment when the apparition, whatever it might be, had disappeared from our view; Jack's account agreed in every particular with mine. Phil himself had seen nothing more than we had, or failed to see as much. The plot thickened.

Arrived upstairs, he took up his station in the archway, a light on the bracket at his elbow, and Shot at his feet. Jack and I stood on either side of the open doorway of our room, partly in the shadow. The house was perfectly silent—Mrs. Brown and her spouse having retired to rest some two hours before—and no sound broke the intense stillness but that of our own quick breathing, an occasional low whine from Shot, and an answering growl from his master.

For my own part, I must confess to a very fervent hope that this, our fourth vigil, would be an undisturbed one, and did not like Wentworth's nervous irritability and excitement over the mystery; and, though I was anxious enough to get at the bottom of it, I hardly knew whether to treat the matter in jest or in earnest: whether to advise Phil to leave it alone, or to take further steps to discover the cause of these midnight disturbances. I was not converted to the ghost theory, but I began to think there was something uncanny about the house.

We waited there perhaps a quarter of an hour; Phil changed his position impatiently; Jack looked at his watch and held it out to me with a significant glance; I nodded assent, and then started. A light footstep fell on the polished floor not ten yards from us, and came nearer, advancing slowly and cautiously it seemed. Shot crouched down lower at his master's feet, and showed his gleaming white teeth in a long, furious growl. Phil turned round full face to the end of the passage, completely filling up the doorway with his tall, heavily-built figure. I looked straight out into the darkness, as Jack was doing, with a fixed, fascinated gaze. Ere we had time to think, the soft footfall seemed to pass us. I could not move a finger, could not stretch out my hand to feel what was to us so strangely invisible, and yet must have some shape or form. I heard a brief, stern word from Wentworth; and then that awful cry, more fearful, more despairing, if possible, than before. The spell seemed gone, and I turned my head just in time to see a look of awful horror and dismay in Phil's face that almost froze my blood.

"Take it away; for mercy's sake, take the cursed thing away!" he muttered hoarsely, putting his hand over his eyes; and then he staggered a little and fell heavily, before I could step forward to save him.

We were both kneeling beside him in a moment, and Jack turned the ashy grey face to the light, and laid his fingers on the wrist hurriedly. There was no sign of life or movement, and the head fell back again. He looked at me.

"Charlie," he groaned, "he's dead!"

"Dead! No—no!" I shouted desperately. Tearing open the shirt, I placed my hand upon the heart, that had already ceased to beat.

Alas! it was too true; poor Phil Wentworth was dead. The kindest, truest friend man ever had! We raised his head again, fetched water and brandy, and then carried him to the bed in my room. It was all in vain.

I need not enter into all the details of that terrible night. The alarm, the hastening for the doctor, the desperate remedies, the lingering hope, resigned at last, and then the awful silence of death, and the darkened room upstairs; or of the days that followed, full—it seemed to me—of hurrying to-and-fro, of strange, painful scenes, and faces of mingled curiosity and sorrow. Heart disease and undue excitement, the doctors in their wisdom pronounced it, and I suppose they were right: doctors always are; but I know what Jack thought and what I thought myself—that there was something else besides undue excitement. Poor Phil undoubtedly saw something that night: what it was I do not know—I scarcely dare to think.

It was not until months after that I could bear to have the subject mentioned, or hear the strange wild legend of that haunted gallery— a legend that had almost died out with the decay of the old house: of a fair ancestress of the Wentworths, with a sweet, childlike face, and a heart as hard and cruel as her face was fair, condemned for her many crimes, and a wickedness conspicuous even in the dark and wicked age in which she lived, to wander for ever up and down the gloomy passages and galleries of her earthly home, in the most hideous form that the mind of man can conceive, and shrieking out the never-ending torture and despair of a lost soul—a fearful vision, appearing only to the heir of the house in every third generation.

I do not know whether to believe the story or not: it is no great matter. I only know that I lost my dearest friend that night, and though I shall go to him, he will never come back to me. As for the strange apparition in the garden, it will, I suppose, for ever remain a mystery. I had no heart to make further investigations and inquiries. But the sweet, childish face I saw that summer night in the shrubbery rises before me even now when I think of my poor friend. Was it—could it have been—one with the hideous vision that filled his brave heart with such sudden horror and dismay? I will think of it no more.

It all came to an end at last, and we went back to town the joint possessors of Aldrum and the Aldrum estate, by a codicil in poor Wentworth's will dated only a few days before he joined us for that fatal holiday. From that day to this we have never, either of us, set foot on our property. The house is kept in some sort of repair, and the estate fairly well managed, I believe, but I cannot make up my mind to go and see. I'll leave my responsibility to that bright, fair-haired lad who comes rushing in at the window for a ball of string and some advice about his kite, and wonders audibly why his father is looking so dull over those bothering papers.

"Your advice is sound and good, Charlie, my boy. The papers shall be shoved into the drawer, and we will go and fly kites."

THE EYNESHAM GHOST

A PERSONAL EXPERIENCE

CAPTAIN ARTHUR COLLINS

Time, 1880

"The coverts haven't been disturbed for years, so I *know* the shooting will be all right; the house, they tell me, is comfortable, though it is so old; and I *believe* there's a ghost, if you care for such things: you must try and come."

Somehow or other no one ever thought of refusing Lord Rannoch anything; certainly I never did, for I was very fond of my young kinsman; so I said I would go, though it involved throwing over two engagements of long standing. Perhaps, too, the curiosity I felt about Eynesham Manor—the place he referred to—had something to do with my ready assent. Being a cadet of the clan that hailed Harry Rannoch for chief, I had heard a good deal about it in an indefinite mysterious kind of manner when quite a boy; in one's youth, too, the retina of the mind is so unclouded, that what few impressions are received become indelibly printed, to wax faint perhaps as years roll by, still liable to be revived at any moment by some chance allusion or happening that half awakens remembrance, like the action heat or particular chemicals have on some writing fluids.

Strangely enough this was to be its present owner's first visit as well as mine; a yachting accident, and that modern scourge, typhoid, had disposed of three good lives in as many months, and Harry was recalled suddenly from a West Indian station, where he was leading the busy *insouciant* life of a sub-lieutenant in Her Majesty's navy, to find himself 'an hereditary legislator,' the possessor of several large estates and an enormous rent-roll, and the aim and prize of high calling of half the match-making mothers in England, none of whom *en attendant* would have allowed their daughters to dance with him the previous season.

Eynesham Manor was one of the estates I have referred to, situate in a wild and lonely part of Blankshire. The late Lord Rannoch had never resided there, nor, to the best of my belief, had his predecessor. Some mystery—some deed of violence or wrong, that had doubtless been a blot on the fair scutcheon of the race at the time, but had been so condoned by the long softening of years as to have all the shame taken out of it, and indeed had probably become quite a respectable family tradition—still hung over the gray old feudal house like a pall.

In the intervals of whist, as the Flying Dutchman was whirling us thither next day, I tried in vain to recall the old nurse's tales of my youth about it. "Perhaps I may discover some clue, extract some information from the traditionary oldest inhabitant in the place," I thought at last, and settled my attention to making the most of the bad hands persistently dealt to me that afternoon, whereby the good player is to score over the indifferent one—at least so runs the dogma.

It was late when we reached the house, for a long drive supplemented our railway journey. Very comfortable and alluring it looked, its many mullioned windows all aglow, and a ruddy patch of light streaming from the open hall-door on to the graveled drive. On crossing the threshold of a haunted house, I ought no doubt to have felt a thrill of indefinable horror, had I been properly constituted. As a matter of fact, however, cold and the pangs of hunger made me callous to all but the probable condition of my bedroom fire and the dinner-hour.

Family portraits and armour, rare tapestry, richly carved-oak furniture, and an elaborate plaster ceiling—moulded into many a curious cipher and armorial bearing—gave quite an old-world character to the hall in which we dined, while an admirably-constructed horseshoe-table enabled the entire party to face and enjoy the genial warmth of the huge wood-fire. An early adjournment was made; for all were tired with the long journey, and wished to be fresh and in good fettle next day for the shooting, of which excellent reports were given.

To make what follows clear, I must rather minutely describe my bedroom and its position. One other room adjoined it, occupied by my cousin Rannoch; and these two were separated from the rest of the bedrooms by a passage and the drawing-room—an up-stairs apartment, so customary in houses of that date. My room was large and lofty, and the walls paneled in dark oak; the bed immediately on the left on entering, the window facing it; and beside that, and at an opposite angle to the other one, the door leading into Harry's room, down a short flight of steps. A third door—the only other one in the room—was close beside it, seemingly little used, and securely fastened. I was too tired, however, to make many investigations that night; but went straight to bed, and was soon fast asleep.

Some two or three hours must have elapsed—for the fire had become low and flickering—when I awoke with a start. No perceptible sound or sight had aroused me; but awake I was—most thoroughly; every nerve tense, every faculty keen. There was just sufficient light from the expiring embers to enable me to notice the door at the head of my bed silently open and as silently close. An icy wind seemed to pervade the apartment; and as it passed by me, almost instantaneously the third door in the opposite corner, which I had thought so securely fastened, opened and closed in the same mysterious manner.

Was I dreaming? could I believe my eyes? Then, before I had time to recover from my astonishment, from beyond the door just closed came the cry of a child—not the petulant accents of temper or momentary pain, but a cry so pitiful and despairing, so instinct with terror and agony, that my blood curdled in my veins, the next moment to course headlong through them, every spark of manhood roused to succour the helpless and tormented. I rushed to the door, and tried in vain to force it open. Again the cry; and this time I caught the words: "Ah, not there! not there!" followed by a low fiendish laugh, a struggle, and the sound of a body falling down a flight of stairs, and alighting with a dull thud at the bottom.

Calling loudly to Harry to come and help me, I redoubled my efforts to force the door. Suddenly it opened *into* my room. Again I felt the same chill breath, and the door closed; the one into the passage opened and shut. Though I saw no form, heard no foot-steps, yet I *felt* some Presence, some awful Thing, had passed me; and, mad with anger and awe, I hurried into my cousin's room, and quickly roused him. He noticed my evident agitation, and lis-tened attentively to what I told him of the horrible visitation; but he had heard nothing, and naturally thought I had been dreaming, or suffering from a prolonged nightmare. He came into my room, and we carefully examined the third door. It was closely fastened, and defied our combined efforts to open it.

"We must leave it till the morning, old fellow," he said at last, with a yawn; "but I'll exchange rooms with you, if you like."

This I would not hear of, and we sought our respective beds, leaving the door of communication between our rooms open. I could sleep no more; the horror and supernatural fear I had at first experienced by degrees became absorbed in the mortification I felt I had been so helpless in giving aid where it was apparently so needed. The plaintive boyish tones, "Ah, not there! not there!" rang in my ears at intervals all night. Then the whole scene would pass before me like some hideous phantasmagoria: the mysterious opening and closing of the doors; the piteous appeal, answered by the cruel fiendish laugh; the struggle; the dull thud of the falling body; and then the dead silence, and unseen unheard passage of the Presence through my room.

We agreed the next morning not to mention the occurrence to the rest, but to sit up and watch carefully ourselves that night, to see if we could unravel the mystery. The shooting was varied and excellent, but my nerves were unhinged, and I could hit nothing. Pleading a bad headache, I returned to the house after luncheon, determined, if possible, to discover something myself. First I care-fully examined the third door in my room. It seemed as though it had been fastened for years; on striking its panels, however, there was a hollow reverberating sound, as though there was a passage the other side of it. I next extended my scrutiny to the exterior of the house. Two sides looked on to an old bowling-green and a flower-garden, the other on to the carriage-drive, and the fourth—where our rooms were—on to the little church, only separated from the dwelling-house by an unusually large yew hedge. Judging from the position of our windows, I made out there must be a large space of outside wall unaccounted for, so to speak, by the rooms within. This was thickly overgrown with ivy. After some research, and with the help of a gardener's ladder, I discovered the tracery of a window beneath the luxuriant evergreen. It appeared to have been bricked up; and this strengthened a conviction I felt there must be a passage the other side of the locked door in my room, leading to some apartment on a lower level, now disused, and to which doubtless the blind window pertained. A secret chamber was nothing wonderful in so old a house. No doubt such chambers existed in many old houses, and are always curious and interesting—strange relics, more moving than any history of the time when a man was not safe in his own house, and when it might be necessary to secure a refuge, beyond the reach of spies or traitors, at a moment's notice. Such a refuge was a necessity of life to a great mediaeval noble. But after the terrible sounds I had heard the previous night, I felt more inclined to connect this one with some secret deed of wrong and violence, nay, possibly murder. I did not, however, like to take any further steps without consulting Rannoch.

That night we sat up late over whist, and it was long after midnight before we separated. Harry, fatigued with his long day's shooting, was rather inclined to pooh-pooh the ghost business, as he called it, but I persuaded him to watch one hour with me. We wheeled an old-fashioned couch round to my bedroom fire, piled up the logs on the andirons, and, lighting our cigarettes, awaited what might happen. With his usual kind thoughtfulness, seeing how morbid and nervous I was, my cousin tried to interest me in everyday topics. He was full of admiration for the Manor House—the shooting so good; declared he would spend a few months of every year there. Then followed schemes for improvement—a billiard-room to be improvised, new stables built, the old bowling-green the very place for lawn-tennis.

"And, of course," he added laughingly, "we'll lay your ghost for you, even if it entails a bishop to manage the job."

The words were hardly out of his mouth when the door from the outside corridor slowly opened, the icy draught seemed to pass us, and the mysterious portal in the opposite corner flew back on its hinges and then immediately closed. In an agony of fear I listened for what I seemed to know *must* follow; ah, too horrible! again the heart-rending little voice praying for mercy, followed by the low cruel laugh, the straggle, the fall, and a dead silence. Rannoch rushed to the door with an oath, and, as I had done the previous night, tried to force it open. Suddenly it seemed to yield to his efforts, and he sprang through; but an irresistible power impelled him back into the room, and seemed to crush him down, while the door again closed behind him. The chill breath had passed me, and the other door opened and shut, before he had risen half stunned and dazed from his knees. Like all men of a happy sunny temperament, it required a great deal to rouse my cousin, and I had never before seen him so thoroughly enraged. He swore solemnly he would have the mystery solved if he had to pull down the house brick by brick; no Glamis secret should cast its baneful shadow over his race. Curiously enough it never occurred to either of us to attribute the circumstance to any trick or design of others, there was something much too horrible and real about it for that. Rannoch passed the rest of the night on the couch beside the fire in my room, and I heard him muttering and moaning in his fitful slumbers at intervals during the few remaining hours of the night.

We once more agreed to say nothing of the matter to the rest of the party, but to watch again by ourselves. I pondered deeply over what had happened all day; an idea struck me—to sprinkle the floor with flour, and so try and detect the traces of the mysterious visitant. I mentioned this to Harry, and he promised to have the necessary preparations made. That evening the doctor from the adjacent country town dined with us, a man who had lived all his long life in the neighbourhood, and so I thought I might learn something from him. Watching my opportunity, I drew him apart from the rest, and asked him if he had ever heard the Manor House was haunted.

"Yes," he answered, instinctively lowering his voice and glancing round to see whether my cousin was near us, "yes, it has long had that reputation. Our host's father was only here once, and never put foot inside the place again; what it was that made him take such a dislike to it no one knows, and he was not the kind of man, as you I daresay remember, people cared to put idle questions to. You are aware, of course, this estate came to your family from the distaff side; Lady Joan Eynesham, who married the third Lord Rannoch, was sole heiress of this Manor. She seems to have been a hard vindictive woman, and had an extraordinary dislike for her eldest son. The story goes she flogged him to death for never writing in his copybooks without blotting them—poor lad, a heavy punishment surely for so slight an offence; certain it is that about thirty years ago, when they were making some alterations in this house, they found hidden away amongst the joists of an old window-sill a bundle of copybooks, bearing the date when Lady Joan lived here, and answering to the description given, each page in them blotted and smeared. Another legend about her is, that she used to shut up the unfortunate boy in a kind of dark room for hours together, and that one day, when he struggled against this fate, she threw him violently down some stairs, and so injured his spine that he shortly after died. Have you noticed her portrait in the gallery here? It is a very remarkable face, and remarkable as a painting too—one of Holbein's best. There is one of the poor boy there also. Needless to add her ghost is supposed to haunt one of the bedrooms—I think in the western wing—rather apart from the others. I only know the servants—always too ready to believe in such tales—will not go near the room after dark."

Here the rest of the party joined us, and the garrulous little doctor quickly turned the conversation. But what he had told me seemed to tail-in strangely with the sounds we had heard in the hidden passage, and I confess I disliked more than ever our self-inflicted vigil, so soon to commence. Shortly after, all had retired, and Harry and I found ourselves alone in our remote room; he was no longer inclined to laugh at the matter, but was rather sternly resolved to sift it thoroughly. We sprinkled the flour thickly between the doors, and then sat down beside the fire to watch for what might follow. Rannoch had brought a heavy-loaded stick, and there was a dangerous gleam in his blue eyes, and a set resolution in the lines round his mouth, very alien to his usual careless happy expression. Suspense became intolerable as time went on, and we sat there, silent and intent, waiting for what, or for whom? Yes, at last the door, on which our straining eyes had been so long fixed, swung noiselessly back on its hinges, the same icy wind blew chilly through the chamber; and then with dismay and horror we saw footprints, apparently those of a woman and a child, printing themselves off, one by one, on the level spotless surface—footprints plain and palpable, but of the dreadful Presence nothing more.

Rannoch started to his feet and seized his life-preserver directly the first door moved; before I could restrain him, he rushed into the hidden passage as the other one opened, and the next moment it closed on him. Of what followed I have but a confused remembrance; the struggle sounded louder and seemed more protracted; the boyish cry, the mocking cruel laugh, and Harry's muttered oaths were mingled in a hideous hell of discord; then dull sounds of bodies falling, and silence broken only by groans. The next moment—so it seemed—the rest of the party were crowding into the room, aroused by my shouts and ringings. We speedily burst open the closed door, and sprang into the passage. At the further end of it was a landing, and some dilapidated-looking stairs leading to a chamber beneath; there—stretched on the floor, a strange ghastly-looking heap, in his gay-coloured velvet smoking-suit—lay my dear young cousin, insensible, nay more, to all appearance dead. With difficulty and all loving care we lifted him up, and carried him far away from the hateful accursed chamber, to one quite the other side of the house. For weeks he hovered between life and death, and brain-fever of the worst and most virulent type made us tremble for his reason for a still longer period. But youth and a naturally strong constitution pulled him through at last. The winter was past, though, before he could venture out of his room, a gaunt pale shadow of his former self, tottering on my arm. I had, of course, avoided all reference to that awful night, fearing it would excite him. On the second day, however, that he was able to leave his room, we were moving slowly down a corridor, hung with pictures, leading from it, when I suddenly felt his arm stiffen in mine, and with difficulty I prevented his falling.

"Look!" he cried, with a pained expression, "look! there she is, that accursed woman! Ah, take me away—quick, she is on me!"

I hurried him back to his room, and it was some time before he regained his composure. I took an early opportunity of examining the picture that had so alarmed him; beneath it I saw the name, Lady Joan Eynesham; and instantly it occurred to me this must be the portrait the doctor had spoken of. It was indeed a remarkable one, life-sized, a canvas instinct with Holbein's genius and stiff mannerisms. It represented a lady of more than average height, dressed in black, with the long white coif and wimple worn by widows of that period; a hard, cruel, pitiless face—a face once seen never to be forgotten—I can see it now as I write. This, then, was the effigy of our mysterious visitant, whose footprints I had seen only. Poor Harry's instant recognition of a picture he had never seen before proved it so beyond a doubt. Close by I found the picture of her son—a boy endowed with all the hereditary beauty of his race, with comely limbs and graceful mien and wistful pathetic blue eyes—a child one could imagine a mother worshipping and treasuring with deepest affection, not ruthlessly tormenting and persecuting even unto the death.

That evening Rannoch voluntarily told me what befell him in the secret passage. Instead of finding it in darkness, as he feared, he said it was lit by a strange distinct light. At the farther end he saw a woman, answering in every detail of dress, form, and face to the Holbein portrait he had noticed a few hours before. A boy, apparently about twelve, was struggling with her as she was dragging him to the head of the broken staircase.

"As I rushed up the corridor to his rescue, this incarnate fiend turned on me. The same irresistible power that had forced me back into your room the first night we watched together now seemed to sweep me, with the boy, headlong over the stair-landing. I remember no more. And now let this be a sealed subject between us for ever; I cannot bear to discuss it. Take me away, too, from this curse-stricken house directly I can be moved."

I have little more to add. My cousin had all the family pictures removed from Eynesham to Castle Rannoch. There was one exception—the Holbein of Lady Joan. This he deliberately had burnt, though the Committee of the National Gallery prayed for it at his own price. The portrait of the ill-fated boy hangs in his own sitting-room at Rannoch. The marvellous pathetic beauty of the face attracts all who see it there; but to any inquiries he simply answers, "An ancestor of mine;" and perhaps, as the little doctor said of his father, "He is not the kind of man people care to put idle questions to."

Eynesham Manor is turned into a farmhouse; the western wing, with its secret chamber and blood-stained memories, was razed to the ground.

THE OPEN DOOR
MRS. OLIPHANT

Blackwood's Edinburgh Magazine, 1882

[Inscribed to a dear and happy Memory.]

I took the house of Brentwood on my return from India in 18—, for the temporary accommodation of my family, until I could find a permanent home for them. It had many advantages which made it peculiarly appropriate. It was within reach of Edinburgh, and my boy Roland, whose education had been considerably neglected, could go in and out to school, which was thought to be better for him than either leaving home altogether or staying there always with a tutor. The first of these expedients would have seemed preferable to me, the second commended itself to his mother. The doctor, like a judicious man, took the midway between. "Put him on his pony and let him ride into the Academy every morning; it will do him all the good in the world," Dr. Simson said; "and when it is bad weather there is the train." His mother accepted this solution of the difficulty more easily than I could have hoped; and our pale-faced boy, who had never known anything more invigorating than Simla, began to encounter the brisk breezes of the North in the subdued severity of the month of May. Before the time of the vacation in July we had the satisfaction of seeing him begin to acquire something of the brown and ruddy complexion of his schoolfellows. The English system did not commend itself to Scotland in these days. There was no little Eton at Fettes; nor do I think, if there had been, that a genteel exotic of that class would have tempted either my wife or me. The lad was doubly precious to us, being the only one left us of many; and he was fragile in body, we believed, and deeply sensitive in mind. To keep him at home, and yet to send him to school—to combine the advantages of the two systems—seemed to be everything that could be desired. The two girls also found at Brentwood everything they wanted. They were near enough to Edinburgh to have masters and lessons as many as they required for completing that never-ending education which the young people seem to require nowadays. Their mother married me when she was younger than Agatha, and I should like to see them improve upon their mother! I myself was then no more than twenty-five—an age at which I see the young fellows now groping about them, with no notion what they are going to do with their lives. However, I suppose every generation has a conceit of itself which elevates it, in its own opinion, above that which comes after it. Brentwood stands on that fine and wealthy slope of country, one of the richest in Scotland, which lies between the Pentland Hills and the Firth. In clear weather you could see the blue gleam—like a bent bow, embracing the wealthy fields and scattered houses—of the great estuary on one side of you; and on the other the blue heights, not gigantic like those we had been used to, but just high enough for all the glories of the atmosphere, the play of clouds, and sweet reflections, which give to a hilly country an interest and a charm which nothing else can emulate. Edinburgh, with its two lesser heights—the Castle and the Calton Hill—its spires and towers piercing through the smoke, and Arthur's Seat, lying crouched behind, like a guardian no longer very needful, taking his repose beside the well-beloved charge, which is now, so to speak, able to take care of itself without him—lay at our right hand. From the lawn and drawing-room windows we could see all these varieties of landscape. The colour was sometimes a little chilly, but sometimes, also, as animated and full of vicissitude as a drama. I was never tired of it. Its colour and freshness revived the eyes which had grown weary of arid plains and blazing skies. It was always cheery, and fresh, and full of repose.

The village of Brentwood lay almost under the house, on the other side of the deep little ravine, down which a stream—which

ought to have been a lovely, wild, and frolicsome little river—
flowed between its rocks and trees. The river, like so many in that
district, had, however, in its earlier life been sacrificed to trade,
and was grimy with paper making. But this did not affect our pleasure in it so much as I have known it to affect other streams. Perhaps our water was more rapid—perhaps less clogged with dirt and
refuse. Our side of the dell was charmingly *accidenté,* and clothed
with fine trees, through which various paths wound down to the
river-side and to the village bridge which crossed the stream. The
village lay in the hollow, and climbed, with very prosaic houses,
the other side. Village architecture does not flourish in Scotland.
The blue slates and the grey stone are sworn foes to the picturesque; and though I do not, for my own part, dislike the interior
of an old-fashioned pewed and galleried church, with its little
family settlements on all sides, the square box outside, with its bit
of a spire like a handle to lift it by, is not an improvement to the
landscape. Still a cluster of houses on differing elevations, with
scraps of garden coming in between, a hedgerow with clothes laid
out to dry, the opening of a street with its rural sociability, the
women at their doors, the slow waggon lumbering along—gives a
centre to the landscape. It was cheerful to look at, and convenient
in a hundred ways. Within ourselves we had walks in plenty, the
glen being always beautiful in all its phases, whether the woods
were green in the spring or ruddy in the autumn. In the park
which surrounded the house were the ruins of the former mansion
of Brentwood, a much smaller and less important house than the
solid Georgian edifice which we inhabited. The ruins were picturesque, however, and gave importance to the place. Even we, who
were but temporary tenants, felt a vague pride in them, as if they
somehow reflected a certain consequence upon ourselves. The old
building had the remains of a tower, an indistinguishable mass of
mason-work, overgrown with ivy, and the shells of walls attached
to this were half filled up with soil. I had never examined it closely, I am ashamed to say. There was a large room, or what had been
a large room, with the lower part of the windows still existing, on
the principal floor, and underneath other windows, which were
perfect, though half filled up with fallen soil, and waving with a

wild growth of brambles and chance growths of all kinds. This was
the oldest part of all. At a little distance were some very commonplace and disjointed fragments of building, one of them suggesting
a certain pathos by its very commonness and the complete wreck
which it showed. This was the end of a low gable, a bit of grey
wall, all encrusted with lichens, in which was a common doorway. Probably it had been a servants' entrance, a back-door, or
opening into what are called "the offices" in Scotland. No offices
remained to be entered—pantry and kitchen had all been swept
out of being; but there stood the doorway open and vacant, free to
all the winds, to the rabbits, and every wild creature. It struck my
eye, the first time I went to Brentwood, like a melancholy comment upon a life that was over. A door that led to nothing—closed
once, perhaps, with anxious care, bolted and guarded, now void
of any meaning. It impressed me, I remember, from the first; so
perhaps it may be said that my mind was prepared to attach to it
an importance which nothing justified.

The summer was a very happy period of repose for us all. The
warmth of Indian suns was still in our veins, and we did not feel
the cold. It seemed to us that we could never have enough of the
greenness, the dewiness, the freshness of the northern landscape.
Even its mists were pleasant to us, taking all the fever out of us,
and pouring in vigour and refreshment. In autumn we followed
the fashion of the time, and went away for change, which we did
not in the least require. It was when the family had settled down
for the winter, when the days were short and dark, and the rigorous reign of frost upon us, that the incidents occurred which alone
could justify me in intruding upon the world my private affairs.
These incidents were, however, of so curious a character, that I
hope my inevitable references to my own family and pressing personal interests will meet with a general pardon.

I was absent in London when these events began. In London
an old Indian plunges back into the interests with which all his
previous life has been associated, and meets old friends at every
step. I had been circulating among some half-dozen of these—
enjoying the return to my former life in shadow, though I had
been so thankful in substance to throw it aside—and had missed

some of my home letters, what with going down from Friday to
Monday to old Benbow's place in the country, and stopping on
the way back to dine and sleep at Sellar's, and to take a look into
Cross's stables, which occupied another day. It is never safe to
miss one's letters. In this transitory life, as the Prayerbook says,
how can one ever be certain what is going to happen? All was perfectly well at home. I knew very well (I thought) what they would
have to say to me: "The weather has been so fine, that Roland has
not once gone by train, and he enjoys the ride beyond anything."
"Dear papa, be sure that you don't forget anything, but bring us
so-and-so, and so-and-so"—a list as long as my arm. Dear girls
and dearer mother! I would not for the world have forgotten their
commissions, or given the sight of their little letters, for all the
Benbows and Crosses in the world.

But I was confident in my home-comfort and peacefulness.
When I got back to my club, however, three or four letters were
lying for me, upon some of which I noticed the "immediate," "ur-
gent," which old-fashioned people and anxious people still believe
will influence the post-office and quicken the speed of the mails.
I was about to open one of these, when the club porter brought
me two telegrams, one of which, he said, had arrived the night
before. I opened, as was to be expected, the last first, and this
was what I read: "Why don't you come or answer? For God's sake,
come. He is much worse." This was a thunderbolt to fall upon a
man's head who had one only son, and he the light of his eyes! The
other telegram, which I opened with hands trembling so much
that I lost time by my haste, was to much the same purport: "No
better; doctor afraid of brain fever. Calls for you day and night.
Let nothing detain you." The first thing I did was to look up the
timetables to see if there was any way of getting off sooner than
by the night-train, though I knew well enough there was not; and
then I read the letters, which furnished, alas! too clearly, all the
details. They told me that the boy had been pale for some time,
with a scared look. His mother had noticed it before I left home,
but would not say anything to alarm me. This look had increased
day by day; and soon it was observed that Roland came home at a
wild gallop through the park, his pony panting and in foam, himself

"as white as a sheet," but with the perspiration streaming from his forehead. For a long time he had resisted all questioning, but at length had developed such strange changes of mood, showing a reluctance to go to school, a desire to be fetched in the carriage at night—which was a ridiculous piece of luxury—an unwillingness to go out in the grounds, and nervous start at every sound, that his mother had insisted upon an explanation. When the boy—our boy Roland, who had never known what fear was—began to talk to her of voices he had heard in the park, and shadows that had appeared to him among the ruins, my wife promptly put him to bed and sent for Dr. Simson—which, of course, was the only thing to do.

I hurried off that evening, as may be supposed, with an anxious heart. How I got through the hours before the starting of the train, I cannot tell. We must all be thankful for the quickness of the railway when in anxiety; but to have thrown myself into a post-chaise as soon as horses could be put to, would have been a relief. I got to Edinburgh very early in the blackness of the winter morning, and scarcely dared look the man in the face, at whom I gasped "What news?" My wife had sent the brougham for me, which I concluded, before the man spoke, was a bad sign. His answer was that stereotyped answer which leaves the imagination so wildly free—"Just the same." Just the same! What might that mean? The horses seemed to me to creep along the long dark country-road. As we dashed through the park, I thought I heard some one moaning among the trees, and clenched my fist at them (whoever they might be) with fury. Why had the fool of a woman at the gate allowed any one to come in to disturb the quiet of the place? If I had not been in such hot haste to get home, I think I should have stopped the carriage and got out to see what tramp it was that had made an entrance, and chosen my grounds, of all places in the world,—when my boy was ill!—to grumble and groan in. But I had no reason to complain of our slow pace here. The horses flew like lightning along the intervening path, and drew up at the door all panting, as if they had run a race. My wife stood at the open door with a pale face, and a candle in her hand, which made her look paler still as the wind blew the flame about. "He is sleeping," she said in a whisper, as if her voice might wake him. And I replied, when I could find my voice, also in a whisper, as though the jingling of the horses' furniture and the sound of their hoofs must not have been more dangerous. I stood on the steps with her a moment, almost afraid to go in, now that I was here; and it seemed to me that I saw without observing, if I may say so, that the horses were unwilling to turn round, though their stables lay that way, or that the men were unwilling. These things occurred to me afterwards, though at the moment I was not capable of anything but to ask questions and to hear of the condition of the boy.

I looked at him from the door of his room, for we were afraid to go near, lest we should disturb that blessed sleep. It looked like actual sleep—not the lethargy into which my wife told me he would sometimes fall. She told me everything in the next room, which communicated with his, rising now and then and going to the door of communication; and in this there was much that was very startling and confusing to the mind. It appeared that ever since the winter began, since it was early dark, and night had fallen before his return from school, he had been hearing voices among the ruins—at first only a groaning, he said, at which his pony was as much alarmed as he was, but by degrees a voice. The tears ran down my wife's cheeks as she described to me how he would start up in the night and cry out, "Oh, mother, let me in! oh, mother, let me in!" with a pathos which rent her heart. And she sitting there all the time, only longing to do everything his heart could desire! But though she would try to soothe him, crying, "You are at home, my darling. I am here. Don't you know me? Your mother is here!" he would only stare at her, and after a while spring up again with the same cry. At other times he would be quite reasonable, she said, asking eagerly when I was coming, but declaring that he must go with me as soon as I did so, "to let them in." "The doctor thinks his nervous system must have received a shock," my wife said. "Oh, Henry, can it be that we have pushed him on too much with his work—a delicate boy like Roland!—and what is his work in comparison with his health? Even you would think little of honours or prizes if it hurt the boy's health." Even I! as if I were an inhuman father sacrificing my child to my ambition. But I would not increase her trouble by taking any notice.

After a while they persuaded me to lie down, to rest, and to eat—none of which things had been possible since I received their letters. The mere fact of being on the spot, of course, in itself was a great thing; and when I knew that I could be called in a moment, as soon as he was awake and wanted me, I felt capable, even in the dark, chill morning twilight, to snatch an hour or two's sleep. As it happened, I was so worn out with the strain of anxiety, and he so quieted and consoled by knowing I had come, that I was not disturbed till the afternoon, when the twilight had again settled down. There was just daylight enough to see his face when I went to him; and what a change in a fortnight! He was paler and more worn, I thought, than even in those dreadful days in the plains before we left India. His hair seemed to me to have grown long and lank; his eyes were like blazing lights projecting out of his white face. He got hold of my hand in a cold and tremulous clutch, and waved to everybody to go away. "Go away—even mother," he said,—"go away." This went to her heart, for she did not like that even I should have more of the boy's confidence than herself; but my wife has never been a woman to think of herself, and she left us alone. "Are they all gone?" he said, eagerly. "They would not let me speak. The doctor treated me as if I was a fool. You know I am not a fool, papa."

"Yes, yes, my boy, I know; but you are ill, and quiet is so necessary. You are not only not a fool, Roland, but you are reasonable and understand. "When you are ill you must deny yourself; you must not do everything that you might do being well."

He waved his thin hand with a sort of indignation. "Then, father, I am not ill," he cried. "Oh, I thought when you came you would not stop me,—you would see the sense of it! What do you think is the matter with me, all of you? Simson is well enough, but he is only a doctor. What do you think is the matter with me! I am no more ill than you are. A doctor, of course, he thinks you are ill the moment he looks at you—that's what he's there for—and claps you into bed."

"Which is the best place for you at present, my dear boy."

"I made up my mind," cried the little fellow, "that I would stand it till you came home. I said to myself, I won't frighten mother and the girls. But now, father," he cried, half jumping out of bed, "it's not illness,—it's a secret."

His eyes shone so wildly, his face was so swept with strong feeling, that my heart sank within me. It could be nothing but fever that did it, and fever had been so fatal. I got him into my arms to put him back into bed. "Roland," I said, humouring the poor child, which I knew was the only way, "if you are going to tell me this secret to do any good, you know you must be quite quiet, and not excite yourself. If you excite yourself, I must not let you speak."

"Yes, fill her," said the boy. He was quiet directly, like a man, as if he quite understood. When I had laid him back on his pillow, he looked up at me with that grateful sweet look with which children, when they are ill, break one's heart, the water coming into his eyes in his weakness. "I was sure as soon as you were here you would know what to do," he said.

"To be sure, my boy. Now keep quiet, and tell it all out like a man." To think I was telling lies to my own child! for I did it only to humour him, thinking, poor little fellow, his brain was wrong.

"Yes, father. Father, there is some one in the park,—some one that has been badly used."

"Hush, my dear; you remember, there is to be no excitement. Well, who is this somebody, and who has been ill-using him? We will soon put a stop to that."

"Ah," cried Roland, "but it is not so easy as you think. I don't know who it is. It is just a cry. Oh, if you could hear it! It gets into my head in my sleep. I heard it as clear—as clear;—and they think that I am dreaming—or raving perhaps," the boy said, with a sort of disdainful smile.

This look of his perplexed me; it was less like fever than I thought. "Are you quite sure you have not dreamt it, Roland?" I said.

"Dreamt?—that!" He was springing up again when he suddenly bethought himself, and lay down flat with the same sort of smile on his face. "The pony heard it too," he said. "She jumped as if she had been shot. If I had not grasped at the reins,—for I was frightened, father—"

"No shame to you, my boy," said I, though I scarcely knew why.

"If I hadn't held to her like a leech, she'd have pitched me over her head, and never drew breath till we were at the door. Did the pony dream it!" he said, with a soft disdain, yet indulgence for my foolishness. Then he added slowly: "It was only a cry the first time, and all the time before you went away. I wouldn't tell you, for it was so wretched to be frightened. I thought it might be a hare or a rabbit snared, and I went in the morning and looked, but there was nothing. It was after you went I heard it really first, and this is what it says." He raised himself on his elbow close to me, and looked me in the face. "'Oh, mother, let me in! oh, mother, let me in!'" As he said the words a mist came over his face, the mouth quivered, the soft features all melted and changed, and when he had ended these pitiful words, dissolved in a shower of heavy tears.

Was it a hallucination? Was it the fever of the brain? Was it the disordered fancy caused by great bodily weakness? How could I tell? I thought it wisest to accept it as if it were all true.

"This is very touching, Roland," I said.

"Oh, if you had just heard it, father! I said to myself, if father heard it he would do something; but mamma, you know, she's given over to Simson, and that fellow's a doctor, and never thinks of anything but clapping you into bed."

"We must not blame Simson for being a doctor, Roland."

"No, no," said my boy, with delightful toleration and indulgence; "oh no; that's the good of him—that's what he's for; I know that. But you—you are different; you are just father, and you'll do something,—directly, papa, directly,— this very night."

"Surely," I said. "No doubt it is some little lost child."

He gave me a sudden, swift look, investigating my face as if to see if, after all, this was everything my eminence as "father" came to,—no more than that! Then he got hold of my shoulder, clutching it with his thin hand: "Look here," he said, with a quiver in his voice; "suppose it wasn't living at all!"

"My dear boy, how then could you have heard it?" I said.

He turned away from me with a pettish exclamation—"As if you didn't know better than that!"

"Do you want to tell me it is a ghost?" I said.

Roland withdrew his hand; his countenance assumed an aspect of great dignity and gravity; a slight quiver remained about his lips. "Whatever it was—you always said we were not to call names. It was something—in trouble. Oh, father, in terrible trouble!"

"But, my boy," I said—I was at my wits' end—"if it was a child that was lost, or any poor human creature— but, Roland, what do you want me to do!"

"I should know if I was you," said the child, eagerly. "That is what I always said to myself— Father will know. Oh, papa, papa, to have to face it night after night, in such terrible, terrible trouble! and never to be able to do it any good. I don't want to cry; it's like a baby, I know; but I can't help it;—out there all by itself in the ruin, and nobody to help it. I can't bear it, I can't bear it!" cried my generous boy. And in his weakness he burst out, after many attempts to restrain it, into a great childish fit of sobbing and tears.

I do not know that I ever was in a greater perplexity in my life; and afterwards, when I thought of it, there was something comic in it too. It is bad enough to find your child's mind possessed with the conviction that he has seen—or heard—a ghost. But that he should require you to go instantly and help that ghost, was the most bewildering experience that had ever come my way. I am a sober man myself, and not superstitious—at least any more than everybody is superstitious. Of course I do not believe in ghosts; but I don't deny, any more than other people, that there are stories, which I cannot pretend to understand. My blood got a sort of chill in my veins at the idea that Roland should be a ghost-seer; for that generally means a hysterical temperament and weak health, and all that men most hate and fear for their children. But that I should take up his ghost and right its wrongs, and save it from its trouble, was such a mission as was enough to confuse any man. I did my best to console my boy without giving any promise of this astonishing kind; but he was too sharp for me. He would have none of my caresses. With sobs breaking in at intervals upon his voice, and the rain-drops hanging on his eyelids, he yet returned to the charge.

"It will be there now—it will be there all the night. Oh think, papa, think, if it was me! I can't rest for thinking of it. Don't!" he cried, putting away my hand—"don't! You go and help it, and mother can take care of me."

"But, Roland, what can I do?"

My boy opened his eyes, which were large with weakness and fever, and gave me a smile such, I think, as sick children only know the secret of. "I was sure you would know as soon as you came. I always said—Father will know: and mother," he cried, with a softening of repose upon his face, his limbs relaxing, his form sinking with a luxurious repose in his bed—"mother can come and take care of me."

I called her, and saw him turn to her with the complete dependence of a child, and then I went away and left them, as perplexed a man as any in Scotland. I must say, however, I had this consolation, that my mind was greatly eased about Roland. He might be under a hallucination, but his head was clear enough, and I did not think him so ill as everybody else did. The girls were astonished even at the ease with which I took his illness. "How do you think he is!" they said in a breath, coming round me, laying hold of me. "Not half so ill as I expected," I said; "not very bad at all." "Oh, papa, you are a darling!" cried Agatha, kissing me, and crying upon my shoulder; while little Jeanie, who was as pale as Roland, clasped both her arms round mine, and could not speak at all. I knew nothing about it, not half so much as Simson, but they believed in me; they had a feeling that all would go right now. God is very good to you when your children look to you like that. It makes one humble, not proud. I was not worthy of it; and then I recollected that I had to act the part of a father to Roland's ghost, which made me almost laugh, though I might just as well have cried. It was the strangest mission that ever was intrusted to mortal man.

It was then I remembered suddenly the looks of the men when they turned to take the brougham to the stables in the dark that morning: they had not liked it, and the horses had not liked it. I remembered that even in my anxiety about Roland I had heard them tearing along the avenue back to the stables, and had made

a memorandum mentally that I must speak of it. It seemed to
me that the best thing I could do was to go to the stables now
and make a few inquiries. It is impossible to fathom the minds
of rustics; there might be some devilry of practical joking, for
anything I knew; or they might have some reason in getting up a
bad reputation for the Brentwood avenue. It was getting dark by
the time I went out, and nobody who knows the country will need
to be told how black is the darkness of a November night under
high laurel-bushes and yew-trees. I walked into the heart of the
shrubberies two or three times, not seeing a step before me, till I
came out upon the broader carriage-road, where the trees opened
a little, and there was a faint grey glimmer of sky visible, under
which the great limes and elms stood darkling like ghosts; but it
grew black again as I approached the corner where the ruins lay.
Both eyes and ears were on the alert, as may be supposed; but I
could see nothing in the absolute gloom, and, so far as I can recollect, I heard nothing. Nevertheless there came a strong impression
upon me that somebody was there. It is a sensation which most
people have felt. I have seen when it has been strong enough to
awake you out of sleep, the sense of some one looking at you. I
suppose my imagination had been affected by Roland's story; and
the mystery of the darkness is always full of suggestions. I stamped
my feet violently on the gravel to rouse myself, and called out
sharply, "Who's there?" Nobody answered, nor did I expect any
one to answer, but the impression had been made. I was so foolish
that I did not like to look back, but went sideways, keeping an eye
on the gloom behind. It was with great relief that I spied the light
in the stables, making a sort of oasis in the darkness. I walked
very quickly into the midst of that lighted and cheerful place,
and thought the clank of the groom's pail one of the pleasantest
sounds I had ever heard. The coachman was the head of this little
colony, and it was to his house I went to pursue my investigations.
He was a native of the district, and had taken care of the place in
the absence of the family for years; it was impossible but that he
must know everything that was going on, and all the traditions of
the place. The men, I could see, eyed me anxiously when I thus
appeared at such an hour among them, and followed me with their

eyes to Jarvis's house, where he lived alone with his old wife, their
children being all married and out in the world. Mrs. Jarvis met
me with anxious questions. How was the poor young gentleman?
but the others knew, I could see by their faces, that not even this
was the foremost thing in my mind.

"Noises?—ou ay, there'll be noises—the wind in the trees, and the
water soughing down the glen. As for tramps, Cornel, no, there's
little o' that kind o' cattle about here; and Merran at the gate's a
careful body." Jarvis moved about with some embarrassment from
one leg to another as he spoke. He kept in the shade, and did not
look at me more than he could help. Evidently his mind was perturbed, and he had reasons for keeping his own counsel. His wife
sat by, giving him a quick look now and then, but saying nothing.
The kitchen was very snug, and warm, and bright—as different as
could be from the chill and mystery of the night outside.

"I think you are trifling with me, Jarvis," I said.

"Triflin', Cornel? no me. What would I trifle for? If the deevil
himsel was in the auld hoose, I have no interest in't one way or
another—"

"Sandy, hold your peace!" cried his wife, imperatively.

"And what am I to hold my peace for, wi' the Cornel standing
there asking a' thae questions? I'm saying, if the deevil himsel—"

"And I'm telling ye hold your peace!" cried the woman, in
great excitement. "Dark November weather and lang nichts, and
us that ken a' we ken. How daur ye name—a name that shouldna
be spoken?" She threw down her stocking and got up, also in great
agitation. "I tell't ye you never could keep it. It's no a thing that
will hide and the haill toun kens as weel as you or me. Tell the
Cornel straight out, or see, I'll do it. I dinna hold wi' your secrets:
and a secret that the haill toun kens!" She snapped her fingers with
an air of large disdain. As for Jarvis, ruddy and big as he was, he
shrank to nothing before this decided woman. He repeated to her
two or three times her own adjuration, "Hold your peace!" then,
suddenly changing his tone, cried out, "Tell him then, confound
ye! I'll wash nay hands o't. If a' the ghosts in Scotland were in the
auld hoose, is that ony concern o' mine!"

After this I elicited without much difficulty the whole story. In the opinion of the Jarvises, and of everybody about, the certainty that the place was haunted was beyond nil doubt. As Sandy and his wife warmed to the tale, one tripping up another in their eagerness to tell everything, it gradually developed as distinct a superstition as I ever heard, and not without poetry and pathos. How long it was since the voice had been heard first, nobody could tell with certainty. Jarvis's opinion was that his father, who had been coachman at Brentwood before him, had never heard anything about it, and that the whole thing had arisen within the last ten years, since the complete dismantling of the old house: which was a wonderfully modern date for a tale so well authenticated. According to these witnesses, and to several whom I questioned afterwards, and who were all in perfect agreement, it was only in the months of November and December that "the visitation" occurred. During these months, the darkest of the year, scarcely a night passed without the recurrence of these inexplicable cries. Nothing, it was said, had ever been seen—at least nothing that could be identified. Some people, bolder or more imaginative than the others, had seen the darkness moving, Mrs. Jarvis said, with unconscious poetry. It began when night fell, and continued, at intervals, till day broke. Very often it was only an inarticulate cry and moaning, but sometimes the words which had taken possession of my poor boy's fancy had been distinctly audible—"Oh, mother, let me in!" The Jarvises were not aware that there had ever been any investigation into it. The estate of Brentwood had lapsed into the hands of a distant branch of the family, who had lived but little there; and of the many people who had taken it, as I had done, few had remained through two Decembers. And nobody had taken the trouble to make a very close examination into the facts. "No, no," Jarvis said, shaking his head, "No, no, Cornel. Wha wad set themsels up for a laughin'-stock to a' the country-side, making a wark about a ghost? Naebody believes in ghosts. It bid to be the wind in the trees, the last gentleman said, or some effec' o' the water wrastlin' among the rocks. He said it was a' quite easy explained: but he gave up the hoose. And when you cam, Cornel, we were awfu' anxious you should never hear. What for should I have spoiled the bargain and hairmed the property for no-thing?"

"Do you call my child's life nothing!" I said in the trouble of the moment, unable to restrain myself. "And instead of telling this all to me, you have told it to him—to a delicate boy, a child unable to sift evidence, or judge for himself, a tender-hearted young creature—"

I was walking about the room with an anger all the hotter that I felt it to be most likely quite unjust. My heart was full of bitterness against the stolid retainers of a family who were content to risk other people's children and comfort rather than let a house lie empty. If I had been warned I might have taken precautions, or left the place, or sent Roland away, a hundred things which now I could not do; and here I was with my boy in a brain-fever, and his life, the most precious life on earth, hanging in the balance, dependent on whether or not I could get to the reason of a *banal,* commonplace ghost-story! I paced about in high wrath, not seeing what I was to do; for, to take Roland away, even if he were able to travel, would not settle his agitated mind; and I feared even that a scientific explanation of refracted sound, or reverberation, or any other of the easy certainties with which we elder men are silenced, would have very little effect upon the boy.

"Cornel," said Jarvis, solemnly, "and *she'll* bear me witness— the young gentleman never heard a word from me—no, nor from either groom or gardener; I'll gie ye my word for that. In the first place, he's no a lad that invites ye to talk. There are some that are, and some that arena. Some will draw ye on, till ye've tellt them a' the clatter of the toun, and a' ye ken, and whiles mair. But Maister Roland, his mind's fu' of his books. He's aye civil and kind, and a fine lad; but no that sort. And ye see it's for a' our interest, Cornel, that you should stay at Brentwood, I took it upon me mysel to pass the word—'No a syllable to Maister Roland, nor to the young leddies—no a syllable.' The women-servants, that have little reason to be out at night, ken little or nothing about it. And some think it grand to have a ghost so long as they're no in the way of coming across it. If you had been tellt the story to begin with, maybe ye would have thought so yourself."

This was true enough, though it did not throw any light upon my perplexity. If we had heard of it to start with, it is possible that all the family would have considered the possession of a ghost a distinct advantage. It is the fashion of the times. We never think what a risk it is to play with young imaginations, but cry out, in the fashionable jargon, "A ghost!—nothing else was wanted to make it perfect." I should not have been above this myself. I should have smiled, of course, at the idea of the ghost at all, but then to feel that it was mine would have pleased my vanity. Oh yes, I claim no exemption. The girls would have been delighted. I could fancy their eagerness, their interest, and excitement. No; if we had been told, it would have done no good—we should have made the bargain all the more eagerly, the fools that we are. "And there has been no attempt to investigate it," I said, "to see what it really is?"

"Eh, Cornel," said the coachman's wife, "wha would investigate, as ye call it, a thing that nobody believes in? Ye would be the laughin'-stock of a' the countryside, as my man says."

"But you believe in it," I said, turning upon her hastily. The woman was taken by surprise. She made a step backward out of my way.

"Lord, Cornel, how ye frichten a body! Me!—there's awfu' strange things in this world. An unlearned person doesna ken what to think. But the minister and the gentry they just laugh in your face. Inquire into the thing that is not! Na, na, we just let it be—"

"Come with me, Jarvis," I said, hastily, "and we'll make an attempt at least. Say nothing to the men or to anybody. I'll come back after dinner, and we'll make a serious attempt to see what it is, if it is anything. If I hear it—which I doubt—you may be sure I shall never rest till I make it out. Be ready for me about ten o'clock."

"Me, Cornel!" Jarvis said, in a faint voice. I had not been looking at him in my own preoccupation, but when I did so, I found that the greatest change had come over the fat and ruddy coachman. "Me, Cornel!" he repeated, wiping the perspiration from his brow. His ruddy face hung in flabby folds, his knees knocked together, his voice seemed half extinguished in his throat. Then he began to rub his hands and smile upon me in a deprecating, imbecile way. "There's no-thing I wouldna do to pleasure ye, Cornel," taking a step further back. "I'm sure, *she* kens I've aye said I never had to do with a mair fair, weel-spoken gentleman—" Here Jarvis came to a pause, again looking at me, rubbing his hands.

"Well?" I said.

"But eh, sir!" he went on, with the same imbecile yet insinuating smile, "if ye'll reflect that I am no used to my feet. With a horse atween my legs, or the reins in my hand, I'm maybe nae worse than other men; but on fit, Cornel— It's no the—bogles;—but I've been cavalry, ye see," with a little hoarse laugh, "a' my life. To face a thing ye didna understan'—on your feet, Cornel."

"Well, sir, if *I* do it," said I, tartly, "why shouldn't you!"

"Eh, Cornel, there's an awfu' difference. In the first place, ye tramp about the haill country-side, and think naething of it; but a walk tires me mair than a hunard miles' drive: and then ye're a gentleman, and do your ain pleasure; and you're no so auld as me; and it's for your ain bairn, ye see, Cornel; and then—"

"He believes in it, Cornel, and you dinna believe in it," the woman said.

"Will you come with me?" I said, turning to her.

She jumped back, upsetting her chair in her bewilderment. "Me!" with a scream, and then fell into a sort of hysterical laugh. "I wouldna say but what I would go; but what would the folk say to hear of Cornel Mortimer with an auld silly woman at his heels?"

The suggestion made me laugh too, though I had little inclination for it. "I'm sorry you have so little spirit, Jarvis," I said. "I must find some one else, I suppose."

Jarvis, touched by this, began to remonstrate, but I cut him short. My butler was a soldier who had been with me in India, and was not supposed to fear anything—man or devil,—certainly not the former; and I felt that I was losing time. The Jarvises were too thankful to get rid of me. They attended me to the door with the most anxious courtesies. Outside, the two grooms stood close by, a little confused by my sudden exit. I don't know if perhaps they had been listening—at least standing as near as possible, to catch any scrap of the conversation. I waved my hand to them as I went past, in answer to their salutations, and it was very apparent to me that they also were glad to see me go.

And it will be thought very strange, but it would be weak not to add, that I myself, though bent on the investigation I have spoken of, pledged to Roland to carry it out, and feeling that my boy's health, perhaps his life, depended on the result of my inquiry,—I felt the most unaccountable reluctance to pass these ruins on my way home. My curiosity was intense; and yet it was all my mind could do to pull my body along. I daresay the scientific people would describe it the other way, and attribute my cowardice to the state of my stomach. I went on; but if I had followed my impulse I should not have gone on, I should have turned and bolted. Everything in me seemed to cry out against it; my heart thumped, my pulses all began, like sledge-hammers, beating against my ears and every sensitive part. It was very dark, as I have said; the old house, with its shapeless tower, loomed a heavy mass through the darkness, which was only not entirely so solid as itself. On the other hand, the great dark cedars of which we were so proud seemed to fill up the night. My foot strayed out of the path in my confusion and the gloom together, and I brought myself up with a cry as I felt myself knock against something solid. What was it? The contact with hard stone and lime, and prickly bramble-bushes, restored me a little to myself. "Oh, it's only the old gable," I said aloud, with a little laugh to reassure myself. The rough feeling of the stones reconciled me. As I groped about thus, I shook off my visionary folly. What so easily explained as that I should have strayed from the path in the darkness? This brought me back to common existence, as if I had been shaken by a wise hand out of all the silliness of superstition. How silly it was, after all! What did it matter which path I took? I laughed again, this time with better heart—when suddenly, in a moment, the blood was chilled in my veins, a shiver stole along my spine, my faculties seemed to forsake me. Close by me at my side, at my feet, there was a sigh. No, not a groan, not a moaning, not anything so tangible—a perfectly soft, faint, inarticulate sigh. I sprang back, and my heart stopped beating. Mistaken! no, mistake was impossible. I heard it as clearly as I hear myself speak; a long, soft, weary sigh, as if drawn to the utmost, and emptying out a load of sadness that filled the breast. To hear this in the solitude, in the dark, in the night (though it was still early), had an effect which I cannot describe. I feel it now—something cold creeping over me, up into my hair, and down to my feet, which refused to move. I cried out, with a trembling voice, "Who is there!" as I had done before—but there was no reply.

I got home I don't quite know how; but in my mind there was no longer any indifference as to the thing, whatever it was, that haunted these ruins. My scepticism disappeared like a mist. I was as firmly determined that there was something as Roland was. I did not for a moment pretend to myself that it was possible I could be deceived; there were movements and noises which I understood all about, cracklings of small branches in the frost, and little rolls of gravel on the path, such as have a very eerie sound sometimes, and perplex you with wonder as to who has done it, *when there is no real mystery;* but I assure you all these little movements of nature don't affect you one bit *when there is something.* I understood *them.* I did not understand the sigh. That was not simple nature; there was meaning in it—feeling, the soul of a creature invisible. This is the thing that human nature trembles at—a creature invisible, yet with sensations, feelings, a power somehow of expressing itself. I had not the same sense of unwillingness to turn my back upon the scene of the mystery which I had experienced in going to the stables; but I almost ran home, impelled by eagerness to get everything done that had to be done, in order to apply myself to finding it out. Bagley was in the hall as usual when I went in. He was always there in the afternoon, always with the appearance of perfect occupation, yet, so far as I know, never doing anything. The door was open, so that I hurried in without any pause, breathless; but the sight of his calm regard, as he came to help me off with my overcoat, subdued me in a moment. Anything out of the way, anything incomprehensible, faded to nothing in the presence of Bagley. You saw and wondered how he was made: the parting of his hair, the tie of his white neckcloth, the fit of his trousers, all perfect as works of art; but you could see how they were done, which makes all the difference. I flung myself upon him, so to speak, without waiting to note the extreme unlikeness of the man to anything of the kind I meant. "Bagley," I said, "I want you to come out with me to-night to watch for—"

"Poachers, Colonel," he said, a gleam of pleasure running all over him.

"No, Bagley; a great deal worse," I cried.

"Yes, Colonel; at what hour, sir?" the man said; but then I had not told him what it was.

It was ten o'clock when we set out. All was perfectly quiet indoors. My wife was with Roland, who had been quite calm, she said, and who (though the fever of course must run its course) had been better ever since I came. I told Bagley to put on a thick greatcoat over his evening coat, and did the same myself—with strong boots; for the soil was like a sponge, or worse. Talking to him, I almost forgot what we were going to do. It was darker even than it had been before, and Bagley kept very close to me as we went along. I had a small lantern in my hand, which gave us a partial guidance. We had come to the corner where the path turns. On one side was the bowling-green, which the girls had taken possession of for their croquet-ground—a wonderful enclosure surrounded by high hedges of holly, three hundred years old and more; on the other, the ruins. Both were black as night; but before we got so far, there was a little opening in which we could just discern the trees and the lighter line of the road. I thought it best to pause there and take breath. "Bagley," I said, "there is something about these ruins I don't understand. It is there I am going. Keep your eyes open and your wits about you. Be ready to pounce upon any stranger you see—anything, man or woman. Don't hurt, but seize—anything you see." "Colonel," said Bagley, with a little tremor in his breath, "they do say there's things there—as is neither man nor woman." There was no time for words. "Are you game to follow me, my man? that's the question," I said. Bagley fell in without a word, and saluted. I knew then I had nothing to fear.

We went, so far as I could guess, exactly as I had come, when I heard that sigh. The darkness, however, was so complete that all marks, as of trees or paths, disappeared. One moment we felt our feet on the gravel, another sinking noiselessly into the slippery grass, that was all. I had shut up my lantern, not wishing to scare any one, whoever it might be. Bagley followed, it seemed to me, exactly in my footsteps as I made my way, as I supposed, towards the mass of the ruined house. We seemed to take a long time groping along seeking this; the squash of the wet soil under our feet was the only thing that marked our progress. After a while I stood still to see, or rather feel, where we were. The darkness was very still, but no stiller than is usual in a winter's night. The sounds I have mentioned—the crackling of twigs, the roll of a pebble, the sound of some rustle in the dead leaves, or creeping creature on the grass—were audible when you listened, all mysterious enough when your mind is disengaged, but to me cheering now as signs of the livingness of nature, even in the death of the frost As we stood still there came up from the trees in the glen the prolonged hoot of an owl. Bagley started with alarm, being in a state of general nervousness, and not knowing what he was afraid of. But to me the sound was encouraging and pleasant, being so comprehensible. "An owl," I said, under my breath. "Y—es, Colonel," said Bagley, his teeth chattering. We stood still about five minutes, while it broke into the still brooding of the air, the sound widening out in circles, dying upon the darkness. This sound, which is not a cheerful one, made me almost gay. It was natural, and relieved the tension of the mind. I moved on with new courage, my nervous excitement calming down.

When all at once, quite suddenly, close to us, at our feet, there broke out a cry. I made a spring backwards in the first moment of surprise and horror, and in doing so came sharply against the same rough masonry and brambles that had struck me before. This new sound came upwards from the ground—a low, moaning, wailing voice, full of suffering and pain. The contrast between it and the hoot of the owl was indescribable; the one with a wholesome wildness and naturalness that hurt nobody—the other, a sound that made one's blood curdle, full of human misery. With a great deal of fumbling—for in spite of everything I could do to keep up my courage my hands shook—I managed to remove the slide of my lantern. The light leaped out like something living, and made the place visible in a moment. We were what would have been inside the ruined building had anything remained but the gable-wall which I have described. It was close to us, the vacant doorway in it going out straight into the blackness outside. The light showed the bit of wall, the ivy glistening upon it in clouds of dark green, the bramble-branches waving, and below, the open door—a door that led to nothing. It was from this the voice came which died out just as the light flashed upon this strange scene. There was a moment's silence, and then it broke forth again. The sound was so near, so penetrating, so pitiful, that, in the nervous start I gave, the light fell out of my hand. As I groped for it in the dark my hand was clutched by Bagley, who I think must have dropped upon his knees; but I was too much perturbed myself to think much of this. He clutched at me in the confusion of his terror, forgetting all his usual decorum. "For God's sake, what is it, sir!" he gasped. If I yielded, there was evidently an end of both of us. "I can't tell," I said, "any more than you; that's what we've got to find out: up, man, up!" I pulled him to his feet, "Will you go round and examine the other side, or will you stay here with the lantern?" Bigley gasped at me with a face of horror. "Can't we stay together, Colonel?" he said—his knees were trembling under him. I pushed him against the corner of the wall, and put the light into his hands. "Stand fast till I come back; shake yourself together, man; let nothing pass you," I said. The voice was within two or three feet of us, of that there could be no doubt.

I went myself to the other side of the wall, keeping close to it. The light shook in Bagley's hand, but, tremulous though it was, shone out through the vacant door, one oblong block of light marking all the crumbling corners and hanging masses of foliage. Was that something dark huddled in a heap by the side of it? I pushed forward across the light in the doorway, and fell upon it with my hands; but it was only a juniper-bush growing close against the wall. Meanwhile, the sight of my figure crossing the doorway had brought Bagley's nervous excitement to a height: he flew at me, gripping my shoulder. "I've got him, Colonel! I've got him!" he cried, with a voice of sudden exultation. He thought it was a man, and was at once relieved. But at that moment the voice burst forth again between us, at our feet—more close to us than any separate being could be. He dropped off from me, and fell against the wall, his jaw dropping as if he were dying. I suppose, at the same moment, he saw that it was me whom he had clutched. I, for my part, had scarcely more command of myself. I snatched the light out of his hand, and flashed it all about me wildly. Nothing,—the juniper-bush, which I thought I had never seen before, the heavy growth of the glistening ivy, the brambles waving. It was close to my ears now, crying, crying, pleading as if for life. Either I heard the same words Roland had heard, or else, in my excitement, his imagination got possession of mine. The voice went on, growing into distinct articulation, but waving about, now from one point, now from another, as if the owner of it were moving slowly back and forward. "Mother! mother!" and then an outburst of wailing. As my mind steadied, getting accustomed (as one's mind gets accustomed to anything), it seemed to me as if some uneasy, miserable creature was pacing up and down before a closed door. Sometimes—but that must have been excitement—I thought I heard a sound like knocking, and then another burst, "Oh, mother! mother!" All this close, close to the space where I was standing with my lantern—now before me, now behind me: a creature restless, unhappy, moaning, crying, before the vacant doorway, which no one could either shut or open more.

"Do you hear it, Bagley? do you hear what it is saying?" I cried, stepping in through the doorway. He was lying against the wall— his eyes glazed, half dead with terror. He made a motion of his lips as if to answer me, but no sounds came; then lifted his hand with a curious imperative movement as if ordering me to be silent and listen. And how long I did so I cannot tell. It began to have an interest, an exciting hold upon me, which I could not describe. It seemed to call up visibly a scene any one could understand—a something shut out, restlessly wandering to and fro; sometimes the voice dropped, as if throwing itself down—sometimes wandered off a few paces, growing sharp and clear. "Oh, mother, let me in! oh, mother, mother, let me in! oh, let me in!" every word was clear to me. No wonder the boy had gone wild with pity. I tried to steady my mind upon Roland, upon his conviction that I could do something, but my head swam with the excitement, even when I partially overcame the terror. At last the words died away, and there was a sound of sobs and moaning. I cried out, "In the name of God who are you?" with a kind of feeling in my mind that to use the name of God was profane, seeing that I did not believe in ghosts or anything supernatural; but I did it all the same, and waited, my heart giving a leap of terror lest there should be a reply. Why this should have been I cannot tell, but I had a feeling that if there was an answer it would be more than I could bear. But there was no answer; the moaning went on, and then, as if it had been real, the voice rose a little higher again, the words re-commenced, "Oh, mother, let me in! oh, mother, let me in!" with an expression that was heart-breaking to hear.

As if it had been real! What do I mean by that? I suppose I got less alarmed as the thing went on. I began to recover the use of my senses—I seemed to explain it all to myself by saying that this had once happened, that it was a recollection of a real scene. Why there should have seemed something quite satisfactory and composing in this explanation I cannot tell, but so it was. I began to listen almost as if it had been a play, forgetting Bagley, who, I almost think, had fainted, leaning against the wall. I was startled out of this strange spectatorship that had fallen upon me by the sudden rush of something which made my heart jump once more, a large black figure in the doorway waving its arms. "Come in! come in! come in!" it shouted out hoarsely at the top of a deep bass voice, and then poor Bagley fell down senseless across the threshold. He was less sophisticated than I,—he had not been able to bear it any longer. I took him for something supernatural, as he took me, and it was some time before I awoke to the necessities of the moment. I remembered only after, that from the time I began to give my attention to the man, I heard the other voice no more. It was some time before I brought him to. It must have been a strange scene; the lantern making a luminous spot in the darkness, the man's white face lying on the black earth, I over him, doing what I could for him. Probably I should have been thought to be murdering him had any one seen us. When at last I succeeded in pouring a little brandy down his throat, he sat up and looked about him wildly. "What's up?" he said; then recognising me, tried

to struggle to his feet with a faint "Beg your pardon, Colonel."
I got him home as best I could, making him lean upon my arm.
The great fellow was as weak as a child. Fortunately he did not for
some time remember what had happened. From the time Bagley
fell the voice had stopped, and all was still.

"You've got an epidemic in your house, Colonel," Simson said to
me next morning. "What's the meaning of it all? Here's your butler
raving about a voice. This will never do, you know; and so far as I
can make out, you are in it too."

"Yes, I am in it, doctor. I thought I had better speak to you.
Of course you are treating Roland all right—but the boy is not
raving, he is as sane as you or me. It's all true."

"As sane as—I—or you. I never thought the boy insane. He's
got cerebral excitement, fever. I don't know what you've got.
There's something very queer about the look of your eyes."

"Come," said I, "you can't put as all to bed, you know. You had
better listen and hear the symptoms in full."

The doctor shrugged his shoulders, but he listened to me patiently. He did not believe a word of the story, that was clear; but
he heard it all from beginning to end. "My dear fellow," he said,
"the boy told me just the same. It's an epidemic. When one person
falls a victim to this sort of thing, it's as safe as can be—there's
always two or three."

"Then how do you account for it?" I said.

"Oh, account for it!—that's a different matter; there's no
accounting for the freaks our brains are subject to. If it's delusion;
if it's some trick of the echoes or the winds—some phonetic disturbance or other—"

"Come with me to-night, and judge for yourself," I said.

Upon this he laughed aloud, then said, "That's not such a bad
idea; but it would ruin me for ever if it were known that John
Simson was ghost-hunting."

"There it is," said I; "you dart down on us who are unlearned
with your phonetic disturbances, but you daren't examine what
the thing really is for fear of being laughed at. That's science!"

"It's not science—it's commonsense," said the doctor. "The thing has delusion on the front of it. It is encouraging an unwholesome tendency even to examine. What good could come of it? Even if I am convinced, I shouldn't believe."

"I should have said so yesterday; and I don't want you to be convinced or to believe," said I. "If you prove it to be a delusion, I shall be very much obliged too, for one. Come; somebody must go with me."

"You are cool," said the doctor. "You've disabled this poor fellow of yours, and made him—on that point—a lunatic for life; and now you want to disable me. But for once, I'll do it. To save appearance, if you'll give me a bed, I'll come over after my last rounds."

It was agreed that I should meet him at the gate, and that we should visit the scene of last night's occurrences before we came to the house, so that nobody might be the wiser. It was scarcely possible to hope that the cause of Bagley's sudden illness should not somehow steal into the knowledge of the servants at least, and it was better that all should be done as quietly as possible. The day seemed to me a very long one. I had to spend a certain part of it with Roland, which was a terrible ordeal for me—for what could I say to the boy? The improvement continued, but he was still in a very precarious state, and the trembling vehemence with which he turned to me when his mother left the room, filled me with alarm. "Father!" he said, quietly. "Yes, my boy; I am giving my best attention to it—all is being done that I can do. I have not come to any conclusion—yet. I am neglecting nothing you said," I cried. What I could not do was to give his active mind any encouragement to dwell upon the mystery. It was a hard predicament, for some satisfaction had to be given him. He looked at me very wistfully, with the great blue eyes which gazed so large and brilliant out of his white and worn face. "You must trust me," I said. "Yes, father. Father knows—father knows," he said to himself, as if to soothe some inward doubt. I left him as soon as I could. He was about the most precious thing I had on earth, and his health my first thought; but yet somehow, in the excitement of this other subject, I put it aside, and preferred not to dwell upon Roland, which was the most curious part of it all.

That night at eleven I met Simson at the gate. He had come by train, and I let him in gently myself. I had been so much absorbed in the coming experiment that I passed the ruins in going to meet him, almost without thought, if you can understand that. I had my lantern; and he showed me a coil of taper which he had ready for use. "There is nothing like light," he said, in his scoffing tone. It was a very still night, scarcely a sound, but not so dark. We could keep the path without difficulty as we went along. As we approached the spot we could hear a low moaning, broken occasionally by a bitter cry. "Perhaps that is your voice," said the doctor; "I thought it must be something of the kind. That's a poor brute caught in some of these infernal traps of yours; you'll find it among the bushes somewhere." I said nothing. I felt no particular fear, but a triumphant satisfaction in what was to follow. I led him to the spot where Bagley and I had stood on the previous night. All was silent as a winter night could be—so silent that we heard far off the sound of the horses in the stables, the shutting of a window at the house. Simson lighted his taper and went peering about, poking into all the corners. We looked like two conspirators lying in wait for some unfortunate traveller; but not a sound broke the quiet. The moaning had stopped before we came up; a star or two shone over us in the sky, looking down as if surprised at our strange proceedings. Dr. Simson did nothing but utter subdued laughs under his breath. "I thought as much," he said. "It is just the same with tables and all other kinds of ghostly apparatus; a sceptic's presence stops everything. When I am present nothing ever comes off. How long do you think it will be necessary to stay here? Oh, I don't complain; only, when *you* are satisfied, *I* am— quite."

I will not deny that I was disappointed beyond measure by this result. It made me look like a credulous fool. It gave the doctor such a pull over me as nothing else could. I should point all his morals for years to come, and his materialism, his scepticism would be increased beyond endurance. "It seems, indeed," I said, "that there is to be no—" "Manifestation," he said, laughing; "that is what all the mediums say. No manifestations, in consequence

of the presence of an unbeliever." His laugh sounded very uncomfortable to me in the silence; and it was now near midnight. But
that laugh seemed the signal; before it died away the moaning we
had heard before was resumed. It started from some distance off,
and came towards us, nearer and nearer, like some one walking
along and moaning to himself. There could be no idea now that it
was a hare caught in a trap. The approach was slow, like that of a
weak person with little halts and pauses. We heard it coming along
the grass straight towards the vacant doorway. Simson had been a
little startled by the first sound. He said hastily, "That child has
no business to be out so late." But he felt, as well as I, that this was
no child's voice. As it came nearer, he grew silent, and, going to
the doorway with his taper, stood looking out towards the sound.
The taper being unprotected blew about in the night air, though
there was scarcely any wind. I threw the light of my lantern steady
and white across the same space. It was in a blaze of light in the
midst of the blackness. A little icy thrill had gone over me at the
first sound, but as it came close, I confess that my only feeling was
satisfaction. The scoffer could scoff no more. The light touched
his own face, and showed a very perplexed countenance. If he was
afraid, he concealed it with great success, but he was perplexed.
And then all that had happened on the previous night was enacted
once more. It fell strangely upon me with a sense of repetition.
Every cry, every sob seemed the same as before. I listened almost
without any emotion at all in my own person, thinking of its
effect upon Simson. He maintained a very bold front on the whole.
All that coming and going of the voice was, if our ears could be
trusted, exactly in front of the vacant, blank doorway, blazing full
of light, which caught and shone in the glistening leaves of the
great hollies at a little distance. Not a rabbit could have crossed
the turf without being seen;—but there was nothing. After a time,
Simson, with a certain caution and bodily reluctance, as it seemed
to me, went out with his roll of taper into this space. His figure
showed against the holly in full outline. Just at this moment the
voice sank, as was its custom, and seemed to fling itself down at
the door. Simson recoiled violently, as if some one had come up

against him, then turned, and held his taper low as if examining something. "Do you see anybody!" I cried in a whisper, feeling the chill of nervous panic steal over me at this action. "It's nothing but a — confounded juniper-bush," he said. This I knew very well to be nonsense, for the juniper-bush was on the other side. He went about after this round and round, poking his taper everywhere, then returned to me on the inner side of the wall. He scoffed no longer; his face was contracted and pale. "How long does this go on?" he whispered to me, like a man who does not wish to interrupt some one who is speaking. I had become too much perturbed myself to remark whether the successions and changes of the voice were the same as last night. It suddenly went out in the air almost as he was speaking, with a soft reiterated sob dying away. If there had been anything to be seen, I should have said that the person was at that moment crouching on the ground close to the door.

We walked home very silent afterwards. It was only when we were in sight of the house that I said, "What do you think of it?" "I can't tell what to think of it," he said, quickly. He took— though he was a very temperate man—not the claret I was going to offer him, but some brandy from the tray, and swallowed it almost undiluted. "Mind you, I don't believe a word of it," he said, when he had lighted his candle; "but I can't tell what to think of it," he turned round to add, when he was half-way upstairs.

All of this, however, did me no good with the solution of my problem. I was to help this weeping, sobbing thing, which was already to me as distinct a personality as anything I knew—or what should I say to Roland? It was on my heart that my boy would die if I could not find some way of helping this creature. You may be surprised that I should speak of it in this way. I did not know if it was man or woman; but I no more doubted that it was a soul in pain than I doubted my own being; and it was my business to soothe this pain—to deliver it, if that was possible. Was ever such a task given to an anxious father trembling for his only boy? I felt in my heart, fantastic as it may appear, that I must fulfil this somehow, or part with my child; and you may conceive that rather than do that I was ready to die. But even my dying would not have advanced me—unless by bringing me into the same world with that seeker at the door.

Next morning Simson was out before breakfast, and came in with evident signs of the damp grass on his boots, and a look of worry and weariness, which did not say much for the night he had passed. He improved a little after breakfast, and visited his two patients, for Bagley was still an invalid. I went out with him on his way to the train, to hear what he had to say about the boy. "He is going on very well," he said; "there are no complications as yet. But mind you, that's not a boy to be trifled with, Mortimer. Not a word to him about last night." I had to tell him then of my last interview with Roland, and of the impossible demand he had made upon me—by which, though he tried to laugh, he was much discomposed, as I could see. "We must just perjure ourselves all round," he said, "and swear you exorcised it;" but the man was too kind-hearted to be satisfied with that. "It's frightfully serious for you, Mortimer. I can't laugh as I should like to. I wish I saw a way out of it, for your sake. By the way," he added shortly, "didn't you notice that juniper-bush on the left-hand side!" "There was one on the right hand of the door. I noticed you made that mistake last night." "Mistake!" he cried, with a curious low laugh, pulling up the collar of his coat as though he felt the cold,—"there's no juniper there this morning, left or right. Just go and see." As he stepped into the train a few minutes after, he looked back upon me and beckoned me for a parting word. "I'm coming back to-night," he said.

I don't think I had any feeling about this as I turned away from that common bustle of the railway which made my private preoccupations feel so strangely out of date. There had been a distinct satisfaction in my mind before that his scepticism had been so entirely defeated. But the more serious part of the matter pressed upon me now. I went straight from the railway to the manse, which stood on a little plateau on the side of the river opposite to the woods of Brentwood. The minister was one of a class which is not so common in Scotland as it used to be. He was a man of good family, well educated in the Scotch way, strong in philosophy, not so strong in Greek, strongest of all in experience,—a man who had "come across," in the course of his life, most people of note that had ever been in Scotland—and who was said to be very sound in doctrine, without infringing the toleration to which old men, who are good men, so often come. He was old-fashioned; perhaps he did not think so much about the troublous problems of theology as many of the young men, nor ask himself any hard questions upon the Confession of Faith—but he understood human nature, which is perhaps better. He received me with a cordial welcome. "Come away, Colonel Mortimer," he said; "I'm all the more glad to see you, that I feel it's a good sign for the boy. He's doing well?—God be praised—and the Lord bless him and keep him. He has many a poor body's prayers—and that can do nobody harm."

"He will need them all, Dr. Moncrieff," I said, "and your counsel too." And I told him the story—more than I had told Simson. The old clergyman listened to me with many suppressed exclamations, and at the end the water stood in his eyes.

"That's just beautiful," he said. "I do not mind to have heard anything like it; it's as fine as Burns when he wished deliverance to one—that is prayed for in no kirk. Ay, ay! so he would have you console the poor lost spirit? God bless the boy! There's something more than common in that, Colonel Mortimer. And also the faith of him in his father!—I would like to put that into a sermon." Then the old gentleman gave me an alarmed look, and said, "No, no; I was not meaning a sermon; but I must write it down for the 'Children's Record.'" I saw the thought that passed through his mind. Either he thought, or he feared I would think, of a funeral sermon. You may believe this did not make me more cheerful.

I can scarcely say that Dr. Moncrieff gave me any advice. How could any one advise on such a subject? But he said, "I think I'll come too. I'm an old man; I'm less liable to be frighted than those that are further off the world unseen. It behooves me to think of my own journey there. I've no cut-and-dry beliefs on the subject. I'll come too: and maybe at the moment the Lord will put into our heads what to do."

This gave me a little comfort—more than Simson had given me. To be clear about the cause of it was not my grand desire. It was another thing that was in my mind—my boy. As for the poor soul at the open door, I had no more doubt, as I have said, of its existence than I had of my own. It was no ghost to me. I knew the creature, and it was in trouble. That was my feeling about it, as it was Roland's. To hear it first was a great shock to my nerves, but not now; a man will get accustomed to anything. But to do something for it was the great problem; how was I to be serviceable to a being that was invisible, that was mortal no longer? "Maybe at the moment the Lord will put it into our heads." This is very old-fashioned phraseology, and a week before, most likely, I should have smiled (though always with kindness) at Dr. Moncrieff's credulity; but there was a great comfort, whether rational or otherwise I cannot say, in the mere sound of the words.

The road to the station and the village lay through the glen—not by the ruins; but though the sunshine and the fresh air, and the beauty of the trees, and the sound of the water were all very soothing to the spirits, my mind was so full of my own subject that I could not refrain from turning to the right hand as I got to the top of the glen, and going straight to the place which I may call the scene of all my thoughts. It was lying full in the sunshine, like all the rest of the world. The ruined gable looked due east, and in the present aspect of the sun the light streamed down through the doorway as our lantern had done, throwing a flash of light upon the damp grass beyond. There was a strange suggestion in the open door—so futile, a kind of emblem of vanity—all free around, so that you could go where you pleased, and yet that semblance of an enclosure—that way of entrance, unnecessary, leading to nothing. And why any creature should pray and weep to get in—to nothing: or be kept out—by nothing! You could not dwell upon it, or it made your brain go round. I remembered, however, what Simson said about the juniper, with a little smile on my own mind as to the inaccuracy of recollection, which even a scientific man will be guilty of. I could see now the light of my lantern gleaming upon the wet glistening surface of the spiky leaves at the right hand—

and he ready to go to the stake for it that it was the left! I went
round to make sure. And then I saw what he had said. Right or
left there was no juniper at all. I was confounded by this, though
it was entirely a matter of detail: nothing at all: a bush of brambles waving, the grass growing up to the very walls. But after all,
though it gave me a shock for a moment, what did that matter!
There were marks as if a number of footsteps had been up and
down in front of the door; but these might have been our steps;
and all was bright, and peaceful, and still. I poked about the other
ruin—the larger ruins of the old house—for some time, as I had
done before. There were marks upon the grass here and there, I
could not call them footsteps, all about; but that told for nothing
one way or another. I had examined the ruined rooms closely the
first day. They were half filled up with soil and debris, without
brackens and bramble—no refuge for any one there. It vexed me
that Jarvis should see me coming from that spot when he came up
to me for his orders. I don't know whether my nocturnal expedi-
tions had got wind among the servants. But there was a significant
look in his face. Something in it I felt was like my own sensations
when Simson in the midst of his scepticism was struck dumb. Jarvis felt satisfied that his veracity had been put beyond question. I
never spoke to a servant of mine in such a peremptory tone before.
I sent him away "with a flea in his lug," as the man described it
afterwards. Interference of every kind was intolerable to me at
such a moment.

But what was strangest of all was, that I could not face Roland.
I did not go up to his room as I would have naturally done at
once. This the girls could not understand. They saw there was
some mystery in it. "Mother has gone to lie down," Agatha said;
"he has had such a good night. But he wants you so, papa!" cried
little Jeanie, always with her two arms embracing mine in a pretty
way she had. I was obliged to go at last—but what could I say! I
could only kiss him, and tell him to keep still—that I was doing
all I could. There is something mystical about the patience of a
child. "It will come all right, won't it, father!" he said. "God grant
it may! I hope so, Roland." "Oh yes, it will come all right." Perhaps he understood that in the midst of my anxiety I could not

stay with him as I should have done otherwise. But the girls were more surprised than it is possible to describe. They looked at me with wondering eyes. "If I were ill, papa, and you only stayed with me a moment, I should break my heart," said Agatha. But the boy had a sympathetic feeling. He knew that of my own will I would not have done it. I shut myself up in the library, where I could not rest, but kept pacing up and down like a caged beast. What could I do! and if I could do nothing, what would become of my boy! These were the questions that, without ceasing, pursued each other through my mind.

Simson came out to dinner, and when the house was all still, and most of the servants in bed, we went out and met Dr. Moncrieff, as we had appointed, at the head of the glen. Simson, for his part, was disposed to scoff at the Doctor. "If there are to be any spells, you know, I'll cut the whole concern," he said. I did not make him any reply. I had not invited him; he could go or come as he pleased. He was very talkative, far more so than suited my humour, as we went on. "One thing is certain, you know, there must be some human agency," he said. "It is all bosh about apparitions. I never have investigated the laws of sound to any great extent, and there's a great deal in ventriloquism that we don't know much about." "If it's the same to you," I said, "I wish you'd keep all that to yourself, Simson. It doesn't suit my state of mind." "Oh, I hope I know how to respect idiosyncrasy," he said. The very tone of his voice irritated me beyond measure. These scientific fellows, I wonder people put up with them as they do, when you have no mind for their cold-blooded confidence. Dr. Moncrieff met us about eleven o'clock, the same time as on the previous night. He was a large man, with a venerable countenance and white hair—old, but in full vigour, and thinking less of a cold night walk than many a younger man. He had his lantern as I had. We were fully provided with means of lighting the place, and we were all of us resolute men. We had a rapid consultation as we went up, and the result was that we divided to different posts. Dr. Moncrieff remained inside the wall—if you can call that inside where there was no wall but one. Simson placed himself on the side next the ruins, so as to intercept any communication with the

old house, which was what his mind was fixed upon. I was posted
on the other side. To say that nothing could come near without
being seen was self-evident. It had been so also on the previous
night. Now, with our three lights in the midst of the darkness, the
whole place seemed illuminated. Dr. Moncrieff's lantern, which
was a large one, without any means of shutting up—an old-fashioned lantern with a pierced and ornamental top— shone steadily,
the rays shooting out of it upward into the gloom. He placed it on
the grass, where the middle of the room, if this had been a room,
would have been. The usual effect of the light streaming out of the
doorway was prevented by the illumination which Simson and I on
either side supplied. With these differences, everything seemed as
on the previous night.

And what occurred was exactly the same, with the same air of
repetition, point for point, as I had formerly remarked. I declare
that it seemed to me as if I were pushed against, put aside, by
the owner of the voice as he paced up and down in his trouble,—
though these are perfectly futile words, seeing that the stream of
light from my lantern, and that from Simeon's taper, lay broad
and clear, without a shadow, without the smallest break, across the
entire breadth of the grass. I had ceased even to be alarmed, for my
part. My heart was rent with pity and trouble—pity for the poor
suffering human creature that moaned and pleaded so, and trouble
for myself and my boy. God! if I could not find any help—and
what help could I find?—Roland would die.

We were all perfectly still till the first outburst was exhausted,
as I knew (by experience) it would be. Dr. Moncrieff, to whom it
was new, was quite still on the other side of the wall, as we were
in our places. My heart had remained almost at its usual beating
during the voice. I was used to it; it did not rouse all my pulses
as it did at first. But just as it threw itself sobbing at the door (I
cannot use other words), there suddenly came something which
sent the blood coursing through my veins and my heart into my
mouth. It was a voice inside the wall—the minister's well-known
voice. I would have been prepared for it in any kind of adjuration,
but I was not prepared for what I heard. It came out with a sort of

stammering, as if too much moved for utterance. "Willie, Willie! Oh, God preserve us! is it you?"

These simple words had an effect upon me that the voice of the invisible creature had ceased to have. I thought the old man, whom I had brought into this danger, had gone mad with terror. I made a dash round to the other side of the wall, half crazed myself with the thought. He was standing where I had left him, his shadow thrown vague and large upon the grass by the lantern which stood at his feet. I lifted my own light to see his face as I rushed forward. He was very pale, his eyes wet and glistening, his mouth quivering with parted lips. He neither saw nor heard me. We that had gone through this experience before, had crouched towards each other to get a little strength to bear it. But he was not even aware that I was there. His whole being seemed absorbed in anxiety and tenderness. He held out his hands, which trembled, but it seemed to me with eagerness, not fear. He went on speaking all the time. "Willie, if it is you—and it's you, if it is not a delusion of Satan,—Willie, lad! why come ye here frighting them that know you not? Why came ye not to me?"

He seemed to wait for an answer. When his voice ceased, his countenance, every line moving, continued to speak. Simson gave me another terrible shock, stealing into the open doorway with his light, as much awestricken, as wildly curious, as I. But the minister resumed, without seeing Simson, speaking to some one else. His voice took a tone of expostulation—

"Is this right to come here? Your mother's gone with your name on her lips. Do you think she would ever close her door on her own lad? Do ye think the Lord will close the door, ye fainthearted creature? No!—I forbid ye! I forbid ye!" cried the old man. The sobbing voice had begun to resume its cries. He made a step forward, calling out the last words in a voice of command. "I forbid ye! Cry out no more to man. Go home, ye wandering spirit! go home! Do you hear me?—me that christened ye, that have struggled with ye, that have wrestled for ye with the Lord!" Here the loud tones of his voice sank into tenderness. "And her too, poor woman! poor woman! her you are calling upon. She's no here.

You'll find her with the Lord. Go there and seek her, not here. Do
you hear me, lad? go after her there. He'll let you in, though it's
late. Man, take heart! if you will lie and sob and greet, let it be at
heaven's gate, and no your poor mother's ruined door."

He stopped to get his breath: and the voice had stopped, not
as it had done before, when its time was exhausted and all its
repetitions said, but with a sobbing catch in the breath as if over-
ruled. Then the minister spoke again. "Are you hearing me, Will?
Oh, laddie, you've liked the beggarly elements all your days. Be
done with them now. Go home to the Father—the Father! Are you
hearing me?" Here the old man sank down upon his knees, his
face raised upwards, his hands held up with a tremble in them,
all white in the light in the midst of the darkness. I resisted as
long as I could, though I cannot tell why,—then I, too, dropped
upon my knees. Simson all the time stood in the doorway, with
an expression in his face such as words could not tell, his under
lip dropped, his eyes wild, staring. It seemed to be to him, that
image of blank ignorance and wonder, that we were praying. All
the time the voice, with a low arrested sobbing, lay just where he
was standing, as I thought.

"Lord," the minister said—"Lord, take him into Thy everlast-
ing habitations. The mother he cries to is with Thee. Who can
open to him but Thee? Lord, when is it too late for Thee, or what
is too hard for Thee? Lord, let that woman there draw him inower!
Let her draw him inower!"

I sprang forward to catch something in my arms that flung
itself wildly within the door. The illusion was so strong, that I
never paused till I felt my forehead graze against the wall and
my hands clutch the ground—for there was nobody there to save
from falling, as in my foolishness I thought. Simson held out his
hand to me to help me up. He was trembling and cold, his lower
lip hanging, his speech almost inarticulate. "It's gone," he said,
stammering,—"it's gone!" We leant upon each other for a moment, trembling so much both of us that the whole scene trembled
as if it were going to dissolve and disappear; and yet as long as I
live I will never forget it—the shining of the strange lights, the
blackness all round, the kneeling figure with all the whiteness of

the light concentrated on its white venerable head and uplifted hands. A strange solemn stillness seemed to close all round us. By intervals a single syllable, "Lord! Lord!" came from the old minister's lips. He saw none of us, nor thought of us. I never knew how long we stood, like sentinels guarding him at his prayers, holding our lights in a confused dazed way, not knowing what we did. But at last he rose from his knees, and standing up at his full height, raised his arms, as the Scotch manner is at the end of a religious service, and solemnly gave the apostolical benediction— to what? to the silent earth, the dark woods, the wide breathing atmosphere—for we were but spectators gasping an Amen!

It seemed to me that it must be the middle of the night, as we all walked back. It was in reality very late. Dr. Moncrieff put his arm into mine. He walked slowly, with an air of exhaustion. It was as if we were coming from a deathbed. Something hushed and solemnised the very air. There was that sense of relief in it which there always is at the end of a death-struggle. And nature, persistent, never daunted, came back in all of us, as we returned into the ways of life. We said nothing to each other, indeed, for a time; but when we got clear of the trees and reached the opening near the house, where we could see the sky, Dr. Moncrieff himself was the first to speak. "I must be going," he said; "it's very late, I'm afraid. I will go down the glen, as I came."

"But not alone. I am going with you, Doctor."

"Well, I will not oppose it. I am an old man, and agitation wearies more than work. Yes; I'll be thankful of your arm. To-night, Colonel, you've done me more good turns than one."

I pressed his hand on my arm, not feeling able to speak. But Simson, who turned with us, and who had gone along all this time with his taper flaring, in entire unconsciousness, came to himself, apparently at the sound of our voices, and put out that wild little torch with a quick movement, as if of shame. "Let me carry your lantern," he said; "it is heavy." He recovered with a spring, and in a moment, from the awestricken spectator he had been, became himself, sceptical and cynical. "I should like to ask you a question," he said. "Do you believe in Purgatory, Doctor? It's not in the tenets of the Church, so far as I know."

"Sir," said Dr. Moncrieff, "an old man like me is sometimes not very sure what he believes. There is just one thing I am certain of—and that is the loving-kindness of God."

"But I thought that was in this life. I am no theologian—"

"Sir," said the old man again, with a tremor in him which I could feel going over all his frame, "if I saw a friend of mine within the gates of hell, I would not despair but his Father would find him still—if he cried like *yon*."

"I allow it is very strange—very strange. I cannot see through it. That there must be human agency, I feel sure. Doctor, what made you decide upon the person and the name!"

The minister put out his hand with the impatience which a man might show if he were asked how he recognised his brother. "Tuts!" he said, in familiar speech—then more solemnly, "how should I not recognise a person that I know better—far better—than I know you?"

"Then you saw the man?"

Dr. Moncrieff made no reply, he moved his hand again with a little impatient movement, and walked on, leaning heavily on my arm. And we went on for a long time without another word, threading the dark paths, which were steep and slippery with the damp of the winter. The air was very still—not more than enough to make a faint sighing in the branches, that mingled with the sound of the water to which we were descending. When we spoke again, it was about indifferent matters—about the height of the river, and the recent rains. We parted with the minister at his own door, where his old housekeeper appeared in great perturbation, waiting for him. "Eh me, minister! the young gentleman will be worse?" she cried.

"Far from that—better. God bless him!" Dr. Moncrieff said.

I think if Simson had begun again to me with his questions, I should have pitched him over the rocks as we returned up the glen; but he was silent, by a good inspiration. And the sky was clearer than it had been for many nights, shining high over the trees, with here and there a star faintly gleaming through the wilderness of dark and bare branches. The air, as I have said, was very soft in them, with a subdued and peaceful cadence. It was real, like every natural sound, but came to us like a hush of peace and relief. I thought there was a sound in it as of the breath of a sleeper, and it seemed clear to me that Roland must be sleeping, satisfied and calm. We went up to his room when we went in. There we found the complete hush of rest. My wife looked up out of a doze, and gave me a smile; "I think he is a great deal better: but you are very late," she said in a whisper, shading the light with her hand that the doctor might see his patient. The boy had got back something like his own colour. He woke as we stood all round his bed. His eyes had the happy half-awakened look of childhood, glad to shut again, yet pleased with the interruption and glimmer of the light. I stooped over him and kissed his forehead, which was moist and cool. "It is all well, Roland," I said. He looked up at me with a glance of pleasure, and took my hand and laid his cheek upon it, and so went to sleep.

For some nights after, I watched among the ruins, spending all the dark hours up to midnight patrolling about the bit of wall which was associated with so many emotions; but I heard nothing, and saw nothing beyond the quiet course of nature: nor, so far as I am aware, has anything been heard again. Dr. Moncrieff gave me the history of the youth, whom he never hesitated to name. I did not ask, as Simson did, how he recognised him. He had been a prodigal—weak, foolish, easily imposed upon, and "led away," as people say. All that we had heard had passed actually in life, the Doctor said. The young man had come home thus a day or two after his mother died—who was no more than the housekeeper in the old house—and distracted with the news, had thrown himself down at the door and called upon her to let him in. The old man could scarcely speak of it for tears. To me it seemed as if—heaven help us, how little do we know about anything!—a scene like that might impress itself somehow upon the hidden heart of nature. I do not pretend to know how, but the repetition had struck me at the time as, in its terrible strangeness and incomprehensibility, almost mechanical—as if the unseen actor could not exceed or vary, but was bound to re-enact the whole. One thing that struck me, however, greatly, was the likeness between the old minister and my boy in the manner of regarding these strange phenomena. Dr. Moncrieff was not terrified, as I had been myself, and all the rest of us. It was no "ghost," as I fear we all vulgarly considered it, to him—but a poor creature whom he knew under these conditions, just as he had known him in the flesh, having no doubt of his identity. And to Roland it was the same. This spirit in pain—if it was a spirit—this voice out of the unseen—was a poor fellow-creature in misery, to be succoured and helped out of his trouble, to my boy. He spoke to me quite frankly about it when he got better. "I knew father would find out some way," he said. And this was when he was strong and well, and all idea that he would turn hysterical or become a seer of visions had happily passed away.

I must add one curious fact which does not seem to me to have any relation to the above, but which Simson made great use of, as the human agency which he was determined to find somehow. We had examined the ruins very closely at the time of these occurrences; but afterwards, when all was over, as we went casually about them one Sunday afternoon in the idleness of that unemployed day, Simson with his stick penetrated an old window which had been entirely blocked up with fallen soil. He jumped down into it in great excitement, and called me to follow. There we found a little hole—for it was more a hole than a room—entirely hidden under the ivy and ruins, in which there was a quantity of straw laid in a corner, as if some one had made a bed there, and some remains of crusts about the floor. Some one had lodged there, and not very long before, he made out; and that this unknown being was the author of all the mysterious sounds we heard he is convinced. "I told you it was human agency," he said, triumphantly. He forgets, I suppose, how he and I stood with our lights seeing nothing, while the space between us was audibly traversed by something that could speak, and sob, and suffer. There is no argument with men of this kind. He is ready to get up a laugh against me on this slender ground. "I was puzzled myself—I could not make it out—but I always felt convinced human agency was at the bottom of it. And here it is—and a clever fellow he must have been," the Doctor says.

Bagley left my service as soon as he got well. He assured me it was no want of respect; but he could not stand "them kind of things." And the man was so shaken and ghastly that I was glad to give him a present and let him go. For my own part, I made a point of staying out the time, two years, for which I had taken Brentwood; but I did not renew my tenancy. By that time we had settled, and found for ourselves a pleasant home of our own.

I must add that when the doctor defies me, I can always bring back gravity to his countenance, and a pause in his railing, when I remind him of the juniper-bush. To me that was a matter of little importance. I could believe I was mistaken. I did not care about it one way or other; but on his mind the effect was different. The miserable voice, the spirit in pain, he could think of as the result of ventriloquism, or reverberation, or—anything you please: an elaborate prolonged hoax executed somehow by the tramp that had found a lodging in the old tower. But the juniper-bush staggered him. Things have effects so different on the minds of different men.

NO FICTION
J. G. P.
Macmillan's, 1882

The Editor is in possession of the name of the author of the following singular narrative, and of the place at which it happened, and has every reason to be satisfied of the entire *bona fides* of the writer, a clergyman of the Church of England.

Early in January, 1879, clerical duty called me into the north-west of England. In the midst of a heavy fall of snow, my family and I took possession of the official residence provided for us.

It was an old, stone house of one story; roofed, in part with ancient stone slabs, in part with modern slates; and standing in a garden bare of trees. A wide passage ran back from the entrance towards the kitchen, where there were two doors; the one leading into the yard, the other into the larder, which was, in fact, a roomy cellar at the foot of a flight of very old stone steps. The five bedrooms all opened on a square landing.

"How about the roof!" I asked of the man in charge.

"All right, sir; everything has been carefully seen to; and, when the thaw comes, I'll warrant you'll not be troubled, anything to matter."

In a few days we had shaken down; and the verdict on our new home was, "Not grand, but decidedly cosy."

A tall, solid, fleshy, rosy young woman had undertaken to be our one servant. Sparing of words was she, but not sparing of work.

"The incarnation of stupidity and stolidity," said my son Primus.

"The very thing for us," said his mother.

This girl's name being Stillwell, soon became corrupted into Stillwater; or, for short, Still.

It was splendid skating weather. The low-lying meadows were flooded to the depth of a foot or more, and one glided along over acres of smooth, green, transparent ice. Every day we sallied forth, my three boys, their sister and I, to take our fill of enjoyment in this icy paradise; coming back to bask all the evening before the bright golden sunshine and the silvery ashes of a north-country coal fire.

My wife has the weak habit of going to "tuck up" her boys after they are in bed. One night, their voices sounded so angry, that she ran up in haste, to see what was wrong. On entering their room, she found the two elder boys sitting up in bed, hurling injurious and derisive epithets at some person or persons unknown.

"Let me just find out who you are, and you'll get such a jolly good licking as you'll remember," announced Primus, gazing wrathfully at the ceiling.

"Oh, you blooming idiot! I wish I'd your boots. I'd throw them at your head. Be off! I'm taking a sight at you," shouted Secundus, nose and fingers up-turned in the same direction.

"Are you both mad!" inquired the stern, maternal voice.

"It's that fellow, Mother, that I told you about. He's on the roof again. Just listen to the row he makes."

"Nonsense," said his mother: but she stood listening for some time.

"Oh, you coward!"

"Ah, you funk!" proceeded from the two beds. Not a sound above.

"I have heard no row on the *roof,*" remarked Mother, with dignified emphasis; and, having performed the usual ceremony, she departed; and came and told me of the whole affair, concluding with, "I wonder if it can be rats."

"Not a doubt of it."

Next morning the boys were full of their nocturnal visitor; and declared that, no sooner had the drawing-room door shut, than the scrambling and trampling began again.

"History tells of a certain cat who wore top boots; but I never heard of rats adopting the fashion," I remarked.

"Rats, Father! why we know the sound of them well enough. And they run between the ceiling and the roof. But this is unmistakable boots, with plenty of hobnails in them too, on the outside of the roof. We expected every moment to see the fellow's legs come through plaster and all. I think I may be permitted to speak with authority on the subject of boots and roofs in conjunction."

He certainly might, for he had perambulated the roofs of all the outhouses at S—, to the great detriment of tiles and slates.

"Well then," continued Primus, with the air of an adept, "I am so sure it was a boy of my size in hobnailed boots, that I feel as if I had seen them. I could swear to them."

"Come out and have a look," was my reply.

There lay the white mantle, smooth and glistening in the sunshine, and untrodden by so much as the foot of a tom-cat.

The boys looked at each other in amazement. "I don't care," said Secundus, defiantly, "I shall always believe it was a boy."

"It's the rummest thing I ever knew," slowly remarked Primus.

"If Boots comes again, the only thing you have to do is to wish him a good-night, and to cover up your ears," was my recommendation.

That evening, just as we were about to begin prayers, we were all startled by some tremendous blows on the cellar door. My wife, thinking there must be some one at the back door, told Stillwater to go and see who could be knocking in that outrageous way.

The girl did not stir. After a moment, she said, "It's the cellar door."

"Impossible!" said her mistress, "go quickly and see what it is."

We heard the unlocking and relocking of the yard door. When the girl came back, she said there was no one there. Presently, while I was reading, there came more loud blows, as if struck by a heavy fist; and unmistakably against the cellar door.

When prayers were ended, we went to make acquaintance with our mysterious captive. On opening the door, there was nothing to be seen but the flight of steps.

My wife and I exchanged glances which said very plainly, "A sweetheart." So, as the youth appeared shy, I gave him an encouraging invitation to come forth and show himself. No reply.

"I am determined to know who you are," said I, nobly plunging into the abyss, the boys at my heels. Nothing whatever to be seen, and not a corner in which anything bigger than a mouse could hide. The window! It was tightly closed up for the winter, and was, besides, blocked with snow. I was certainly mystified; but I sent the young ones off to bed with an assurance that wind, in an old house, was capable of making the most extraordinary noises; and, in illustration, we all in turn shook the door; not, however, producing anything like the previous effect.

"It *must* have been at the back door," said my wife, with a searching look at Stillwater.

"No; it's the cellar-door that does it," quietly replied the girl.

"How can it make that noise of itself!"

"I don't know."

"Did you ever hear it before!"

"Yes; this evening, when Miss was at the piano."

We decided that we must watch Stillwater.

In the course of the night, we were awoke by the agreeable sound of "Drip, drip, drip," in one corner of the room. My wife put a basin beneath, with a towel in it, to deaden the sound. Presently "drip, drip," again, just outside the door, which we always kept open.

"There's a sudden thaw, and we're in for it," said I. "Let's go to sleep. It won't hurt the floor-cloth."

But there was no going to sleep; for the drip came faster than ever, until it increased to a little stream. There were no matches in the room; but I managed to find my bath, and to set it, with a blanket inside it, under the spot whence the sound came.

When, at breakfast, I announced the sad news of the sudden thaw, there was a chorus of exclamations, "Why! everything is as hard as iron," &c., &c.

The mother, meanwhile, was directing her handmaiden to dry up the water which had come in during the night. The girl stared. When she came into the room again, her mistress asked her what she had done with the wet blanket. She stared more expressively, and was mute.

"Don't you understand?"

"Yes, Ma'am. But there is no wet blanket, and no water to wipe up."

Up stairs went mistress and servant; and, in two minutes, back came my wife, looking quite bewildered.

"There's not a trace of water anywhere," said she; "and yet, after you were asleep, I heard it drip fast upon the counterpane, just at my feet."

Our delighted offspring settled it that mother had been dreaming; and Primus irreverently hinted that I had generously lent my bath in order to escape my morning's shudder.

When Tertius was being tucked up that night, he asked, "Who was that person who came and looked at me after I was in bed!"

"Stillwater, I suppose."

"Oh! no. It was an old woman, and she had a funny cap on."

"You dreamed her, dear."

"But I hadn't been to sleep. And I turned my head to the wall, and when I looked for her again she had gone away."

"You must have been half-asleep. Now go to sleep quite, and finish the dream."

The next night Primus began—

"Mother, I wish you would tell that old party not to come into my room without knocking. I had just got into bed, happened to glance across to the drawers, and there she stood, coolly looking at me. I was disgusted, and turned my back upon her. Presently, I looked out of the tail of my eye, to see what she was doing, but she'd cut."

"You don't know who it was!"

"No. She looked like one of the charwomen—Boots's mother, I dare say. These people are cool enough for anything."

My wife called to Stillwater, to ask if Mrs. Brown or Mrs. Jones had been in that evening. She was answered that no one had been.

"Then you must have been half-asleep, although you did not know it, and have dreamed."

"Yes, I suppose so. But it seemed very real. At any rate, I'm half-asleep now," murmured Primus.

Night after night we were roused by the voice of this or that child. Their mother always went to them, and always found them sleeping peacefully; though, a minute before, there had been sobbing and moaning. It was bitterly cold, and I persuaded her not to go at the first call. Then there was whimpering on the stairs.

One night, we had both been lying awake for some time, listening to what seemed like cautious steps, first on the landing, and then in our room itself. We had tried to persuade ourselves that it might be mice. But no; there were distinct steps, as of a person walking. Yet, though we followed the sound with our eyes, we saw nothing. Suddenly, there was a howl of anguish, like the cry of a large animal in pain. It thrilled us with horror, for it came from our daughters' room, though it was not possible for it to be their voices. When we reached their bedside, they were calmly sleeping; and were not even roused by our entrance with the light. I made quiet observations next day, both inside and outside of the house.

"If you please, Ma'am, may I have my sister to sleep with me!" said Stillwater to her mistress.

"Are you afraid to sleep alone?"

"No, I'm not afraid."

"Then why do you wish it!"

No answer; only a very earnest look.

"Why! Stillwell, you look as if you had seen a ghost," said her mistress, laughingly.

"Yes, Ma'am, I have," she replied, very quietly.

"And what did it look like!"

"Like Mrs. X——, just as she was of afternoons."

"Come, come! she ought to have been all in white, you know."

"No, she was not in white. She had on the same sort of cap she always wore, and the same dress and white apron."

"I hope you asked her what she wanted."

"No, Ma'am; I lay still and looked at her; and then I sat up and looked at her hard; and presently I could not see her."

"It was no doubt a dream, and you will probably never have such another."

"No, I am sure it was not a dream. Besides, I have seen her twice before, when I was walking about."

"Out of doors!"

"No, Ma'am; in the house. One afternoon, towards dusk, she came and looked at me through the window. I wondered how she could be there, and I looked at her for a good little time."

"And then!"

"And then she was not there. And I went to the window and looked out, but she was gone."

"What was the use of going to the window, when you knew she was dead!"

"I don't know. She looked just as if she was alive. The other time, I was kneeling down on the rug, making your fire burn up. She passed straight before me."

"Oh! nonsense. She would have set fire to her clothes."

Still looked injured; but quietly persisted—

"She did, Ma'am. She passed straight between me and the fire."

"How could she do that? Really, Still, for a sensible young woman, you are very full of fancies."

"It was not a fancy; either of the times, Ma'am. I did see her, I did indeed. I hope you will believe me."

"Yes; I quite believe that you *think* you saw Mrs. X—. You may have your sister to sleep with you."

Now it is not a pleasant thing for any man, still less for one of my profession, to confess that he has felt "creepy" on account of certain inexplicable sounds. But, as this is a perfectly true account, I am compelled to acknowledge that it happened to me again and again, during the time of my dwelling in the Old Lodge. And I also declare that my wife and I were perfectly well in health; and that we had never before been the victims of similar terrors. Furthermore; though we spoke of the noises, we, at first, abstained from mentioning our sensations to each other.

After an hour's sleep, I would be aroused; as if at the command of some person, unseen indeed, but certainly in the room. Then a small something, say a marble, would be gently dropped, more than once, on the carpet, close at my bedside; sometimes on the floor-cloth, just outside the open door. Then the marble would be gently rolled on the boards of the room, and up against the skirting board.

It was an immense relief when, one night, we encountered each other's eyes as we lay listening, and both made a clean breast of our terrors. Yes, nothing short of that word will do. We agreed that the first sufferer should wake the other. But my wife found it not always possible to carry out this determination. "What did you hear!" I asked her once.

"The chest of drawers was dragged over the floor," she replied. "I am thankful you spoke to me, for I have for some time been trying to wake you, but was not allowed. In fact, I have been kept perfectly motionless."

I had heard precisely the same sound, yet the drawers did not appear to have been actually moved. The sounds were so distinct that we always connected them with some special article. Now, it was a chair, or the towel-horse, that was moved. Now, it was the loud snapping of a thick stick in the hall. Now, it was a violent blow on the hall table, struck as if with my own walking-stick, which I remembered to have left there, and which I found there in the morning. Once, the heaviest book on my writing-table appeared to be dropped, as if from the height of a man, on the floor-cloth in the hall. Then a smaller one. I always myself shut the doors of the rooms leading into the hall.

Of course, I tried in every way to account for the mystery; but, after a time, I could only resign myself to lie awake and wonder. The nights were bitterly cold. On one occasion, when there had been a persistent dropping of nuts in a corner of the room, I jumped up, in desperation, and held the light close to the spot. In a second, the sound was behind me. I whisked round, but— tapping to right of me, tapping to left of me, tapping in every direction, without a second's intermission. No sooner did I look towards one spot than the dropping of nuts was at the other end of the room. It was as if some mischievous elf were enjoying himself at my expense.

Our boys had gone to spend a day or two with some friends; and their mother, not liking the look of the empty room, had closed the door in passing; giving it a push, to make sure that it was fast. That night, we heard the door shut with a tremendous bang. Even had it been left open, there was no wind to move it.

Another night, when we had been awoke in the usual way, there was an agreeable variety in the entertainment. A delicate, flute-like sound proceeded from the closed dining-room. Again and again, a distinct and long-sustained musical note, as of some small pipe. Then the fifth of that note, then the octave, repeated many times; then the seventh and octave, over and over again. We were greatly puzzled. The piano was not in that room. And the sound certainly suggested a wind instrument of sweet tone.

I went down early next morning, and found to my surprise, a concertina lying on a table. I lifted the handle, and there came forth a long-drawn note, the very note I had heard in the night. My wife called out to me from upstairs, "That's it! that's it! What is it!"

Without attempting to disentangle her speech, I held up the concertina.

"Oh! that is Phil's. He must have left it behind. But it was the very note; there is no doubt of it."

We locked the thing up in its box, and put it inside a book-case; and next night, we were treated to a repetition of the musical notes, only muffled.

It was not only during the night that the noises were heard. For instance: I was reading by the fading afternoon light, when a chair on the other side of the room seemed to be moved from its place; so that I instinctively turned my head to see who had entered the room. Again, I was about to go down the cellar steps, in the afternoon, when I heard a heavy pickling pan dragged along the stone floor below. I quite thought some one was down there; but, as usual, there was no one to be seen, and the pan was in its place.

At eleven o'clock, a. m., my wife and Still were on the landing. The girl was telling her mistress that she had heard Mrs. X—'s voice the evening before. Her mistress told her she was giving way to fancies.

"But Mary Jones heard it too. She had just brought in the eggs, and stood listening to the singing in the drawing-room. Then I heard Mrs. X—'s angry voice again, on the stairs, and Mary said, 'Who's shouting!' I said I didn't know, and she said, 'It must be the missis. Lor! how angry she is to holler like that. Doesn't she like 'em to sing?'"

"In an old house like this," began my wife, "there may be many noises caused by—"

Suddenly, a noise, as if a shower of small pieces of the ceiling came down sharply on the floorcloth, caused mistress and maid to start back in affright, and involuntarily to look up. There was not a crack to be seen. Then the two pairs of eyes searched the floor in every direction; their owners cautiously standing within the shelter of two doorways. Not a morsel of any kind could they discover.

"What was that, Ma'am?" inquired Stillwater, fixing her sleepy gaze on her mistress.

"I cannot tell," was the only reply that occurred to that intelligent lady.

One morning, the post brought me orders to "move on." Instead of grumbling, I hailed them with delight. For we seldom got a decent night's rest, and my wife's nerves were beginning to be weakened by the constant strain upon them.

The Old Lodge had been for years in the charge of Mrs. X—, who had borne the character of a highly respectable old lady, with the drawback of being somewhat misanthropical and very avaricious.

I am perfectly aware of the ridicule with which stories of this nature are generally received. I can only repeat that I have related an absolutely true experience, for which I am utterly unable to account. I have no theory on the subject. I have always felt a strong distaste for so-called Spiritualism. I perceive the inconsequence and even childishness of my story; and yet, it will always remain, to the storyteller, a serious Fact.

NO. 11 WELHAM SQUARE
HERBERT STEPHEN

The Cornhill Magazine, 1885

I

We were sitting in the drawing-room of our house at Bayswater one evening after dinner, in high good-humour. I had that day been appointed to a certain post at the British Museum which would afford me ample opportunity for the studies in which I was most interested, and put me in possession of what I expected to find an ample competence. We had been talking over my prospects, and the only cloud I could discern upon the horizon was that I should have to be at my post at an earlier hour in the morning than was comfortably compatible with the three-mile walk from our house to the Museum.

"What a pity," said my youngest sister Patricia, "that we don't still live in the dear old house in Welham Square! You could have got to the Museum from there in five minutes."

I was born after we left Welham Square, but Patricia was six years my senior, and could remember her nursery days there.

"Not at all," said my father, very abruptly; "the walk will do you all the good in the world."

As the old gentleman had been, to all appearance, fast asleep for at least ten minutes, I was rather surprised at the energy with which he spoke. Looking up, I saw my mother making anxious signals to Patricia, which she followed up by instantly changing the subject.

A few days afterwards, as I descended reluctantly into the bowels of the earth at the Edgware Road Metropolitan Station, on the way to my new work for the first time, this episode recurred to my mind, and I began to speculate upon what might be the reasons that made the mention of Welham Square distasteful to my parents. I determined to consult my eldest sister Ellen on the subject, and from her, and some other sources, I gradually accumulated the facts which I will present here in the form of a continuous narrative.

No. 11 Welham Square has always been the freehold property of my family. It was built, together with several adjoining houses, about the beginning of the eighteenth century by the owner of a plot of land in which the houses stand, a retired attorney, who had two nephews. These were Andrew Masey, my great-great-great-grandfather, and his cousin, Ronald Masey. Ronald, who was generally thought to be his uncle's favourite, and probable heir, was an exceedingly tall and powerful young man, with a forbidding and melancholy expression of countenance. As a boy he was singularly backward, and his incapacity for mental exertion seemed to develop, as he grew up, into something not far removed from downright idiocy. His weakness of mind caused him to be remarkably subject to the influence of those with whom he lived, and in particular his cousin Andrew, my ancestor, was supposed to exercise over him an influence almost amounting to fascination, and to be able to mould him to all the purposes of an exceptionably vigorous will. Shortly after the building of the houses in what is now Welham Square, the uncle of these young men died, and Andrew took possession of all his property under the provisions, as he asserted, of a will, the existence of which no one except Ronald had any interest in disputing, and which no one except Andrew, the sole executor and devisee, ever saw. Shortly before his uncle's death, Ronald had become engaged to a young lady named Lettice White, to whom he was passionately attached, and it was generally supposed among the neighbours that upon his accession to the avuncular wealth the marriage would take place. But when a barely decent interval had occurred since the old gentleman's obsequies, the fair Lettice was led to the altar, not by the impecunious Ronald, but by his more fortunate cousin Andrew. The newly married pair took up their residence in No. 11, and Ronald came to live with them.

When it was represented to Andrew by some of his few intimate acquaintances that this arrangement was so singular as
almost to be thought improper, he curtly gave them to understand
that Ronald's mental condition was not such as to permit of his
only living relation allowing him to live alone, and that he was
compelled by the merest considerations of family affection to take
the unfortunate young man into his own household. So the three
lived on in the stately and somewhat gaunt mansion, Andrew collecting his rents with methodical regularity, and otherwise giving
his neighbours but little concern. As for Ronald, there soon came
to be little doubt in anyone's mind of his confirmed imbecility. He
appeared seldom, and when he did, was for the most part silent,
regarding his cousin and former betrothed with an expression of
the profoundest submission, which at times merged into a look
of wild and hardly human apprehension, "like a terrified brute-
beast," as it was put by an old lady who was one of the few friends
occasionally privileged to partake of the gloomy hospitality of this
uncomfortable establishment. Nothing more was ever known of
the condition in which my ancestor, his wife, and his cousin lived,
and no one was specially interested when, about six years after the
marriage, Ronald, who had not been seen for many months, died,
and was buried in a frugal manner.

Before he had been dead a year, Andrew and Lettice suddenly
left their house and took up their abode elsewhere, and after a
while a tenant was found for No. 11. Thirty years later, the lease
of the house having expired, Andrew's son, who had succeeded to
his father's property, came to reside there, but not for long. He left
the house suddenly after a few years, and a rumour went abroad
that it was haunted, probably by the ghost of the unfortunate
Ronald. From this time No. 11 descended from father to son, the
adjoining property being sold piecemeal as the family necessities
dictated. Occasionally the successive freeholders made attempts
to live there, but they never stayed more than a few months, and
on each occasion of their removal the rumours of ghostly possession were renewed. These, however, would die away, and tenants
would after a time be found, who never suffered from any incon-
venience. The last occupation by the owner was that of my father,

who moved into the house when my sister Patricia was a little girl. After living there a year he left precipitately, but Ellen could give me no particulars of his reasons for doing so, and knew only that he disliked any reference to the house, and never mentioned it himself. The house was now let to a stockbroker with a family.

II

Five years had elapsed since the conversation I related at the beginning of the previous chapter. My parents had both died, and Patricia was married and living with her husband in a provincial town. My career at the Museum had been a prosperous one, and I was now entrusted with a more responsible and better paid office. The tenant of No. 11 Welham Square had just given me notice of his intention to depart from it, and it occurred to me that it would be interesting to follow what seemed to be the family destiny, and try living in the house myself, to say nothing of the fact that it was admirably suited to my requirements. I felt fully capable of confronting any number of ghosts, and my wife was neither timid nor superstitious. Accordingly at the beginning of the new year we established ourselves, with our two babies, and my sister Ellen, who lived with us, in Welham Square, greatly delighted with the proximity of my work, with the solid masonry, spacious apartments, and roomy passages of our new abode, and with the remnant of eighteenth-century fashion and grandeur which seemed to pervade the neighbourhood. And in Welham Square we lived prosperously, without any kind of disturbance, for upwards of six months.

In the course of July my wife and the children left home to spend a couple of months at the sea-side. I intended to join them when the time came to take my holiday, and in the meantime I stayed in London, going daily to my work. Ellen stayed on with me to keep house in the absence of her sister-in-law.

One evening, four or five days after my wife's departure, I was sitting in my study, a large room with a door leading into the drawing-room, and a heavy curtain hung over my side of the door. It was past eleven; my sister had retired half an hour before, and the two maids who were left in the house were presumably in bed and asleep. I was therefore surprised to hear heavy and somewhat

slow footsteps, apparently those of a large man, ascending the
stairs from the ground-floor. The front door I knew was locked
and chained, nor had I heard anyone ring. The steps paused for
a moment on the landing outside my door, and then I heard the
intruder proceed to go up the next flight of stairs leading to the
bedrooms on the second floor. I sprang up, seized a candle, and
opened the door. As I stood on the threshold of my room I seemed
to hear footsteps, as of a man heavily mounting the stairs at the
top of the flight leading up from my door. But, though I held the
light above my head, I could see no one. Everything wore its usual
aspect. I walked quickly up the stairs, but nobody was visible. I
searched all the empty rooms, but with no result. I called up Ellen
and the maids, but none of them had seen or heard anything. I am
ashamed to say that I made a specially rigorous investigation of
a large room at the back of the house, which we used for a night
nursery, and which tradition declared to have been the abode of
my ill-fated kinsman Ronald Masey. I then went downstairs and
completed my search of the entire premises. Everything was in
order, and at the end of an hour I went back to my study and my
book, rather annoyed with myself for having spent so much time
in so fruitless an exploration, and determined to think nothing
more about the matter.

It was the next night after this that I suddenly started up very
wide awake with a conviction that somebody was in my bedroom.
I seemed to hear still ringing in my ears the sound of a long-drawn
human sigh. I sat up, trembling with excitement, and looked about
in the dim twilight of dawn in late July. I could see no one, but I
did not feel alone. The feeling of suspense became unbearable. I
jumped out of bed, and walked with nervous determination to the
window, where I turned round and faced the room, such light as
there was being behind me. I saw no one. Again I walked across
the room, and as I did so I felt unmistakably that wave of air that
meets one walking in the streets when someone on foot passes
close to him in the opposite direction. I seemed to feel the light
graze of a passing substance against my nightgown. I was dimly
conscious of a faint, indescribable odour, calling up recollections
of a time of life long but indefinitely past. And while I stood fixed

to the spot with surprise and horror, my heart beating violently, I heard distinctly four long heavy steps passing from me towards the window. The floor creaked under their weight. The next instant I felt that I was alone. But it was not until long after the morning was as light as noon that I fell asleep again..

I awoke much troubled in mind, and doubting whether I should not, like my fathers, be compelled to leave this uncanny dwelling; but when in some measure restored by breakfast, I determined to say nothing to my sister at present, but to wait and see whether the situation would in any way develop itself. My resolution was fated to be put to the test sooner than I expected.

I did not get home that evening till close upon dinner-time. When I entered the drawing-room Ellen greeted me with, "Oh, Edward! what do you think has happened? Sikes is dead!"

Now Sikes was a grey parrot belonging to my wife. He was so called because when he first came to us it was affirmed of him, perhaps rather libellously, that, like the hero of Mr. Calverley's poem, he "habitually swore." He certainly did from time to time blaspheme somewhat unreservedly.

I was secretly not altogether sorry to hear of his demise. So I answered with much composure, "Did the cat eat him?"

"No," said Ellen, "he died in the most horrible convulsions."

I went up to get ready for dinner, thinking more of how to prevent my wife from replacing Sikes by another clamorous bird than of the manner of the lost one's death, but in the course of our meal it occurred to me that his fate was an odd one.

"How did Sikes come to have convulsions?" I asked.

"Why, it was most curious," answered Ellen. "I was going to tell you about it. I was in the drawing-room writing letters, and suddenly I heard a tremendous screaming and flapping, and I looked up, and there was Sikes turning over and over in the air, and pecking, and clawing, and flapping his wings, and screaming, and before I could get to him he suddenly twisted his head right round two or three times, and tumbled down dead on the floor."

"But do you mean," I said, "that he was carrying on these gymnastics up in the air?"

"Yes; when I saw him he was quite up above his cage, which was on the little table, and in his struggles he must have wrung his own neck."

"That seems rather remarkable."

"Yes; and another remarkable thing was that he must have opened the door of his cage and got out all by himself, which I never heard of his doing before, because I had been feeding him with cake after lunch, and I know the door was fastened then. I found it open when he was dead."

"Had he been out long?"

"No. He must have been seized almost directly he got out, because it so happened that about five minutes before he began to scream, I fancied I heard the door open, and looked up to see if anyone was coming in, and no one was there, but I happened to see the parrot, and he was in his cage just as usual."

"Well," I said, "I suppose he's dead, and there's an end of it; but it is a very singular catastrophe. I hope Marion won't be inconsolable."

During the rest of dinner I was conscious of being rather poor company. Following close upon the mysterious occurrences I have described, Sikes's unhappy fate troubled me. My suspicions were, however, so undefined, and seemed even to me, when I tried to contemplate them from an impartial point of view, so ridiculous, that I could not bring myself to communicate them to Ellen, and incur the contempt which would be the deserved portion of a grown-up man who confessed to being seriously disturbed by an odd sound in an empty house, and by a commonplace nightmare. I have no hesitation in revealing these sentiments now that subsequent events have justified them. But that evening I again determined to wait. I did not have to wait long.

It was a cold evening, and, after bidding good-night to my sister, I lighted a fire in my study and sat down to enjoy a new novel I had long been wishing to read. I was about halfway through my volume when I suddenly felt a sensation of cold. I looked up. The fire was burning brightly, but I did not feel its warmth. It was as though some opaque body, or a large glass screen, had been interposed between me and it. A moment afterwards I felt the heat fall on my face again. Had I heard the muffled sound of a footstep on the hearth-rug close to me? I put out my hand and felt nothing but the warmth of the fire. As I gazed about the room in surprise my eye fell on an arm-chair standing on the other side of the fire. It was a nearly new chair, which I had bought shortly after coming to Wei ham Square. It had a leather seat, smooth and unworn, with particularly good and yielding springs. Hung upon its back was an antimacassar, worked aesthetically in crewels. As I looked at this chair it struck me that the seat was considerably depressed, as though some one had recently sat down upon it, and the seat had failed to resume its ordinary level. This surprised me, for I had sat in the chair that morning and felt sure the springs had then been in good order. I looked at the antimacassar. Towards the top it was pushed up in wrinkles. As I looked, it occurred to me that it was impossible for it to hang in such a manner by itself. It looked for all the world as if an invisible but substantial human frame was then actually sitting in the chair. When this notion occurred to me, I sat dazed with an indescribable horror, staring stupidly at the chair, which did not move. In an access of frenzied terror, I hurled the book I was reading at the chair. Did it strike the seat, or did it glance away a few inches from the edge and fall on the hearth-rug? The next instant the seat of the chair rose up audibly to its normal level, and the antimacassar fell out into its usual folds, still preserving, however, the traces of its previous wrinkles. I started up, and rushing to the chair, began to prod it. I could discover nothing unusual in its condition. As I was doing so I felt a hand, beyond all doubt, laid steadily on my shoulder. I faced round and saw nothing. "Who are you?" I shouted. "What do you want?" But no answer came. I was alone.

I sat cogitating till one o'clock, and then I went to bed. Just as I was getting into bed it occurred to me that perhaps I might be annoyed in the dark, and though I had not yet seen anything, the prospect seemed rather awful, and with a slightly trembling hand I lighted a night-light. When I had done so, and got into bed, I was rather disposed to be ashamed of myself, and thought I would put it out, but, partly no doubt from a disinclination to get out of bed, I determined that in any case it would do no harm, and that I would leave it as it was. It occurred to me what an odd thing it is that one feels safer in bed than anywhere else, whereas in fact one is never in a more defenceless situation. Then I went to sleep.

I do not know what time I woke. It seemed to me that the air was blowing in upon my chest where the bedclothes should have covered me up. And—yes, certainly there was an odd depression in my pillow, close in front of my face, as if some heavy weight were pressing it down. I put up my hand to investigate. I touched something on the pillow. I caught hold of it, and turned cold with terror. For I held tightly in my hand, another hand, neither cold nor warm, but large and solid. My light was still burning, and there was no one to be seen. The hand was suddenly jerked away from me. I sprang out of bed, and rushed to the fireplace with a despairing feeling that someone followed close behind me. I seized the poker, turned round, and struck wildly at the air. Whether I hit anything or not I do not know. I remember only that as I was recovering myself from a frantic lunge at nothing, I received a sharp and stunning blow on the back of my head. When I came to myself it was six in the morning, and I was lying on the floor where I had fallen. The night-light was out, and the morning sunlight was streaming in at my window. There was a very large and painful bruise where I had been struck.

III

I felt that this was getting beyond a joke. It was all very well to frighten me, but when my ghostly enemy took to knocking me down like a ninepin, I was not going to keep it to myself any longer. I had no intention of surrendering, for the blood of the Maseys was up, and the fact that each of my ancestors since the house was built had sooner or later evacuated the premises made me all the more determined not to be driven away without making some further resistance. So I unbosomed to my sister Ellen the whole of my experience in the matter. She was decidedly sceptical about the ghost, if ghost it could be called, and suggested that I was not well. I vowed that I was as well as any man with a great hole in the back of his head could be, and she consented to the

arrangement that I proposed—that she should sit up for a night or
two in the drawing-room, while I was in my study, with the door
open between us, and that if any remarkable incident occurred,
I should call her in. In order not to be wholly without male assistance in case I should be attacked, I invited a college friend
of mine named Prescott, a strong, sensible, and energetic young
doctor who lived near us, to keep my sister company in the drawing-room. He, when he heard my story, was, as befitted a scientific
young professional man, exceedingly facetious at my expense, but
he willingly consented to share our watch, and to sleep in the
house. That evening I sat up as usual in my study, while Prescott
and Ellen beguiled the hours in the drawing-room with light literature, until about half-past two, when, nothing having occurred,
we settled to go to bed, and separated; Prescott divided between
high spirits at the temporary triumph of incredulity, and a tinge
of disappointment at the non-occurrence of anything in the shape
of a row, and Ellen rather indignant with me for having kept her
up so long to no purpose. After the stormy experiences of the two
preceding nights I thoroughly enjoyed an unbroken sleep.

I prevailed upon my sister and my friend to give the ghost
one more chance, and the next evening saw us again comfortably
established in the two rooms, separated only by the curtain which
hung over the door of communication.

It may have been eleven o'clock when I heard a board creak
just behind my chair. Uttering a shout, I sprang up, and dashed at
the spot from which the noise had come. I came into heavy contact
with what felt like a gigantic human figure. Prescott and Ellen
hurried into the room and beheld me wildly grappling, apparently
with nothing at all. "By Jove!" said Prescott, "he has got them."
"Them" I believe meant some kind of hallucinations upon which
Prescott professed to be an authority, but I was struggling furiously with my unseen antagonist, and had no breath for explanations.

"Seize him! seize him!" I cried.

At that moment my prey burst from me, hurling me with pro-
digious violence across the room.

Prescott rushed forward, and as he did so was tripped up by
what he afterwards described as a heavy kick from an unseen foot,

and sent sprawling on the floor. Fortunately I was prostrate at the other end of the room, and could not be suspected of having had a hand, or a foot, in this outrage.

As we struggled to our feet, while Ellen stared wildly about, we all heard two or three hurried steps, as of a man running; there was a tremendous crash, and all was still. But the curtains had swung violently back into the window, and the window itself, plate-glass, frame, and all, was burst clean away outwards.

Prescott was as white as a sheet, and the sensible and strong-minded Ellen was actually crying, which impressed me more than anything else in the scene.

"Let us leave this horrible house," she said; "something worse will happen if we stay."

But I was filled with an unreasonable kind of courage at having, as it seemed, put our inexplicable visitor to flight; and I was besides conscious of a certain degree of pride in the assurance that Prescott had been converted, and would hardly talk again about my having "got them."

"We can't go to-night," I said, "and as our gentleman seems to have taken himself off for the present, we had better consider what's to be done next. I am sure Prescott wants to stay and investigate the phenomenon."

We shut the shutters over the wreck of the window, and sat talking over the event until late at night. By degrees I contrived to infuse into my companions some of my courage, and at last, no further disturbance having taken place, we all went to bed in pretty good spirits. I placed a loaded double-barreled pistol on the table by my bedside, thinking that if a ghost could be struggled with, he ought to be able to be shot, and Prescott placed within reach a large bowie-knife, which he had brought back from America, and had long been wishing for an opportunity to make use of.

When I woke I thought my last hour had come. My throat was tightly grasped by two extremely strong hands. A crushing weight was on my chest. I tried to shout, but could not. I was rapidly being strangled. And as I lay writhing, my eyes, forced half out of their sockets, glared through the light of the night-light at the opposite wall, which looked precisely as usual, except that, as the squeezing of my throat grew more and more intolerable, my view of the room slowly darkened. But of the horrible and only too palpable form that was killing me I could see no trace. In unavailing despair I clutched at the iron wrists that held me down. In another moment I believe I should have become unconscious. Then, a last gleam of hope, the thought of my pistol, flashed through my mind. I stretched out my hand, and as I lay I could just reach the end of the barrel. I drew it towards me, and with an expiring effort pushed the muzzle of it close against what I took to be the invisible body of my tormentor, and fired. We never found the bullet, or any trace of it afterwards. Instantly the hands relaxed their gripe on my throat a little, and with a violent effort I wrenched my neck away; then a heavy body fell sideways from my bed to the ground, and I fell too, grappling with it. At that moment Ellen and Prescott, who had been aroused by the sound of the shot, burst into the room. There they saw me struggling, partly on the floor, and partly kneeling apparently on space. They rushed to my assistance. Both of them felt the thing, both of them grappled with it. The struggles of our enemy became fainter. Managing to get one hand free I repossessed myself of the pistol, which had fallen on the floor, and emptied the second barrel into what I judged to be the breast of the spectre. I fired straight downwards, apparently at the floor, but of that bullet we saw no more than of the other. Meanwhile Prescott stabbed furiously with the bowie-knife, and each time he dashed the blade down its progress was arrested before it reached the carpet. Then the struggles ceased, and nothing was heard except our rapid panting. We were all kneeling on and holding down what looked like space, and felt like the form of a tall and athletic man.

"We've done for it, whatever it is," said I hoarsely.

Prescott burst into a foolish giggle. "By Jove!" he said, "we'll make a cast of it and see what it's like."

As he spoke the form of our victim was agitated by a desperate convulsion, which shook us all off. Before we could seize it again a deep groan burst from the place where we had held it, and the word "Lettice!" rang through the room in a tone of sepulchral melancholy. Then there was silence.

I threw myself on the floor—not, as I had intended, on the prostrate figure. We searched the room, and then the house, but we could find absolutely nothing. Nor from that day to this has anyone, to the best of my knowledge, seen, heard, or felt anything whatever of this ghastly being.

After much consideration we determined to keep the adventure to ourselves, for a time at any rate. Indeed, it was only last summer, when we had lived in the house for a good number of years without any kind of ghostly interruption, that I described the circumstances herein narrated to my wife. She doesn't believe them, and I am sorry I told her.

Was it the ghost of Ronald Masey? Did it voluntarily depart and leave us alone because it considered that the annoyances it had inflicted upon my ancestors and me were sufficient, and that the tale of its vengeance upon our house, for the wrongs, whatever they were, inflicted upon Ronald in his lifetime by Andrew and Lettice, was complete? Or did we actually kill it? Perhaps we did. He was a poor weak creature when he was alive.

Edward Masey.

11 Welham Square, 1885.

BY ONE, BY TWO, AND BY THREE
ADRIAN ROSS
Temple Bar, 1887

I

It was while I was at Cambridge that I first came to know Angus Macbane. We met casually, as undergraduates do, at the break-fast-table of a mutual friend, or rather acquaintance; and I remember being struck with the odd cynical remarks my neighbour threw out at rare intervals, as he watched the argument we had started, about Heaven knows what or what not, and were maintaining on either side with the boundless confidence and almost boundless ignorance peculiar to freshmen. I seem to see him now, leaning back after his meal in a deep arm-chair, with his host's cat purring her contentment on his knee. He never looked at the semicircle of disputants round the fire, but blew beautiful rings of cigarette smoke into the air, or gazed with a critical expression, under half-shut lids, at the photographs of actresses forming a galaxy of popular beauty above the mantlepiece. Then he would emit some sentence, sometimes sensible, oftener wildly nonsensical; but always original, unexpected—a stone dropped with a splash and a ripple into the stream of conversation.

I do not think that he showed any very particular power of mind at the breakfast-party, or indeed afterwards. What made one notice him was the faint aroma of oddity that seemed to cling to him, and all his ways and doings. He was incalculable, indefinable; this was what made a good many dislike him, and made me, with one or two others, conceive a queer liking for him. I always had a taste, secret or confessed, for those delicate degrees of oddity which require a certain natural bent to appreciate them at all. Extravagance of any kind commands notice, and compels a choice between admiration and contempt; moreover, it generally (and not least at a University) invites imitation. No one ever either admired or despised Macbane, as far as I know; and no one could ever have imitated him. The singularity lay rather in the man himself than in any special habit. For Macbane was not definably different from other young men. He was of medium height, slightly made, but not spare; his face had hardly any colour, and his hair and moustache were light. His eyes were of a tint difficult to define—sometimes they seemed blue, sometimes grey, sometimes greenish; and he had a trick of keeping them half-shut, and of looking away from any one who was with him. This peculiarity is popularly supposed to be the sign of a knave; in his case it was merely a part of the man's general oddity, and did not create any special distrust.

Our acquaintance, thus casually begun, ripened into a strange sort of friendship. Macbane and I saw very little of each other; we did not talk much, nor go for walks and rows together, nor confide to each other our doings and plans, as friends are supposed to do. On rainy afternoons I would stroll round to his rooms and enter, to find him generally seated before the fire, caressing his cat. We did not greet each other; but I generally took up one of the numerous strange and rare books that he contrived to accumulate, though he spent very little money. This I would read, occasionally dropping a remark which he would answer with some cynical, curt sentence; and then both of us relapsed into silence. Tea would be made and drunk, and we sometimes sat thus till dinner-time, or later. Yet though I always felt as if I bored Macbane, I still went to his rooms; and when I did not go for some time, he would generally, with an air of extreme lassitude and reluctance, come round to my quarters, there to sit and smoke and turn over my books in much the same way as I did when I visited him.

Angus Macbane never told me anything much about himself or his family; he was one of the most reticent of mortals. All he ever did in that way was to say once in an abrupt manner that some of his ancestors had been executed for witchcraft; and when I vented some of the usual commonplaces on the barbarous ignorance and cruelty of those times, he cut me short by remarking in a tone of profound conviction that he thought his ancestors thoroughly deserved their fate, and that their condemnation was the only oasis of justice in a desert of judicial infamy.

From other sources, however, I discovered that Angus Macbane was an only son, whose parents had both died soon after his birth, leaving nothing behind them but their child. An uncle, a rich Glasgow merchant, had provided in no very lavish way for the boy's education, and was supposed to be intending to leave him a large share of his property. This was all I gathered from those people who made a point of knowing everything about everybody; and there is no lack of them at Universities.

Two striking peculiarities there were about Macbane, which stood out from the general oddity of the man. The first was his fondness for cats, or, to speak more accurately, the fondness of cats for him. He had always one pet cat—generally a black one—in his rooms, and sometimes more; and when he had two, they were invariably jealous of each other. But he seemed to have an irresistible attraction for cats in general: they would come to him uncalled, and show the greatest pleasure when he noticed or caressed them. He did not stroke a cat often, but when he did, it was with a certain delicate and sensitive action of the hand that seemed to delight the animal above everything. So marked was the attraction he exercised, that a scientific acquaintance accused him of carrying valerian in his pockets.

The other peculiarity was in his books. He had picked up, in ways only known to himself, a very fine collection of early works on demonology and witchcraft. A more complete account, from all sides, of "Satan's invisible world" was seldom accumulated. There were books, pamphlets and broadsheets in Latin, French, German, English, Italian and Spanish, and some old family manuscripts relating to the arts or trials of warlocks and witches. There was even an old Arabic manual of sorcery, though this I am sure he could not read. Most of these works were of the sixteenth and seventeenth centuries, since which period, indeed, civilisation has ordained a "close time" for witches; and any treatises on the black art dated after that time Macbane not only did not buy, but as a rule refused to accept as gifts. "Early in the eighteenth century," he once remarked, "men lost their faith in the devil; and they have not as yet recovered it sufficiently to produce any witchcraft worthy of the name." And indeed he had the greatest abhorrence and contempt for modern Spiritualism, mesmerism, esoteric Buddhism, &c.; and the only occasion during his Cambridge life on which I saw him really lose his temper was when a mild youth, destined to holy orders, called on him and asked him to join a society for investigating ghostly and occult phenomena. He turned on the intruder with something like ferocity, saying that he did not see why people wanted to be wiser than their ancestors, and that the old way of selling oneself to the devil, and getting the price duly paid, was far better both in its financial and moral aspects than paying foreign impostors to show the way to his place of business. "Though what the devil wants at all with such souls as yours," he added meditatively, "is the one point in his character that I have never been able to understand. It is a weakness on his part—I am afraid it is a weakness!" The incipient curate turned and fled.

A few sayings of this kind, reported and distorted in many little social circles, gave Angus Macbane an evil reputation which he hardly deserved. The College authorities looked askance on him, and some of them, I believe, would have been thankful if his conduct had given them a pretext for "sending him down," whether for a term or for ever. But no offence or glaring irregularity could be even plausibly alleged against him. He attended the College chapel frequently, and never lost an opportunity of hearing the Athanasian Creed. "When I hear all those worthy people mumbling their sing-song formulas, without attaching any meaning to them, and chanting forth vague curses into the air," he once said to me, "I close my eyes, and can sometimes almost fancy myself on the Brocken, in the midst of the Witches' Sabbath."

This devout assiduity was only reckoned as one point more against him; for Angus Macbane belonged by birth to the very straitest of Scotch Presbyterians, and evinced no desire to quit them, or to dispute the harshest and most repulsive of the doctrines handed down from his ancestors. Yet to my knowledge he never went near any Presbyterian chapel, but preferred, as his worthy uncle said, "to bow in the house of Rimmon."

This uncle, as I gradually divined, was the one being whom my friend regarded with something like hatred. Mr. Duncan Macdonald was the brother of Macbane's mother. He was a big, red, sandy man, rich, unmarried, and not unkindly in nature; and an ordinary person with a little tact could have managed him, if not with complete satisfaction, at any rate to no small profit. It is true, the manufacturer was one of those self-made men who think that no man has any business to be otherwise than self-made; but by flattering his pride, he could easily have been induced to support his nephew in ease, and even in luxury and extravagance, if enough show were made for the money. But he was a Philistine of the Philistines, two-thirds of his life dominated by gain, and the rest by a rigid sense of duty. Material success and respectability were his two golden calves; and to both of these his nephew's every thought and act did dishonour. Angus Macbane could not have been made a successful man by any process less summary and complete than the creation of a world for his needs alone; and not even this would have given him respectability. He could not live without aid from his uncle; but he accepted from him a mere pittance, which, grudgingly taken, soon came to be as grudgingly given. Yet when he forced himself to compete for scholarships and prizes which would have made him partly independent, he missed them in a way which would have been wilful in any other man. His essays were a byword among examiners for their cynical originality, perverse ability, and instinctive avoidance of the obvious avenues to success. Thus he was constrained to depend on that scanty income of which every coin seemed flung in his face. With his developed misanthropy and contempt for ordinary men, he would at all times have been intolerant of the mere existence of such a man as his uncle; and that he himself should be hopelessly indebted to such a creature for every morsel he ate, for every book he read, was a sheer monstrosity to his mind—or so I should conjecture from what I knew of the two. Angus seldom willingly mentioned his uncle; and when he did so, it was with a deadly intensity of contempt in his tone—not his words—such as I never heard before or since.

II

An end comes to all things; and my time at Cambridge, which had passed as swiftly for me as for most men, and left me with the usual abundant third year's crop of unfulfilled purposes, came to its end in due course. Angus Macbane had "gone down" before I did, with a high second-class degree in mathematics, chiefly gained, as I happened to hear from an examiner, by a very few problems which hardly any one else solved. A serious quarrel with his uncle followed on this ill-success; but from motives of family duty and respectability Mr. Macdonald continued to pay his nephew enough to maintain life. No relation of his, he felt, must come to the workhouse.

For a year or two I lost sight of Macbane; and when I saw him again, he was living in lodgings in an obscure street of a London suburb. I had learnt his address from another old college friend, Frank Standish by name, who had kept up relations with Angus. Frank was a complete contrast to Macbane; he was a tall, hearty, handsome, athletic fellow, successful in everything he undertook, and was now making his way as an engineer, and likely to do well. It was this opposition in their natures that had begotten their friendship. I have seen them sitting together at Cambridge, Standish chatting on by the hour, and Macbane watching him in contented silence. As some one remarked, it was like the famous friendship of a race-horse and a cat.

I was myself now an under-master at a large day-school, and my evenings were in general free; so one night I called for Standish at his lodging, and together we trudged off to find Macbane. Our path led through one of those strange uncanny wildernesses that lie about the outskirts of every great and growing town. Skeletons of unfinished houses, bristling with scaffolding poles, loomed on us at intervals through the rainy mist; the roads were long heaps of brickbats and loose stones, already varied with blades of coarse grass. The path we followed was seamed across with the ruts of heavy carts that had gone-to and from the half-built houses; and we stumbled over posts and through plashy pools, along the ghostly highway, completely deserted now that the workmen were gone, and stretching its miles of raw ruin through the autumn mist.

Standish whistled cheerily as he strode on through the desolation, and I was comforted to have him with me—I think I should
almost have felt afraid but for his presence. We crossed the No
Man's Land of chaotic brick and mortar, and found ourselves in
a street of mean new houses. At No. 21, Wolseley Road, Standish
paused and rang; a slatternly maid-of-all-work answered the bell,
and ushered us into the presence of Angus Macbane.

He was sitting by a poor little fire, in a shabby arm-chair, with
his black cat on his knee as usual, and a volume of demonology in
his hand; and, save that the room was small, cheaply furnished and
hideously papered, and the occupant looked thinner and wearier,
we could have fancied ourselves at Cambridge again. But after the
first greetings, I soon noticed that Macbane was changed for the
worse since I had seen him last. He did not seem at all dissipated, nor had he acquired the air of meanness and shiftiness that
marks the needy adventurer; but there was a genuineness, almost
a desperation, in his cynical utterances, which they had not had
before—a hopelessness of expression and an irritability which I
did not like. The misanthropy at which he had played before was
now in grim earnest.

He told us a little—very little, and that reluctantly—of his
own way of life. He was doing nothing of any moment—a struggling unknown writer, spasmodically trying to secure some literary foothold, and failing always, whether by the fatality which
attended him specially, or by the same chances as befall any
author. Added to this misery was the consciousness of his dependence on his uncle, which was bitterer to him, I could see, than
ever. He began to talk about Mr. Macdonald of his own accord,
and that was always a bad sign.

"Do you know," he said, with a bitter laugh, "my worthy relative is coming out here before long? He writes me that he is due in
London on business in a fortnight or so, and will pay me a visit to
see if I am still given over to the same reprobate mind as before,
and opposed to what he calls my duty. Won't you come and see the
fun, you two? I think I know how to aggravate him now, perfectly
well. I assure you, at my last interview with him, I made him swear
within three minutes—and he an elder!"

"I say, Macbane," Standish put in, in his good-natured way, "don't carry that game too far. The old chap is good for a lot if only you don't rub him up the wrong way. If you rile him this time, ten to one he cuts you off with a shilling—and then where will you be?"

"If he only would die!" Macbane went on, not seeming to hear his friend's remonstrance. "Fellows like that have no sense of fitness. When I saw him last he reminded me of one of those big fat coarse speckled spiders, that you want to kill, only they make such a mess. I should so like to murder him, if I could do it by deputy."

He was joking, of course, but there was more earnestness than I liked in his manner. I looked at Standish, and he at me, before I spoke.

"If those are your sentiments," I said, echoing his light tone, "we had better come to prevent bloodshed."

"Yes, do come," Angus resumed; "and if you will kindly take off his head outside, I shall be greatly obliged to you. Bring a delightful rusty old axe, Standish, with plenty of notches in the blade. It will be so nice to be like one of those dear Italian despots, and get one's assassination done for one. Though there are better than hiring a bravo, even. An ancestor of mine—" and here he stopped suddenly.

"Well, what did your ancestor do?" asked I.

"Oh," said Macbane coolly, "he raised a devil of some sort and got scragged by it himself."

As he spoke these trivial words, there came a faint sound at the door as of something scratching very gently on the panels. I turned to Macbane and asked—

"Is that your dog, Mac?"

"My dog!" he said with a shudder, "why, I *hate* dogs. I never have one near my room by any chance—except when the landlady sends me up sausages."

"Perhaps it is another cat come to make friends with you," suggested Standish. "There it is again. I will let it in, whatever it is."

He flung the door open, and the chill air rushed in from the draughty passage and stairs. There was nothing outside or in sight, and he shut the door again with a bang.

"I heard it distinctly," he said, in the aggrieved tone of one who fancies he has made himself ridiculous. "What could it have been?"

"Wind, perhaps, or a rat," said Macbane lightly. "There are plenty of rats in the place, and I am glad of it, for it is the only thing that prevents me from expecting the house to fall every moment. When it is going to fall the rats will all run out, and my cat Mephistopheles will run out after them, and I shall run out after Mephistopheles; and the landlady and the first-floor lodgers, and the landlady's cat that eats my tea and sugar, will all be squelched together, to the joy of all good cats and men—eh, Mephisto? Why, what ails the cat?"

For Mephistopheles was standing upon his master's lap, with back arched and tail rigid and bristling, glaring into the darkest corner of the little room, and hissing in a passion of mingled rage and fear. Then, before any one could stop him, the cat made one leap at the window, with a yell and a great crash of glass, and was gone, leaving us staring at each other.

Angus Macbane spoke first, with a forced laugh.

"There goes my cat," he said, "and there goes one-and-nine for broken glass. Cats I may get again, but one-and-ninepence—never. A cat with nine lives, a shilling with nine pence—all lost, all lost!"—and he went on laughing in a shrill hysterical way that I did not at all like. During the pause that followed, Standish looked at his watch.

"It is pretty late now," he said, "and I have a lot of working drawings to prepare to-morrow. Good-night, Macbane. If I come across your cat, I'll remonstrate with him for quitting us so rudely. But no doubt he will come back of himself."

As Standish said this, the rest of the large pane through which the cat had leaped suddenly fell out with a startling crash into the street, making us all wince.

"It was cracked already," remarked Angus; "and the glazier does not allow for the pieces. Good-night, both of you. I fancy I have something to do myself, too."

I was surprised, and a little hurt, at being thus practically turned out by my friend (for I had expressed no intention of departing, and it was not really very late); but I was not sorry to go now, and have the solace of Standish's cheery company home. A curious undefined feeling of apprehension was creeping over me, and I wanted to be out in the night air, and shake off my uneasiness by a brisk walk.

We went downstairs, leaving Macbane brooding in his chair. As the landlady saw us out, I slipped a half-crown into her hand.

"Mr. Macbane's window got broken to-night," I said. "Will you have it mended, and not say anything about it to him?"

I knew that he would probably forget the occurrence if not reminded of it. Standish nodded approval, and we went out into the mist. We walked on in silence till we turned out of the lamp-lit and inhabited part, and then my companion remarked abruptly—

"That makes one-and-three-pence I owe you, Eliot"—and relapsed into silence, not even whistling as he strode along.

We had reached nearly the middle of the long artificial desert, where a street was some day to be, when Standish stopped and caught me by the arm.

"Eliot, what is that?" he whispered.

We both stood still and listened. From the waste land beyond one of the skeleton houses came a fearful cry, whether of a child or an animal we could not tell—a scream of mere pain and terror, intense and thrilling, neither human nor bestial. Then there was a deep snarling growl, and the yell died into a choking gurgle, and suddenly fell silent.

"Come on," Standish gasped, and ran with all his speed in the direction of the sound.

I followed as fast as my shorter legs and wind would take me over the stiff slimy clay of the waste land, and after a few minutes found him bending over a little dark heap on the ground at the edge of a puddle.

"Have you got a match?" he said.

I nodded—I was too much out of breath to speak—and pulled out my match-box. I struck a light, screening it with my hand, and we both looked earnestly at the black lump at our feet.

"Bah!" said Standish, as he mopped the perspiration from his face. "Why, it's only a cat, and it sounded like a baby!"

It was the body of a large black cat, still warm and quivering, but quite dead. The throat was almost entirely severed, and the blood had streamed out, darkly streaking the thick yellow water of the pool. Of what had killed it there was no sign or sound, only, in the soft clay beside the puddle, there were marks which seemed those of the poor cat's feet, and other footprints like these, but larger. I pointed them out to Standish.

"I see what it was," he said, as we trudged laboriously back to the road. "The cat was out there, and some beast of a dog caught it and killed it—though what cat or dog should be doing there is more than I can say. What teeth the brute must have! Ugh! I hope he's not waiting round to take another bite!"

We got back to the road unbitten, and went on our way in silence, till I said—

"Standish, do you know, that cat was very like Macbane's?"

"Do you know, Eliot," was his answer, "that is just what I was going to tell you?"

And not another word did he utter, till I left him at his door and said good-night.

III

Macbane was never a good correspondent, but he duly informed us of the date of his uncle's expected visit; and when the day came, I called for Standish in the evening as before, and we trudged off through another sloppy mist. Standish, good thoughtful fellow, had brought with him, in his overcoat pocket, a bottle of very fine old Irish whiskey, which he had long been treasuring up for some festal occasion, but now intended to devote to the mollifying, if possible, of Mr. Macdonald.

"Every glass he takes of this," he solemnly assured me as we went on, "will be worth a hundred a year to Macbane."

We did not go by the same dreary road that we had taken before. Frank declared, with a shudder, that the last cry of that cat was still ringing in his ears, and that he could not stand the ghastly place again. I was rather surprised at his unwonted nervousness, but readily acquiesced in it. So we went a mile or so out of our way, keeping along endless streets of shabby-genteel houses, which were sufficiently hideous, but not appalling; and about nine in the evening we reached Wolseley Road.

I was surprised and almost shocked to notice the change that had passed over Macbane in the few weeks since I had seen him last. He did not seem worse in health—on the contrary, there was at times a nervous alacrity about his movements which I had not remarked before. But his face and expression seemed to have darkened, as it were, and grown evil. His college cynicism had already turned into misanthropy; and now, I thought, it had developed into a positive malevolence. He still was silent and brooding, after the first greetings; but he no longer seemed dejected. Altogether a transformation of some kind had come to him, such that I— though not very impressionable—was rather inclined to fear than to pity him.

The conversation, as was natural, turned on the uncle, who might appear at any moment now. Standish and I joined in urging on our friend the necessity of attempting conciliation, of showing some semblance of submission. We had more than once induced him to do so before, though his perverse temper generally made him unable to do more than avert an instant stoppage of the supplies; but to-night he was obstinate, and even spoke as if he were the aggrieved party, and his uncle the one to make advances.

"If the old fool cares to be civil," he said fiercely, "then there's an end of it; and if not, there's an end too. I am tired of humouring him."

As he spoke, the "old fool's" heavy tread was heard on the stairs, and in another minute he entered. He was a big, strong, red-faced, coarse-looking fellow, with sandy whiskers and grizzled hair, who nodded awkwardly to us, and gave a surly greeting to his nephew, who sat still in his arm-chair, looking into the fire with half-shut eyes.

Mr. Duncan Macdonald seemed disconcerted by our presence, and I offered to withdraw; but Macbane would not let us.

"You see, uncle," he remarked, still keeping his eyes averted, and using the familiar title solely, I am convinced, because he knew the uncle did not like it, "these gentlemen know all about our little affairs, and they had better hear your version of matters now than my version afterwards. Besides, one of them is going to be a literary man, and write a tale with Scotch characters in it; and you will be quite a godsend for him, as raw material for a study. If you want to swear at me, pray don't mind him; there is nothing that tells more in literature than a little aboriginal profanity, properly accented."

This was a bad beginning for an interview; and would have been worse still had Mr. Macdonald been able fully to understand his nephew's speech. What he did understand, however, obviously offended him; and he began to address Macbane in no very conciliatory tones, though at first with a forced moderation of language and strained English accent which were evidently the result of the young man's taunt. Then, as Macbane did not answer, but sat still looking into the fire, his uncle began to lose temper. His language grew broader and stronger, both as Scotch and as reproach. He addressed us with a sort of rough eloquence on the subject of his nephew's miserable laziness, shiftlessness, effeminacy—pointing at him, and showering down vigorous epithets on him. In the midst of his tirade, as he paused for breath, came a low sound of scratching at the door.

"There's that confounded rat again!" cried Standish, glad of any pretext for interrupting the miserable business. "Dead, for a ducat, this time!" He dashed open the door as he spoke, but there was nothing to be seen. Only the gaslight in the passage, flickering and flaring in the draught, sent strange shadows flitting across the walls.

Frank came back and sat down, and busied himself in uncorking his bottle of whiskey, and setting the kettle on to boil. I took up a book, so as not to seem to observe a scene which I knew must be so painful and humiliating for Macbane. The uncle again plunged into the stream of his invective, and I kept my eyes on the nephew. I knew that he was really quite as passionate as the elder man, and I was afraid of what he might do if he once lost his self-control; but though a little shiver passed over him sometimes, he was quite silent, leaning back in the arm-chair, with his head resting on his right hand, and his left arm hanging listlessly over the side of the chair. Presently he began to move the hands languidly to and fro, with the fingers outstretched, and the palm horizontal and slightly hollowed, keeping it more than a foot from the carpet. It was a curious gesture, but he had many odd tricks of the kind.

At last Mr. Macdonald, having spent his store of abuse without any response, began, I fancy, to feel a little ashamed of himself, and became more conciliatory, letting fall some hints as to the terms on which he might even yet receive his prodigal nephew back to favour. The manner of his overtures was far more offensive than their substance, and to one who could make allowance for the man's coarse nature, there was even a trace of a feeling that might be called kindness. But Macbane was always far more sensitive to externals than other men, and his uncle's condescension, I could see, irritated him far more than his anger. He left off moving his hand to and fro, sat up and clutched the arms of his chair. Then, when the older man had done, he cast one deadly look at him, and shook his head as if he would not trust himself to speak.

"Winna ye speak, ye feckless pauper loon?" roared his uncle, with a string of oaths.

Macbane was silent, but that good fellow Standish interposed at what he thought was the right moment.

"Come, Mr. Macdonald," he said frankly, "I don't think you should talk like that. After all, Macbane is your own sister's son, and he is not well now, and you must not come down on him too heavily. Let us have a glass of toddy all round now and part friends, and we three will talk it all over, and make matters smooth to-morrow. We can't do any good to-night."

As he spoke, he got out some tumblers from the cupboard and wiped them clean. The Glasgow manufacturer seemed a little mollified; nobody could help liking Standish or his whiskey, and all might yet have been well if the devil had not seemed to enter suddenly into Angus Macbane. Standish had poured out a generous measure of the fragrant spirit, and was turning to take the kettle off the hob, when Macbane sprang up like a cat, in a white heat of rage, took the tumbler from the table and flung it right into the grate. The glass rang and crashed, and the flame leapt out blue like a tongue of hell-fire; and Angus stood at the table, quivering all over, with his right hand opening and shutting as if feeling for a weapon. Standish caught him by the arm and pulled him back into his chair.

"Are you mad, Mac?" he exclaimed. Macbane did not seem to hear, but sat glowering at his uncle. As for Mr. Duncan Macdonald, he turned purple with anger. The complicated atrocity of the insult—an outrage at once on kinship, hospitality, thrift and good whiskey—had smitten him dumb for a moment with surprise and rage. He clenched his fist and struck blindly at his nephew, who was fortunately out of reach; then he spoke in a husky but distinct voice, slowly, as if registering a vow.

"De'il throttle me," he said, "if ever you see bawbee of mine again." And he took up his hat and umbrella and turned to the door.

"Done with you, in the devil's name!" cried Macbane.

Without another word the uncle flung the door open, and shut it after him with a crash that shook the house. Then we heard him heavily stamping down the stairs and along the passage, till another great bang proclaimed that he had left the house. This last noise seemed to rouse Macbane from a sort of trance. He sprang up again and rushed to the door and threw it open, as if to pursue his uncle. We were going to stop him, for he looked murderous enough; but instead of dashing downstairs, he stopped, flung out his hand with a strange gesture, as if he were pointing at something, and muttered a few words that I could not catch. Then he shut the door and came back slowly to his old seat, as pale as a dead man.

In the excitement of the scene, we had none of us noticed the time; but now the cheap little clock on the mantlepiece struck twelve, and recalled the fact that two of us were far away from our lodgings. Standish and I looked at each other; we neither of us liked to leave Macbane alone yet. The man's expression as he flung the glass into the fire—still more his look as he pointed down the stairs—was black enough for anything; and if we went now, he seemed quite capable of going out and murdering his uncle, or staying and murdering himself. Standish winked at me, and went out quietly. In ten minutes he came back and addressed Macbane, who was sunk in one of his reveries again.

"All right, old fellow," he said cheerily, "your landlady tells me her first floor is vacant, and she will put us two up for the night. So cheer up, Mac. It is a bad business, but we will see you through it, never fear. Now let's brew some punch and be jolly to-night at any rate, as we needn't go."

Macbane woke up again at this, with a sudden feverish gaiety. He eagerly took the steaming tumbler Frank prepared for him, and drained it at a draught—he whose strongest stimulant was coffee. The whiskey did not seem to affect his head, however. More than this, he hunted out a soiled pack of cards from an obscure drawer, and proposed—he who hated all games—that we should play to pass the time. Dummy whist he thought too slow, and I proposed three-handed euchre, generally called "cut-throat." The name seemed to amuse our friend vastly. He insisted on learning the game, and we started at once. His spirits were almost uproarious; I had never seen him like this before. Yet his gaiety was very unequal. Sometimes he would out the wildest jokes, till in spite of our uneasiness about him we shrieked with laughter; and again he would sink back in his chair, forgetting to play his hand, and seeming as if he listened for some sound. After some time he went to the door and flung it open, declaring that he was "stifling in this hole of a room." Then he sat down again to play, but fidgeted about in his chair impatiently. He was studying his cards, which he held up in his left hand, when I happened to look at the other arm hanging down by his chair.

"For goodness sake!" I exclaimed, "what have you done to your hand, Macbane?"

He held up his right hand as I spoke, and looked at it. Palm and fingers were dabbled and smeared with watery blood, fresh and wet. For a moment we stared at each other with pale faces.

"I must have cut my hand over that confounded tumbler or something," said Macbane at last with an evident effort. "I will go and wash it off in my bedroom and be back in a moment."

He slipped out as he spoke, and we heard him washing his hand, muttering to himself all the time.

Then in a few minutes he came back, keeping his hand in his pocket, and resumed the game. But his former high spirits were gone, and another tumbler of punch failed to recall them. He made constant mistakes, played his hand at random, and at last suddenly threw all his cards down on the table, laid his head on them, and burst into a terrible fit of hysterical sobbing.

We did not know what to do with him, but Standish laid him on the hard sofa, and in a little time he seemed better, though greatly shaken, and managed to control himself. He thanked us in a whisper, and told us to go, and he would get to bed alone. We were still rather anxious about him, but there seemed no reason for staying with him now against his will. The natural reaction had followed on all the strain and excitement, and I, for one, was glad that it was no worse. So we left him beginning, in a slow and dazed way, to get to bed, and descended to try and snatch a little sleep in the genteel misery of the first-floor lodgings.

IV

We passed a rather disturbed night in our strange quarters. There were rats in the walls, the windows rattled, and altogether there were more queer noises than one generally hears in houses so new. However, we did get to sleep, and did not wake again till the grey dull sodden dawn was making ghastly the little strip of sky visible over the grimy roof of the house opposite. We rose and dressed quickly and went up to Macbane's room. I peered in, but he was still sleeping heavily; so we busied ourselves, as quietly as we could, in preparing breakfast, intending, if our friend did not wake, to go off to our own work for the day, leaving a message for him. We purposed, in a rather vague manner, to do something for poor Macbane. Standish hoped to work on the better feelings of his uncle; I had resolved to devote some of my little savings to keeping my friend out of the workhouse.

We were half through our scanty and silent meal, when a heavy tread was heard on the stairs, making apparently for the room where we were. "What luck!" said the sanguine Standish; "here's the penitent uncle, come back after the whiskey. Now leave me alone to manage him. There is half the bottle left."

The steps came up to the door and paused: then there was a single sharp rap, and in walked—not Mr. Macdonald, but a policeman. If Standish and I had been thieves or coiners taken in the act, we could hardly have shown more confusion. My first thought was that perhaps Macbane had done something wrong; and this suspicion was confirmed by the officer's first words.

"Beg your pardon, gentlemen," he said; "but is either of you Mr. A. Macbane?"

"No," said Standish; "Mr. Macbane is asleep in the next room. What do you want with him?"

"I want him to come with me to the station, as soon as convenient, sir," was the reply.

"What for?" persisted Standish. "Nothing wrong, I hope?"

"Nothing wrong about him; leastways, I don't suppose so, sir," said the man. "But there's been foul play somewhere. There's been a body found in the road out a mile off, and a card in the pocket with Mr. Macbane's name and address on it; and we want him to come and identify the corpse."

"Do you know the man's name?" I demanded, divining, as I asked, what the answer would be.

"His linen was marked 'Macdonald,' sir," was the cautious reply.

"And how had he been killed?" asked Standish breathlessly.

"Throat cut from ear to ear," said the constable, with terrible conciseness.

We looked at each other, and shuddered. Neither of us had any kind feelings for the man thus suddenly cut off; in fact, we had been thoroughly disgusted with his coarse and sordid temper, and had hoped—in jest, it is true—that he might break his neck over the dismal road he had to traverse. But this sudden, mysterious, hideous murder—for such it must be—struck us with a chill of horror. My first collected thought, I believe, was a feeling of intense thankfulness that we had not left Macbane alone the night before. Now, at any rate, no suspicion could attach to him.

The policeman looked curiously from one to the other of us.

"Perhaps" he said at length, "one of you two gentlemen would know him?"

"If it is the man I suppose," answered Standish, "we certainly do know him. Mr. Macdonald is Mr. Macbane's uncle, and was here last night. We both saw him leave before twelve o'clock, and have not seen him since."

"Then, sir," said the policeman, "perhaps one of you will wake Mr. Macbane and bring him along as soon as he can come, and the other will go to the station at once, for there is never any time to lose in these cases."

I went into Macbane's bedroom, and Standish took up his hat and followed the policeman out. I touched my friend on the shoulder. He gasped, yawned, then sat up, rubbed his eyes, and stared wildly round him, till his gaze rested on me. Then the recollection of what had happened seemed to come back on him in a flash, and he laid his head back on the pillow.

"Is that you, Eliot?" he said. "I have had such a horrible dream. Thank you for waking me. Must I get up now?"

"Yes, you must, Macbane," I replied gravely. "I will tell you why afterwards."

"Moralities and mysteries!" said he, in his cynical way. "Well, I shall soon hear, if I am a good boy, and don't take long over my dressing. Reach me my trousers, there's a good fellow."

As I did so, I saw that his right hand was again streaked thinly with dried blood, and I could not help an exclamation.

"Ah!" said he, as I called his attention to it. "That thing has been bleeding again, I see. Well, I can soon wash it off." And he sprang up in his nightshirt, and ran to his washstand.

"Look here!" he cried, as he plunged his hand into the water; "shouldn't I make a lovely Lady Macbeth? 'Here's the smell of the blood yet. Oh! oh! oh! All the perfumes of Araby—' How does it go? 'Yet who would have thought the old man had so much blood in him?'"

"For God's sake, be quiet!" I screamed. "Your uncle is lying at the police-station with his throat cut! Be thankful you had nothing to do with killing him!"

Macbane turned faint and sick, and sat down on his bed again; but he bore the news much better than I had thought he would. To be sure, he had no love for his uncle, and could not be expected to sorrow for him; but the shock did not seem somehow to affect him greatly, except by a mere physical repulsion at the horrid manner of his uncle's death. He soon got up again, and went on dressing, listening meanwhile as I told him all I yet knew about the matter; and as soon as he was ready, we went out together.

The police-station was soon reached, and we were admitted into a back room where Mr. Macdonald's body lay on a table, covered with a piece of sacking. There was no difficulty in identifying the corpse. The throat was cut, or rather, as it seemed to me, torn almost through with a frightful wound; but the face was uninjured, and still bore an expression of sudden horror and surprise that was very ghastly. We did not care to look on the sight long. When the covering had been replaced, the constables told us all they knew. Some workmen, coming to their work at one of the unfinished houses in the new road, had found the body, lying on its back in a pool of clotted blood. There were no marks of a struggle that they noticed. They had put the corpse on a short ladder left in one of the houses, and carried it to the police-station. The nearest surgeon had been called in, and had pronounced that life had been extinct for some hours. A purse and gold watch were found in the pockets. As to the hand or the weapon that had done the deed, neither the surgeon nor the police would offer any suggestion; and we could not help them. Only, as we left the station, the police-sergeant remarked that he thought he had a clue to the murderer. "Do you hear that, Standish?" said Macbane in a mocking tone; "*he* thinks he has a clue."

We walked back to Wolseley Road and left Macbane there; and then Standish and I trudged off to our work—for work must be done, whoever has died. And all that afternoon and evening, whenever I was within sight or sound of a main street, my eyes were greeted with sensational placards, and my ears deafened with the shouts of newsboys, reiterating the same burden—"Third Edition! Awful Murder in Craddock Park! A Glasgow Merchant Murdered!" and over every placard I seemed to see the vision of the dead face, and that gash in the throat.

The inquest was held a few days afterwards, and of course we all attended it. The story of the quarrel with Angus Macbane came out, in its main outlines, from his evidence and ours; and I could tell from the Coroner's pointed questions, that he suspected our friend. But there was no reasonable doubt that Duncan Macdonald had been killed within an hour after he left the lodging-house; and it was perfectly clear from our evidence and the landlady's that Angus Macbane had been in his room long after this, and practically certain that he had never left the house at all that night. The medical evidence, when it came, was conclusive; the distinguished surgeon who had made the postmortem examination gave it as his opinion that the wound in the throat could have been inflicted with no species of weapon with which he was acquainted; and as far as he could venture to form a hypothesis, death had been caused by the bite of some animal armed with exceedingly large and powerful cutting teeth. This unexpected statement caused quite a sensation in court; and Standish jumped up. "By Jove, I forgot the cat!" he said to me; and then, advancing to the Coroner, he informed him that he had an addition to make to his former statement. He was sworn again, and told the story of the mysterious death of poor Mephistopheles in a straightforward way that evidently impressed the jury. I confirmed his tale in every particular.

There were no more witnesses, and the Coroner summed up. He began by stating that all the evidence that could be collected still left this terrible affair in a very mysterious state. So far as he could see, however, there was happily no reason for regarding it as a murder. There had been no robbery of the body, though robbery would have been perfectly easy; and though there might have seemed some *primâ facie* grounds for suspecting one person of complicity in the act—here the worthy Coroner glanced at Macbane, who smiled slightly—yet it had been proved by reputable witnesses, whose testimony had not been impugned (here Standish blushed, and I think I did, too), that the person in question could not possibly have been present on the scene of Mr. Macdonald's death at the hour when it took place, and had apparently confined the expression of his ill-will to mere words, which it would be unfair to invest with any special significance—and so on, in the usual moralizing vein of coroners. The medical evidence, he went on to say, pointed to the theory that the death of the deceased was caused by some savage animal; and the further statement of two of the witnesses seemed to indicate that some such ferocious beast, perhaps a dog, was loose in the neighbourhood. It would be for the jury, however, to review all the facts, and return a just and impartial verdict upon the case.

The jury deliberated for some time, and finally determined that the deceased died from the bite of some savage animal, but what animal they were unable to say. A rider to the verdict directed the police to use all possible diligence to track out and destroy so dangerous a beast, and suggested that a reward should be offered for its capture or death. This was done by the local authorities, but with no result; and as weeks went on, and no fresh victim fell to the "ravenous beast or beasts unknown," men ceased to go armed, or to apprehend attacks, and the Craddock Park Mystery was forgotten.

Mr. Duncan Macdonald had left no will; and though he had torn up a testament providing for his nephew, he had not yet executed his threat of disinheriting him. So Macbane, as the only near relative, came in for the manufacturer's very considerable fortune. He sold out his uncle's share in his business, and his first act, almost, was to purchase an old, half-ruinous place, called Dullas Tower, which had been (as I gathered from the scanty letter he wrote me about it) the ancestral seat of the Macbanes before the family fell into poverty and ill repute in the old witchcraft days.

I was prevented by my school duties from seeing Macbane, now that he had gone north; and about this time Standish got a good appointment on an Indian railway in course of construction, and had to sail at once. Thus we three friends were parted for long, and it might be for ever. I was sorry enough to lose Standish; I think it was rather a relief to see no more of Macbane. He was stranger than ever, now that his sudden prosperity had come upon him—alternately gay and sullen, exalted and depressed, and disquieting enough in either mood. I occasionally sent him a line, and at still rarer intervals received an answer; but, on the whole, I thought he had dropped out of my life permanently, and I was not sorry to have it so, now that he needed no help. I did not dream of the strange way in which we were once again to be brought together.

V

It was some months after Standish had left for India, and I had already received one letter from him, when I was startled by a brief paragraph among the Indian telegrams in the *Times*. It ran thus—"I regret to state that Mr. F. Standish, the young and talented engineer superintending the construction of the Salampore Junction Railway, has been killed, it is supposed by a tiger." This was all—terribly simple, brief and direct, as messages of evil are now. I was greatly shocked and grieved at this sudden death of my old friend; for though I was not likely to see him again for many years, and college friendships fade sadly when college life is over, yet we had been much together before he left, and my remembrance of him was still warm and affectionate. As soon as I recovered from the blow of the news, I wrote at once to Lieutenant Johnson, a young officer whom Standish had mentioned as being stationed near his quarters, and as being an acquaintance of his, to ask for some particulars of my friend's death.

The answer was forwarded to me about the end of August. I was not at the time in London, but had been invited by an old friend of my family to stay with him and have some shooting (though this was mere pretence on my part) at his place in Yorkshire. Lieutenant Johnson's letter was sent on from my lodgings to Darton Manor, where I was. It was a good letter, showing in its tone of manly regret how familiar and dear Standish had grown in the short time of intercourse with his new neighbours; but what I turned to most eagerly was of course the account of my poor friend's death. It was brief and rather mysterious. Standish had gone out for an early walk in the cool of the morning, taking his gun with him, as was his custom. He had walked along the line of the new railway a little distance, and then turned off into the country. As he did not come back at his usual time, two of his servants had gone out to look for him, and found him lying on his back in a path, quite dead. His throat was fearfully torn, but there was no other wound on him. There had been no struggle, and the gun was still loaded. Footprints of some animal were observed in a patch of soft ground near by, but it was not certain whether this was the beast that had killed Standish; for while the footmarks were like those of a small panther, the wound seemed rather as if inflicted by the teeth of a tiger. A large hunting-party had beaten the neighbouring country without finding any dangerous wild animal.

This narrative set me on a very gloomy train of thought. The details of Standish's end were horribly like those of Mr. Duncan Macdonald's—the suddenness, the stealth, the mystery, the ferocity of the attack were the same in both cases. Yet, what possible connection could there be between the Craddock Park mystery and the death of an engineer on the Salampore railway? Still, I could not keep this haunting feeling of some impending doom from shadowing my mind. Four men had met in that little room in Wolseley Road on that memorable night in November; two of the four had already perished by the same mysterious and horrible death. Was it possible that the same end was reserved for the other two, and, if so, who would be the next victim? It was a wild idea, I felt; but I simply could not get it out of my head, and it made me very gloomy and depressed at the dinner-table that night.

My kindly old host noticed this, and his genial nature could not rest satisfied till all around him were as cheery as himself. So when our *tête-à-tête* dinner was done—we had been very late in dining that day—he resolved to have up a bottle of a certain very rare old wine, which he kept under special lock and key for great occasions. This precious liquor he was now resolved to devote to clearing away my melancholy.

He would never trust a butler with the key of his cellar—least of all would he let a servant touch this priceless vintage. He was going to fetch the bottle himself, but of course I interposed and insisted on going for him. With a sigh of resignation, he gave me his bunch of cellar-keys, carefully instructing me as to their particular uses, and the treasures to which they respectively gave access. Then he dismissed me, and I went down to the cellar.

The cellar of Darton Manor was far older than the house. It was hewn out of the rock on which the hall stood, and was large and lofty. I think that when the old castle, whose walls are still to be traced in the Manor garden, was standing, the vaults beneath must have been the storehouse of the garrison. When the modern house was built, two windows were cut up through the rock to give light to the cellars; but the present owner had protected these openings with double gratings, and put an iron-plated door, with a strong and cunning lock, to defend his precious wines.

I took up a candle, lit it, and went down the winding stair that led to the cellar. The vault below was so lofty and so far beneath the floor of the hall, that the staircase, cut in the rock, seemed as if it would never end; I felt like one descending into a sepulchre. The clash of the keys swinging from my hand was the only sound in the chilly silence, except when noises came, muffled and faint, from the house above. At last I reached the heavy door of the cellar, and, with some labour, unlocked it and swung it back. Then I drew out the key, as I wanted another on the bunch for releasing the precious bottle I had been sent to fetch. For a moment I stood in the doorway, holding my light high, and gazing round me into the great cavernous room. I could not see all of it; but the long rows of casks and the racks of bottles were very impressive in their silent array of potential conviviality. Then I glanced up at the windows, whose gratings were now and then made visible by a flicker of summer lightning across the sky; and as I did so, I suddenly heard a crash as of glass, far up in the house above. Then, as I still listened, came a faint sound of footfalls rapidly growing louder, as if something was coming down the winding stair with long leaps.

I did not stop to face whatever this might be; I did not pause to think what I should do. In a blind and fortunate impulse of overpowering terror, I flung the heavy door to, plunged the key into the lock and shot the bolt home. How I managed to do it in the one instant left to me, I never could understand; I had found the door hard enough to open before. As I gave the key a last turn, something came against the iron outside with a thud that almost shook the hinges loose. Then there was a moment of quiet, and I, listening behind the door, could catch a quick, hoarse, heavy panting, as of some beast of prey. Then came another great shock, and another; and at every blow the good door creaked and shook, but held firm. Next there was a grating, rending sound, as if teeth and claws were tearing at this last obstacle between my life and its destroyer—and still I stood silent, transfixed with horror, as in a nightmare, expecting to feel the fangs of the unseen Thing close through my throat. How long I stood thus, tasting all the bitterness of death, I cannot tell. It was years in agony—it may have been only minutes of time. To feel that something fiendish, brutal and merciless was slowly tearing its way to me, and to know nothing of It save that It was death, this was the deadly and over-mastering terror. My trance cannot have lasted long. With a start, I awoke to the consciousness that life was still mine, and that a chance of escape yet remained. The frozen blood again coursed through my veins, and my dead courage revived. I sprang to the nearest large barrel that lay on its side and rolled it close against the door, to keep the panels from giving way. Then I took up an iron bar that I found lying on the floor—perhaps a lever for mov-ing the casks—and stood ready to give one last blow for my life. The sound of tearing ceased; I heard one deep snarling growl of disappointed rage; and then the quick steps seemed to recede up the stair. I stood there delivered, for a moment.

Only for a moment, however. My candle, which was a mere stump, suddenly flared, flickered and left me in total darkness, made darker by the little patch of sky seen through the nearer window, across which still ran an occasional flicker of summer lightning. In trying to strike a light, I dropped the match-box on the rock floor. While I was groping for it, I suddenly looked up and saw two eyes.

Two eyes, I say, but they were rather two flames, or two burn-ing coals. For a moment I stood glaring, fascinated, at the orbs that glared into mine. Then, as the Thing turned what seemed its head, and the eyes were averted for a moment, I saw, or thought I saw, a dim phosphorescent mass obscuring the faint light of the window. Then the eyes were on me again, and I heard the sound of tearing and wrenching at the outer grating—for there were two, one above the window and one inside. The outer bars were old and rusty—strong enough to resist any common shocks, but not to hold against the unknown might that was rending at them. I heard them creaking, cracking, and then—oh heaven! the whole grating gave way, and I heard it ring as it was hurled aloft and fell far out on the stones. Next instant the strong glass of the window flew in shivers on the floor—and there were those awful eyes looking into mine now, with only a few bars between us. Then the wrenching began once more at the last barrier. It bent—it shifted—I thought it was giving way, and in a frenzy I rushed forward, whirling the iron bar round my head, and struck with all my force through the grating. Another horrible growl answered the blow, and the bar was seized and dragged from my grasp. It was found next day, deeply indented, on the ground, a hundred yards away.

But now that the prey seemed given over disarmed to its teeth, the devilish fury of the Thing seemed to triumph over the devilish cunning that had directed it. It gave up the persistent assault on the grating, and writhed against the bars in a transport of hissing rage, biting the air, grinding its jaws on the tough iron. And yet— this was the horror of it—I could see nothing distinctly—only a phosphorescent shadow, twisted and tortured with agonies of rage, and turning upon me sometimes those eyes which seemed to redden with the growing frenzy of the Thing, till they were like blood-red lamps. I think I had lost all fear for my life now. I did not think of danger or resistance; but so mighty was the sheer hor- ror of that bestial rage, that I groveled down in the darkest corner of the vault, and hid my eyes and stopped my ears, and cried to Heaven to deliver me from the presence of the Thing.

Suddenly, as I crouched there, the end came. The noise ceased. I turned and saw that the eyes were gone. I stood up and stretched out my arms, and a cool air blew through the shattered window on my streaming forehead. Then every tense fibre of my body seemed to give way, and I fell like one dead on the floor.

I was wakened from my swoon by a thundering at the door, and the sound of voices—human voices once more. I staggered to the door, pushed away the cask, and after long wrenching—for my hands seemed to have lost all strength—got the lock open, and stumbled into the arms of my good host. Above him, on the stairs, were two or three of the men-servants, their pale frightened faces looking ghastly in the light of the flaring candles.

"My dear boy!" he cried. "Thank God you are alive! We have been so frightened about you."

I told him faintly that I had fallen in a swoon. I could not yet speak of what I had gone through, and, indeed, it now seemed like a hideous dream.

"Well, do you know," he said, as he took my arm, and helped me up the stair, "we had such a scare upstairs! Just a few minutes after you had gone, when I was wondering whether you would find the right wine, smash came something right through the dining-room window, and over went the big candlestick, and we were in the dark. And when we got a light again, you never saw such a scared set as we were; but there was nothing to be seen. Did you have a visit, too?"

"Something did come down here," I managed to articulate; "but don't ask me about it—not to-night. I want to sleep first."

"I think we all want that," he said briefly, as we reached the lighted hall again; and I, for one, felt as if I had come up from the grave alive.

VI

I slept late into the following morning, and should have slept later still had I not been aroused about ten o'clock by the butler, who held in his hand a yellow telegram envelope. As soon as I could shake off my drowsiness in part, I tore open the missive, and unfolding the paper, found to my surprise that it was from Macbane. He knew my address, indeed, from a letter that I had sent him; but knowing his ways, I never expected even a note from him, much less a telegram. When I read the message, my surprise was not diminished.

"If safe, and wishing to see me alive," it ran, "come at once. If unable, forget me. Nearest station, Kilburgh."

What could this mean? Could Macbane know anything of my mysterious danger of last night? and if so, was the doom that had missed me impending over him? Or was it merely that he was ill and desponding, and thought himself dying? Turn and twist the message as I could, it puzzled me; but one thing was plain—Macbane was, or thought himself to be, in deadly need of me, his only friend, as far as I knew: and if I did not go, it was possible that he

might lose the last chance of any friendly human care in his solitary life. I resolved at once, shaken and weary as I still felt, to start
for Dullas Tower. I rose and dressed hurriedly, and snatched some
breakfast alone—for my good old host was too much exhausted by
the excitement of the last night to come down yet. While eating, I
was studying a railway guide, and discovered that by driving to the
nearest station at once, I could catch a train which would enable
me by devious junction lines to make my way to Kilburgh (a little
place in a wild part of a Lowland county) by the evening. While
the horse was being put into the dog-cart, I scribbled a note to my
host, explaining the reason for my speedy departure, and promising to return as soon as possible; and then I stepped into the cart
and was driven off, arriving just in time to catch the train.

My journey was of the exasperatingly tedious character known
to all who have ever tried to go any distance by means of cross-
lines and local lines and junctions. Twice I got some food during
my long intervals of waiting at stations; and all the time, whether
travelling or resting, I was possessed with a haunting perplexity, a
shadowy fear. Through my brain incessantly beat, keeping time to
the pulsating roar of the wheels, a text, or something like one—I
know not how or why it suggested itself—"One woe is past; be-
hold another woe cometh." The mysterious peril of the last night
seemed already to have happened years ago; the dim terror of the
future would be ages in coming; and between them, and in the
shadow of both, I was still going on and on, slowly but endless-
ly—a dream myself, and in a dream.

It was about eight in the evening, I think, when I reached Kilburgh station; but my watch had stopped, and I could not be sure.
As I stepped out on the platform, I was conscious of an intense
sultry heat in the dense night air, and a sudden little gust of wind
smote on my cheek like a breath from a furnace. The train went on
again, plunged with a doleful wailing shriek into a tunnel, and was
lost to sight; and when its rumble died away, the utter stillness was
strange after the noise and rattle in which I had passed the day. I
cast a hasty glance round me, and could just make out the lights of
a few houses in the valley below the station, and the dark outlines

of hills around, some of them serrated with black pines, and the sky dense with cloud, and with a denser mass of gloom labouring slowly up from the west. There was the weight of a coming storm in the air.

I asked the station-master where Dullas Tower was, and how I was to reach it.

"Dullas Tower?" he said meditatively; and then, with a sudden flash of comprehension—"Oh, it's the De'il's Tower ye'll be meaning, sir—Macbane's?"

I nodded acquiescence; this popular corruption of the name seemed ominous, but somehow natural.

"Then ye've a matter of ten miles to go," he said deliberately; "and gin I might offer an opeenion, ye'll do better to tak' Jimmy Brown's bit giggie. The man frae Macbane's tauld him to be ready the morn."

Guided by the cautious "opeenion" of the station-master, I found Brown's trap waiting outside the station. He was English, as I could tell by his accent; and this perhaps accounted for the slight tinge of contempt in the worthy official's reference to him and his vehicle. His horse, as far as I could tell by the station lamp, seemed a poor one; but it showed a remarkably vicious temper when I tried to get in—kicking and backing, and seeming possessed by an irrational desire to do me some bodily harm.

"Whoa, then, will ye, ye beast?" called Brown, as he caught bold of the rein and dexterously foiled the brute's instant attempt to bite him. "You're a harm to others and no good to your owner. You're just like Macbane's muckle cat, that killed two men, and the third was Macbane."

I had gained my place on the seat at last, but this remark nearly shook me off it again.

"What do you mean by that?" I almost screamed at the man. He turned a puzzled face up to mine, as he climbed into his place and took the reins.

"Oh, I don't know, sir," he answered, as we rattled off. "It's just a saying the folks have about here. It's some story about an old warlock Macbane that had the Tower long ago, I believe. Nothing

to do with this one, sir—of course not. I got into the way of saying
it from hearing it often, that's all."

I did not answer him, as we drove on between high banks of
earth and rock, with now and then a tree nodding threateningly
above us. I was faint and tired, and unable to think in a connected
manner. The grim old proverb, like the Scriptural or quasi-Scrip-
tural phrase, transformed itself into a dreary refrain, which rang
in time to the beat of the horse-hoofs on the dry road: *"Killed* two
men, and the *third* was Mac*bane*—*killed* two men, and the *third*
was Mac*bane"*—it seemed a part of me, a pulse in my very brain,
till it grew meaningless with incessant repetition.

We drove on westward, toiling up hills, rattling down them,
always moving towards the storm, as the storm moved towards us.
Now and then I heard the muttering of thunder—now and then a
livid gleam of lightning glanced across the face of the cloud, or a
moaning gust of hot wind swept up the dust, and fell silent again.
I took little note of the scenery on either tide; and indeed I could
see but little of it in the darkness. The lightning, growing brighter
and nearer, occasionally revealed some bare cliff-face, some solemn black row of pines, some thread or sheet of water—I hardly
saw anything. It was all a part of my dream still, and it seemed
natural to me when a black grove of tall trees, and in the midst a
denser black mass, with one or two lights twinkling in it, rose up
before us, and the driver told me this was the De'il's Tower.

As we came up to it, and I roused myself from my lethargy
a little to observe my journey's end, I could see that part of the
building seemed ruinous and broken down; the walls ended in a
slope bristling with bushes. One grim-looking tower at the corner
loomed high above us, apparently uninjured, and half-way up it
shone a faint light.

I alighted, paid the driver, who seemed in a hurry to get away,
rang, and when an old woman came to the door, asked if Macbane
was at home. She said in reply that he was ill, and could see no
one; but when I gave my name she conducted me through a long
passage—part of it almost ruinous, part in better repair—to the
foot of a winding stair. Here she told me to go up and knock at

the first door I came to, and stood at the foot of the steps with her candle to light me up. When I reached the door—which was some way up—I could hear her hobble away, leaving me in darkness, only relieved by an occasional gleam of lightning through the narrow slits that let in light and air to the staircase. I knocked gently, and a voice said "Come in." I felt along the iron-studded door till I found and turned the handle of the latch. As I entered I saw Macbane sitting back in an old chair with a shaded lamp on the table beside him, and some books and papers in its circle of light. The room was small and circular, and was, as I conjectured, half-way up the tower that had given its name to the building. A window, made visible from time to time by the lightning, opened on the outer air; and I noticed with a sort of dull wonder that there seemed to be a set of strong bars defending it—perhaps a relic of old times when the room was a prison; I cannot tell.

My friend did not rise from his chair to greet me. He motioned languidly to a seat near him, and for some minutes I sat and looked at him, and he stared at the door. I noticed a new and alarming change in him, since I had seen him last. Then, his look had been almost malevolent, instinct with a positive hatred for men; now all passion, all life, good or bad, seemed extinct in him. He looked worn and wasted; but it was the settled stony hopelessness of his face that struck me most: and the pity that I had felt for him in his old days of poverty now revived tenfold.

After a long pause, only broken by the muffled growls of the nearer thunder, he spoke.

"I hardly thought you would come," he said; "but now you are here, you had better read this. There is not much time to explain"—and he pointed to a yellow and torn old manuscript lying on the table.

I was perplexed by this—for why should I have been sent for in hot haste to read an ancient document of this sort? But I did not inquire or object. It all seemed part of the inexplicable dream in which I was moving. I took up the roll and began to look into it.

It was crabbed and quaint in writing and style, and it would only be perplexing to give its antique phraseology and obsolete

Scotch law-terms and phrases, even if I remembered them. But the substance of it was plain. It was a record of the trial and condemnation of Alexander Macbane of Dullas Tower for witchcraft, early in the seventeenth century. After many preliminaries, over which I passed hastily, the narrative came to the confession of the wizard. This was apparently volunteered, and not extorted by any torture; but such cases were by no means rare at that time, I think. The peculiarity of this confession was that it was clear, consistent, rational even (if so wild a tale could be called rational), and did not involve any one besides the wizard himself. Actual torture was applied, it would seem, to make Alexander Macbane implicate an old crone tried at the same time, but in vain. "The devil," he had said, "was no fool; he had better servants than these poor women." These particulars, petty though they may be, struck my attention at the time; and I have never been able to forget them since.

Briefly put, the gist of Alexander Macbane's confession was as follows. He admitted that he had, by certain magic processes which he refused to reveal (because their very simplicity might lead others to use them), secured the services of a strange familiar. This Thing owned him as master and did his bidding, though only in one way—it could slay, and nothing more. He had killed by it two men, kinsmen of his, one his enemy and one his friend, who had in fact (a marginal note stated) died in a sudden and strange manner. But that which he had regarded as his servant (the confession went on to say) had become his master, and he a bondslave to its devilish power. It was jealous of all he did; it had cut off any beast for which he showed a fondness, and it had driven him to cast off all his friends, and to give up all friendly feeling for men. One man, whom he loved, he had bidden it slay, or else it would have slain himself. The Thing needed to have victims pointed out to it at certain intervals, or it turned on its master. Being asked how he knew the intentions of his familiar, the wizard answered that he could not tell how, but he divined its thoughts, even as, he felt sure, it read his. To the inquiry what form his demon assumed, he said that at first it was invisible to him as to others, but could be felt; and that gradually it took visible form as a beast black and catlike, with a great mouth.

The judges here asked the reason why Alexander Macbane had turned against his demon; the answer, given in quaint but still pathetic language, was that he had married a woman whom he loved, and had been happy with her for some months, and now he knew that he must choose between her and himself as a sacrifice to his familiar. In making his confession, he knew that he was devoting himself to death the same night; but he was resolved to do this. Better, he said, was it to die horribly thus, than to live alone with his sin and its punishment. "And so," the record concisely ended, "the said Alexander Macbane, being remanded to his prison, was there found dead the next day, with his throat rent through, and the bars of the window broken. Whereby it was thought that he had said the truth as to himself."

As I read the last words, I dropped the roll; for the lightning glared into my very face, and a moment after a ringing crash of thunder burst over the building as if sky and earth were coming together. Then the roar leaped and rolled through the clouds, and died muttering far away; and through the rush of rain and wind I heard Macbane's voice.

"You understand now," he said, with that dreadful hollow sameness in his tone; "I am glad any way that you will be left, and not I; I always liked you better than Standish. Perhaps it was a tiger after all that killed him, poor fellow. You are quite safe now; it is coming for me to-night. I thought it would have killed me last night, when I called it back—" a crash of thunder drowned his last words.

"Macbane!" I cried, finding my power of speech at last; "it shall not be! Whether it is real or a dream, I do not know; but you shall not die that way. I kept the Thing out; cannot you do it? Never give up hope. Cannot you save yourself?"

Macbane smiled hopelessly. "Listen," said he, and held up his hand; and in a pause of the rain I heard, low and distinct, *a scratching on the door.*

"Open it, Eliot," he said calmly. "It must come, and the sooner the better. Then go down and wait; for it will not be a pleasant thing to see."

I sprang to the door, but not to open it. With frenzied speed I locked and double-locked it, and drove the heavy bolts into their sockets. But no rush came against the door—no tearing or grinding of teeth. I could hear nothing—not even a breath; and the stillness was more terrifying than any sound.

"It is no use," said my friend; "you could keep yourself safe; you cannot save me. It will have help to-night."

A gust of wind swept round the tower as he spoke; and mingling in its wail I seemed to hear—or was it but my fancy?—the long deadly howl of the Thing that I felt was be near us. For a few moments there was silence. Then, with a crash, the lightning fell close to the tower, and a great pine, shattered by the stroke, rushed down right against the window, and its top crashed into the room, rending away the iron bars like rotten sticks. The wind of the fall extinguished the lamp; but in the darkness and the roar of thunder I could *feel* something pass by me with a mighty leap: and next moment a fainter flash showed me a picture which was but for an instant, but in that instant was branded in on my memory. Macbane stood upright with arms folded, gazing calmly forward and upward—and before him crouched, as if for a spring, a black mass with blood-red burning eyes—the same eyes that had glared on me the night before. So much I saw; then, suddenly, the world was one blinding flame, one rending crash around me, and I fell stunned and senseless.

When I lived again, the dawn's grey glimmer was dimly lighting the tower; and outside the blackened and shattered window a bird was singing. As I opened my eyes, my glance fell on something lying in the centre of the room; it was Macbane's body. I crawled to him and looked into the dead face. There was no wound or mark on him, and there even seemed a faint smile on his lips; and near his feet lay a little heap of grey ash.

A SHADOW OF GOLD
VIDA D. SCUDDER
The Overland Monthly, 1887

"Why, auntie," said I, "you have never showed me this before."

I was sitting, my lap filled with odds and ends of sketches, in the sunny window of Aunt Ellen's bright little study. She was not much of an artist, this dear old aunt of mine; but she took an unfailing delight in the laborious production of the stiff, minute little pen and ink drawings that had been the fashion in her girlhood. Disconsolate elms always waved in feeble and feathery manner in these landscapes, while beneath their shadow cattle of remarkable anatomy gazed at themselves in preternatural pools. It was with a good deal of surprise that from these familiar productions, to which I was awarding absently the praise that rejoiced auntie's heart, I saw fall one of a very different nature. Not a feather-elm this time, not even a pen and ink sketch; but a girl's head, outlined by vague, fragmentary touches, and defined mainly by faint washes of soft color.

"It's because you never finished her, I suppose," I remarked critically, "that she has such a curious expression of suspense—what papa would call a look of arrested development. I don't see what there is in the face that repels me so strongly. It is rather weak, of course, but that may be because the washes are so faint. She seems to be looking through a mist, and she lacks form. But she's pretty, very pretty."

"Yes, that's just it; but she couldn't have much form, you know," said Aunt Ellen, absently; "and she *is* pretty, poor child."

"Is, auntie? She doesn't look real. I never thought of her being a portrait. Is she still alive?"

Aunt Ellen's knitting dropped in her lap, and she looked straight at me. Aunt Ellen always answered the exact truth to a question.

"I don't know, my dear," she said seriously.

"Why, auntie! Who is she, and how did you come to know her?"

"Her name was Martha Clinton, Alice. I do not think that I will tell you the story of our acquaintance."

"Oh, but you must; for your hints are so mysterious that she'll just haunt me night and day if I don't know all about her. Is she one of your numerous adopted daughters? And did she tell you her love affairs, and all the secrets of her heart? They always do, you know, dear little Mother Ellen. You say you don't know whether she is alive or not? How dreadful!"

"After all, why not?" asked auntie of the calla lily. The calla had no possible reason to give; so after an abstracted little pause, she settled her cap—auntie's dainty caps were apt to be a trifle awry—and began:—

"It was about four o'clock on a January afternoon that I first saw little Martha. You were a child at school and don't remember; but your Uncle Henry had invited us all that year to spend the holidays at the old homestead farm at Bayford. Your cousin Harry was at home from college, and we had quite a company of young people, and a very jolly time. Pretty Mabel Lee was there among the others—such a fresh, sunny, wholesome child! She was my great pet, the prettiest of all the girls there in my opinion, and I could see that Harry, for one, quite agreed with me.

"Well, a mild, sunshiny afternoon had come, and I was taking a stroll along the river path with old Mrs. Shrieve. We were chatting away cosily, when Bridget came running from the house with a big yellow envelope in her hand. I hate telegrams, and our family is so large that something may always have happened to somebody. But I pulled it open; and I'm ashamed to say that the first thing I felt was a sense of relief.

"'My old uncle, Stephen Hunt, is dead, Mrs. Shrieve,' I said, 'and I shall have to go to Oakton to settle his affairs. He was on my father's side, you know, and I am the nearest living relative.'

"As I spoke my eyes wandered to the little river, which had not frozen that winter, and was flowing peaceably by the side of the road. Not a breath of wind was stirring, and the smooth surface reflected perfectly each snowy twig and shriveled leaf of the bushes on the bank above. There's nothing but pen and ink to render effects like that. But to my surprise and perplexity, I saw amid the reflections of the low alder bushes, that of a slight girlish figure, dressed in a clinging garment of a peculiar reddish tint. I saw at once that she was not one of the girls in the house. She had no wrap on, not even a hat, and my first thought was that she was a very imprudent child. Her attitude, so far as I could judge it inverted, was that of arrested attention, surprise, and it seemed to me, delight.

"How did a graceful young girl come to be standing in that thicket of snowy brambles on the other side of the river? I looked up quickly, meaning, whoever she was, to order her to go straight home and wrap herself up.

"There was no one to be seen! The branches of the alder thicket shone lustrous black beneath their white burdens; the late sunshine slanted quietly across the frosty ground, and in the spot where I had looked for a young lady two wee sparrows were peacefully hopping and twittering. Thoroughly bewildered, I caught a last echo of good Mrs. Shrieve's rather lengthy condolences.

"'Did you know your uncle well?' she was saying.

"Now I am forced to confess that I had forgotten all about Uncle Stephen and the telegram. I hadn't met him for years, and he had been a very disagreeable old man, whom I had avoided thinking of as much as possible. He lived all by himself in a forlorn old house at Oakton, and people said that he was a skinflint, a regular miser of the old-fashioned type, who spent all his time fingering and patting the piles of money which he had accumulated. There were some excuses for him, I suppose. My grandfather had been a hard man, and I had heard people say that Stephen's moroseness and meanness had developed themselves rather late in life, after some contest with his father. But I always remembered him as I had seen him once when I was a little girl—an old-looking

man already, with an evil, pinched face, patting a bulgy pock-
etbook from which he gave me with much preamble a two-cent
piece. I know I threw the penny away and rubbed my little hand
hard when I left him.

"But of course I was not going to gossip with old Mrs. Shrieve
about my dead uncle; so I went back to the house, and soon after
supper left the young people playing dumb crambo, and climbed
up to my room. I had chosen to be in an L all by myself, for dear-
ly as I love young people, I wasn't young myself, even then, and
I love to have my quiet, especially at night. There was not much
furniture in the room, I remember, except a tall, old mirror in the
corner opposite the fire.

"Well, when my packing was finished, I sat down before the
fire with my Emerson. To tell the truth I didn't expect to read
much; for I was very sleepy, and thought it likely that I should
take a series of nice little naps, until it should be ten o'clock and
my principles should allow me to go to bed. But I grew less and
less sleepy every minute, and yet I found it absolutely impossible
to fix my attention on the 'Over-Soul.' My thoughts would per-
sist in wandering off in the least agreeable direction. I had never
remembered my uncle Stephen's existence when he was alive; but
now that he was dead, some power external to myself forced me
to think over one scene after another in his forlorn old life. I
saw him chuckling as he smoothed dirty money against his wrinkled cheek; or hiding it with a hideous leer in a hole in the wall;
or finally dying, parched and dreary, with no companion but his
shining coins. The strange thing was, that whereas I had known
my uncle, and had always thought of him, as an elderly man, his
ghostly face seemed in my vision to be constantly struggling after
youthfulness. One moment it would appear to me smooth, handsome, almost merry; the next, the lines of care and avarice would
creep into cheek and forehead, and the gay smile become fixed in
a thin-lipped, greedy grin. But at last these horrible impressions
faded away, and were succeeded by another, even more unpleasant.
I felt that some one was looking at me; yes, my dear, I felt it so
strongly that I put up my hand and straightened my cap. I stood

it as long as I could; but I never did believe, as some women do, in enduring things just for the pleasure of the discomfort. So I pushed away my chair, and stepped back into the room.

"Of course there was no one to be seen. But as I now stood, I could look straight into the depths of the corner mirror, and became aware of a slight disturbance there. A puff of smoke had blown out from the fire, and hung poised, a delicate veil inter- posed between my sight and the reflected wall behind. As I looked, the smoke, instead of being dissipated, seemed to become more dense, to take upon itself an opaline and rosy tint. A moment more, and I saw—I cannot say distinctly, yet I saw—emerging from faint wreaths of fire-lit smoke, a face. A girl's face, whose wistful eyes, fixed firmly on my own, gazed at me through a shift- ing veil of vapor, and whose pale cheeks glowed as if illuminated by the very heart of the fire behind. The golden threads of her curling hair floated away from her and vanished, melted into the circles of shining smoke which had spread through all the room. The contour of her face evaded me constantly, lost in the thin veil that hung before her, swayed by an unfelt breeze; but the soft eyes and yellow hair, gleaming vaguely through the dimness, reminded me of the old, half-effaced frescoes of saints that one sees on blurred Italian walls. Yet there was in the expression, despite its girlish pathos, an undefinable but disagreeable suggestion. Now and again a quiver of suffering would run across the pale cheeks and lips; and as I looked more carefully, a shuddering sense of horror seized me—for it was evident that the fire light, which pervaded the smoky haze and shone with dusky effulgence through the girl's fair youthful face, did not proceed from the cheerful little blaze that crackled on my hearth. I knew at once that this was the same girl whom I had seen in the river; and as I watched longer the tremulous, searching face, I perceived that the lips were moving. Soon I became aware of a voice, a whisper, a breath; it came, not from the mirror, but from a point a little behind me, in the room itself.

"'Pity, pity, pity,' it was saying.

"'Who are you that I may pity you?' The words must have been mine, for I could see my lips moving in the mirror.

"An instant's dispersion of the smoky veil; a flicker of little white hands clasped in triumph, and the voice went on, low, musical, monotonous.

"'At last, at last,' it said: 'I knew that you must hear me and see me at last, for I have willed, and you are kind and good. You saw me for an instant in the garden, but I could not stay. Now you will not leave me till I have told you, and you will help me. You must, you shall, for there is no one else, and the time has come.'

"'Who are you, that I may help you?'

"'Oh, you must know my story, for I have been telling it to you all the evening.' As the voice went on, its strange, unearthly monotony gave place in a measure to pathetic cadences, to sweet, girlish breaks and delicate inflections; and at the same time a quieter steadfastness crept into the mirrored face. 'Perhaps you thought that it was only about him; but what has been my life, ever, but a part of his? And I have waited, waited so long! But now he is coming back to me; death has brought him back, and the waiting is over. You told me that this afternoon; and for the news I thank and bless you. He is coming back to me, my lover, and it is you who shall show him the way.'

"'He! I! Of whom are you speaking?' I was completely bewildered.

"'Who? But I have been telling you about him all the evening. Stephen Hunt, my Stephen, my noble young lover. . . . Once I seem to remember that I had thoughts and even feelings that were not his: but that was long ago, before I stepped into the water. It was dark and cold, the water; but the letter burned and burned till I was glad of the coolness. It was such an unhappy letter—my poor Stephen! His father forbade him seeing me again, ever, and he said good-by. He did not know, nor did I till after I stepped into the river, that the time would come when no father could prevent him, yes, when he would be sent to me. We all come where we most want to be, you know, after the change. And so I have stayed here, where I had known him and been happy; and the time has been filled with hope and memory. And now he is dead, dead at last, and he can come to me.'

"As she spoke, the dim haze that shrouded her grew fainter and fainter, till her eager young face looked out from its dark background glowing with lovely life.

"'But you must help him,' she resumed: 'He will want me, but he will not know where to find me; and I cannot go to him. We are so weak; we who are no longer men and women. But you can go, and this is what you shall do for me. In every room in the house, but chiefly in the room where he lived and died, you shall say: 'Martha Clinton waits, and loves, and remembers, in the old homestead at Bayford. Come to her, come!'

"The sweet, young lips ceased moving; once more dense waves of shining smoke rolled up and wrapped her in its misty foam; slowly the atmosphere cleared, and the familiar pictures smiled at me from the walls; and I—well, Alice dear, I sank in my arm-chair by the fire again, and cried as hard as I could cry.

"The next day at noon I found myself at Oakton, in the desolate, rickety old house where my Uncle Stephen had lived his miserable life. Not the commonplace detail of the journey, nor the dreary round of duties to be gone through with on my arrival, lessened for an instant my belief in the reality of my night vision. My heart was filled with tender and solemn pity for the sad young spirit whose secret was in my keeping, and the unseen world seemed very near to me. Every whisper of the wind was a message from the invisible; in the depths of every mirror I sought for shadowy figures, and in every room of the deserted house I repeated the message that had been given me: 'Martha Clinton waits, and loves, and remembers, in the old homestead at Bayford. She calls you to her, come!'

"But if I looked for any answer, I looked in vain. I did not even feel that sense of an invisible presence so common in houses lately visited by death. I am an old woman, my dear, and that sense is well known, almost welcome, to me; but never before had I felt this terrible impression of utter lifelessness and desolation. In bare, dismantled room and gusty passage I called aloud, but there was no answer. I waited, but there came no sign. At last the hollow emptiness grew simply unbearable. I felt haunted by sheer vacuity; the horror of solitude gathered around me; and as soon as the funeral was over I collected the papers—that it was my duty to examine, and hastened back to Bayford. I did not dread the place where Martha's fair young spirit had showed herself to me; I felt that the companionship even of one long dead would be a comfort and a blessing.

"The family at Bayford, busily popping corn about the great wood fire, gave me a hearty welcome. Pretty Mabel flew to me and laid her warm little cheeks against mine; Harry saluted me directly after, with more gallantry than the occasion strictly demanded; and all the young people begged that auntie would sit down and toast her toes with them. But auntie was tired and soon excused herself—I was shattered and weary, and the contrast between this bright, full young life and that of the poor, waiting spirit who might, for all I knew, be standing in their midst, was more than I could bear.

"Once in my own room, I settled myself to the reading of Uncle Stephen's letters. They were for the most part insignificant, but I found one old yellow package carefully tied with string and labeled 'M's letters,' which I eagerly opened; but out of it fell a tress of hair, which gave me a shiver, so like was it to the ghostly gold that I remembered. There was a daguerreotype, too, of a man, young and handsome, with a weak mouth, and eyes in which I traced a curious, cold glitter. With a sense almost of desecration I unfolded and began to read the letter.

"As I read, the indications that they furnished, joined to hints heard in by-gone years, made clear to me the whole sad little story. It was not an uncommon one, that of the pretty, poor young cousin, beloved by the son of the house, and separated from him by the anger of a practical father. I saw how the girl's essential weakness of character had caused her to succumb, selfishly and completely, as soon as her hope of personal happiness was crushed, and I saw also how her death had hardened my uncle, and determined for evil a character that a strong and pure love might have saved. There was something very touching in the childlike trust of her letters, far more convincing than the fiery protestations of his

answers, which were also in the packet. It was with no surprise
that, glancing up, as I finished one of these last, I saw in the mirror the dim image of the girl herself leaning over me. The look of
unrest in her troubled eyes was greater than before; but she smiled
faintly as I looked into their depths.

"'I have not seen these for so long,' she said with subdued
pathos. 'Show me more, please.'

"I turned to the next letter, which was in my uncle's bold but
rather undecided hand. 'Life of my life,' it began.

"'You see how he loves me,' she murmured; and together we
read the letters, which during her brief life in the flesh she had
written and received. It was strange enough to catch glimpses in
the glass of her slender, shadowy figure, behind my wrinkled face,
and to remember that while she was writing these musty yellow
pages, I had been a baby girl, scampering after butterflies.

"As silently we turned from sheet to sheet, Martha's quiet
content changed for a vague uneasiness. She would lift her head
every moment, and glance about with a troubled air of expectation. Once she glided to the window, and looking out into the
night, called gently, 'Stephen! Stephen!' Then she returned, and
looked once more over my shoulder in silence.

. . . "'a love that time cannot alter, nor death destroy,' said the
letter.

. . . "'that time cannot alter, nor death destroy,' she repeated
softly. 'Ah, he understood it, even then.'

"'May I come in, Aunt Ellen?' said a ringing voice at the door—
and Mabel Lee, bright with the freshness and life of the present,
came dancing into the room. As she entered, the face of the spirit-
girl grew grey and faint; softly she vanished from my sight, and
nothing was left me but Mabel, holding my cheeks between her
two warm little hands.

"'I knew you were busy, but I couldn't wait another moment to
tell you. Auntie, dear auntie, can you guess what I have to tell?"

"And looking at her fluttering lashes, and rosy, uplifted face, I
felt that indeed I needed no words to tell me of the young delight
that had come to her and to my nephew Harry.

"The next morning I spent in wandering through the farm, trying to overcome the great sadness that filled my heart. I would have rejoiced in the happiness of Mabel and Harry, echoes of whose clear laughter floated to me through the keen, frosty air; but I could not think of their bright young faces without seeing between them the vision of another face, on which the look of youth remained, without that ineffable charm of promise which is the essence of all youthful beauty. The ghostly girl whose life had lost all noble purpose, all thought, all memory, to whom nothing remained but the glowing heat of her selfish passion—could my bright Mabel ever be like her? As I thought of the two with equal tenderness, I found myself on the little bridge that spans the river, watching listlessly the world reflected in its depths, broken and blurred by the slight breeze that played upon the surface of the water. On a sudden beside my own I saw the dim and wavering image of another face, so distorted with despairing wonder, that I should hardly have recognized it but for the golden glory of silky hair that melted into the sunlit water. The ripples danced, and rose, and sank, in points of shimmering light and the face of Martha Clinton came and went, one moment clearly seen in almost terrible beauty of illumined color, the next all but hidden by shifting and tremulous shadow. At the same time the sighing of the breeze resolved itself into a voice, charged with agonized suspense, now rising to a wail, now sinking to a shuddering whisper.

"'What have you done with him?' it cried. 'He has not come. I have waited, and looked, and called, all night, and he has made no sign. I trusted you; I thought you kind; and you have played me false. You never gave my message!'

"'I did, I did, poor spirit. In every room I repeated the words you taught me; but there came no answering sign.'

"'Yet he is there,' she murmured. 'He is surely there. And if he knows he will come, for there can be nothing in the way.'

"'But you, my dear. Can you not go to him?' I asked, pityingly.

"'It is forbidden,' she murmured, with a sideways look of what seemed rather fear than reverence.

"'And if one disobeys?'

"A gleam of light passed across her face; then a quivering sigh breathed in my ear.

"'I have not life enough.'

"'As the words died away, the face in the water turned slightly. Was it the flickering sunshine, or did there flash into the narrowed eyes and contracted lips a look of hate, of cunning, and of power? An instant more, and it was gone, and in its place I saw the frank blue eyes and rebellious curly hair of little Mabel. She was laughing musically at my surprise and discomfiture; and in her sweet, wholesome presence I strove to banish all thoughts of ghostly visitants, of ghostly joys and sorrows. Yet I shivered with a vague apprehension that was not for myself, as I remembered that the next day would find me far away from Bayford and its dear inmates. My hurried departure from Oakton had left many things undone, which would take at least a week to attend to; and I had no adequate excuse to give for neglecting my duties there.

"The day after my last interview with Martha found me accordingly once more an inmate of the damp, rickety house at Oakton. I found awaiting me the same sense of blank emptiness, which oppressed me even more than before. All my time, except my working hours, 1 spent out of doors in the quiet village street. There at least the birds twittered, the squirrels chattered, the wind swayed the branches, and I could escape from the death-like immobility within.

"On the third day after my arrival, I was strolling down the street, when I saw a slight figure advancing towards me with a swift and easy motion. At first I resisted the conviction borne in upon me that to none except to her who was a woman, yet not a woman, could that gliding step belong; but as she approached there came over me for the first time in all this strange experience, a shuddering thrill of horror and of supernatural fear. I felt in every fiber of my being that she who stood before me did not belong to the dear world of human life. Yet how did Martha Clinton, seen heretofore only in the shadow-land of mirror or of river, come to confront me here, in the world of realities? There was a subtle change about her, too. In spite of the sense of mystery, remoteness, almost of terror, that grew upon me in her presence, she appeared far less removed than formerly from the world of sense. Coloring and outline were no longer vague or blurred; she stood in the twilight air so distinct against the dusk of the evening that I could almost have touched her, had not an undefined shrinking held me back.

"'Your suggestion was a good one. I have broken the rules.' There was a new and curiously metallic ring to her voice.

"'And the means?'

"'They were not easy.' The light faded from the sky, and around us there gathered the sense of separation from the world of men. 'But I am here; I have come to him.'

"'And can you stay—until the end?'

"'There will be no end; we shall be together forever and ever. Take me to him, you. To the room where he lived and died.'

"Silently and swiftly we walked up the tranquil street. Here and there on the steps an old woman sat knitting. The bells of the church were tolling for an early evening service. The great sun hung poised in the west, a fiery ball of light. Long shadows from white houses and spreading maples slanted across the fields; but below the feet of Martha Clinton the grass lay bathed in unbroken sunshine, and as we advanced the depth of color and clearness of form which I had noticed in her, waned with the waning light, and left her once more mist-like, shadowy.

"'Yes, the strength is passing,' she answered to my look. 'But it has done its work.'

"As we entered the hall of my uncle's house, I made a strange discovery. Instead of shutting out the light of the late evening, the walls seemed to enclose and concentrate within themselves the red glow of the sunset; and the house, which had oppressed me with its emptiness, was filled by ghostly life, bathed and irradiated with this unearthly and lurid radiance. Everywhere they crowded and jostled, confused, uncertain, shadowy figures, a shifting vision of light and color. 1 recognized them all; the remembered friends of my childhood, the ancestors familiar to me through family legend, from the time when the old house was built—they drifted past me, a changing phantasmagoria of vaporous, luminous forms.

"'My grandfather was one of the most upright of men,' I exclaimed involuntarily. 'But where is he? My Aunt Margaret was a saint upon earth. I do not see her here.'

"'They are—elsewhere,' said Martha impatiently. 'Have I not told you that where the heart was, the spirit will linger? This is the room. Come.'

"It was indeed the room in which my uncle Stephen had passed his sordid days. But on the threshold she paused with a shiver, as if struck by an icy blast.

"'It is cold,' she murmured—'cold as life.'

"As we entered, there became visible to me, as through a pale gray haze, a ghostly shape seated by the table—the shape of my uncle Stephen; but alas! not that of the gay young lover of Martha's memories. He was a man old, bent, and withered, with an ugly look about the half-closed eyes and the corners of the flabby mouth. Cold indeed was the figure, with the chilling cold of those dense fogs that seem sometimes to be eating their way into the heart of the world. Before him on the table lay a heap of shadow-gold. He was clawing it with greedy fingers, and counting in a hollow voice.

"'Sixteen—seventeen—eighteen,' he said with a chuckle.

"I looked at Martha. She was standing, drawn to her full height, her dark eyes fixed with perplexity, sorrow, and dawning recognition on the forlorn old ghost. Turning to me she said imperiously:

"'Where is my lover? Where is Stephen Hunt?'

"I pointed silently to the figure at the table. Silent she too stood for a moment, with all the woman in her face; then with a sudden rush of pity and tenderness she glided forward and laid her hand on his shoulder, and called him by his name.

"'Stephen,' she said. 'Stephen!'

"He did not move, nor notice her in any way. Still the dimly shining coins dropped one by one from his grey fingers.

"'Twenty-one—twenty-two,' he counted.

"'Dear,' she murmured, slipping down on her knees before him—'dear, do you not know me? Stephen, it is so many years, so many long, long years! I know it now. I did not think the time had been so long until I saw you. Time passes quickly when one loves

and waits. And you have grown gray, dear, quite gray—did you
know it? and your face is wrinkled, that was so fair and smooth.
Have they been hard years, my Stephen?'

"She paused. There came no change in the old ghost's sullen form, no answer beyond the sound of the dropping gold and
the monotonous count. It was a strange sight. Through the face
of the spirit-woman there passed as she pleaded flushes of lovely
color, deepening and paling like the fire in the heart of the opal;
while the gray, vague, cruel figure beside her remained untouched,
unmoved.

"After an instant, she resumed: 'They are over now, those years
of waiting, Stephen, and I have come to you at last. Ah! I know
now why you did not heed my message. It was because you feared
me, dear, feared that I should not love you now that your back
is bent and your beard is white. You did not know, you did not
understand. It was your very self whom I loved, the thought of
whom made the years of waiting pass like one weary night. And if
I cared for you then, oh! I care for you now so much more tenderly! And I will be with you and cheer you and love you, and never
leave you again forever, dear.'

"'Twenty-nine—thirty—thirty-one.' That was all. Not a look,
not a sign, to show that he even saw the kneeling spirit at his feet.
She laid her hands about his arm, her face upon his knee. He never
turned. She implored him with passionate beseeching to give her
one word, one glance. His words and glances were for his gold
alone.

"Then, soft and low, she began to recall to him the memory
of their dead love. Of the day when he had first seen her; of that
when they had looked into each other's eyes and known the truth;
of the dream-world in which they had lived, oblivious of all, indifferent to all without.

"And as she spoke, slowly a dim uneasiness crept into the shadowy form. From time to time he raised his head, and passed his
claw-like hand across his deep-set sunken eyes. The look of greedy
contentment gave place to one of struggle, of vague and clouded
effort. 'What was it?' he murmured to himself once or twice.
'What was it? I can't think.'

"But the struggle always died away; and bending once more over his gold, he resumed his dreary count. Then as the sweet voice pleaded, he would raise his head and gaze at her with dim, unseeing eyes.

"At last a look of dull, faint recognition came across him. His troubled glance remained fixed on the gleaming head at his knee, on which the last slanting sunbeam had settled. She waited breathless. Slowly, with vague, uncertain motion, he stretched his hand to the table and gathered in his skinny fingers one ghostly, golden coin. For one instant, he laid it gently against her shining hair, and gazed at her with pitiful, bewildered eyes. Then the cloudy darkness gathered once more about him; he gave one tremulous sigh, and shaking mournfully his withered head, laid the coin on the table.

"'Thirty-three—' he counted.

"Then she sank on the floor beside him, with a wailing, sobbing cry. 'He does not know me; he does not even hear me!'

"The light died out of the room, and left it damp and dull. Fainter and fainter grew the figures of the lovers; and as they faded from my sight, there came to me, I know not whence, a word to say:

"'He does not hear you. He never will hear you. You fixed your love on the changing, and it has changed. "Where the heart has been, there the spirit must abide." His heart was with his gold, and his gold he will finger forever, blind and deaf to all beside, while you, poor ghost, forever struggle in vain to recall to him the dead love that died with his youth.'

"Scarcely knowing what I did, I hurried from the house and took the train for Bayford. The evening air restored me, and it was with a sense of sadness and of solemn calm, that I got out six hours later, at the little station. At the door of our house, my brother Henry met me, with strangely troubled face.

"'Ellen!' he exclaimed. 'But I am grateful. We need you here.'

"'What has happened?'

"'I hardly know. Everything is in confusion, and no one understands. Dear little Mabel fell into a swoon at four o'clock this afternoon. No one can rouse her, and she lies as if dead.'

"I sent them all away, even my poor Harry, from the room where the white, lovely form was lying. For nearly an hour I worked and watched her. At last the pale lids quivered, the dilated eyes met mine, and she put out feebly a transparent little hand, which looked as if every particle of blood had been withdrawn from it.

"'What does it mean, Aunt Ellen?' she sighed. 'I—we—were talking, Harry and I,—on this sofa. And as we talked, there glided into the room,—Aunt Ellen! I do not know what she was. She came straight to me and hissed in my ear. 'Why should you rejoice while I suffer?' she said, 'And—'

"The awe-struck little voice died away. The death-like swoon had gathered her again.

"But she did not die. You have heard, Alice, of the long and terrible illness that followed so mysteriously on her engagement, and of how she was won back to life again by the tenderness and devotion of your cousin Harry. You know too, how frail ever since has been her hold on existence. The doctors call the trouble nervous prostration, I believe. A convenient word, my dear, that covers a great many things."

THE GREEN LADY
WALTER HERRIES POLLOCK

Longman's Magazine, 1888

It was some time since I had seen my friend Morton, and the last I had heard of him was that in one of his many whims he had taken an old country house for a year and had gone to live there with his sister, vowing that he had done with London for ever. At the time of which I write he had been in the house for nearly a month; therefore I confidently expected to see him very soon in town. Nor was I deceived in this, for one fine morning as I was coming out of a club to which we both belong, I heard him asking if Mr. Latimer was in the club. I went up and spoke to him, and he turned round and shook hands with me with unusual warmth.

"You," he said, "are the very man I wanted to see. Come into the smoking-room—there'll be nobody there now—and I'll tell you all about it."

I followed him, not in a very curious frame of mind, for I felt a certainty that "it" was some more or less ingenious excuse which he had invented to himself for leaving the country house after the first month of the twelve for which he had taken it. In this belief, as will be seen, I was mistaken. After we had sat down he remained silent for a space, gazing alternately straight into the empty fire-place and then sideways at me with a queer look as of one who had a confidence to make but shrank from making it. Once or twice indeed he almost began to speak and suddenly stopped himself. Finally I broke the silence by saying, "Well, old chap, what about the house?"

He replied eagerly, and as if relieved, "That's just it, Darsie; that's what I want to talk to you about."

"I suppose," I answered, "that you want to give it up and would like to pass on the agreement if it can be arranged."

"Give it up be hanged!" said Morton; "I was never so bent on staying in a place in my life."

"Indeed," I continued with the surprise natural to one who knew his restless character, "is it so very agreeable?"

"On the contrary," he made answer, "it's so deuced disagreeable. Now don't interrupt"—I had done nothing of the kind—"and I'll tell you all about it." He had said that before, but I was not indiscreet enough to tell him so, and he proceeded with his narrative.

"When I took Grey Towers" (that was the name of the country house) "you were not in London, or I should have called you into council." I bowed acknowledgment, well knowing that if he had done so it would have been for the purpose of having somebody to disagree with.

"It belongs to a relation of mine who never lives there, and it had been empty for a considerable time. Too large for most people, but I like to have lots of room."

"That," I said, "is true enough," remembering Morton's habit of constantly changing and interchanging the purpose of every room in his house.

"Yes, yes," he said impatiently. "Well, I knew what kind of house it was although I'd never been there—an Elizabethan mansion, moat, family pictures, owner's and my own ancestors, shaven lawn, peacocks, cut yews, box edgings, priest's room, haunted room; all the bag of tricks, in fact. Drainage had been lately put in perfect order; climate excellent; fine old library left open for my use: everything perfect, in fact."

"Then," I said, in a moment of forgetfulness, "I don't quite understand your sticking to the place."

"Didn't I tell you," replied Morton with a touch of irritation, "that there turned out to be something very much the reverse of perfect in it? If you'll only let me get in a word edgeways I'll explain."

"Do so, Barkins, do so," I answered, quoting a great actor.

"My sister," Morton went on, "was delighted with the place. So was I. So were the servants. So was even the Incomparable One." (This was the name by which Morton's confidential valet was known among us.) "In fact I feared that, as you hinted just now, the place might turn out to be far too perfect to suit me."

"Yes," I observed, "perfection is monotonous, and you don't like that."

"I can assure you," said Morton, "that I have had mighty small chance of trying it at Grey Towers. It was for a very brief period— two or three days, I forget which—that the sameness of excellence endured. And when it ceased—" Morton here exhibited as eloquent an aposiopesis as I have heard, or rather as I have *not* heard.

"Why, what happened?" I asked.

"That," retorted Morton, "is precisely what I am anxious to find out. Part of what happened I can tell you in a very few words, but 'the greatest is behind,' and that is what I want to get at."

"So," I interposed, "the whole for once is really greater than a part."

"Just so," replied my companion; "but let me tell you the part. At the expiration of two or three days one of the housemaids gave warning, making some rather hollow excuse and saying that she was sorry to leave so good a place, but really had no choice in the matter. The next day another one followed suit, and then came the kitchen-maid. Then the housekeeper was closeted with my sister for some time, and then my sister came and begged me to see the housekeeper. This I did, and when she came in I said, 'What is all this, Mrs. Thompson?'

"'Well, sir,' she replied, 'I wish I rightly knew; but my belief is that if things goes on much longer as they are going on now there won't be a servant as will be left in the place in a few days' time.'

"'The Haunted Room, Mrs. Thompson?' I said interrogatively.

"'No, sir,' she replied, 'not that particularly. I've been in old houses like this before, and most of them has a Haunted Room, and I have noticed that it's generally next door to the priest's room; but I've never known much trouble come of the regular Haunted Room before. Besides, if that was all, sir, you could have it shut up. No, it's more than that, sir. It's all over the place like.'

"'What is all over the place?' I asked.

"'Well, sir, things as oughtn't to be, from what I make out.'

"'Indeed. I hope you don't believe any of this nonsense, Mrs. Thompson?'

"'I don't rightly know what to believe, sir.'

"'Well, what do these silly girls say they've seen?'

"'With some it's seeing and with some it's hearing, sir. Martha, that was the under-housemaid, there was a picture of an old man in the top room she slept in, and she said it came down and stood by her bedside and looked at her in a dreadful threatening way the first night, and just when she was going to scream it vanished away; and the second night it came down again, and just as she was putting her head under the bedclothes it put a cold hand on her forehead and she nearly fainted away. Then there was Jane, the housemaid, sir; she heard voices in the corner of her room, one shrill and like a woman's that said in a cruel way, *Shall I do it now?* and the other deep and gruff that answered, *No; wait for two nights;* and they said this over and over again, and she said she'd rather not wait. Then there was Selina, that's the kitchen-maid; she was sent into the kitchen garden to gather some herbs that the gardener had forgotten, and just as she was rising up from stooping to gather them if there wasn't—that's what she says—a little grey man in an old-fashioned-looking suit, with a spud in his hand, right in front of her; and he laughs a nasty chilly kind of laugh, and says he, *Herbs you call 'em,* he says; *you was born two hundred years too late.* With that she gave a screech, not knowing quite why, and there was nothing in front of her but a tall bush."

"'Extremely probable,' I said. 'All this is the talk of ignorant, superstitious girls. May I ask if you have seen or heard anything odd, Mrs. Thompson?'

"Mrs. Thompson folded her hands and looked straight up to the ceiling.

"'Come, come, Mrs. Thompson,' I said, 'let us have it all out. In talking to you I am speaking with a woman of sense, and it is important you should tell me all you can that may throw light on this business.'

"'Well, sir,' said Mrs. Thompson, 'it may be fancy or it may not be, but goodness knows I was thinking of nothing of the kind when I saw—or seemed as if I saw—a procession of monks going up the great grass walk between the moat and the ha-ha.'

"'Monks! how do you know they were monks?' I asked.

"'They was dressed like those in *Faust* at the Lyceum,' said Mrs. Thompson, not an imaginative person, and the answer so far was conclusive.

"'Thank you, Mrs. Thompson; that will do,' I said. 'I must consider what steps it is best to take in this business.'

"Well," Morton went on, "things did not get any better after my interview with Mrs. Thompson. My sister came down to breakfast the next morning looking very white and worn; but she is not a talkative person and I asked her no questions. Indeed, if I had she would not have answered them. Presently the butler—a model of discretion—wished to speak with me. He slept in a room overlooking the moat, and through his window, which was left open, he had heard a noise as of people paddling about and talking to each other in hoarse whispers. He did not suggest any ghostly explanation, and of course I did not, but while I entrusted him with a double-barreled gun I could not help remembering that the old boat which was still moored in one corner of the moat was more than half rotten. Then the boy, a pert youth, said he wouldn't stay in a place where the moment he'd cleaned the knives they got dirty again and looked as if somebody had been trying to saw wood with them; and the footman explained that he was not used to practical jokes and could not think it due to himself to remain where they were played. It appeared that he had found the pepper-box filled with snuff, the salt-cellar with sugar, the mustard-pot with treacle, and the marmalade-jar with chutney."

"Looks like Brownies," I interposed.

"Yes," said Morton somewhat wearily; "we have 'em of all sorts, as you will see. In the garden is a rockery with a fountain and cascade, and the gardener intimated that he was not accustomed to a waterfall making faces at him and wouldn't stay where he was expected to put up with it."

"Kühleborn," I said. "I should not have thought it of him."

"Nor I, Darsie," replied Morton; "but after the loss of his niece what can you expect? However, in this part of the proceedings there was a touch of humour. Not so with other branches of the affair. We managed to get a man-servant to sleep for one night in the room where the maid had heard voices, and the next day he left. He too had heard voices, but with a difference. He described a whispering and muttering as of many persons holding secret counsel together, and then a dead, cold silence, broken by a fierce whisper of *Is it time?* Then many voices seemed to say with a horrible hiss *Yes;* and then he said he felt, although he saw nothing, that a man was standing over him with a knife, and then he fainted. I needn't tell you all the things I heard of, but here is one more. One of my nephews came to stay with us for a few nights, and his first night in the house I put him in a cheery-looking oak-paneled room. I had noticed, as it happened, that there was a space between the wall on one side of this room and the room next to it. There might formerly have been a passage there, or it might have been a hiding-place in troublous times—a kind of supplement to the Priest's Room. Anyhow there was nothing remarkable in the fact. But the boy told me that he was waked in the small hours by some one chanting prayers and psalms in Latin in a low weak voice just outside his room. Then he heard a tramp of feet and a rattle of steel, and then a miserable groan and a heavy fall, and then all was still. He is a nervous boy, but plucky, and after he had lain quaking a little while he made up his mind that it was nightmare and rats, and wanted to sleep in the same room again. However I made some excuse for preventing that, and soon afterwards he left us without having been disturbed again."

Morton paused awhile, and I struck in with, "Have you yourself, Morton, seen or heard anything of this strangely inclusive assortment of Presences?"

"Well," he answered with some hesitation, "not absolutely, but it may be that Bruno" (his favourite mastiff) "has."

"How was that?" I asked.

"In this way," he replied." There was something wrong with the lock of my study door, and I had had it put in order by the village locksmith. My sister and the servants had gone to bed, and Bruno and I were alone in the study at night, when it occurred to me to try the result of the locksmith's handiwork. I locked, unlocked, and relocked the door several times, and finally, having locked it, I happened to think suddenly of a passage I wanted to look up in Apuleius, and acting on the thought, took the book from its shelf and sat down in my armchair with Bruno at my feet. I got interested and absorbed, and it may have been half an hour before my attention was aroused by a low growl from Bruno. At the same time I felt a cold wind on the back of my neck."

"Ausgespielt," I ventured to interpose.

"Deuce a bit," said Morton; "it was a real draught. I looked round and saw the door that I had locked, and which opened outwards, slowly unclosing itself and swinging inwards. As it opened so did Bruno retreat backwards, still growling, with his eyes and coat both staring horridly, until when it was wide open he gave a dolorous whine, dropped down with his head between his fore paws, and lay there trembling and whimpering."

"And what did you do?" I asked.

"I went and shut the door," he replied with a manner that prevented me from asking if he had had any difficulty in doing so.

"You saw and heard nothing?"

"Nothing but what I have told you."

"You are sure the door was locked and opened the wrong way?"

"I can't swear to it, but I'm sure about the dog."

"Ah! What of the Incomparable One?"

"He says he has heard strange sounds and seen odd sights, but he doesn't mind them. I don't think he's much of a 'sensitive.'"

"Well," I went on, "it appears to me that you have got some very undesirable and uninvited guests at Grey Towers."

"That is my impression," returned Morton; "and now perhaps you understand why I am bent on sticking to the house."

"Quite so. At the same time you can't live there without any servants, and if these disturbances, however caused, go on, that is what it will come to."

"Exactly," Morton said, "and that is why I have come to you for help and counsel."

"If," I said, "you like to try an experiment—"

"Why, of course I do," he interrupted

"You will get into a hansom with me and come to a certain house in the Adelphi."

"I am with you," said Morton, and we accordingly started.

When I discharged the cab we found ourselves opposite the door of a house divided into chambers, with the names of the owners written up in the passage. "First floor and ground floor, Mr. Peregrine," I read out from this list; "that's our man."

"Peregrine?" said Morton. "Haven't I seen his name in connexion with a private inquiry office?"

"Yes," I replied, "but not a private inquiry of an ordinary kind, as you will soon find out. He is an old friend of mine and a somewhat remarkable person. Quite young still; has travelled a good deal, knows many languages, is very agreeable, and takes a great interest in magic, which he studied in the East."

"Come, come, Darsie," said Morton, "your taking all the Grey Towers stories so quietly was odd enough, but I thought it was explained when I saw that this Peregrine was a kind of head of a detective office."

"So he is," I replied.

"But now you say he's a sort of magician."

"So he is," I repeated. "But instead of speculating about him, let us come up and see him. I think he may be able to help you, but I cannot be sure."

"Very well," said Morton, shrugging his shoulders, and we ascended to Peregrine's office. This was like most offices in that it had an office chair and table, but unlike most in having walls hung with good pictures and little tables covered with articles of bigotry and virtue. In the office chair, with the mouths of various speaking tubes within his reach, sat Peregrine himself—a slight, tallish man of between thirty and forty, clean shaven and with a curiously Oriental cast of face. He rose and came forward to shake hands with me, and then I introduced Morton, whom he received with pleasant if elaborate courtesy. We talked awhile *de omnibus rebus,* and then Morton proceeded to tell Peregrine what it was that troubled him, making the narrative as concise as possible but not forgetting any of the points that he had told me. Peregrine sat listening with a note-book in front of him, but so far as I could judge confined himself to entering each variety of Mysterious Appearance as Morton detailed it. When Morton had finished his story Peregrine considered for a moment and then said, "You have not told me how long the house had been empty before you took it. Do you know?"

"Yes," replied Morton; "five years."

"And do you happen to know if it had any reputation for being—well, let us say strange before then?"

"I have made all possible inquiries," answered Morton again, "and I cannot find that six years ago there was supposed to be anything more odd about it than a vague tradition of the figure of a priest being sometimes seen in the Priest's Room."

"Ah! common enough," rejoined Peregrine in a dry, business-like tone. "Five years ago. Let me see." With this he gave a turn to a revolving bookstand that stood at his elbow and took from one of its shelves a thick manuscript volume, the leaves of which he turned over with deliberate swiftness. "Five years ago," he continued, half to himself, as he looked at page after page; "it fits exactly. Black Abbey burnt down, Grange Mount rebuilt, the room at Drippingwell Hall stripped to the stone walls and new paneled, the Convent Walk at St. Jude's unturfed and graveled, and—yes, here's another—of course that is it. As for the practical jokes, they're not worth tracing. Might happen anywhere. Kühleborn—a piece of impertinence, but not ill-meant. Well—well." All this Peregrine said with his face bent down towards his manuscript book, while Morton looked at me in much surprise, raising his eyebrows as if to question whether Peregrine was playing the fool or was, indeed, something more than a fool. Suddenly Peregrine looked up.

"Any old women about the passages?" he asked in a sharp tone, as a doctor might say, "Any pains in the head?"

"No," said Morton, still astonished, "none that I know of."

"No ladies in purple or grey, or any other colour, that come to meet you and suddenly vanish, eh?"

"No," said Morton again, "none that I know of."

"Back a woman against the lot," said Peregrine, again dropping into his half-aside tone, and then resumed his direct address to Morton by saying, "Sooner or later I think I can set this all right for you. May be able to put things in train at once. Will you allow me?"

So saying he whistled into a speaking-tube, and having heard an answering whistle, called down it, "Is the Green Lady at home?"

"I'll see, sir," came the answer, quickly followed by an assurance that the Green Lady was at home.

"Ask her to speak to me for a moment," said Peregrine, and immediately afterwards whistled down the tube again. Again came an answering whistle, but one quite different from that which had previously been heard. This one, though not so loud, was of so strange a quality that both Morton and I involuntarily started, while Peregrine looked at us with a quiet, benevolent smile. The sound seemed to carry more with it than any whistle, low or loud, ought to carry; it had some far-off kinship with the whistle which Signor Boïto gives to his Mefistofele, and yet it was not like that. Indeed, it was not like anything one had heard before, but had a strangeness all its own, and seemed charged not so much with terror as with the peculiar sense of uneasiness and disquiet that goes before a thunderstorm. Peregrine smiled again, and again spoke down the tube in a language which sounded Oriental, but with which neither Morton nor I was acquainted. Only here and there we caught the name *Grey Towers*. An answer came up through the tube, seemingly in the same language which Peregrine had employed, and in a tone of which the effect corresponded closely enough to that produced by the whistle. Peregrine looked over at us with an expression of amused content, and spoke down the tube again, this time in English, and as I thought for the express purpose of puzzling us.

"Thank you, my dear," he said. "You can start as soon as you like, and if you can engage one or two of the well-behaved ones so much the better. You know the terms and the commission. Only, mind, the place must be cleared in a week. And now, Mr. Morton," he said, turning to my friend, "I see you are not unwilling to have an explanation of all this, and you shall have one if, as I expect, all goes well, in a very short time. Just for the present I must ask you

to be content not to burst but to rest in ignorance. Do you pro-
pose returning to Grey Towers before the week which you heard
me mention has elapsed?"

"I had thought of going back to-night and asking Latimer to
accompany me," replied Morton, who was by this time in the state
of a man whom nothing can surprise.

"There can be no objection," observed Peregrine; "only I must
beg, if my plan is to succeed, to make one condition with you. It
is not a difficult one. If you should meet a lady in a—in somewhat eccentric attire on the staircases, or in the passages, or in
the grounds, or, in short, anywhere about, please do not notice or
interfere with her in any way. This is important. You will undertake this? Thank you. If you will kindly speak to my head clerk
as you go out he will make all business arrangements with you.
One moment. Perhaps it might be as well if you could devise some
story to account for the presence of a—a strange lady to whatever
servants are still staying with you. It may save trouble." And with
this Peregrine bowed us out.

"This is an odd business," said Morton when we got into the
street; "but as I've consulted Peregrine I'll go by his advice and see
it out according to his instructions. We shall just catch the next
train if we start now."

We occupied part of our time on the journey—the day of the
week was Tuesday—in devising a more or less plausible tale to
account for the presence which Peregrine had told us to expect
of a strange lady, and arrived at Grey Towers in time for dinner.
Morton's sister informed us that nothing new had happened in the
way of disturbance, but that some of the old experiences had been
repeated and that some more servants had given warning. He in
return took her into confidence concerning our visit to Mr. Peregrine. I watched with some curiosity to see how she would receive
his story; she is a woman of strong nerve, strong judgment, and
little speech. She heard him out and said quietly, "I think Mr.
Peregrine is a man of sense." She went to bed early, and Morton
and I went to the billiard room, where presently entered to us the
Incomparable One with bottles and glasses. Having put his tray
down, he stopped and looked inquiringly at Morton.

"Well, what is it?" asked Morton.

"Beg pardon, sir," replied the confidential valet, "but I told you about those lights and noises."

"Yes; what of them?"

"They were there again to-night, sir, and a curious thing happened."

"What was it?"

"The lights were flashing and hopping about in the passage to the anteroom, and I heard mutterings and whisperings all round, when the lights grew gradually dim, and I saw—or I thought I saw—a woman taller than any of the women in the house come along the passage. I could not hear her footfall, but I thought I could hear the rustle of her dress, and she seemed to lift up her hand with a commanding gesture, and then the lights all went out and the noises ceased. I thought you might like to know, sir."

"Thank you. Did you see how she was dressed?"

"No, sir; it was too dark."

"Very good. I rely upon you not to say a word of this to anyone else. And if you see this woman again don't take any notice."

"Very good, sir," said the essence of discretion, and left us.

"The Green Lady!" said I to Morton.

"May be," he replied. "Let us go to the room where my nephew slept."

We went, taking glass-shaded candles with us. Now both Morton and I remembered the story his nephew had told about the room, and therefore it cannot be denied that imagination may have caused us to think that on entering the room we heard a scuffle behind the wainscoting, followed by the clank of steel, which gave way to a rustling sound as of a silk dress, which in its turn was succeeded by absolute silence. We left the room and exchanged our impressions, which were as above recorded.

The next day, as was once said in evidence before a Grand Jury by an engaging pawnbroker's boy who came to a sudden stop in the midst of a too fluent and probable story—"the next day nothink 'appened." But in the evening, after Morton's sister had gone to bed, an idea occurred to me. "What was it you told me about strange doings in the moat?" I asked Morton. *"Singular Conduct of a Rotten Boat* might have been the heading in a newspaper, might it not?"

"Yes," Morton replied; "it was something of that kind that the butler told me."

"Then," said I, "let us go down to the moat." There was just enough moon to show us our way without the help of a lantern, and we took up our station just opposite to the butler's window. In about five minutes we heard a distinct splashing in the water.

"Water rats," I whispered to Morton.

"Hush!" he whispered back angrily; "listen!"

I did, and presently through the gentle plash, plash which still went on we both heard a low curious voice say, *No! I will not have it.* Then the splashing ceased and all was quiet.

We looked at each other.

"The same voice," I said.

"Yes," replied Morton, "not a doubt of it. I think that will do for to-night." So we went back and played one game at billiards and then went to bed.

The morning of the following day, Thursday, we spent in idleness and lawn tennis, and, whether by design on each person's part or by chance, no reference was made to the Singular Manifestations until we all met at luncheon. Then Morton's sister said: "Have you been in the grass walk this morning?"

We replied that we had not, and I ventured to ask why the inquiry was made.

"For this reason," she answered. "You remember Mrs. Thompson's story about what she called the Monks?"

"Quite well," replied Morton. "Anything new about them?"

"This much. Either she was not far wrong or some strange folk got into the garden this morning, for as I was going up the grass walk I distinctly saw a person, either in a long brown ulster or in a brown monk's frock, going quickly into a by-path, followed by a woman in a green dress. You may imagine that I pursued them, but when I got to the path there was nothing there."

"Was she tall?" asked Morton.

"She was tall. Perhaps it was Mr. Peregrine's Green Lady."

"Perhaps it was," said Morton, and then we went back to lawn tennis.

On Friday morning at about twelve the new gardener asked for an interview with Morton, with whom I was sitting at the time in the smoking-room.

"Coming to give warning?" I said to Morton, interrogatively. "More Appearances?"

"Not so sure," Morton answered. "I'll have him in. Don't you go. Stay and see it out."

Accordingly the new gardener came in bashfully. He stood first on one leg, then on the other, twirling a hat characteristic of gardening between his hands, and twice addressed himself to motion as he would speak, and ended in a kind of crowing gape.

"Come, Williams," said Morton, "speak out. Don't be afraid of astonishing me."

"Well, sir," said the gardener, taking heart, "since you say so. I did hear, sir, that the last gardener left on account of something wrong with the cascade."

"Wrong," said Morton. "Well—why—yes—you may call it wrong."

"There was something, sir, if I'm not mistaken—and I'm here to be set right, sir, if I am—about what he called a face that made shapes at him in the water. Childish stuff it seemed to me, sir, till—" here the gardener stopped short and twirled his hat again.

"Till what?" cried Morton, eagerly. "What is it?"

"Well, sir," replied the gardener, "if you wouldn't mind coming to see for yourself. I know I'd never a' believed it."

"Come along, Darsie, quick," said Morton. "You lead the way, Williams, to where you saw—whatever it is."

"Kühleborn," I gasped out to Morton as we ran at top speed to the cascade, and again he replied, "We shall see."

We did see. There most unmistakably was a distinct though constantly shifting face—a face as distinct, that is, as can be made by falling water—in the very centre of the cascade, the face of an old, old man, with long hair and beard; and though the features were, of course, somewhat blurred, there was no doubt that what passed for the mouth seemed curled in innumerable varieties of derision; indeed, as the gardener had said, made "shapes" at us continually, while the clatter and echo of the falling water sounded like broken conscienceless laughter. We looked at each other in silence, a silence broken by the low piercing sound of the whistle we had heard in Peregrine's rooms. This strange sound overpowered for the moment all others, and even as it was heard the face in the water seemed to vanish into fantastic but meaningless jets and bubbles. I thought, indeed, that I saw the expression change rapidly to fury, and then to fear, but that may have been fancy.

"I don't think you'll have any more trouble, Williams," said Morton, and we walked away.

"Explicit de Kühleborn," I observed.

"Yes," replied Morton. "Poor old chap!"

There remained but one more task that we knew of for our honoured but mysterious and practically unseen guest, and that was accomplished with dexterity, skill, and much more than punctuality—for she had had a full week allowed to her—on Friday night. Morton and I were sitting in his study late at night, deep in argument, when suddenly Bruno, who was lying on the rug, gave a low growl. With the same impulse we both looked at the door, which this time of course was not locked. It slowly opened *inwards,* and the more it opened the more Bruno growled uneasily. When the door had opened about half-way it very slowly and as if unwillingly swung back again. Bruno rose to his feet, and as the door suddenly clapped to with a bang he lolloped towards it, barking with delight. Morton and I ran to the door before him, flung it open outwards, and rushed into the passage just in time to see a green skirt disappearing round the corner.

The next day we met the Green Lady. She was standing at the top of the stairs as we came up them, a tall commanding presence in an old-fashioned green silk dress with a fur tippet round her neck. Mindful of Peregrine's warning, we passed on as if unmindful of her being there, and whether we walked through her or whether she vanished exactly as we approached her, I do not know. Anyhow she was there one moment and not there the next. We turned to compare notes as to her appearance and entirely agreed, but neither of us could speak a word as to her features. After this, for the three weeks that we stayed in the house, Morton, his sister, and I saw her frequently, but we never exchanged any sign of recognition. Whether the servants—the missing places were soon filled now that the house was quiet—whether the servants saw her or not I do not know. The Incomparable One had undertaken to keep them quiet if they did. Morton of course wrote to thank Peregrine. So, save for her fitful appearances, to which we were accustomed, life went on just as it might in any other country house of the same kind as Grey Towers; and of course before the month was up Morton was tired of it and we went up to London with an intention on his part to get rid of the remainder of his term if he could.

The day after our departure he and I met at the club, and he proposed to call on Peregrine, to which I at once assented. We found him, as before, ensconced in his luxurious office, and he welcomed us even more warmly than before.

"I was on the very point of writing to you," he said.

"Nothing wrong, I hope?" said Morton, answering his tone rather than his words.

"Well—no—not now at least, I hope. You see, the fact is the Green Lady took such a liking to you or to the house, or both, that I began to fear she never would come back. Now that you have deserted the Towers I shall probably see her very soon. She does not like solitude, and of course she couldn't ask any of the old lot back. Her loss would have been very great to me. She is a most invaluable—a—person."

I saw Morton was getting more and more eager in curiosity, and so struck in with, "You promised, Peregrine, that you would exp—"

"So I will," he interrupted. "It is really quite simple. Those—a—people who worried you were in wonderful luck to find such a refuge as Grey Towers when they were turned out of their own places. Wonderful luck—and a fine time they must have had of it. But they're wanting in judgment and sense. Now, the Green Lady has both to a remarkable degree, is of the very oldest—a—descent, and knows a great deal more than all of them put together. A mixed lot those—a common lot (barring Kühleborn), but nasty to tackle. I knew she would make a clean sweep of them. But I really don't know a single other—a—person who could have dealt with such a crew so neatly and so quickly. When her own place fell to pieces some time ago she was glad enough to come to me: I had only just started the agency then. I have never known her take such a fancy to a place before. To be sure it's the best and oldest house she has been sent to yet, to say nothing of other attractions. But, upon my word, I was getting quite alarmed—quite alarmed. Ah! there she is!" he said with a pleased smile as the peculiar whistle came up the speaking-tube. "All's well that ends well. Now you won't think me rude, but I shouldn't like her to know that you're here, so I'll say good-bye. You understand it all now."

"There is no room for misapprehension," said Morton. And we went away.

MY UNCLE'S CLOCK
ANONYMOUS

Macmillan's Magazine, 1888

I have heard people talk a good deal about my grandfather's clock, but I really think that my uncle's clock was a more remarkable thing. I did not notice anything peculiar about it in his lifetime, except that it was always stopped, being in this respect the exact opposite of that well-known clock of everybody's grandfather which went on ticking to the exact moment of the old gentleman's death. My uncle's clock stood in his bed room, on the mantelpiece; and I always wondered that he, who liked everything about him to be in order, wound up, and working punctually, should allow this solitary specimen of incapacity to stare him in the face night and morning with a lying account of the hour. Once or twice when my uncle has been ill and I have gone to see him, I have walked up to that clock with the intention of setting it going and putting it right, but my uncle always stopped me with the significant remark: "I rather think I'd let that clock alone, if I were you, James."

I took the hint without asking any questions. My uncle was not the sort of man who would stand a catechism very well; indeed, there were some points concerning his personal history, and the manner in which he had made his fortune, about which his most intimate friend, if at all a prudent man, would judge it best to make few inquiries. I do not mean that my uncle was not an honourable member of society, and a very useful one too: many owners of valuable estates, many county families remember him still with respectful gratitude; but his occupation was of a very peculiar sort, one which would not bear much talking about: he was, in fact, a remover of ghosts.

What he did with the ghosts when he had got them nobody could guess. He did not travel with much luggage, and could not have carried them away in his boxes. They were not in his own home: a quieter, better-ordered establishment than that never existed: the very rats were not allowed to make a noise there. One thing only was certain, that when he undertook to remove a ghost that ghost never went back again: it was heard of no more. His knowledge of the world of phantoms was immense: I think I may say unique. He had studied all the existing literature of the subject, until there was not a ghost anywhere in the three kingdoms with whose habits, weaknesses, and prejudices he was not familiar. Not a phantom of them all could resist him: he could twist the whole spectre-world (it is not, I believe, a very intelligent world) round his little finger. There was nothing he enjoyed more than facing an obstinate and self-opinionated old ghost—a ghost of a few hundred years' standing, with a conceit to match his age—having it out with that old ghost, and reducing him to submission.

My uncle never advertised himself in any way, and had to be approached cautiously by all who desired his services. He kept his ghost-laying within the strict limits of a profession, though one not generally acknowledged or frequently followed, and refused wages, though he would take a fee. His first effort was, I believe, achieved solely to oblige a friend: afterwards a whisper of his extraordinary powers went round, and every man who had a haunted house which he could not let, every family pursued by a dogged phantom which stuck to the ancestral residence after its natural term was over, every person afflicted by an attendant spectre, applied to my uncle for relief. He never refused it, when it was properly asked for. On receiving a summons to the practice of his profession, he packed up his traps and went off with his manservant. Sometimes it would take him weeks to remove a ghost: sometimes he would do it in half an hour. The fees he received for his services varied from a hundred pounds (he never would take less,—rather than that, he did his work for nothing) to a thousand. There was one old gentleman who had been very much bothered for many years by an irritating phantom, who was always washing his hands in his presence, and asking him for a towel—an under-bred ghost that, and one without any sense of the fitness of things! When this old gentleman was relieved of his trouble his gratitude was so great that, besides paying the customary fee, he left in his will five thousand pounds and perpetual right in the ghost, to my uncle and his heirs for ever. *I* was my uncle's heir, but I did not know of the whole extent of his possessions when I stepped into them.

Well, my uncle died, and the secret of the ghosts, and what he had done with them, died with him. He left everything to me, and I immediately determined to have that clock put to rights. I could not do away with it, because there was a special clause in his will that it was to be left where it was, in the same room, on the same mantelpiece, facing the bed in which I intended to sleep. If I sent away that clock I forfeited my uncle's fortune: the estate and the clock went together, and were by no means, nor at any time, to be separated. However, if I could not get rid of this piece of furniture, I could make it go; and this I resolved to do.

The first night that I slept in that particular room I had reached home late after a long journey, and, being very tired, forgot my resolution. I never had a better night's sleep in my life. But the next morning when I awoke, the clock faced me with its fingers impudently and lyingly pointing to half-past two, when, as a matter of fact, I knew that it was just eight. I sprang out of bed and attacked that false witness. It wound up easily, and ticked regularly. Its internal organisation had evidently suffered nothing from a prolonged holiday. Throughout the whole of that day it ticked cheerfully and kept well up to time; and as I put my head on the pillow that night, and heard it ticking industriously in the darkness, I felt that I had begun well my stewardship of the fortune left to me: the only thing which wanted doing in my uncle's house I had promptly done. Then followed the peace of a well-earned sleep.

Rats! could it be rats making that noise! Were there ever such impudent, ingenious, multifarious, abominable, and riotous rats as these? I don't know how long I had been asleep, but the noise which awoke me was something distracting. I sat up in bed and listened. No, it could not be rats. Rats could not groan dismally, rats could not giggle foolishly, nor could they wail hysterically. They might run about the passages with the sound as of a hundred pattering feet, but they could not talk in confidential whispers, nor could they appeal piteously for help, nor could they denounce one another in angry human tones.

A happy thought occurred to me. The servants were indulging in private theatricals. They had presumed on my youthful inexperience, and relied on the soundness of my slumbers: they were doubtless giving a ball or some similar entertainment to their friends in the small hours of the night. I got out of bed and made for the door. The passage beyond was in utter darkness. I thought I heard the sound of scuttling feet; then all was still. As I groped my way towards the butler's room, some one seemed to be following me with stealthy steps. I felt for a match, which I had in my pocket, and struck it: no one was near me, but an icy breeze rushed past me as from an open window, and my match went out. I groped my way on to the butler's door and banged at it.

"Timpkins," I said, "what is the meaning of all this?"

There was a moment's pause, and then a tremulous and husky voice answered from inside, "Is that you, sir?"

The fellow's teeth were absolutely chattering from fright: I could hear them, and the sound rejoiced me: it was well that he should feel a wholesome dread of my righteous wrath.

"Of course it's me. Open the door instantly!"

"I daren't, sir, not if it cost me my place"; and the teeth chattered audibly.

"Look here, Timpkins, you'd better not be such a fool as this. Why, man, I sha'n't slay you for it!"

"You, sir!" in an undoubted accent of astonishment, "it's not you that I'm afraid of. Oh, sir"—here the teeth chattered again— "can't you manage them better than this!"

"I'd better begin by managing you," I answered angrily; but he did not seem to hear me.

"Not a servant will stay with you if you let it happen again! They all left before, every one of them, and they'll do it again. I only stopped because your uncle swore to me that it should occur no more, and it didn't. What he did to them, and where he put them, I can't say. But he managed them somehow. There's a noise beginning. Oh, sir, do you think they are coming again!"

"What are you talking about, fellow?—the servants?"

"The servants! Goodness gracious, no, sir! Do you think I'd let them carry on like that! It's not the least use, sir, rattling at that door, for I will *not* open it, not if I leave before breakfast to-morrow! This is not my business, sir, it's yours: you know that well enough, and I really think you might manage it a little better." Here he shuddered till the bed shook under him.

"I'll break the door in, Timpkins, if you don't tell me what you mean. The servants must have been making that awful row, and you know it."

"Not the servants, sir," he answered in a quavering voice; "it was the ghosts!"

The ghosts! the man was mad, or drunk. At that instant somebody certainly laughed a little mocking laugh in my ear, and I did not wait to argue the case any further. I bolted back to my room along the draughty passage, shut the door and locked it. At least there was no more noise that night. I did not sleep, but a peaceful silence prevailed, through which the clock ticked with undiminished cheerfulness.

The following morning Timpkins waited upon me at breakfast with irreproachable demeanour. When the meal was cleared away he respectfully requested permission to speak of the incidents of the night. The other servants had, he said, asked him, as the most experienced of them all in the ways of the house, to lay their grievances before me. I had not quite decided with what front it was best to face the awkward subject of the mysterious disturbance, so I just told him to go forward with what he had to say.

"Every one of them has something to complain of," he began. "There's the under-housemaid declares as a young man came and hanged himself in her room: a most unpleasant thing to happen to any respectable person, and, as the girl herself says, gentlemen should keep to their own rooms and ladies to theirs, even if they do happen to be ghosts. There's not one of them that did not see something last night. I did myself, but I'd rather not speak of it. When I hear a thing in confidence, even from a ghost, I prefer to keep it to myself."

"Do so, by all means. I am not going to believe those ridiculous stories. I heard plenty of noise, but I saw nothing."

"I fancy, sir," he said significantly, "that would be because the ghosts don't properly know that your uncle's gone, so they dare not venture into his room. He had great control over them: I hope you'll manage to get some in time, or you'll have your house empty."

"I don't believe in the ghosts," I answered, with more irritation than truth.

"Well, sir, we all know, though it is not commonly spoken of, that your uncle was a—ahem! a ghost-collector. He went to places, and he brought 'em away with him, but what he did with 'em, and where he put 'em, nobody knew. Once or twice they broke out, and there was an awful row, but that hasn't happened for years. Last night, when the noise began, I said at once, 'They've broken loose again.' I do hope, sir, for your own sake, that you'll somehow manage to get the upper hand of them. Your uncle never gave you, I suppose, sir, a hint how to do it?"

"Never a word!"

"That's bad, but it'll happen come to you. I've spoken to the servants. They all wanted to leave this very day, but I've said to them: 'The new master's young and not experienced in the management of ghosts. Give him a fair trial, and he'll perhaps get them under, as the old master did.' They've agreed to stop for a week, and see how things go on. And I am sure, sir, you've the good wishes of us all that you may get well through with it soon." Then the respectable Timpkins departed, leaving me as much amazed and subdued in spirit as he desired the ghosts to become under my treatment. My treatment, indeed! I felt no ability left within me to cope with the rebellious phantoms who had broken loose.

Timpkins was right in his surmise, for the next night the ghosts invaded my bedroom. I awoke to find them in full possession. They seemed to be enjoying themselves amazingly in their own eccentric manner. There was a regular crowd of them. A lady in patches and high heels was dancing a minuet on the hearth-rug.

A wicked-looking man with a gray beard was depositing a skull and a few other relics of crime in a corner of the room: his manner was really amusingly secretive when you came to consider the crowded state of the apartment, but it did not amuse me at the time. A young man in a Cavalier dress was proposing in the shelter of the window-curtain to a young lady in a Puritan garb. A mad violinist was practising scales at the foot of the bed. A small boy, who produced the effect of having been deserted on the top of a mountain by a wicked uncle (I don't know how he did it in the circumstances, but ghosts have a peculiar talent for the histrionic art, and appear to be quite independent of scenic accessories), was screaming for assistance at the top of his voice. A philosopher was taking notes in my easy-chair. Last, but not least, a highwayman was explaining the details of his execution to me at one side of the bed, while a gentleman in a powdered wig, and holding a snuff-box, related to me old but not venerable Court anecdotes on the other side.

The rest of that night I decline to describe. I reasoned with those ghosts. I stormed at them, I threatened them. Then I began to throw the furniture at them, but they did not even dodge: the missiles went clean through them without damaging them in the least: I broke the looking-glass and the water-bottle, that was all. Most of the ghosts took no notice whatever of my proceedings, but remained absorbed, like lunatics, in their own. One or two paused for a moment to smile at my helpless rage, and the young lady on the hearth-rug actually giggled with amusement. Clearly these ghosts were too many for me!

The next morning at breakfast I informed Timpkins that my portmanteau must be packed at once. I was going away for some time. He smiled a smile of satisfaction. "Very right indeed, sir, and I hope that you'll be successful and bring none of them back when you come!"

Evidently he thought that I was taking the ghosts away, whereas I was only flying from them; but I kept my own counsel, and departed by the midday train. A week's absence from home, in cheerful society and with cheerful surroundings, revived my spirits somewhat. I began to hope that the ghosts would have tired themselves out and gone: they could not always be working so hard. I would, at any rate, run down home and see what was happening there. The place looked so beautiful as I approached it—for my uncle had spared no expense in making it all that a gentleman's residence should be—that I felt quite ashamed of having been driven away from it by a set of paltry ghosts, a mere phantom collection gathered together by my own uncle, principally for his profit, but partly also for his amusement, and out of a sort of virtuoso curiosity. "The finest collection of spectres in the world," so he had been proud to consider them; and was I, the owner of the museum, to be afraid of my own specimens! The idea was absurd. I was received by Timpkins, whose air was preternaturally solemn.

"I'm afraid, sir, that you did not pack them as well as you thought," he remarked gravely. "Some of them must have got loose somehow, for they were at it as bad as ever the night after you left."

"Were they indeed!" I answered grimly.

"And for several nights after that," he went on. "The servants have all left. They stayed their week, and then they went. And as it happened the ghosts have been quiet ever since."

"Exactly so," I answered irritably, "I always said the servants were at the bottom of it."

He looked at me with surprise. "You don't think so, I'm sure, sir. It's just what they call a co-hincidence!"

Coincidence or not, the ghosts let me alone that night, but I got up the next morning in a very bad temper, notwithstanding. My uncle's servants had been admirably chosen, and knew their work thoroughly. It was tiresome to lose them all at one fell swoop of fate. I should have been absolutely alone in the house but for the faithful Timpkins, who still evidently hoped that I should "manage them." He had got the gardener's wife to come and cook for me in our temporary difficulty, and I ought to have been more grateful to him than I was. I am afraid that I wanted an excuse for being savage. I found one in the clock, which had run down in my absence, and had not been attended to. I had not noticed this the night before.

"I declare, Timpkins," I remarked to that ill-used individual, "I think that my own room might at least be taken care of: I can understand that the rest of the house must be at sixes and sevens, but the place I sleep in ought to be in order!"

Timpkins, in whose experienced eye I saw compassion for my pitiable situation, expressed regret that anything had been neglected. He had not been aware of it.

"It's the clock," I answered angrily: "it has not been wound up, a thing that can be done in three minutes!"

"Oh, the clock!" responded Timpkins, his countenance clearing. "I beg pardon, sir, but the old master never allowed any one to touch it. The last housekeeper (a very valuable person, sir) was sent away because she tried to make it go. If you want that clock winding up, sir, I'll take it as a particular favour if you'll do it yourself!"

I felt inclined to quarrel with him on the spot, but on the whole decided that I wouldn't; so I wound up the clock myself. That night, as the intelligent reader will be already aware, the ghosts came again. The intelligent reader has had the advantage of what I may call "selected circumstance" from which to draw his deductions: I was struggling with multifarious circumstances altogether unselected, which I have not put before him. Selected circumstance is what reveals to us the end of novels while the actors in them are struggling in a hopeless fog: this it is which makes us so much wiser than the philosophers, and so much sharper than the detectives, in the books we read. We are not really so clever as we think on most occasions.

Well, the ghosts came again, and I think that on the whole, they behaved rather worse than before. They talked, screamed, groaned, and proposed at the very top of their voices, and without any regard to the proprieties. They quite disturbed the philosopher at his notes, and he looked at me in a remonstrant way, as who should say, "I really do think, you know, that you let them go too far."

But what was I to do! At first I could only add my groans to theirs. After a time the sound of the clock ticking joyously on through all the noise struck me oddly. I ceased my groans to listen to it: a saving thought flashed through my mind: the coincidence existed not with the servants, but with the clock. I leaped out of bed, I rushed through those ghosts as if they had been air—very chilly air they seemed to be too—and I put my finger on the swinging pendulum. There was a low wail of deep dismay, then— oh, joy! oh, happiness! oh, relief! the ghosts were gone!

I drew my breath with a long sigh of satisfaction, and felt the solitude like a Paradise. But my troubles were not all over. The silence lasted about a minute, then I heard a slight sound, as if some one in the corner of the room was trying to speak to me. The voice was faint and uncertain: it trembled and nearly ebbed away, then took body and went on. "I—er—really must protest. I—er—really can't consent to this. It—er—is not fair, not in the contract. You—er—have a perfect right not to wind it up, but to stop it—er—that was never agreed to."

I looked in the corner of the room and saw that the old philosopher had almost gone, but not quite; or, to speak more correctly, he had partly come back again. His form was as indistinct as his voice, it wavered like a candle in a breeze, and tried hard to keep itself together, that his limbs might not part company, like clouds before a tempest. "If you—er—would just let it go again while I talk to you," he pleaded, "the others—sha'n't—come back, and I'll tell you all—er—all about it." He nearly went out then and there, and only by a violent effort braced himself up into comparative solidity. He was a courageous old phantom.

I stood hesitating, with my finger on the clock. A wise man would have let well alone; but I was not wise. I wanted to know "all about it." I wanted to hear the secret of the clock and of the ghosts.

"You are sure they won't come back!" I asked.

"I—er—promise—honour of a gentleman. Just give me a few ticks; so hard to speak without. Ah—er—*thank you*—" in a clear voice of great relief, as I set the clock ticking.

Then the old gentleman began to gesticulate, and to talk violently, not to me, but to the other ghosts. Apparently they were gradually convinced by his eloquence (the details of which I could not quite catch), for it became less and less vehement; and at last

the philosopher turned to me (he was now looking perfectly solid), and said with a smile, "It's all right, they have agreed to leave
the negotiation in my hands. I always had great influence with
them. Your uncle often consulted me on difficult affairs. Now we
can sit down and talk comfortably together.

"Before I go any further in my communication," the phantom
went on, with a glance at the clock which was comfortably ticking in front of us, "I must make one bargain with you, really a
very moderate one. I have a great deal of valuable information to
give you, and you cannot expect to have it, even from a ghost, for
nothing."

"Tell me your terms," I responded with a brevity in strong contrast to his courteous circumlocution.

"They are very simple, very simple, indeed," he said, rubbing
his hands together gently, and keeping his ghostly eye on me;
"just that you should undertake to wind this clock up once a year.
Merely that."

"That will, as I understand," I replied, frowning, "be equal to
an invitation to the—er—to your agreeable friends to come back
and make as much hubbub as they like."

"For eight days only, eight days, or nights, as I should more
accurately say. What are those in a whole year! I must have something in return for what I tell you. Those at any rate are my terms."
He pressed his unsubstantial lips firmly together. To be brief, I
consented. It was again a foolish thing to do, but I was never very
wise, and my curiosity was aroused. I wanted to know about these
curious people who lived somewhere on my premises. I can boast
of as ancient a descent as most people, and one of my earliest
ancestresses (some say the very earliest, but the point is now dis-
puted) brought a good deal of trouble into our family by too
curious a desire to know the flavour of an apple. I had inherited
her curiosity. She was a very distinguished woman, and I am not
going to blush for the family failing which owed its introduction
to her. I consented then. The ghost sat down in my easy chair,
crossed his legs, and began his story with great affability.

"Your uncle was a very admirable man, and I should not wish
to say a word against him. He had unusual powers. Everybody

with unusual powers has a right to exercise them at the expense of weaker creatures. That is, I believe, an axiom of your most advanced thinkers. Having then such powers, he looked about for a subject to give them full scope, and he found—*us*. We were, each in our different spheres, pursuing our appointed tasks with great credit to ourselves and satisfaction to the community. Men respected us, women feared us: we had power, sir, and influence. There was not one of us who had not secured a comfortable situation, and was not doing his best to fulfil his duty in it. We were active then, and useful. We kept alive the past in the memory of the vulgar, who do not read and will not think: we threw out hints of the supernatural: we awakened the emotions of awe, wonder, compassion. Are not these the feelings, sir, which it was the ambition of your mighty poets in the past to inspire by their tragedies? You can all of you reverence Æschylus; but who is grateful to a ghost! However complaints are useless. Your uncle brought us from our various avocations, and shut us up together in a museum, like a set of mummies. What could we do there but become the trivial, miserable, deteriorated beings that we are? The dignity of our profession was gone. We could not frighten one another. We could not act without a public. We became mere puppets, and might as well have been worked by strings."

At this juncture I interrupted him. "Would you mind telling me the locality of that museum?" I asked.

"Not in the least," he answered courteously, "but it would be difficult for you to visit it, and unadvisable. Your uncle had it built on purpose for us. It is an immense underground vault, in a lonely spot in the park; after it was finished, the entrance was walled up and soil thrown over the whole, as before. There is no way in or out, except for ghosts. Your uncle did his best to make it comfortable for us. It is well furnished with secret passages, old pictures, oak-chests, bones, cupboards, curtains, and other articles for which he thought we had a fancy. It is in fact a playground for us, but we wanted to work. Your uncle never could understand that: this was strange, because he understood it well enough for himself. We became so unhappy in that place, that at times we broke out, in spite of our respect for him, and our dread of his punishments, which were very ingenious, very ingenious indeed," added the phantom musingly, as if he remembered one or two which few men would have thought of. I wished that I could think of them.

"At last things got so bad between us, that I was appointed ambassador. I said to your uncle, 'Now look here, let us talk it over as man to man. Ghosts have not many rights, but they have a few, and really, you know, you should not trample them under foot. Our feelings may seem superficial, but they exist, you ought to remember that in dealing with us.' Your uncle listened to me quite kindly, and I put the matter before him still further. 'We don't want much: a very little satisfies us. Some ghosts are content to appear only once in a hundred years or so, but I never heard of a ghost who had not his appointed day out at some time or other. It is not reasonable, it is not fair to deprive him of it. We go on practising our parts down there, and we must have some chance, just the ghost of a chance, as I may say, to appear in them before the public. There must be a possibility of it to keep our minds easy. You ought to allow us that.' 'Very well,' said your uncle, 'I'll drive a bargain with you. Will you undertake that it shall be kept by all the others as well as yourself?' I answered that I was appointed to speak for the rest. 'Then,' said your uncle, 'I offer you this. You are free to come out and enjoy yourselves as you like, whenever that clock on my mantel-piece is going, *but at no other time.*' That was the main feature of the compact we made: there were other small conditions, as that the clock was not to be removed from its place, or wilfully damaged in any way; the room was not to be kept locked up; no one except himself was to know the secret concerning it. These conditions I insisted upon, to give us a real chance of an occasional holiday, and your uncle agreed to them; but, would you believe it, sir," the phantom concluded with a deep sigh, "your uncle had such power of will that never, by any accident, was the clock wound up from that day until the hour of his death."

"And now," I responded gloomily, "I have actually undertaken to wind it up once a year."

"You have received a great deal of information in return," said the ghost cheerfully.

"Which will never be of the slightest use to me," I answered sadly, for the apple was eaten, and the family troubles were before me.

"I wish," I remarked to the philosopher, "that you could induce your friends to behave with a little more moderation when they come to see me next."

"I will use all my influence in that direction," he answered, with a polite bow of farewell. The dawn was breaking, and, like a puff of cold wind, he went past me to his subterranean dwelling.

I next had an interview with Timpkins, and tried to put the situation before him cheerfully. We engaged new servants, who were to arrive in eight days, and for the next few nights we put up with the ghosts as well as we could. Timpkins stood by me manfully during the period, and when the clock had run down, peace prevailed.

The year that followed was a pleasant one. Nobody meddled with the clock, and the ghosts practised their parts silently underground. I liked my uncle's house, and I enjoyed the use of his fortune. I almost forgot at times that it included a collection of phantoms. But the months went on, and the season came when I was obliged to face my difficulties. I dismissed my servants for ten days' holiday, and shut up all the house except my own rooms. I engaged Timpkins to remain with me during the awful week, for a fee of a hundred guineas: this money was to buy his silence also.

"I am afraid, Timpkins," I said sadly, "that we may expect the ghosts again. I am obliged—er—to have a little talk with them."

"That's a pity, sir," said Timpkins, with an air of gloom. "It isn't well to give too many liberties to them creatures. The old master never did it, and it isn't good for 'em, gives them notions, and puts them up to mischief."

"It won't happen often," I answered, apologetically, "only once a year."

"Once a year! Indeed, sir! That's very bad!" said Timpkins severely. He departed then, and I was left alone with the clock.

I took the key in my fingers, and I looked at the innocent timepiece with hatred. Something very like murder was in my heart. Should I dash it to my feet in a thousand fragments!

Such was certainly my inclination, but I doubted the wisdom of indulging it. The ghosts would regard such an act of violence as a destruction of their agreement with my uncle, and would swarm all over the premises at once and for ever. At present they seemed to have the impression (foolish creatures!) that I had the power of keeping them to their treaty as my uncle would have done, and of enforcing penalties for breach of contract. It was as well that they should remain in this delusion: I had no wish to destroy it by any rude shock, nor to enlighten them as to the real depths of my weakness and the poverty of my resources. No, I would do no act of violence: I would keep my word with the phantom philosopher and wind up the clock; therefore I began my task with self-control and outward calmness. But the works were rusty: the damp had got into the inner chimney-wall during the recent rains, and had damaged the clock. Still I persisted in my conscientious efforts to turn the key: still the clock resisted. Then suddenly there was a crack and a whirr, and the key turned round with the greatest ease, for the mainspring was broken.

I sunk down in the easy-chair and rang the bell for the butler, who came running in alarm.

"Timpkins," I said incoherently, "you can send for the servants as soon as you like. It's all right: they'll never come again."

Timpkins looked at the open clockface, and at the key in my hand.

"I understand, sir," he remarked with significance; "I was always sure that had something to do with it. *You've broken the clock!*" Evidently he approved of my action: perhaps he thought I had done it on purpose. I did not undeceive him. It was to the ghosts, and not to him, that I was answerable.

We sent for the servants to return to their duties at once. I telegraphed invitations to some of my friends to come and have a jolly week with me; and a jolly week we had. I never felt so happy in my life, nor so free. Now I can keep my compact with the phantom without fear. I shall turn the key round next Christmas with a light heart, for nothing will follow. And the ghosts have no right to complain, for the thing happened entirely by accident. But I shall not have the clock mended: that was not in the contract.

A NEW GHOST STORY
ANONYMOUS

Belgravia, 1890

It was a wild, wailing evening in December—that melancholy
month when nature pipes in such a minor key that it almost seems
as if the dying year were yielding up its existence reluctantly;
and as on the evening in question there was an occasional rumble of thunder in the air, and the sea was sobbing as well as the
wind, when the waves broke fretfully against the rocky pediment
on which Kinver Castle stood, it might fairly be said that the dia-
pason of dreary sounds had achieved itself.

Nevertheless, though the weather was so inclement, and the
scene without so chill and cheerless—indoors, that is to say inside
the pleasant drawing-room at Kinver, everything spoke of warmth
and comfort, and all the means and appliances of enjoyment were
at hand. For a bright fire was crackling and sparkling in the grate
and diffusing a rich, crimson glow through the room; a fascinating little table, with the green baize cover which connotes whist,
was drawn up before it, and round it were gathered a group of
four merry fellows, who, having cut for partners, were just sitting
down to play their ante-prandial rubber, when one of them, whose
name was Granby and who was the master of the house, suddenly surprised all the others by uttering an exclamation of dismay.
But the fact was, that having chanced to look out of the opposite
window whilst he was seating himself, he caught sight of an object
approaching the house, which at once sent his feelings into an
uncongenial channel and caused him to exclaim ruefully, "O'Mara,
by all that's unfortunate! Was there ever anything so tiresome? He

277

will spoil our rubber, he will bore us to extinction with his long stories, and as I see he has got his portmanteau with him he will never know when to go. Oh, I say, what *is* to be done?"

"Why did you ask him to come, Bobbie dear?" called out Miss Granby from the further end of the room, where she was engaged in playing a game of chess with an old maiden aunt who was a sort of duenna to her and at the same time helped her to do the honours of her brother's bachelor establishment.

"Oh, it was done in a weak moment, confound it! I merely said that if he happened to pass this way he might look us up. But I had no idea the beggar would take me at my word, and so soon too. However, that is neither here nor there nor anywhere at the present juncture. The question is, now that he has come what's to be done with him?"

"Put him in the haunted room, Bobbie," suggested Miss Granby sweetly, "and if you do, you'll find he will not stay long enough to wear out his welcome."

"My dear Nea, you're a mine of wealth to me!" cried her brother delightedly. "The very thing. Of course I'll put him there; and if that doesn't drive him away in less than no time I'll eat my hat. It is a most extraordinary thing," added Granby, turning to his friends, "but no one has ever been able to sleep in that room in my memory, the noises are so fearful. The last person who persisted in spending a night there was an old aunt of mine, and she was found dead in her bed in the morning. Of course, it may only have been a coincidence—indeed I feel pretty sure it was nothing more—but then it was a coincidence of such a very disagreeable nature that it has given the room an additionally evil reputation, and so terrified the servants that none of them would enter it after dark for any consideration. But excuse me for a moment, boys, I must tell Johnson where the portmanteau is to go." And with these words Captain Granby quitted the room.

Meanwhile the unwelcome and ill-fated guest had driven up to the door and got into the hall, where he soon found himself in the hands of the butler and the footman. And when with their assistance he had uncoiled his manifold wraps and emerged from them, he looked so long and narrow that his figure suggested the

idea of a house which had been run up by contract and not made
to last. His face, too, was thin and sallow, and so devoid of all
comeliness, that on one memorable occasion when he was going to
be photographed, his best friend advised him to be taken praying
in his hat. Moreover, his career from first to last had been most
unsuccessful—he used to say himself that at his initial exam., at
Sandhurst, the only thing he passed in was health, and since then,
failure had become chronic with him—and when to these things
are added that he had a somewhat lugubrious tone of voice and a
good deal of the Emerald Isle on the tip of his tongue, it will be
admitted that he was rather heavily handicapped all round. And
yet he was not without his points. For he had a sort of mother-wit
which stood him in good stead sometimes; he possessed a soft
heart and an even temper; and there were many who declared that
he was not such a fool as he looked by any means. Be that as it
might, however, on this particular evening when he was ushered
into the drawing-room, instead of spoiling the rubber, as his host
had anticipated, he at once went over to the other end of the room
and joined the ladies, to whom, presumably, he made himself most
agreeable, as his droll sayings and racy anecdotes elicited many a
merry laugh from them during the next hour or so. Indeed, one of
the whist-players—a gallant dragoon named Herrick, who was very
much smitten with Miss Granby—looked rather indignant when
he perceived that she derived so much amusement from the Irishman's society. And when he found that "the same sort of thing"
went on all through dinner and after it, his indignation deepened
into spleen, which he vented by declaring to his host after the party had broken up, that O'Mara's jokes made him sick, and that he
thought him the most consummate ass he had ever met in his life!

"Well, I think he behaved rather well this evening on the
whole," said Granby; "he didn't bother *us,* and he certainly seemed
to get on swimmingly with the ladies. As for my sister, I have not
heard her laugh so heartily for ages."

"Oh, that was merely her good nature," objected Herrick. "I
am sure the fellow bored her horribly—indeed, I saw a look of
boredom on her face once or twice, only she was too kind to let
him see it."

Howbeit, as a matter of fact, the young lady instead of being bored, subsequently informed her brother that she had spent quite a pleasant evening and so had her aunt. "I declare, Bobbie," she said, "your interesting Islander isn't half bad—in short, both auntie and I found him most entertaining—I am rather glad he came after all."

"Nevertheless, I don't think you would like him to stay," returned her brother. "I fancy you'd find that a little of him is quite enough. But now I must go up and see, or rather hear, how he is getting on in the haunted room. I daresay by this time he is buried in slumber."

"Well, I don't think you will say *Requiescat in pace* to him!" cried the lively girl, laughingly.

"No, certainly not—the very reverse of that, whatever it may be. And now good-night, my pet, don't stay up any longer or you'll lose your roses." And turning away as he spoke, Granby forthwith began ascending the stairs—very noiselessly—and in a few minutes afterwards he had reached the door of the room occupied by his victim, who at first appeared to him to be conversing with somebody, though afterwards it became evident that he was merely talking to himself.

"Well, if this is English hospitality it's cold comfort!" ejaculated the shivering Irishman, evidently drawing the bedclothes more closely round him as he spoke, for owing to the craziness of the door every sound he made was distinctly audible to the listening ear. "I must say me friend Granby was a cool customer to put me in such a draughty hole, for those confounded windows seem to think it is their business to let in the air instead of excluding it, and, as for the noise, I do believe the rats are dancing a jig at this moment in the wainscoting. Well, Granby, me boy, when you come to O'Mara Castle—though that stately edifice only exists in the air at present—I'll give you a warmer reception than you've given me." And with this generous resolve the soliloquist turned over, and in a short time afterwards it was easy to gather from his regular and very stertorous breathing that he had at least found temporary oblivion of all his worries and discomforts in the pleasant land of dreams.

It may readily be imagined that great anxiety was felt and mani-
fested next morning to know how O'Mara had got on through the
night. But when he at length appeared at breakfast he looked such
an altered being that no one thought of chaffing him; and while
the ladies of the party almost started on first seeing him, Granby
certainly experienced some very unpleasant qualms of conscience
at having subjected him to an ordeal which had affected him so
strangely. The fact was, O'Mara was no longer the same man that
he had been the day before. Pale, haggard, and heavy-eyed, with a
scared look and a nervous manner, it seemed as if somebody else
had taken his place for the time being. And instead of chatting
easily and unconstrainedly as it was his wont to do, his words were
few and sometimes hardly coherent, while in answer to all inquiries as to how he had fared in the haunted chamber, he returned
the same invariable reply, namely, that he had really nothing whatever to tell.

"Oh, Mr. O'Mara, you must have seen something, or you
wouldn't look so queer and so unlike yourself as you do!" cried
Miss Granby. "Did the old lady who is supposed to haunt that
room appear to you? Or did you hear her? Or was the bed so uncomfortable that you could not sleep? Or what?"

"Oh, thank you. Miss Granby, the room was quite comfortable!" answered O'Mara with polite mendacity. "But I never can
manage to sleep well in a strange bed—that's all—and I positively
have nothing to tell you about the ghost."

"Hah!" said Granby to himself, "there's more in that than meets
the ear, and we must get it out of him." So in accordance with this
determination, as soon as breakfast was over he followed his guest
into the smoking-room, and there cornered him so resistlessly that
the hard-pressed Irishman had to yield in the end, at least to a
certain point, and at last he said with very great reluctance:

"Well, me boy, if you *must* know, there's an end on't. I did see
something, and heard something too—a thing that has made me
feel down-hearted ever since—but what it was I certainly cannot
and will not tell you."

"Oh, but how did it all come about? And what did you see?"
persisted Granby.

"Well, you see, Johnson told me about the room being haunted—so my rest was disturbed by bad dreams—but at two o'clock I awoke to find the whole place enveloped in a sort of vapour, and, through the cloud at the end of my bed, a ghastly, fearful face was peering at me. It was the face of a woman, and looked like that of a corpse—white and livid—and I declare to you, Granby, me blood literally curdled in me veins as I saw the Thing coming nearer and nearer to me until at last it was so close that I could feel its cold breath on me cheek. It then whispered something into my ear which I would have given a great deal not to have heard; but I can't tell what it was because I promised I wouldn't, so don't urge me any more, like a good fellow."

And with these words, which were uttered wildly and in great excitement, O'Mara rose from his seat and hurried from the room to escape further importunities.

"Confound the beggar!" said Granby as he watched his retreating figure. "He seems half daft to-day, and do you know I'm beginning to repent of having put him in that beastly room after all. It seems hardly fair, or—"

"Oh, nonsense, Granby!" exclaimed Herrick. "The poor chap is in a blue funk, that's all! I can quite believe that he had a nightmare, and I've no doubt he heard noises too, but I'll swear they didn't proceed from anything more formidable than a *ridiculus mus*. Bacon says," he added, "'that nature never puts much that is precious up in a garret four storeys high,' and he is quite right. I never knew a long, lanky, overgrown fellow like O'Mara yet who hadn't the heart of a chicken."

"There you are quite wrong," objected Granby. "O'Mara is not a coward; if he were I would not have put him in that room, anxious as I was to get rid of him, because it wouldn't have been safe."

"Safe!" sneered Herrick. "Surely, Granby, you are not going to tell me that you believe in ghosts or any nonsense of that kind?"

Granby reddened. "No," he said, "I don't believe in them any more than you do, but I believe there is some unexplained mystery connected with that unlucky room, which scares everybody, and, valiant as you are, my friend, I venture to say you would not like to spend a night in it yourself."

"Oh, wouldn't I though?" cried Herrick. "I'll sleep in it this very night if you'll let me. May I?"

"Oh, certainly!" answered Granby. "There is nothing to prevent you from trying it if you like, and if you really intend to sleep in it I shall tell Johnson to put your things there."

And so the matter was settled.

But Granby felt by no means satisfied with the existing aspect of affairs as regarded O'Mara's state of mind. And though he knew that *he* could do nothing more than what he had already done, he had such unlimited faith in his sister's powers of persuasion that he straightway went to her, and explaining to her how uncomfortable he felt, begged her to try what she could effect in the matter.

With this request she willingly complied, and moreover was pretty confident of succeeding in her mission, too. But contrary to her expectations the interesting Islander, as she had dubbed him, proved firm and unyielding, and seemed so determined to stick to his colours that she was obliged to content herself with having at last extorted a reluctant half-promise from him that some time in the course of the ensuing year he might divulge part of the secret to her, though nothing, he said, could induce him to tell it to her or anybody else before that.

Meanwhile, it was observed that on the following morning O'Mara came down looking much brisker and brighter than he had done the previous day. While as for Herrick, whose appearance was so eagerly anticipated, though his cheek was not blanched nor his eye wild (as O'Mara's had been), it was patent to everyone that he, too, had something on his mind which he did not want or wish to talk about. However, in answer to the innumerable questions with which he was plied, he at length admitted that he was awakened in the middle of the night by such a loud noise that he thought at first the walls must be falling in, while at the same time the whole room seemed to be filled with the fumes of sulphur. "Someone was moving about quite close to me, too," he added, "who, after having kept me on tenterhooks for a good while, at last rushed out through the door (which I could swear I shut before going to bed), and thence clattered down the corridor, where the noise finally died away in the distance."

"By Jove! that's deuced strange!" cried Weston, who was a brother officer of Herrick's, "but, my dear fellow, why didn't you get up and pursue the phantom or whatever it was? If you had done that, the whole thing might have been cleared up by this time."

"Oh, I should like to see *you* do it!" exclaimed Herrick sarcastically. "I bet you a pony you don't do it under similar circumstances yourself!"

"Done!" said Weston. "Let *me* sleep there to-night, Granby, and if I don't unravel the mystery for you, I'm a Dutchman."

So the third night the haunted chamber had a new occupant. But while O'Mara and Herrick had little to say for themselves after having encountered its perils and dangers, Weston had simply nothing at all. He appeared at an early hour, looking as fresh as paint and as merry as the Swiss Boy, and turning smilingly to his host, who he saw was looking towards him with great expectations, he said, "I'm really very sorry to disappoint you, Granby, but the truth is I have no revelations whatever to make. I saw nothing, I heard nothing, nor were there any noises except what were made by the rats in the wall, and only that the bed happened to be uncommonly hard and uncomfortable and the cold was simply marrow-piercing, I could have slept quite snugly and undisturbedly there till morning."

Now this was drawing a blank cover with a vengeance, and everybody looked proportionately disappointed. But in the midst of their discomfiture the door opened and in stalked O'Mara, who said he found he would have to leave that day as he had a little matter of business to attend to in Town.

"What day is this?" asked Miss Granby as soon as he had made the announcement.

"The first of January," he answered.

"Oh, then it's next year!" she observed, illogically but emphatically, "and so I claim the fulfilment of your promise, Mr. O'Mara. No, no," she went on, in answer to an incipient demurrer from him. "I shall not let you off, and as you are a man of honour you must not break your word."

"I have no intention of breaking it, me dear Miss Granby, but if you remember, I stipulated that I was to tell the secret to yourself alone. You and I and nobody by, and not *pro bono publico.*"

"So you shall," said the obliging young lady. "If you will come into the next room with me now we shall have it quite to ourselves—it is always empty at this hour." And so saying she rose from her seat and led the way into the library, followed by O'Mara, who, as soon as they' were alone together took up his parable in the following manner:

"Now, me dear young lady, I have a very solemn revelation to make to you, but you must not feel nervous, and, above all, you must bear in mind that you are never to tell what I'm going to confess to you, to anybody—it must remain locked up in your own breast for ever and a day. I know that crusty old bachelors say," continued O'Mara, "that nature made no provision either in the mental or physical economy of a woman for keeping a secret, but I'm proving that *I* don't believe in that ungallant assertion, by making you me confidant now—and here is what I have got to tell you: On the night of my arrival, when I saw the apparition which you have already heard about, I began to shiver and to shake as if I had got a sudden attack of ague, and when the Thing said to me, 'Are you awake, O'Mara?' though I answered promptly and respectfully, 'Yes, ma'am!' I declare you could have knocked me down with a feather if I had been standing up, which luckily I wasn't. 'Then,' said the apparition, 'as you are awake, we can converse a little together, and I have something to give you.' 'Oh, you darlin',' says I, 'that's welcome news, for since I came to this country, the only thing anybody has given me is advice, and I'm sick of that.' 'Ah, well,' says she, 'it's a little bit of the same that *I* have got to give you, too, but then you'll find mine is valuable, so listen to me. Imagination is my name, and I chiefly make my home in Ireland, though of course I'm to be found elsewhere also, and my advice to you is, whenever you are put into a cold, uncomfortable room (where there are better rooms to be had), just *invent* a ghost story, and my word on it, you will find plenty of fools ready to believe everything you say, and lots of fellows only too glad—just for bravado, you know—to occupy your quarters whilst you lie snugly and cosily in theirs.' So having said this the old party vanished away, and now, me dear young lady," added O'Mara, "you've got me secret and me tale, and 'pon me honour, I think you have a bit of me heart too, for yours is the pleasantest face I ever saw, and—"

"Oh, Mr. O'Mara, Mr. O'Mara," said the laughing girl as soon as she could find voice to speak, "it's a bit of your head that I would rather have than anything else, for you have outwitted us all and made fools of every one of us—you have indeed, and most cleverly you did it, too. But before I let you go, will you tell me how you managed to frighten even the doughty Mr. Herrick?"

"With the greatest pleasure in life," returned O'Mara gallantly. "I tied walnut shells to the cat's feet and a lighted cigar steeped in sulphur to her tail, and having first let her softly into the room, as soon as she had made noise enough I then let her softly out again—so there you are!"

"Capital, capital! Most ingenious!" cried Miss Granby in great delight, "and," she added, "I am really glad that you succeeded so well with *him,* because he is so bumptious and conceited."

The Irishman smiled benignly. "Well, now," he said, "is there anything more that you would like to hear before I go, for you know I could refuse you nothing? And I can tell you Miss Granby, that having had to disoblige you temporarily on Thursday gave me a pain in me heart which I'll carry to the grave with me."

"Oh, Mr. O'Mara, how can you say such a thing! What is truth?"

"Fact, I assure you. But what's the good? I'm a fool for me pains—or me pain—for there's not a soul in this house who would ever care to see my ugly face again!"

"You are quite mistaken," cried the young lady graciously, "*I* should." And then with a blush which seemed to the admiring Hibernian the pink of perfection, she added, "And what's more I hope you will come again, and I promise that if you do you shall have a warm reception, and instead of the haunted chamber, the very best room in the house!"

This was satisfactory. In fact eminently so. And as O'Mara observed, it would have added a cubit to his stature only that he tried to keep himself down for the sake of appearances. But though his fair hostess regarded him thus amicably, it was a very different matter with the other members of the community—who one and all received the relation of facts with such very black looks that it was evident they were thoroughly put out by them. Indeed as for Herrick he could hardly be appeased, and at once announced his intention of riding after "the scoundrel," and informing him that neither he nor any other jackanapes should play practical jokes on *him* with impunity.

But Granby, who was a sensible man, and who had regained his equanimity much sooner than the others, said quietly:

"Sit down, my dear fellow, and don't talk nonsense. We are all in the same boat. He has befooled and beaten each of us, as I may say, with our own weapons. But then he did it so cleverly, that I, for one, not only forgive him but feel that we all owe him a vote of thanks for having invented *A new ghost story!*"

THE EMPTY COMPARTMENT
ANONYMOUS
Murray's Magazine, 1890

I am not a racing man, and therefore, looking at others through myself after the manner of my kind, I did not imagine that I should be delayed on my journey homeward by the fact that the day of my return was the great day at F— races.

A fortnight of my summer holiday had been devoted to fly-fishing on certain well-preserved streams in North Wales. I had fished from the bank, I had waded through mountain torrents, and every evening had come back tired and happy, and laden with silver-brown treasures, jewelled with specks of amber and vermilion.

And now the nets were up at sea, and I was waiting, waiting for the great salmon that were surely hurrying towards me, fighting their way against peat-brown swirling water, climbing the salmon-ladders, jumping the granite boulders, towards the flies that lay in ambush for them in my old well-worn flybook.

For days I had pictured their coming, had stood by a pool through which they must pass, had studied the fly, gaudy but not too gaudy, with a glint of peacock amidst its pheasant's colouring, and one touch of crimson in the silk which bound it, which no salmon of any curiosity could resist; for days I had hazarded a guess at the weight of my first take, beginning modestly at 7 lbs. or so, and growing bolder as the days passed until 10, 20, even 30 lbs. seemed possible.

And just then, just when I had heard of fish six miles below me, when weather was perfect, and long patience about to be rewarded, a telegram summoned me home, and blackness settled upon everything.

The landlord sympathized with me at the little Angler's Inn, where I was staying, but when I told him the serious nature of my telegram, he did not like to refer to the pleasures that awaited me if I remained, but only pointed out the dangers on my path if I left: "Those dreadful F— races!"

A frivolous excuse to my mind from a man who had not dared to urge the coming salmon as a reason for remaining. No, I was the junior partner of my bachelor uncle who had money (this last assertion refers to the uncle, and not to the junior partner); he summoned, and I must go.

One train only would get me to London that night; by starting at once I could run to an important Junction, a couple of hours away, change there, and be in town by eight or nine o'clock.

Now this Junction was on the direct line to F— races.

I reached the station a trifle late, for it had been quick work to take my rods to pieces, and get my flies that were on the casts tenderly into my book. However, I was in time, and found a rather noisy set of half-a-dozen men on the platform whom I took to be bookmakers, why I cannot say, as I do not know any signs to distinguish a bookmaker when I see him, and I may be mistaken.

I gathered that one train had passed through too full for them to get seats, and I heard one say to the station-master: "Look here, I gave you a good tip, and it's hard lines if you don't put a carriage on for self and friends if the next's as full as the last."

"The next" was full, if about six above the usual number in each compartment constitutes repletion, and the station-master's gratitude led to the running out of an old carriage from a shed, into one compartment of which jumped "self and friends."

Profiting by their importunity, but not anxious for their company, I got into the next compartment, and was glad to find myself alone. I settled my rods in the rack above my head, disturbing dust and cobwebs as I did so, pulled a newspaper from one pocket, and a travelling cap from another, and read myself to sleep. We had had a long sitting in the smoking-room the night before, over the momentous question of the salmon, and I slept soon and heavily.

How long I slept I cannot say, but I awoke in the roar and rattle of a tunnel—awoke in thick darkness to hear the slow panting of the engine and feel the laboured strain which told me we were going up-hill; also to a more disagreeable consciousness, namely, that I was not alone, that there were other persons in the compartment, and that therefore I must have passed a station.

What a fool I must have looked, sleeping heavily in broad daylight, so heavily that two persons at least had passed me in getting in without disturbing my boorish slumbers. Two at least—for they were talking and I listened for a moment to their conversation, wishing to gather who my companions might be, before daylight showed them to me.

They were very near me, it seemed, on the opposite seat by the door, and the first words I heard were these, spoken in a gentle girlish voice, but with a sad firmness in it:

"I cannot, Harry!"

The answer startled me, it was so roughly given, and the voice was a man's.

"You mean you won't, Kate, and there's an end of it."

Then the girl whispered something that I did not catch, but I could hear the man half push her from him as he exclaimed:

"I am a ruined man without it, and you won't lift a finger to save me."

This would never do; they evidently fancied me still asleep, and would be talking over all sorts of private affairs, so I coughed, moved uneasily, rustled my newspaper, and, as the first distant gleam showed that the train was nearing daylight, planted myself firmly in my corner prepared for apology or defence, and when we rushed out of the darkness—found myself absolutely alone.

This was absurd; I had been asleep indeed, but yet, as I looked around, and turned to the window to see trees and fields gliding past, I knew I was wide awake now, and began to dislike the situation. For I still heard the two talking, though not so clearly, and could only conclude that they were in the compartment occupied by the racing set, that these last had got out at the station we had evidently passed while I slept, and that their places were filled by the two whose voices reached me with such unnatural distinctness.

And yet how improbable that the men who were so evidently going to the races had got out before the Junction. Horror! I thought, the blood rushing to my face at the bare idea, I cannot have slept past the Junction too! No, my watch showed that I had not been forty minutes in the train.

I pulled myself together, and looked round.

The carriage in which I sat was old and dirty, as I have said; opposite to me, just where, with my eyes shut, I could swear that a man and a girl sat talking, the dingy brown cloth was somewhat stained, and there was a long jagged slit, apparently cut with a knife, out of which the stuffing of the cushion hung miserably.

This slit would account for the distinctness of the voices I heard, I argued with a sophistry I would have scorned in another. No, it would not account for it, urged common sense; but it must, or my eyes were playing me false.

Just as I decided this, half-heartedly, a loud guffaw from the racing men assured me that they at least were still in the other compartment.

Then where were my two companions? Talking in whispers, pleading, disputing, with four or five rough, noisy men side by side with them, their voices coming to me through the horrible jagged cut in the faded cloth opposite. Or—or where? Here with me, not to be seen, though I rubbed my eyes, and looked out of the window, and forced myself to look back at the spot where the voices sounded, just above that horrible slit in the cloth. For it was horrible. I confessed this to myself at last, and drew my feet up on the seat of the carriage, and felt the cold dampness of fear creep down my face, as I heard a girl's voice, hoarse and eager, as it seemed to me, striving for calmness against growing terror.

"Listen, Harry," she said. "This money is not mine. You do not understand, so I must tell you, though it is my father's secret. He has owed this sum for ten years, and for ten years has worked and saved and starved for it. Little by little he has gathered it all; and I have watched him growing older, and paler, and seen the stoop in his shoulders, and the dimness in his eyes, until, Harry, my heart has nearly broken for pity. But a week ago the last pound was put in the bank, and he was free."

"A week ago," the man's voice muttered harshly; "and why not pay it a week ago, and have saved tempting me?"

The last words were said so low that I scarcely heard them, and the girl took no notice of them, and hardly even answered his question.

"It was for my brother's sake, dear, the brother you never knew, who is dead, and who, but for his father, would be disgraced as well. He was weak, poor fellow, in body and mind. He was a clerk, and betted, and lost, Harry;" and the poor little voice grew so pitiful here, that I could fancy I saw pleading eyes raised to the other's face, "and he took money, £200, from his master, and—"

"£200!" the shout with which these words were uttered made me tremble. "Never mind the story, Kate; tell it me another time: it's common enough, God knows! Where is the money?"

There was a shrinking movement on the girl's part. I could hear her breathe quickly, and push the man's hands away, while I sat crouching there like a coward, hearing all and afraid to help, afraid to put out my hand across the carriage for fear of what it might touch.

"No, Harry—no," she panted; "you shall not have it. My father— Oh, Harry, let me tell you. My father went to Frank's master and pleaded for him; he swore that if he would forgive the boy he himself would pay the money back, and at last it was agreed. Frank went to Australia, and died there a year after, and my father worked on, faithful to his promise.

"Half way through the time he took £100 to Frank's master. My father thought he was surprised to see the money. A friend said he could not claim it now my brother was dead. Anyway, he told my father he would forgive him the other half; but father would not hear of that. He said for his dead boy's honour he would pay all; and this morning, Harry, he told me to go and get the money from the bank, and to-morrow he will pay it over himself, and be free and happy again. Now, Harry, you understand."

The man's tone was changed when he spoke again.

"Of course, dear, I understand," he said more gently, and I could hear him draw her towards him; "and now you must listen to me. You know you are mine, Kate; you have promised to marry me, and you ought to trust me a little."

"I do, Harry," she whispered, "only you promised to give up betting."

"You talk like a woman, Kate, and a woman with no experience. I tell you most men bet; it all depends how you do it. Now here I am doing nothing rash, I am behind the scenes. I have the trainer's word for it, and John of Gaunt is as sure to win as the bookmakers think he is safe to lose, and that is saying a good deal. With a paltry £5 in my pocket I am safe to make £50, and with £100—think Kate, we could marry to-morrow!"

"I would rather wait than marry so, dear," the gentle voice answered.

"But by George, Kate, I would not,"—the briefly repressed fury burst out again; "and I tell you again the money will save me. Lend it me, child; just for to-night; I'll bring it you doubled to-morrow, Kate. I swear! Doubled! you don't know how I'll multiply it. And hark you, girl—for I see your meek eyes set themselves, and your lips, that can tremble sometimes, press together—you had better know the truth; your brother's story will be mine without this money; I owe more than that weak boy dared venture. I love you, Kate, and I'll marry you if you are true to me; but, by heaven, if you think to put a dead brother before a living husband, I'll be more like killing than marrying."

I heard his teeth grind together as he spoke, and there was an awful silence. The girl must have drawn back from him, for, when she spoke again, her voice sounded further away, and there was a kind of sob in her throat which broke and choked her words.

"I must give you up, Harry; I can never be your wife now. When you are calmer you would despise me, as I should despise myself for lending what was not my own. The money is in a dead hand, I dare not touch it."

A harsh laugh burst from the man close to me, and my hands which were locked together, were wet and cold; I tried to tear them apart; I tried to bite my lip and force the blood into my face, but though I knew how I was cowering, I had no control over the horrible demon of fear which had me in its grasp.

"What do you mean, child?" the man who laughed asked in a hollow voice, "what makes you talk of dead hands? Come near me,

Kate, I will not give you up so lightly; see, we will talk of other things; don't look so frightened, come and kiss me, Kate; you are a brave girl, we'll forget that cursed money."

I heard her creep back to her old place, heard her crying as women cry after a tension of mind and heart has been removed, heard him kiss her, and ask her forgiveness; and then, just as the cold fear that held me seemed about to relax its hold, I felt—no, I felt nothing, but I heard, close to me now in the silence, a movement of a trembling, fumbling hand—a hand that sought something, something secret, something that it would grasp unseen.

The two were not speaking now, or only in murmurs so low that the moving hand which fumbled near me seemed to claim my ear more than their words.

My head throbbed with the tension of listening; all the blood in me seemed to be beating there, leaving my heart stone cold. Suddenly the groping hand passed swiftly close to my face; I felt the waft of the parted air against my wet temples, and then I heard a cry; ah, such a cry of surprise breaking into terror, of terror over-mastering love, as the girl's voice shrieked:—

"No, no, not that, not that; oh, father, help, help—help!"

Help? Against what? What had the girl's eyes seen, what dread had forced that bitter, broken cry from the poor lips? At last I leaned forward, I cried too, "Help, help!" At least I think I did, but if any sound came from my dry throat I knew not; before me I knew the man bent over something, something that moved a little, that moaned, that sighed softly. And after the sigh, the bending form lifted itself and muttered, and searched; I heard the hands tearing at something; then I heard a quick exclamation, a rustle of crisp paper, and then the door at my side was open; I felt the rain on my face, for a heavy shower was passing over us.

The blessed rain! the comforting, commonplace wetness reassured me; I felt my terror passing, and even reached a hand, half-heartedly shut the door, with a dazed feeling that I had had a bad dream.

But some object was dragged against it, was forced through it keeping it open, until I heard a dull thud outside, and then for the last time a harsh voice, now in the doorway, mutter:—

"What devil drives me? There's the Junction, I must leap!"

The train slackened speed, the swinging door fell into its place slowly, as though released from the pressure of a restraining hand, and I looked up and saw a porter run forward as we steamed into the station.

I caught at his arm as he came to the carriage; it was a relief to hold to humanity once more. I saw him look in my face curiously.

"Are you ill, sir?" he asked, "Your carriage door was open, were you getting out?"

I could not answer him.

"You hurt your hand, sir, I suppose; it is not safe to open the door too soon."

"My hand! No, I have not hurt it—why?"

I managed to get the words out at last.

The porter looked at me again queerly. "Well, you were staring at it when I came up as if you thought it would be covered with blood or something like."

"I did—I did! " then realizing what I was saying I broke off. "No—no, it is not hurt, but I am not well; I will stay here an hour or so; I cannot go on just yet."

The porter seemed surprised, but helped me out, and then got out my things. As he did so he exclaimed at the state of the carriage—

"Who has been pulling this stuffing out here? Were you alone, sir? This looks queer—somebody's been cutting the cushion. I must speak to the station-master."

But the station-master was already there. He had noted the delay, and made his way to the carriage, glancing at me rather strangely, and then looking into the compartment I had left.

"Who put this carriage on?" he called out.

The guard came up.

"It was put on at B—, sir. The train was full, and all the stock had been sent on for the races; it was the only one they had, I understood."

"That is so, sir," said one of the racing men, putting his head out of the window, "and dirty enough it is too; but here we are,

and here we mean to stay, and we'll be glad to be moving towards
F—, if convenient."

I thought the station-master looked inquiringly from me to
the man who spoke, and back again to me. His face was pale, and
he seemed about to speak, but looking at his watch, only signalled
with his hands to the guard, and then stood apparently in much
perplexity as the train slowly left the station. Then he glanced at
me.

"You look cold, sir," he said; "come and have a cup of coffee in
my room. I suppose you will go on by the next train?"

I followed him, convinced that he would ask me about that
open door in the old railway carriage. I was not sorry to sift the
matter a little, for I felt bolder now, surrounded by the every-day
details of the small country station. Its dreary refreshment room,
its deserted bookstall, its one porter—his day enlivened only by
the event of the passing trains—all this was ordinary, well known,
and anything but supernatural. When the porter brought me
the stereotyped bun, flat, limp, and currantless, scarcely recovered from obvious compression in the box that conveyed it to the
station, I felt almost reassured. I had been asleep, I knew, what
more satisfactory than to suppose I had been dreaming? But the
station-master, having made some coffee, and handed me a steaming cup, would not let me rest.

"Would you mind telling me, sir," he asked, in the whisper I so
well remembered my small brother adopting in the dead of night
when we were boys, and which always made me feel "creepy," "how
that door came open?"

"That's just what I don't know," I said, in the would-be reas-
suring tone I always used to that small brother, and with the old
result, namely, of blending our fears together, and doubling their
intensity.

"I was asleep—I mean I had been asleep, and perhaps I kicked it."

"Ah!" breathed the station-master.

"Why?" I ventured to ask, after a silence.

"Only that four years ago, on the first day of F— races, that
same carriage ran into our station with its door open, as it did

to-day, and inside was a woman in a dead faint; she came to herself in an hour, and talked of a murder."

"But that carriage—how do you know?"

"This is how I know, sir," and the man got up and shut the door, which opened on to the platform, and pulled his chair near mine when he came back. "Some seven or eight years ago I was master here, and waiting for the train passing through to the races as it might be to-day, and as she came in I saw a door open, and going forward found the compartment in disorder, a knife on the floor, blood on it and on the seat and carpet, and a slit in the stuffing of the cushion at the back just at the height—well, at the height you saw it, sir, if it's as I think. We sent men back along the line, and soon found a girl's body stabbed and thrown on the metals."

"Thrown on the line?"

"Yes, so they said. It was all found out quickly enough when her old father came to identify her; he said she'd been robbed too, for she had £100 in notes on her when she was murdered."

"And the man,—he did not escape?"

"No, the police guessed what he had been up to, and traced him to the races, where they made out he had lost every note he stole. He had been betting largely on one horse—"

"John of Gaunt," I cried eagerly, but with some of the recent terror on me again.

"Yes, that was it, sir; you've heard the story before?"

I shook my head and he went on—

"Well, they followed him pretty well all over the country, public feeling was so hard against him that every one knew he could not hide long, and at last they came upon him half-starved in a barn; he faced them and shot himself, and escaped hanging."

I did not speak, I was going over my recent experience in the train.

"The queer part of it, sir, is this," said the station-master, "after the coroner's jury had been here and seen the carriage—left untouched for them you'll understand—we never used it; somehow the men did not like it, and one market-day they sent it back to the station you came from, sir, and for years it was not used.

Then four years ago, as I said, they hooked it on for the races, every bit of rolling stock being wanted, and then it came in here with its door swinging, and a swooning woman inside, who told a strange story when it could be got out of her. The men liked it less after that, and sent it back again, and now that fool down the line drags it out on race day of all days in the year, and puts you in it, sir, and in my idea it ought to be broken into firewood."

We talked until my train came in, and I told him all I heard on that awful journey.

"Poor soul," he said; "I seem to know that girl."

"By the bye," I asked, as I packed my things into a carriage in the train that was to take me on, carefully choosing a compartment full of smokers, "What was her name? do you remember?"

He curved his hand round his mouth, and leaned towards me—

"Kate Lee," he said.

I do not often tell this story. Sometimes I have told it, and seen an incredulous smile cross the polite faces of my hearers. I cannot account for its incidents, or explain its improbability; but for me it has had one marked result, I never enter an empty railway carriage.

LOUISE

W. L. ALDEN

Cassell's Family Magazine, 1895

I had always maintained that Oswell was a man of genius, and that he was wasting his time and his abilities in the hack work of daily journalism. He lived only a few doors from me, and I had frequent opportunities of preaching to him from the above text. In time my sermons had their effect. Oswell began to write short stories, and these were soon recognised as among the best short stories of the day.

At first he insisted that his success as a story writer was a mere fluke; but he gradually came to perceive that he had found his true vocation. He abandoned journalistic work and shut himself up in order to write a novel. He was at all times an extremely industrious and hardworking man; but, as he became more and more interested in his novel, he worked almost incessantly, and I saw very tittle of him. One evening just after dinner he came into my office, where I usually took my after-dinner cigar, and said:

"Doctor, I have come to consult you. I think that I am either insane already, or in immediate danger of becoming insane."

"I can assure you at once that you are not in the least danger of insanity," said I. "When a man is sane enough to know that he is insane, he is perfectly sane."

"That is rather too much of a paradox to be convincing," he replied. "Wait till you hear what I have to tell you. You will then find either that I am insane, or that the age of miracles has returned."

"Take a cigar first," said I, "and let me assure you that you have the eye and the temperature of a particularly sane and healthy man. However, let us hear what you have to say."

"You know, of course," began Oswell, "that about six months ago I undertook to write a novel for Peters & Sons, and to deliver the manuscript on the first of May next. That gave me only eight months in which to do the work, and as I was anxious to do something that would attract attention, I have been hard at work ever since.

"Now you know I have never been a conceited ass, whatever other varieties of an ass I may have been. But I assure you that I have been doing good work. I have a plot that is absolutely new, and I have done my very best to make my characters live men and women."

"Have you succeeded in that?" I asked as Oswell paused, and seemed to be at a loss what to say next.

"Altogether too well, at least in one instance," he replied. "It is that very fact that brings me here. Can you imagine an author writing of a girl so long and so intently that he finally falls in love with her?"

"Anything is possible provided it is sufficiently idiotic," I replied.

"Of course, of course," he answered hastily. "I know that it was idiotic, but for all that, the girl grew to seem so absolutely alive to me that I ended by loving her. In the first place she is more beautiful than any woman whom you or I ever saw. I made her, and I ought to know. By the bye, did you ever try to see in imagination the face of the heroine of any novel—without the assistance of an artist, I mean? Try it and you will find that it is impossible. You may say to yourself that the girl has eyes and hair of such a colour, that her mouth is small or large, and that she has any sort of nose you choose. Do your best and you cannot make a mental portrait that will be visible to you. The utmost you can do will be to perceive that the girl is either short or tall, plump or thin. Her face will be for ever hidden from you."

"Admitting all this," said I, "what has it to do with your heroine?"

"Only this, that long before I saw her, her face was perfectly familiar to me, even her changes of expression and tricks of manner.

Of all the flesh and blood women whom I have known there is not one whom I can see in memory half as clearly as I could see Louise. It was not merely her wonderful beauty that fascinated me. There was a charm about her that I cannot define, but that to me was irresistible. And then I could not but love her for her nobility of character. Doctor, I tell you that a better, more sincere, more fearless, more high-minded, more noble woman never lived. No man who knew her could have helped loving her, and who could ever know her as well as I, her creator? Now do you think I am insane?"

"I think you are very lucky in not being a married man," I replied. "If there was a Mrs. Oswell, Mademoiselle Louise would seriously complicate things."

"But," urged Oswell, "does what I have said shake your faith in my sanity?"

"Not in the least. Have I not always maintained that you are a man of genius, and as such you have a right to indulge in little eccentricities? If that is all you have to tell me I shall still continue to insist that you are sane."

"That is not all. What would you say if I told you that I had actually seen Louise with my own eyes?"

"I should say that you had been working too hard and needed a rest. Seeing spectres is by no means a rare result of overwork. It does not mean that the man who sees them is insane, but that there is some slight insanity—in other words, derangement—of the optic nerve or the retina. If you have begun to see spectres, you will, if you keep on working, hear voices before long. Even then you will not be insane. But take my advice and knock off work for two or three months, and you will find that Mademoiselle Louise will vanish."

"I am not sure that I want her to vanish, even if that were to be the price of my sanity. But let me tell you how it is that she appears to me. Perhaps you will change your mind as to the spectral theory.

"About two months ago I was working at my book one evening. It must have been about ten o'clock. If you remember, my desk stands in the centre of the room, and there is a mirror directly opposite to it. I happened to lift my eyes and I saw a woman's figure reflected, as I thought, in the mirror. I looked hastily around, but there was no woman in the room. I looked again at the mirror, and saw the woman so plainly that I recognised her as Louise, in spite of the fact that both her face and figure seemed filmy and semi-transparent. She was looking at me. and I thought I could perceive a smile on her lips. I sprang to my feet and went towards the mirror, but the vision suddenly disappeared.

"After satisfying myself that the door was shut, and that it could not be opened from the outside without a key, I sat down again at my desk, a good deal startled. I did not for an instant suppose that the vision was anything but an hallucination, due either to overwork, or, perhaps, to indigestion. So after having convinced myself that it was a matter of no consequence, but that it would be wiser to do no more work that night, I put out my lamp and went to bed.

"The next night I glanced several times at the mirror as I was working, but it showed me nothing except my own face. After a while I got up, intending to rest myself for a few moments by walking up and down the floor. There, directly in front of me, at the other end of the room, I saw Louise.

"This time the vision seemed much less filmy and unsubstantial than it had seemed the first time that I saw it. Still, either the figure or the air of the room between it and me wavered as heated air wavers, and I could distinctly see that the outer edges of the woman's dress were transparent. I had no sensation of fear. How could I have had when I saw before me a woman whom I knew so completely, and whom I loved? I went towards her with outstretched arms, and with a cry on my lips. This time she did not immediately vanish. I seemed to be nearly touching her, and almost on the point of clasping her in my arms, when she melted away, and I found myself alone again."

"There is a steamer to the Cape next Saturday," I said, as Oswell paused again, "Take it, and don't put pen to paper for the next six months."

"Since that night," continued Oswell, without noticing my interruption, "I have seen Louise every night. Gradually her figure has taken more and more of the apparent solidity of actual life. She approaches close to me, and sometimes she puts her arms about my neck. I cannot feel them, but I can see them. I put my arms around her, and I clasp nothing that is tangible. It is only to the sense of sight that she is perceptible.

"She does not speak, but she understands what I say. In her eyes and her expression there is all the vivacity that an actual woman could show. That she loves me there cannot be a shadow of doubt. I can look through her eyes down into her soul. She stands by my desk while I write, and knows without reading it what I am writing of her. Between us there is the most perfect communion of thought. As I said, she is intangible, but, for all that, our souls have kissed one another."

The passion in the man's voice startled me. For the first time I began to think it possible that he was really insane. However, I had, through long experience, gained some little reputation in the treatment of nervous disorders, and I felt reasonably sure that whatever hallucinations Oswell might have, his brain was as yet free from disease.

"Oswell, old man," I said, "there is nothing in the world the matter with you except overwork. Your spectre will disappear as soon as you have given yourself a long rest. Go to the Cape, or, better still, round the world. You'll come back another man. Stay here and work as you have been working, and I won't answer for the consequences."

"You still insist," said Oswell, "that Louise is what you call a spectre and not a visible spirit?"

"Certainly I do. There cannot be the least doubt as to the young person's composition. I have in my library records of a number of cases of men who have been temporarily haunted by spectres. You may read them if you choose."

"I wish I could convince myself that you are either right or wrong. I know that Louise exists and is visible to me; but at the same time I have a constant fear that she does not exist, and that I am a prey to an insane delusion. Can you understand how a man can fully believe and fatally doubt at one and the same time?"

"You are an amateur photographer, if I remember rightly," I said, "Now with the help of your camera you can easily prove

whether Mademoiselle Louise is real or spectral. Have your camera
ready the next time she shows herself, and make a photograph of
her. If she is substantial enough to impress the retina of your eye,
she is substantial enough to impress a photographic plate. If you
find nothing on the plate after developing it, you will be convinced
that your spectre has no objective existence. Am I not right?"

"Thank you," said Oswell. "I accept the test. But what will you
say if I am able to bring you a photograph of Louise? Would that
shake your faith in your theory?"

"There will be time enough to discuss that question when you
bring me the photograph," I replied. "I have no fears as to what
the result will be. Meanwhile, take your passage for the Antipodes.
I'll give you a draught that may be of use to you, though complete
cessation from work is the one thing that you need."

I did not see Oswell the next day, and I felt sure that he stayed
away because he did not want to admit that the photographic test
had proved me to be in the right. However, on the day following
he burst into my office early in the morning, and I saw from his
look that something more than usual had happened.

"Well?" I said. "Sit down and tell me what your spectre thinks
of photography. I am afraid that she doesn't approve of it."

"Look at that," said he, handing me an unmounted photograph
that was as yet hardly dry.

I looked at it and saw the photograph of a young woman, who,
I don't hesitate to say, must have been more beautiful than any
woman since Helen of Troy.

"That is Louise," said Oswell. "I photographed her yesterday
afternoon, and this is the result. Now what do you think of our
test?"

"What do I think?" I said. "I think, or rather I know, that
someone is playing a contemptible practical joke on you. Your
spectre is more real than I supposed she was—that is to say, she is
just exactly as real as Pepper's ghost. I was right in the first place
when I said that I could see no signs of mental derangement about
you. We'll unearth the young woman who poses as a ghost in your
room, and find out who her confederate is. You needn't quit work
after all."

"I know perfectly well how Pepper's ghost is produced," replied Oswell. "It would be an absolute impossibility to produce it in my room. Besides, where in London or elsewhere is the woman who could pose for that photograph? Do you imagine that she could exist without being famous the world over for her beauty?"

I argued with him warmly and at some length, for I was, of course, confident, now that I had seen the photograph, that he was the victim of a trick. But it was impossible to shake his conviction that Louise, as he called her, was the visible projection of his creative thought.

Other patients beginning to arrive, I was forced to dismiss him, and he went away, promising me that in a day or two I should make a thorough inspection of his room.

I went to see him the next afternoon. As he said, it did not seem possible, in view of the situation and furniture of his room, that even the cleverest trickster could have produced, without detection, the figure of the woman whose photograph Oswell had made. I felt myself completely baffled, though I still believed that the apparition was capable of explanation as the work of a practical joker.

As I left him he made a remark which did not strike me particularly at the time, but which I afterwards remembered. He said that Louise had assured him that in the other world they would be always together, and that the sense of her intangibility would not longer trouble him.

For the next three days I was absent from London, having been called away to the North for a consultation. On the morning of my return I was shocked to read in the paper that Oswell had committed suicide.

I went immediately to his rooms and found that the report was true. The coroner's inquest had already been held, and a verdict had been found to the effect that he had committed suicide by taking cyanide of potassium—a chemical which he sometimes used in his photographic operations.

Nothing could be found of the book upon which he had been working, but from the presence of ashes in the grate it was plain that he had been burning papers.

I alone knew that he had gone voluntarily to his death in the hope of joining the woman whom he believed his brain had created.

Of the absolute truthfulness of Oswell it is impossible for me to entertain a doubt. I should, of course, believe that his "Louise" was merely the result of a mental hallucination, were it not for the photograph. With that evidence before me, how was it possible for me to doubt that there was some degree of objective reality to the vision? On the other hand, the explanation which he gave of the matter was certainly incredible. I often think of Oswell's remark that he believed and doubted at one and the same time. I believe that "Louise" was born into visibility by the intense action of Oswell's brain, and I believe that this explanation is both incredible and impossible—a circumstance which goes to support my theory that a man can believe with one lobe of his brain something that the other lobe utterly rejects.

"NUMBER NINETY"
MRS. B. M. CROKER
Chapman's Magazine, 1895

"To let furnished, for a term of years, at a very low rental, a large old-fashioned family residence, comprising eleven bed-rooms, four reception-rooms, dressing-rooms, two staircases, complete servants' offices, ample accommodation for a Gentleman's establishment, including six-stall stable, coach-house, etc."

The above advertisement referred to number ninety. For a period extending over some years this notice appeared spasmodically in the various daily papers. Occasionally you saw it running for a week or a fortnight at a stretch, as if it were resolved to force itself into consideration by sheer persistency. Sometimes for months I looked for it in vain. Other ignorant folk might possibly fancy that the efforts of the house agent had been crowned at last with success—that it was let, and no longer in the market.

I knew better. I knew that would never, never find a tenant as long as oak and ash endured. I knew that it was passed on as a hopeless case, from house-agent to house-agent. I knew that it would never be occupied, save by rats—and, more than this, I knew the reason why!

I will not say in what square, street, or road number ninety may be found, nor will I divulge to human being its precise and exact locality, but this I'm prepared to state, that it is positively in existence, is in London, and is still empty.

Twenty years ago, this very coming Christmas, my friend John Hollyoak (civil engineer) and I were guests at a bachelor's party; partaking, in company with eight other celibates, of a very *recherché* little dinner, in the neighbourhood of Piccadilly. Conversation became very brisk as the champagne circulated, and many topics were started, discussed, and dismissed.

They (I say *they* advisedly, as I myself am a man of few words) talked on an extraordinary variety of subjects.

I distinctly recollect a long argument on mushrooms—mushrooms, murders, racing, cholera; from cholera we came to sudden death, from sudden death to churchyards, and from churchyards, it was naturally but a step to ghosts.

On this last topic the arguments became fast and furious, for the company was divided into two camps. The larger, "the opposition," who scoffed, sneered, and snapped their fingers, and laughed with irritating contempt at the very name of ghosts, was headed by John Hollyoak; the smaller party, who were dogged, angry, and prepared to back their opinions to any extent, had for their leader our host, a bald-headed man of business, whom I certainly would have credited (as I mentally remarked) with more sense.

The believers in the supernatural obtained a hearing, so far as to relate one or two blood-curdling, first or second-hand experiences, which, when concluded, instead of being received with an awestruck and respectful silence, were pooh poohed, with shouts of laughter, and taunting suggestions that were by no means complimentary to the intelligence, or sobriety, of the victims of superstition. Argument and counter-argument waxed louder and hotter, and there was every prospect of a very stormy conclusion to the evening's entertainment.

John Hollyoak, who was the most vehement, the most incredulous, the most jocular, and the most derisive of the anti-ghost faction, brought matters to a climax by declaring, that nothing would give him greater pleasure than to pass a night in a haunted house—and the worse its character, the better he would be pleased!

His challenge was instantly taken up by our somewhat ruffled host, who warmly assured him that his wishes could be easily

satisfied, and that he would be accommodated with a night's lodging in a haunted house within twenty-four hours—in fact, in a
house of such a desperate reputation, that even the adjoining man-
sions stood vacant.

He then proceeded to give a brief outline of the history of
number ninety. It had once been the residence of a well-known
county family, but what evil events had happened therein tradition did not relate.

On the death of the last owner—a diabolical-looking aged person, much resembling the typical wizard—it had passed into the
hands of a kinsman, resident abroad, who had no wish to return
to England, and who desired his agents to let it, if they could—a
most significant proviso!

Year by year went by, and still this "Highly desirable family
mansion" could find no tenant, although the rent was reduced,
and reduced, and again reduced, to almost zero!

The most ghastly whispers were afloat—the most terrible experiences were actually proclaimed on the housetops!

No tenant would remain, even *gratis;* and for the last ten years,
this, "handsome, desirable town family residence" had been the
abode of rats by day, and something else by night—so said the
neighbours.

Of course it was the very thing for John, and he snatched up
the gauntlet on the spot. He scoffed at its evil repute, and solemnly promised to rehabilitate its character within a week.

It was in vain that he was solemnly warned—that one of his
fellow guests gravely assured him "that he would not pass a night
in number ninety for ninety thousand pounds—it would be the
price of his reason."

"You value your reason at a very high figure," replied John,
with an indulgent smile. "I will venture mine for nothing."

"Those laugh who win," put in our host sharply. "You have not
been through the wood yet though your name is Hollyoak! I invite
all present to dine with me in three days from this; and then, if
our friend here has proved that he has got the better of the spirits,
we will all laugh together. Is that a bargain?"

This invitation was promptly accepted by the whole company; and then they fell to making practical arrangements for John's lodging for the next night.

I had no actual hand—or, more properly speaking, tongue—in this discussion, which carried us on till a late hour; but nevertheless, the next night at ten o'clock—for no ghost with any self respect would think of appearing before that time—I found myself standing, as John's second, on the steps of the notorious abode; but I was not going to remain; the hansom that brought us was to take me back to my respectable chambers.

This ill-fated house was large, solemn-looking, and gloomy. A heavy portico frowned down on neighbouring bare-faced hall-doors. The caretaker (an army pensioner, bravest of the brave in daylight) was prudently awaiting us outside with a key, which said key he turned in the lock, and admitted us into a great echoing hall, black as Erebus, saying as he did so: "My missus has haired the bed, and made up a good fire in the first front, sir. Your things is all laid hout, and (dubiously to John) I hope you'll have a comfortable night, sir."

"No, sir! Thank you, sir! Excuse me, I'll not come in! Good night!: and with the words still on his lips, he clattered down the steps with most indecent haste, and—vanished.

"And of course you will not come in either?" said John. "It is not in the bond, and I prefer to face them alone!" and he laughed contemptuously, a laugh that had a curious echo, it struck me at the time. A laugh strangely repeated, with an unpleasant mocking emphasis. "Call for me, alive or dead, at eight o'clock to-morrow morning!" he added, pushing me forcibly out into the porch, and closing the door with a heavy, reverberating clang, that sounded half-way down the street.

I did call for him the next morning as desired, with the army pensioner, who stared at his common-place, self-possessed appearance, with an expression of respectful astonishment.

"So it was all humbug, of course," I said, as he took my arm, and we set off for our club.

"You shall have the whole story whenever we have had something to cat," he replied somewhat impatiently. "It will keep till after breakfast—I'm famishing!"

I remarked that he looked unusually grave as we chatted over our broiled fish and omelette, and that occasionally his attention seemed wandering, to say the least of it. The moment he had brought out his cigar-case and lit up he turned to me and said:

"I see you are just quivering to know my experience, and I won't keep you on tenter-hooks any longer. In four words—I have seen them!"

I am (as before hinted) a silent man. I merely looked at him with widely-parted mouth and staring interrogative eyes.

I believe I had best endeavour to give the narrative without comment, and in John Hollyoak's own way. This is, as well as I can recollect, his experience word for word:—

"I proceeded upstairs, after I had shut you out, lighting my way by a match, and found the front room easily, as the door was ajar, and it was lit up by a roaring and most cheerful-looking fire, and two wax candles. It was a comfortable apartment, furnished with old-fashioned chairs and tables, and the traditional four-poster. There were numerous doors, which proved to be cupboards; and when I had executed a rigorous search in each of these closets and locked them, and investigated the bed above and beneath, sounded the walls, and bolted the door, I sat down before the fire, lit a cigar, opened a book, and felt that I was going to be master of the situation, and most thoroughly and comfortably 'at home.' My novel proved absorbing. I read on greedily, chapter after chapter, and so interested was I, and amused—for it was a lively book—that I positively lost sight of my whereabouts, and fancied myself reading in my own chamber! There was not a sound—not even a mouse in wainscot. The coals dropping from the grate alone occasionally broke the silence, till a neighbouring church-clock slowly boomed twelve! '*The hour!*' I said to myself, with a laugh, as I gave the fire a rousing poke, and commenced a fresh chapter; but ere I had read three pages I had occasion to pause and listen. What was that distinct sound now coming nearer and nearer? 'Rats, of course,' said Common-sense—'it was just the house for vermin.' Then a longish silence. Again a stir, sounds approaching, as if apparently caused by many feet passing down the corridor—high-heeled shoes, the sweeping switch of silken trains! Of course it was all imagination,

I assured myself—or rats! Rats were capable of making such curious improbable noises!

"Then another silence. No sound but cinders and the ticking
of my watch, which I had laid upon the table.

"I resumed my book, rather ashamed, and a little indignant
with myself for having neglected it, and calmly dismissed my late
interruption as 'rats—nothing but rats.'

"I had been reading and smoking for some time in a placid and
highly incredulous frame of mind, when I was somewhat rudely
startled by a loud single knock at my room door. I took no notice
of it, but merely laid down my novel and sat tight. Another knock
more imperious this time. After a moment's mental deliberation I
arose, armed myself with the poker, prepared to brain any number
of rats, and threw the door open with a violent swing that strained
its very hinges, and beheld, to my amazement, a tall powdered
footman in a laced scarlet livery, who, making a formal inclination
of his head, astonished me still further by saying:

"'Dinner is ready!'

"'I'm not coming!' I replied, without a moment's hesitation,
and thereupon I slammed the door in his face, locked it, and resumed my seat, also my book; but reading was a farce; my ears
were aching for the next sound.

"It came soon—rapid steps running up the stairs, and again a
single knock. I went over to the door, and once more discovered
the tall footman, who repeated, with a studied courtesy:

"'Dinner is ready, and the company are waiting.'

"'I told you I was not coming. Be off, and be hanged to you!'
I cried again, shutting the door violently.

"This time I did not make even a pretence at reading, I merely
sat and waited for the next move.

"I had not long to sit. In ten minutes I heard a third loud
summons. I rose, went to the door, and tore it open. There, as I
expected, was the servant again, with his parrot speech:

"'Dinner is ready, the company are waiting, and the master
says you must come!'

"'All right, then, I'll come,' I replied, wearied by reason of his
importunity, and feeling suddenly fired with a desire to see the
end of the adventure.

"He accordingly led the way downstairs, and I followed him, noting as I went the gilt buttons on his coat, and his splendidly turned calves, also that the hall and passages were now brilliantly illuminated, and that several liveried servants were passing to and fro, and that from—presumably—the dining-room, there issued a buzz of tongues, loud volleys of laughter, many hilarious voices, and a clatter of knives and forks. I was not left much time for speculation, as in another second I found myself inside the door, and my escort announced me in a stentorian voice as 'Mr. Hollyoak.'

"I could hardly credit my senses, as I looked round and saw about two dozen people, dressed in a fashion of the last century, seated at the table, which was loaded with gold and silver plate, and lighted up by a blaze of wax candles in massive candelabra.

"A swarthy elderly gentleman, who presided at the head of the board, rose deliberately as I entered. He was dressed in a crimson coat, braided with silver. He wore a peruke, had the most piercing black eyes I ever encountered, made me the finest bow I ever received in all my life, and with a polite wave of a taper hand, indicated my seat—a vacant chair between two powdered and patched beauties, with overflowing white shoulders and necks sparkling with diamonds.

"At first I was fully convinced that the whole affair was a superbly-matured practical joke. Everything looked so real, so truly flesh and blood, so complete in every detail; but I gazed around in vain for one familiar face.

"I saw young, old, and elderly; handsome and the reverse. On all faces there was a similar expression—reckless, hardened defiance, and something else that made me shudder, but that I could not classify or define.

"Were they a secret community? Burglars or coiners? But no; in one rapid glance I noticed that they belonged exclusively to the upper stratum of society—bygone society. The jabber of talking had momentarily ceased, and the host, imperiously hammering the table with a knife-handle, said in a singularly harsh grating voice:

"'Ladies and gentlemen, permit me to give you a toast! Our guest!' looking straight at me with his glittering coal-black eyes.

"Every glass was immediately raised. Twenty faces were turned towards mine, when, happily, a sudden impulse seized me. I sprang to my feet and said:

"'Ladies and gentlemen, I beg to thank you for your kind hospitality, but before I accept it, allow me to say grace!'

"I did not wait for permission, but hurriedly repeated a Latin benediction. Ere the last syllabic was uttered, in an instant there was a violent crash, an uproar, a sound of running, of screams, groans and curses, and then utter darkness.

"I found myself standing alone by a big mahogany table which I could just dimly discern by the aid of a street-lamp that threw its meagre rays into the great empty dining-room from the other side of the area.

"I must confess that I felt my nerves a little shaken by this instantaneous change from light to darkness—from a crowd of gay and noisy companions, to utter solitude and silence. I stood for a moment trying to recover my mental balance. I rubbed my eyes hard to assure myself that I was wide awake, and then I placed this very cigar-case in the middle of the table, as a sign and token that I had been downstairs—which cigar-case I found exactly where I left it this morning—and then went and groped my way into the hall and regained my room.

"I met with no obstruction *en route*. I saw no one, but as I closed and double-locked my door I distinctly heard a low laugh outside the keyhole—a sort of suppressed, malicious titter, that made me furious.

"I opened the door at once. There was nothing to be seen. I waited and listened—dead silence. I then undressed and went to bed, resolved that a whole army of footmen would fail to allure me once more to that festive board. I was determined not to lose my night's rest—ghosts or no ghosts.

"Just as I was dozing off I remember hearing the neighbouring church clock chime two. It was the last sound I was aware of; the house was now as silent as a vault. My fire burnt away cheerfully. I was no longer in the least degree inclined for reading, and I fell fast asleep and slept soundly till I heard the cabs and milk-carts beginning their morning career.

"I then rose, dressed at my leisure, and found you, my good, faithful friend, awaiting me, rather anxiously, on the hall-door steps.

"I have not done with that house yet. I'm determined to find out who these people are, and where they come from. I shall sleep there again to-night, and so shall 'Crib,' my bulldog; and you will see that I shall have news for you to-morrow morning—if I am alive to tell the tale," he added with a laugh.

In vain I would have dissuaded him. I protested, argued, and implored. I declared that rashness was not courage; that he had seen enough; that I, who had seen nothing, and only listened to his experiences, was convinced that number ninety was a house to be avoided.

I might just as well have talked to my umbrella! So, once more, I reluctantly accompanied him to his previous night's lodging. Once more I saw him swallowed up inside the gloomy, forbidding-looking, re-echoing hall.

I then went home in an unusually anxious, semi-excited, nervous state of mind; and I, who generally outrival the Seven Sleepers, lay wide awake, tumbling and tossing hour after hour, a prey to the most foolish ideas—ideas I would have laughed to scorn in daylight.

More than once I was certain that I heard John Hollyoak distractedly calling me; and I sat up in bed and listened intently. Of course it was fancy, for the instant I did so, there was no sound.

At the first gleam of winter dawn, I rose, dressed, and swallowed a cup of good strong coffee to clear my brain from the misty notions it had harboured during the night. And then I invested myself in my warmest topcoat and comforter, and set off for number ninety. Early as it was—it was but half-past seven—I found the army pensioner was before me, pacing the pavement with a countenance that would have made a first-rate frontispiece for "Burton's Anatomy of Melancholy"—a countenance the reverse of cheerful.

I was not disposed to wait for eight o'clock. I was too uneasy, and too impatient for further particulars of the dinner-party. So I rang with all my might, and knocked with all my main.

No sound within—no answer! But John was always a heavy sleeper. I was resolved to arouse him all the same, and knocked and rang, and rang and knocked, incessantly for fully ten minutes.

I then stooped down and applied my eye to the keyhole; I looked steadily into the aperture, till I became accustomed to the darkness, and then it seemed to me that another eye—a very strange, fiery eye—was glaring into mine from the other side of the door!

I removed my eye and applied my mouth instead, and shouted with all the power of my lungs (I did not care a straw if passersby took me for an escaped lunatic):

"John! John! Hollyoak!"

How his name echoed and re-echoed up through that great empty house!—"He must hear *that*," I said to myself as I pressed my ear closely against the lock, and listened with throbbing suspense.

The echo of "Hollyoak" had hardly died away when I swear that I distinctly heard a low, sniggering, mocking laugh—*that* was my only answer—that; and a vast unresponsive silence.

I was now quite desperate. I shook the door frantically, with all my strength. I broke the bell; in short, my behaviour was such that it excited the curiosity of a policeman, who crossed the road to know "What was up?"

"I want to get in!" I panted, breathless with my exertions.

"You'd better stay where you are!" said Bobby; "the outside of this house is the best of it! There are terrible stories—"

"But there is a gentleman inside it!" I interrupted impatiently. "He slept there last night, and I can't wake him. He has the key!"

"Oh, you can't *wake* him!" returned the policeman gravely. "Then we must get a locksmith!"

But already the thoughtful pensioner had procured one; and already a considerable and curious crowd surrounded the steps.

After five minutes of (to me) maddening delay, the great heavy door was opened and swung slowly back, and I instantly rushed in, followed less precipitately by the policeman and pensioner.

I had not far to seek John Hollyoak! He and his dog were lying at the foot of the stairs, both stone dead!

THE STORY OF A GHOST
VIOLET HUNT

Chapman's Magazine, 1895

I

"It is but giving over of a game
That must be lost."

Philaster

"Come, Mrs. Arne—come, my dear, you must not give way like this! You can't stand it—you really can't! Let Miss Kate take you away—do now!" urged the nurse, with her most motherly of intonations.

"Yes, Alice, Mrs. Joyce is right. Come away—do come away— you are only making yourself ill. It is all over, you can do nothing! Oh, do, do come away!" implored Mrs. Arne's sister, shivering with excitement and nervousness.

A few moments ago Dr. Graham had relinquished his hold on the pulse and come away from the bedside of Edward Arne with the hopeless movement of the eyebrows that meant—the end. The nurse had made the little gesture of resignation that was possibly a matter of form with her. The young sister-in-law had hidden her face in her hands. The wife had screamed—a scream that turned them all hot and then cold—and flung herself on the bed over her dead husband. There she lay; her cries were terrible, her sobs shook her whole body.

The three gazed at her pityingly, wonderingly, not knowing what to do next. The nurse, folding her hands, looked towards the

319

doctor for directions, and the doctor drummed with his fingers on the bed-post. The young girl timidly stroked the shoulder that heaved and writhed under her touch.

"Go away! Go away!" the widow reiterated continually in a voice hoarse with fatigue and passion.

"Leave her alone, Miss Kate," whispered the nurse at last; "she will work it off best by herself, perhaps."

She turned down the lamp, as if to draw a veil over the scene, and as she did so, Mrs. Arne raised herself on her elbow, showing a face stained with tears and purple with emotion.

"What! Not gone?" she said harshly. "I tell you I *will* be left. It is my house. Go away, Kate, go away! I don't want you, I want no one—I want to speak to my husband. Oh, if you would only go away—away—all of you. Give me an hour—half-an-hour—five minutes!"

She stretched out her arms imploringly to the doctor.

"Well . . . ," said he, almost to himself.

He signed to the two women to withdraw and followed them out into the passage. "Go and get something to eat," he said peremptorily, "while you can. We shall have trouble with her presently. I'll wait in the dressing-room."

He glanced at the writhing figure on the bed, shrugged his shoulders, and passed into the adjoining room, without however closing the door of communication. Sitting down in an armchair drawn up to the fire, he stretched himself and closed his eyes. The professional aspects of the case of Edward Arne rose up before him in all its interesting forms of complication. . . .

It was just this professional attitude that Mrs. Arne unconsciously resented both in the doctor and in the nurse. They had been kindness itself, but through all their kindness, she realised and resented their scientific interest in her husband as a curious and complicated case; and now that the blow had fallen, regarded them both in the light of executioners. Her one desire, expressed with all the shameless sincerity of blind and thoughtless misery, was to be free of their hateful presence and alone—alone with her dead!

She was weary of the doctor's subdued manly tones—of the nurse's commonplace motherliness, too habitually adapted to the needs of all to be appreciated by the individual—of the childish consolations of the young sister, who had never loved, never been married, did not know what sorrow was! Their clumsy expressions of sympathy struck her like blows, the touch of their hands on her body, as they tried to raise her, irritated her in every nerve. With a sigh of relief, she buried her head in the pillow, pressed her body more closely against that of her husband, and lay still. . . .

The lamp went out with a gurgle. The fire leaped up, and died. She raised her head and stared about her helplessly.

"Edward—dear Edward!" she whispered in his ear, lying down again; "why have you left me? Darling, why have you left me? I can't stay behind—you know I can't. I am too young to be left. It is only a year since you married me and promised to love me and to cherish me for ever! I never thought it was only for a year. *Till death us do part!* Yes, I know that's in it, but nobody ever thinks of that! I never thought of living without you! I meant to die with you. . . .

"No—no—I can't die—I must not—till my baby is born. You will never see it. Don't you want to see it? Don't you? Oh, Edward, speak! Say something, darling, one word—one little word! Edward! Edward! are you there? Are you there? Answer me, for God's sake, answer me!

"Darling, I am *so* tired of waiting. Oh, think, dearest. There is so little time. They only gave me half-an-hour. In half-an-hour they will come and take you away from me—take you where I can't come to you—with all my love I can't come to you! I know the place—I saw it once. A great lonely place full of graves, and little stunted trees dripping with dirty London rain . . . and gas lamps flaring all round . . . but quite, quite dark where the grave is . . . a long grey stone just like the rest. How could you stay there?—all alone—all alone—without me?

"Do you remember, Edward, what we once said—that whichever of us died first should come back to watch over the other, in the spirit? I promised you, and you promised me. What children we were! Death is not what we thought. It comforted us to say that *then*. Now, it's nothing—nothing—worse than nothing! I don't want your spirit—I can't see it, or feel it—I want you, *you,* your eyes that looked at me, your mouth that kissed me, your arms that held me—"

She raised his arms and clasped them round her neck, and lay there very still, murmuring "Love me! Love me!"

The doctor in the next room moved in his chair. The noise awoke her from her dream of contentment, and she unwound the dead arm from her neck and, holding it up by the wrist considered it ruefully.

"Yes, I can put it round me, but I have to hold it there—see? It is quite cold—it doesn't care. Ah, my dear, you don't care! You are dead. I kiss you, but you don't kiss me. Edward I Edward! Oh, for heaven's sake kiss me once, or I shall go mad I Just once! No, no, that won't do—that's not enough! I can't do without you! I must have you back. . . . What shall I do? Pray? . . . I often pray. . . . Oh, if there is a God in heaven, and if He ever answered a prayer, let Him answer mine—my only prayer, I'll never ask another—and give you back to me! As you were—as I loved you—as I adored you! He must listen, He must! My God, my God, he's mine—he's my husband, he's my lover—give him back to me!"

"—Left alone for half-an-hour or more with the corpse! It's not right!"

The muttered expression of the nurse's revolted sense of professional decency came from the head of the staircase, where she had been waiting for the last few minutes. The doctor joined her.

"Hush, Mrs. Joyce! I'll go to her now."

The door creaked on its hinges, as he gently pushed it open and went in.

"What's that? What's that?" screamed Mrs. Arne. "Doctor! Doctor! Don't touch me! Either I am dead or he is alive!"

"Do you want to kill yourself, Mrs. Arne?" said Dr. Graham with calculated sternness, coming forward; "you really must come away now. Come!"

"Not dead—not dead—" she murmured.

"He *is* dead, I assure you. Dead and cold an hour ago! Feel! . . . By God!"

He had taken hold of her, as she lay face downwards, and in so doing he had touched the dead man's cheek—it was warm! Instinctively his finger sought a pulse—

"Stop! Wait!" he cried in his intense excitement. "My dear Mrs. Arne, control yourself!"

But Mrs. Arne had fainted, and fallen heavily off the bed on the other side. Her sister, hastily summoned, attended to her, while the husband she had given over for dead, was, with faint gasps and sighs, and reluctant moans, pulled, as it were, hustled, and pushed back over the threshold of life.

II

"I wonder why you always choose to wear black, Alice?" remarked Esther Graham, carelessly. "You are not in mourning that I know of."

She was Dr. Graham's only daughter and Mrs. Arne's only bosom friend. She sat with Mrs. Arne in the dreary drawing-room of the house in Chelsea. She had come to tea. She was the only person who ever did come to tea there.

She was brusque, kind, and blunt, and had a talent for making inappropriate remarks. Six years ago Mrs. Arne had been practically a widow—for an hour! Her husband had succumbed to an apparently mortal illness, and for the space of an hour had lain for dead. When suddenly and inexplicably he had revived from his trance, the shock, combined with six weeks' nursing, had nearly killed his wife. All this Esther had heard from her father. She herself had only come to know Mrs. Arne after her child was born, and all the tragic circumstances of her husband's illness put aside and forgotten. But her idle question received no answer from the pale absent woman who sat opposite, with listless lacklustre eyes fixed on the green and blue flames dancing in the fire.

"Do say something, Alice!" she implored, after five minutes' silence.

"I beg your pardon, Esther," said Mrs. Arne piteously. "I was thinking."

"What were you thinking of?"

"I don't know, I am sure."

"No, of course, you don't. People who sit and stare into the fire never do think, really. They are only brooding and making themselves ill, and that is what you are doing? You mope, you take no interest in anything, you never go out—I am sure you have not been out of doors to-day?"

"No—yes—I believe not. It is so cold."

"You are sure to get cold if you sit in the house all day, and sure to get ill too! Just look at yourself!"

Mrs. Arne rose and looked at herself in the Italian mirror over the chimney-piece. It reflected faithfully enough her even pallor, her dark hair and eyes, the sweeping length of her eyelashes, the sharp curves of her nostril, and the delicate arch of her eyebrows that formed a thin sharp black line so clear as to seem almost unnatural.

"Yes, I do look ill," she said with conviction.

"No wonder—if you choose to bury yourself alive like this!"

"I do feel as if I lived in a grave sometimes. I look up at the ceiling and fancy it is my coffin lid."

"Don't, please, talk like that!" expostulated Miss Graham, pointing to Mrs. Arne's little girl. "If only for Dolly's sake, I think you should not give way to morbid fancies."

"Oh, Esther," the other exclaimed, stung into something like vivacity, "don't reproach me! I hope I am a good mother to my child!"

"Yes, dear, you are a model mother—and model wife too. Father says the way you look after your husband is something wonderful, but don't you think for your own sake you might try to be a little gayer? You encourage these moods, don't you? What is it? Is it the house? These lovely old Chelsea houses are a little depressing, I always think."

She glanced around her—at the high ceiling, at the heavy damask *portières,* the tall cabinets full of china, the dim oak paneling—it reminded her of a neglected museum. Her eye travelled into the farthest corners, where the faint filmy dusk was already gathering, lit only by the bewildering cross-lights of the glass panels of cabinet doors—to the tall narrow windows—then back again to the woman in her mourning dress, cowering by the fire. She said sharply:

"You should go out more."

"I do not like to—leave my husband."

"Oh, I know that he is delicate, I know you look after him as if he were a baby, but still, does he never permit you to leave him? Does he never go out by himself?"

"Not often!"

"And you have no pets! Now I simply can't imagine a house without animals!"

"We did have a dog once," answered Mrs. Arne plaintively. "But it howled so we had to give it away. It would not go near Edward . . . But please don't imagine that I am dull! I have my child, you know." She laid her hand on the little head at her knee and Miss Graham rose, frowning.

"Ah, you are too bad!" she exclaimed. "You look like a widow exactly, with one child, and you are stroking its orphan head and saying, 'Poor fatherless darling!'"

Voices were heard outside. Miss Graham stopped talking quite suddenly and sought her veil and gloves on the mantelpiece.

"You need not go, Esther," said Mrs. Arne. "It is only my husband."

"Oh, but it is getting late," said the other, crumpling up her gloves in her muff and shuffling her feet nervously.

"Come!" said her hostess, with a bitter little smile, "put your gloves on properly—if you must go—but it is quite early still."

"Please don't go, Miss Graham," put in the child.

"I must. Go and meet your papa like a good little girl."

"I don't want to."

"Unnatural daughter," said Esther absently, still looking towards the door. Mrs. Arne rose and fastened her cloak for her. The white, sad, oppressed face came very close to the cheerful one, as she murmured, in a low voice:

"You don't like my husband, Esther? I can't help noticing it. Why don't you?"

"Nonsense!" retorted the other, with the emphasis of one who is repelling an overtrue accusation. "I do, only—"

"Only what?"

"Well, dear, it is foolish of me, of course, but I am—a little—afraid of him."

"Afraid of Edward!" said his wife slowly. "Why should you be?"

"Well, dear—you see—I—I suppose women can't help being a little afraid of their friends' husbands—they can spoil their friendships with their wives in a moment, if they choose to disapprove of them. I really must go. Good-bye, child, give me a kiss! Don't ring, Alice. *Please* don't. I can open the door for myself—"

"Why should you?" said Mrs. Arne. "Edward is in the hall; I heard him speaking to Foster."

"No, he has gone into his study. Good-bye, you apathetic creature!"

She gave Mrs. Arne a brief kiss and dashed out of the room. The voices outside had ceased, and she had reasonable hopes of reaching the door without being intercepted by Mrs. Arne's husband.

But he met her on the stairs. Mrs. Arne, listening intently from her seat by the fire, heard her exchange a few shy sentences with him, the sound of which died away as they went downstairs together. A few moments after, Edward Arne came into the room and dropped into the chair just vacated by his wife's visitor.

His juxtaposition had the effect of making his wife look at once several years older. Where she was pale, he was well-coloured, the network of little filmy wrinkles that on a close inspection covered her face had no parallel on his smooth skin. He was handsome; soft well-groomed flakes of auburn hair lay over his forehead, and his steely blue eyes shone equably, a contrast to the sombre fire of hers, and the masses of dark crinkly hair that shadowed her brow. The deep lines of permanent discontent furrowed that brow as she sat with her chin propped on her hands and her elbows resting on her knees. Neither spoke. When the hands of the clock over Mrs. Arne's head pointed to seven, the white-aproned figure of the nurse appeared in the doorway, and the little girl rose and kissed her mother very tenderly.

Mrs. Arne's forehead contracted. Looking uneasily at her husband, she said to the child tentatively, yet boldly, as one grasps a nettle, "Say good-night to your father!"

"Good-night!" it said indifferently, in his direction.

"Kiss him!"

"No, please—*please* not."

Her mother looked down on her, curiously, sadly. "You are a naughty spoilt child!" she said, but without conviction. "Excuse her, Edward."

He did not seem to have heard.

"Well, if *you* don't care—" said his wife bitterly. "Come, child!" She caught the little girl by the hand and left the room.

At the door she half turned and looked fixedly at her husband. It was a strange, ambiguous gaze, in which yearning interest and a bitter dislike were strangely commingled. Then she shivered and closed the door softly after her.

The man in the armchair sat on with no perceptible change of attitude, his unspeculative eyes fixed on the fire, his hands clasped idly in front of him. The pose was obviously habitual. The servant brought lights and closed the shutters, drew the curtains, and made up the fire noisily, without however, eliciting any reproof from his master.

Edward Arne was an ideal master, as far as Foster was concerned. He kept cases of cigars, but never smoked them, although the supply had often to be renewed. He did not care what he ate or drank, although he kept as good a cellar as most gentlemen— Foster knew that. He never interfered, he counted for nothing, he gave no trouble. Foster had no intention of ever leaving such an easy place. True, his master was not cordial, he very seldom addressed him or seemed to know he was there, but then neither did he grumble if the fire in his study was allowed to go out, or interfere with Foster's liberty in any way. He had a better place of it than Argentine, Mrs. Arne's maid, who would be called up in the middle of the night to bathe her mistress's forehead with eau-de-Cologne, or made to brush her long hair for hours together to soothe her. Naturally enough Foster and Argentine compared notes as to their respective situations, and drew unflattering parallels between this capricious wife and model husband.

III

Miss Graham was not a demonstrative woman. On her return home she somewhat startled her father, as he sat in his study, up to his eyes in papers and memoranda of all kinds, by the sudden violence of her embrace.

"Why this demonstration?" he asked, smiling and looking up. He was a young-looking man for his age, his thin wiry figure and clear colour belied the evidence of his hair, tinged with grey, and the tired wrinkles that gave value to the acuteness and brilliancy of the eyes they surrounded.

"I don't know!" she replied, "only you are so nice and alive somehow. I always feel like this when I come back from seeing the Arnes."

"Then don't go to see the Arnes."

"I'm so fond of her, father, and she will never come here to me, as you know. Nothing but my affection for her would induce me to enter her tomb of a house and talk to that walking funeral of a husband of hers. I got away to-day without having to shake hands with him, anyhow! . . . Father, I do wish you would go and see Alice."

"Is she ill?"

"Well, not exactly ill, I suppose, but her eyes make me quite uncomfortable, and she says such odd things! I don't know if it is you or the clergyman she wants, but she is all wrong somehow! She never goes out, except to church, she never pays a call, or has any one to call on her! The Arnes never entertain, nobody ever asks them to dinner, and I'm sure I don't blame them—the mere sight of that man sitting like a death's-head at one's table would spoil any party. She is always alone. Day after day I go in and find her sitting over the fire, with that same tired weary brooding expression. I shouldn't be surprised in the least if she were to go mad some day. . . . Father, what is it? What is the tragedy of that house? There is one, I am convinced. And yet, though I have been the intimate friend of that woman for years, I know no more about her than the man in the street. She's utterly miserable, I know that much."

"She keeps her skeleton safe in the cupboard," said Dr. Graham. "I respect her for that. But please don't talk nonsense about tragedies. Alice Arne is only morbid—the malady of the age. And she is a very religious woman."

"Yes, just the kind of woman who turns Roman Catholic in the end. She is always going to Mr. Bligh's services. I wonder if she complains of her odious husband to him."

"Odious?"

"Yes, odious!" Miss Graham shuddered. "I cannot stand him! I cannot bear the touch of his cold froggy hands, and the sight of his fishy eyes! That inane smile of his simply makes me shrivel up. Father, honestly, do *you* like him, yourself?"

"My dear, I hardly know him. It is his wife I have known ever since she was a child, and I a boy at college. Her father was my tutor. I never knew her husband till six years ago, when she called me in to attend him in a very serious illness. I suppose she never speaks of it? No? A very odd affair. For the life of me I cannot tell how he managed to recover. You needn't tell people, for it affects my reputation, but *I* didn't save him! Indeed I have never been able to account for it. The man was given over for dead!"

"He might as well be dead, for all the good he is," said Esther scornfully. "I have never heard him say more than a couple of sentences in my life."

"Yet he was an exceedingly brilliant young man; one of the best men of his year at Oxford—awfully run after in society—poor Alice was wild to marry him!"

"What? Actually in love with that spiritless creature? He is like a house with some one dead in it, and all the blinds down—an empty shell—a husk without a kernel—"

"Come, Esther, don't you be morbid—not to say silly! You're hard on the poor man! He is the ordinary, commonplace, cold-blooded specimen of humanity, a little stupid, a little selfish—people who have gone through a serious illness like that are apt to be—but on the whole, a good husband, a good father, a good citizen—"

"Yes, and his wife is afraid of him, and his child simply hates him!" exclaimed Esther with effect.

"Nonsense!" said Dr. Graham sharply. "The child is spoilt—only children are apt to be—and the mother wants a change, or a tonic of some kind. I'll go and talk to her when I have time. Go along and dress. Have you forgotten that George Graham is coming to dinner?"

After she had gone the doctor made a note on the corner of his blotting-pad, "Mem.: to go and see Mrs. Arne," and dismissed the subject of the memorandum entirely from his mind.

George Graham was the doctor's nephew, a tall weedy sympathetic young man, full of fads and fallacies, with a gentle manner that somehow inspired confidence. He was several years younger than Esther, who loved to listen to his semi-scientific, semi-romantic stories of things met with in the course of his profession. "Oh, I come across very queer things!" he used to say, mysteriously, "you would not believe—?"

He was looking at a photograph on the mantelpiece when she went in to receive him. "Strange!" he murmured, as he turned round to greet her. "It is rather like my little widow!"

"Who is your little widow?" asked Esther after dinner, when, her father having gone back to his study, she and her cousin sat together as usual.

He laughed. "You like to hear of my professional experiences? Well, she certainly interested me," he said, thoughtfully. "She is a queer psychological study in her way. I wish I could come across her again."

"Where *did* you come across her, and what is her name?"

"I don't know her name, I don't want to; she is not a personage to me, only a case. I hardly know her face even. I have never seen it except in the twilight. But I gathered that she lived somewhere in Chelsea, for she came out on to the Embankment with only a kind of lacy thing over her head; she can't live far off, I fancy."

"Tell me about her?"

"It was three weeks ago," said George Graham. "I was coming along the Embankment about ten o'clock. I walked through that little grove there is, you know, just between Cheyne Walk and the river, and I heard in there some one sobbing very bitterly. I looked and saw a woman sitting on a seat with her head in her hands, crying. I was awfully sorry, of course, and I thought I could perhaps do something for her, get her a glass of water, or salts or something. I took her for a woman of the people—it was quite dark, you know. So I asked her very politely if I could do anything for her, and then, I noticed her hands—they were quite white and covered with diamonds."

"Sorry you spoke, I suppose," said Esther.

"She raised her head and said—I believe she laughed—'Are you going to tell me to move on?'"

"She thought you were a policeman?"

"Probably—if she thought at all—but she was in a semi-dazed condition. I told her to wait till I came back, and dashed round the corner to the chemist's and bought a bottle of salts. She thanked me, and made a little effort to rise and go away. She seemed very weak. I told her I was a medical man and bade her sit still awhile. Then I talked to her."

"And she to you?"

"Yes, quite straight. Don't you know that women always treat a doctor as if he were one step removed from their father confessor—not human—not in the same category as themselves? It is not complimentary to one as a man, but one hears a good deal one would not otherwise hear. She ended by telling me all about herself—in a veiled sort of way, of course. It soothed her—relieved her—she seemed to have had no sort of outlet for years, by the way she went on, poor thing!"

"To a mere stranger!"

"To a doctor. And she did not know what she was saying half the time. She was hysterical, of course. Heavens! what nonsense she talked! She spoke of herself as a person somehow haunted, cursed by some malign fate, a victim of some fearful spiritual catastrophe, don't you know? I let her run on. She was so

convinced of the reality of a sort of 'doom' that she fancied had
befallen her. Rot, of course, mere hysterical rot—only interesting
medically! Then it got cold—she shivered—I suggested her going
in. She shrunk back; she said, 'If you only knew what a relief it is,
how much less miserable I am out here! I can breathe . . . I can live
. . . it is my only glimpse of the world that is alive . . . I live in a
grave . . . oh, let me stay!' She seemed positively afraid to go home."

"Perhaps some one bullied her at home?"

"I suppose so, but—she had no husband. He died, she told me,
years ago. She had adored him, she said—"

"Is she pretty?"

"Pretty! Well, I hardly noticed. She's a case to me, not a person, as I told you. Let me see! Oh, yes, I suppose she was pretty—
no, now I think of it she would be too worn and faded to be what
you call pretty."

Esther smiled.

"Well, we sat there together for quite an hour, then the clock
of Chelsea Church struck eleven, and she got up and said 'Good-
bye,' holding out her hand quite naturally, as if our meeting and
conversation had been nothing out of the common. Oh, she is
mad, not a doubt of it! There was a sound like a dead leaf trailing
across the walk and she was gone."

"Didn't you ask if you should see her again, or anything?"

"That would have been a mean advantage to take."

"You might have offered to see her home."

"I saw she did not mean me to."

"She was a lady, you say," pondered Esther. "How was she
dressed?"

"Oh, all right, like a lady—in black—mourning, I suppose.
She has dark crinkly hair, and her eyebrows are very thin and dark
and arched—I noticed that in the dusk."

"Which is the photograph that reminded you of her?" said
Esther suddenly, taking him to the mantelpiece.

"This one."

"Alice Arne! Oh, it couldn't be—she is not a widow, her husband is alive—has your woman any children?"

"Yes, one. She mentioned it."

"How old?"

"Six years old, I think she said. She talks of the 'responsibility of bringing up an orphan.'"

"George, what time is it?" she asked suddenly.

"About nine o'clock."

"Would you mind coming out with me?"

"I should like it. Where shall we go?"

"To St. Adhelms! It is close by here. There is a special late ser-vice to-night, and Mrs. Arne is sure to be there."

"Oh, Esther—curiosity!"

"No, not mere curiosity. Don't you see if it is *my* Mrs. Arne who has been going on like this, it is very serious? I have thought her ill for a long time; but as ill as that!— Shall you know her again?"

"Of course I shall know her—her and her eyebrows."

Esther Graham pointed out a woman who was kneeling beside a pillar in an attitude of intense devotion and abandonment. When the latter rose from her knees, and turned her rapt face up towards the pulpit whence the Reverend Ralph Bligh was holding his im-passioned discourse, George Graham touched his cousin on the shoulder, and motioned to her to leave her place on the outermost rank of worshippers.

"That is the woman!" said he. "That is my little widow!"

IV

"Mem.: to go and see Mrs. Arne." The doctor came across this note in his blotting-pad one day six weeks later. His daughter was out of town. He had heard nothing of the Arnes since her departure. He had promised to go and see her. He was a little conscience-stricken.

Yet another week elapsed before he found time to call upon the daughter of his old tutor.

At the corner of Tite Street he met Mrs. Arne's husband and stopped. A doctor's professional kindliness of manner is, or ought to be, independent of his personal likings and dislikings, and there was a pleasant cordiality about his greeting which ought to have provoked a corresponding fervour on the part of Edward Arne.

"How are you, Arne?" Graham said; "I was on my way to call on your wife."

"Ah—yes!" said Edward Arne, with the ascending inflection of polite acquiescence. A ray of blue from his eyes rested transitorily on the doctor's face, and in that short moment the latter noted its intolerable vacuity, and for the first time in his life felt a sharp pang of sympathy for the wife of such a husband.

"I suppose you are off to your club?—er—good-bye!" he wound up abruptly. With the best will in the world, he somehow found it almost impossible to carry on a conversation with Edward Arne, who raised his hand to his head in token of salutation, smiled sweetly, and was gone.

"He really is extraordinarily good-looking," reflected the doctor as he watched him down the street and safely over the crossing with a certain degree of solicitude for which he could not exactly account; "but he is a regular wet blanket. One feels one's vitality ebbing out at the finger-ends as one talks to him. I shall begin to believe in Esther's absurd fancies about him soon. Ah, there's the little girl!" he exclaimed, as he turned into Cheyne Walk and caught sight of her with her nurse, making violent demonstrations to attract his attention. "She is alive, at any rate. How is your mother, Dolly?" he asked.

"Quite well, thank you," was the child's reply. She added, "She's crying. She sent me away because I looked at her. So I did. Her cheeks are quite red."

"Run away—run away and play!" said the doctor, nervously. He ascended the steps of the house and rang the bell very gently and neatly.

"Not at—" began Foster, with the intonation of polite falsehood, but stopped on seeing the doctor, who, with his daughter, was a privileged person. "Mrs. Arne will see you, sir."

Half way upstairs the doctor paused.

"Mrs. Arne is not alone?" he said interrogatively.

"Yes, sir, quite alone. I have just taken tea in."

Dr. Graham's doubts were prompted by the low murmur as of a voice, or voices, which came to him through the open door of the room at the head of the stairs. He paused and listened while

Foster stood by, merely remarking, "Mrs. Arne do talk to herself sometimes, sir."

It was Mrs. Arne's voice, the doctor recognised it now. It was not the voice of a sane or healthy woman. He at once mentally removed his visit from the category of a morning call, and prepared for a semi-professional inquiry.

"Don't announce me," he said to Foster, and quietly entered the back drawing-room, which was separated by a heavy tapestry *portière* from the room where Mrs. Arne sat, with an open book on the table before her, from which she had been apparently reading aloud. Her hands were now clasped tightly over her face, and when, presently, she removed them and began feverishly to turn page after page of her book, the crimson of her cheeks was seamed with white where her fingers had impressed themselves.

Graham wondered if she saw him, for though her eyes were fixed in his direction, there was no apprehension in them. She went on reading, and it was the text, mingled with passionate interjections and fragmentary utterances, of one of the services of the Church that met his astonished ears.

"'*For as in Adam all die.*' All die—yes, all! It says all! '*For he must reign . . . the last enemy that shall be destroyed is Death—*'"

She paused and raised her head, and Graham made a step forward.

"Death!—death!—always death! Oh, why is there death? And then— '*What shall they do, if the dead rise not at all!*' Not at all! Never! Never! 'I *die* daily. . . .' Daily! No, no, better get it over . . . dead and buried . . . out of sight, out of mind . . . under a stone. Dead men don't come back. . . . Go on! Go on! Get it over. I want to hear the earth rattle on the coffin and then I shall know it is done. '*Flesh and blood cannot inherit!*' — Oh, what did I do? What have I done? Why did I wish it so fervently? Why did I pray for it so earnestly? God gave me my wish—"

"Alice! Alice!" groaned the doctor.

"What? Oh, where was I? I've lost it. . . . '*When this corruptible shall have put on incorruption—*' Oh! can I bear it? . . . Yes, I must. . . . Go on! '*Dust to dust, ashes to ashes, earth to earth—*' Yes, that is it. '*After death, though worms destroy this body—*'"

She flung the book aside and sobbed uncontrollably.

"That was what I was afraid of. My God! My God! Down there—in the dark—for ever and ever and ever! I could not bear to think of it! My Edward! And so I interfered . . . and prayed . . . and prayed till. . . . Oh! I am punished. Flesh and blood could not inherit! I kept him here—I would not let him go—I would not. . . . I prayed. . . . I denied him Christian burial. . . . I did . . . I did. . . . How could I know?"

"Good heavens, Alice!" said Graham, coming forward, "what does this mean? I have heard of schoolgirls going through the marriage service by themselves, but the burial service—!"

He laid down his hat and went on severely, "What have you to do with such things? Your child is flourishing—your husband alive and here—"

"And who kept him here?" interrupted Alice Arne fiercely.

"*You* did," he answered quickly, "with your care and tenderness. I believe the warmth of your body, as you lay beside him for that half-hour, maintained the vital heat during that extraordinary suspension of the heart's action, which made us all give him up for dead. You were his best doctor, and brought him back to us."

"Yes, it was I—it was I—you need not tell me it was I!"

"Come, be thankful!" he said cheerfully. "Put that book away, and give me some tea. I'm very cold."

"Oh, Dr. Graham, how thoughtless of me!" said Mrs. Arne, rallying like a well-bred woman at the slight imputation on her politeness he purposely made. She tottered to the bell and rang it before he could anticipate her.

"Another cup," she said quite calmly to Foster, who answered it. Then she sat down quivering all over with the suddenness of the constraint put upon her.

"Yes, sit down and tell me all about it," said Graham good-humouredly, at the same time observing her closely.

"There is nothing to tell," she said simply, shaking her head, and futilely altering the position of the tea-cups on the tray. "It all happened years ago. Nothing can be done now. Will you have sugar?"

He drank his tea, and made conversation. No subject that he introduced seemed to interest her. Yet he could see that a question trembled on her tongue, and tried to lead up to it.

It came at last.

"Dr. Graham, tell me," she asked tremulously, "do you believe that prayers—wicked unreasonable prayers—are granted?"

He helped himself to another slice of bread-and-butter before answering. "Well—" he said slowly, "it seems hard to believe that every fool who has a voice to pray with and a brain to conceive idiotic requests should be permitted to interfere with the economy of the universe. As a rule, if people were longsighted enough to foresee the result of their petitions, I fancy very few of us would venture to interfere."

Mrs. Arne groaned.

She was a good churchwoman, Graham knew, and he did not wish to sap her faith in any way, so he said no more, but inwardly wondered if a too rigid interpretation of some of the religious dogmas of the Vicar of St. Adhelm's, her spiritual adviser, was not the clue to her distress. Then she put another question—

"Eh! What?" he said. "Do I believe in ghosts? I will believe you if you will tell me that you have seen one."

"You know, Doctor," she went on, "I was always afraid of ghosts—of spirits—things unseen. I couldn't ever read about them. I could not bear the idea of some one in the room with me that I could not see. There was a text that always frightened me that hung up in my room: *'Thou, God, seest me.'* It frightened me when I was a child, whether I had been doing wrong or not. But now," shuddering, "I think there are worse things than ghosts."

"Well, now, what sort of things?" he asked good-humouredly. "Astral bodies—?"

She leaned forward and laid her hot hand on his.

"Oh, Doctor, tell me, if a spirit—without the body we know it by—is terrible; what of a body—" her voice sank to a whisper, "a body—senseless—lonely—stranded on this earth—without a spirit—?"

She was watching his face anxiously. He was divided between a morbid inclination to laugh at the grotesqueness of the image suggested, and the feeling of intense discomfort provoked by this wretched scene. He longed to give the conversation a more cheerful turn, yet did not wish to offend her by changing it too abruptly.

"I have heard of people not being able to keep body and soul together," he replied at last, "but I am not aware that practically such a division of forces has ever been achieved. And if we could only accept the theory of the despiritualised body, what a lot of antipathetic people now wandering about in the world it would account for!"

The piteous gaze of her eyes seemed to seek to ward off the blow of his misplaced jocularity. He left his seat and sat down on the couch beside her.

"Poor child! poor girl! You are ill, you are over-excited. What is it? Tell me," he asked her as tenderly as the father she had lost early in life might have done. Her head sank on his shoulder.

"Are you unhappy?" he asked her gently.

"Yes!"

"You are too much alone. Get your mother or your sister to come and stay with you."

"They won't come," she wailed. "They say the house is like a grave."

"What nonsense! I am sure your sensible mother never said anything of the sort. But you *must* see more people somehow. It's a pity Esther is away. Have you had any visitors to-day?"

"Not a soul has crossed the threshold for eighteen days."

"We must change all that," said the doctor vaguely. "Meantime you must cheer up. Why, you have no need to think of ghosts and graves—no need to be melancholy—you have your husband and your child—"

"I have my child—yes."

The doctor took hold of Mrs. Arne by the shoulder, and held her a little way from him. He thought he had found the cause of her trouble—a more commonplace one than he had supposed.

"I have known you, Alice, since you were a child," he said gravely. "Answer me! You love your husband, don't you?"

"Yes." It was as if she were answering futile prefatory questions in the witness-box. Yet he saw by the intense excitement in her eyes that he had come to the point that she feared, and yet desired, to bring forward.

"And he loves you?"

She was silent.

"Well then, if you love each other, what more can you want? Why do you say you have only your child in that absurd way?"

She was still silent, and he gave her a little shake.

"Tell me, have you and he had any little difference lately? Perhaps something a few words could set right? Is there any—little coldness—any—temporary estrangement between you?"

He was hardly prepared for the burst of foolish laughter that proceeded from the demure Mrs. Arne as she rose and confronted him, all the blood in her body seeming for the moment to rush to her usually pale cheeks.

"Coldness! Temporary estrangement! If that were all! Oh, is every one blind but me? Anything come between us! There is all the world between us—all the difference between this world and the next!"

She sat down again beside the doctor and whispered in his ear, and her words were like a breath of hot wind from some Gehenna of the soul.

"Oh, Doctor, I have borne it for six years, and I *must* speak! No other woman could bear what I have borne, and yet be alive! And I loved him so, you don't know how I loved him! That was it—that was my crime—"

"Crime?" repeated the doctor.

"Yes, crime! It was impious, don't you see? But I have been punished. Oh, Doctor, you don't know what my life is! Listen! *Listen!* I must tell you. I must tell you. To live with a— At first—before I guessed—when I used to put my arms round him, and he merely submitted—and then it dawned on me what I was kissing—! It is enough to turn a living woman to stone—for I *am* living, though sometimes I forget it. Yes, I am a live woman, though I live in a grave. Think what it is! to wonder every night if you will be alive in the morning, to lie down every night in an open grave—to smell death in every corner—every room—to breathe death—to touch it—" Her voice rose to a scream. "You can ask Dolly, she knows it too; she feels it—"

"Be off, Dolly," shouted Graham to the terrified child, who at this moment appeared in the doorway with her nurse.

Mrs. Arne slipped on to the floor, where she lay face downwards, her hand clutching the carpet convulsively. Her words died away in indistinct murmurings, as she entirely lost consciousness.

Yet her last clearly-heard sentence, as the frightened child turned and fled downstairs, seemed to Graham to strike the note of madness.

"The child knows! She knows! She would never kiss him! She knows she has no father now. Her father died before she was born, the very day I lost my husband!"

"Don't let him come near me! Doctor, don't let him come near me!" was Mrs. Arne's cry as she lay tossing on the bed to which she was carried. "I can't get well if you bring him here."

"I won't," Graham would answer soothingly. "Trust me, he shall not come into this room till you say he may."

"I shall never say he may! I never, never shall want to see him again! . . . Need I? Need I? Let him stay down there . . . underground . . . in the dark . . . and not come back to trouble the living . . ."

The doctor reflected that Edward Arne's study was in the basement of the house, and that he often sat there without lights. Still her brutal speech did not quite fit even that meaning.

"What has he done to you, Alice?" he asked gently.

"Nothing! Nothing! It was I who did it. It is my fault. I made a mistake. . . . One should never interfere. But I repent . . . I want to take back my prayer. . . . I want God to take it back. He knows best . . . *'A time to be born, and a time to die . . .'*"

"She lied to me the other day," thought Graham. "She has had a long quarrel with her husband—a quarrel serious enough to have temporarily unsettled her reason!"

"I have lost my patient," Dr. Graham wrote a week later to a medical friend. "I call Edward Arne my patient, but, practically, he was his wife's. I never till now realised what a good and loving woman can do for a man. Such wonders as we physicians cannot think of attempting! And the proof of it is that from the moment she was laid up—three days ago—he began to pine away, and finally went out of being; just like those little heaps of charred ashes of something one has thrown on the fire, that keep their shape till they are disturbed and then fall asunder into nothingness. The servants found him dead in his armchair three days ago. There had been no warnings, no symptoms of serious illness, they tell me. Yet I take some blame to myself, for though I was in the house every day I never saw him. It was never suggested that I should see him. He was a delicate man, as you know, but not precisely an invalid. I took for granted that he had his little regimen of health and would follow the simple rules of life I had laid down for him years ago, even though his wife was not there to see that he did so. A man who had such a narrow escape of death as he had six years ago, might have been expected to be ordinarily careful. He seems though to have been unable to minister to himself, and, when his wife's sudden indisposition deprived him of her care, he had nothing to do but die.

"I am anxious about his wife. Poor Alice Arne has for months, perhaps for years, been on the further side of the line that divides sanity from insanity. I see now that some talk that she and I had one day, was symptomatic of the mental illness from which she is now suffering. She had lately displayed an abnormal abhorrence towards her husband, much at variance with her almost equally abnormal previous devotion to him. This abhorrence is due to an extraordinary hallucination of which she is possessed, in connection with the phenomenon of his recovery, six years ago, from a seemingly fatal complaint.

"As far as I can gather from her disjointed talk she appears to be the victim of a singular delusion. She actually fancies that she has undergone the penalty due to an impious prayer. She thinks that her husband's very preservation and after-existence was the result of the granting of her petition to God—a petition answered in the letter but not in the spirit—on that day, six years ago, when he was given up for dead! Nevertheless, the non-professional observer would not call her insane. It is monomania, the result of severe shock. There is no very obvious disturbance of the nerve centres.

"I attended Arne, as you know. It was a most extraordinary case as I thought at the time, but his recovery was quite within the limits of medical science, although it strained them to an unusual degree.

"Mrs. Arne's hallucination is the outcome of an imagination wrought upon by grief, and resting nevertheless upon a scientific basis of fact—a fact quite extraordinary enough to seem a miracle to a scientifically-ignorant woman—this strange resurrection of her husband! She believes that his spirit was indeed parted from the body and never returned to it, but that her fervent prayer was answered, inasmuch that, though the spirit passed for ever, the body remained on earth, and mocked her with a life in death. For these last six years of their life together he was not, in her estimation, a human being at all, but a ghost of a new sort—a sort in which I think not a few scientific pioneers may be tempted to believe—not a disembodied spirit, but (if one may be allowed to coin a word) a *disinspirited* body. The old-fashioned ghost, to speak with ordinary scientific scepticism, is not a true objective phenomenon, because we neither see nor hear it, we only fancy we do—our senses are only illuded into believing that we see or hear it—but a body that lives and moves without a soul; of that sort of ghost many examples may be in our midst at this moment, and about us all day long!

"When I told her he was dead, she showed no emotion—not even surprise. It was as if she had expected it. She was calmer by then, and she was sitting sewing in the window-seat of her room. She drew her needle out before answering, then she raised her eyes to mine.

"'Yes, Doctor, I gave him up. I could not bear it any longer. I am wiser now. I will pray no more foolish prayers!'"

THE LONG-DISTANCE TELEPHONE
ROBERT BARR

Cassell's Magazine, 1900

As the great steamship slowly approached her berth, Philip Radnor eagerly scanned the sea of faces upturned towards him. The end of the wharf was covered with a dense mass of humanity gathered to welcome friends or relatives arriving by the incoming liner. The drab-coloured crowd was lightened here and there by the white blotch of a fluttering handkerchief, and these blossoms of greeting increased as the thronged vessel neared the pier-head.

There was a pang of disappointment in Philip's heart when, at last, he was forced to admit that the face he sought was not among those on the wharf. He had written to his wife from London telling her not to meet him; the journey would fatigue her; the ship might be delayed; the day of arrival was likely to be stormy at that season of the year; there had been many good reasons why she should not come, yet now her absence caused a feeling of loneliness which almost overpowered him, accentuated by the fact that every other passenger seemed to have one or more friends awaiting him. The enthusiastic gathering below Philip faded from his vision, and he saw instead a boudoir sixty miles distant; a room he contrived especially for his wife, so that she might communicate with him or he with her at any time when space parted them. From a table by a window that looked out over a green lawn arose the crooked arm of the first long-distance telephone that had been installed in the environs of New York. The instrument had been accounted a wonder in its time, for the far-away voice filled the hushed room in ghostly fashion, and one sitting even in the furthest corner

might listen and hear. "The Room of the Whisper," his wife called
this enchanted chamber; a remote nest in an unfrequented part
of the large country mansion, and from its seclusion all outer
sounds were ingeniously excluded, so that it became an awesome
oasis of silence except when animated by that thin spirit-like voice
from afar. From within this room his wife could talk with him in
confidential manner, free from all likelihood of being overheard.
The sixty miles between them vanished into nothingness, conjured
away by that greatest of all necromancers, the modern inventor,
and they spake together, voice to voice, as if distance were non-
existent.

And now it seemed to Philip that space had been annihilat-
ed for sight as well as for sound; every detail of that apartment
was visible to him; all the little touches of decoration by which
a woman's hand humanises, and even emparadises, the four walls
that encompass her. So real was this inward vision that the more
stirring panorama passing before his vacant eyes made no impression on him; the hoisting of the gangway; the slow procession of
the passengers ashore; the greeting of friend and friend; and it was
not until his respectful steward spoke twice to him that he awoke
from his dream. The luggage, it seemed from what the man said,
had been carefully deposited under the letter "R" on the wharf.
The steward emphasised the pains he had taken to see that everything was in its place, so Philip, coming to a realisation of his
obligations, gave the steward the expected fee and went down the
gangway, the last and alone.

The returned traveler did not go to his belongings, as every
other passenger was doing, but hurried to the nearest public telephone station. He knew the town well, even that part of it nearest
the steamer landings. He closed the door of the narrow telephone
room behind him, rang up the central station, became connected
with the hamlet of Pleasantville sixty miles away, and asked for
number 351.

"Hello, hello," he cried, "is that 351? Is that you, Nellie?"

"Yes. Oh, Philip, you have returned. Are you well . . . are you
well, my dearest husband?"

"Never was better in my life, Nell. Had a splendid trip over, too. The only drawback was that you were not with me. And how are you, dear girl? That after all is the main question."

"It is well with me also, Philip, but I have been anxious, anxious about you."

"Nellie, my darling, you worry too much. What on earth could happen to me during a mere trip to England? Why, it's like crossing a ferry. If I had been sure of two such quiet voyages I would have insisted on your coming along. It was like midsummer both going east and coming west, which is amazing at this time of the year. England was a little damp and dismal, but not so much as I expected, from all I had heard. I believe the journey would have done you good, even though I should not have had much time to spend with you in London. I was kept pretty busy."

"I am sure of it. Then you have heard nothing from Herbert?"

"No. What has he been doing?"

"He was to have met you when your ship came in. You saw nothing of him then?"

"Nothing. He probably found something more interesting to do in New York than wait some hours here at the wharf. I don't suppose Herbert is any too anxious to meet me."

"Philip dear, you are mistaken. Will you forgive me, you who are so tender and kind to me, if I speak to you of my only brother, and ask you to bear with him even when you do not approve of his actions?"

"Why, certainly, Nell, but then you must admit that only brothers are in the way of being spoiled by the over-indulgence of sisters who can see no fault in them. Anything I have ever said to or of Herbert has been for his own good, although that was not likely to be the view he took of it. However, the office of candid friend is a thankless one at best, even, or perhaps I should say especially, with one's own brother-in-law, so I shall abandon it as far as Herbert is concerned. What has he been doing? He's been up to something, I know, and you want to shield him. Come, Nellie, what's the trouble?"

"Oh, Philip, Philip, see how quick you are to think evil of him, and that from the slightest of hints! Your frame of mind towards him seems to be naturally antagonistic, and I can't understand why that should be so. If anyone made some vague suggestion coupled with the name of your wife, you would not ask at once what wicked thing she had been doing, now would you, Phil?"

"Certainly not. I'd knock him down. I see what you mean. I am rather prejudiced against Herbert, and so may do him a little less than justice. All right. I promise to reform, and if I disapprove of anything he does, I shall at least have the grace to keep quiet about it. Does that satisfy you, little girl?"

"Not quite, Philip. Are you angry at my persistence? Dear Philip, be patient with me. You have always been patient and forbearing where I was concerned, and oh, Philip, how much I love you—you dearest and best—"

There was a break in the voice and a silence. The man stood listening, wrinkles of perplexity coming across his brow. He murmured to himself, "What on earth has that young villain been doing? No State's Prison offence, I hope. Yet there's something behind all this, or Nellie would not be so worried about it that her first words to me on landing are of that scapegrace. I see how it is. He was to have confessed to me when he met me. Perhaps it's all in the papers, and she wanted him to tell me before I heard of it elsewhere, and he, the coward, has been afraid to face the music. So poor Nellie takes it all on her shoulders as she has so often done before. Curse a poltroon anyway."

"Are you still there, Philip?"

"Yes, dear. Nellie, hadn't you better tell me everything? I have seen nobody, and haven't even bought a paper. What is it that is troubling you, my dear wife? It is better that I should know it now, for I'll have to know it sooner or later, and what appears very serious to you, is very likely not so, in reality. In any case you may be sure I will do everything I can for you or yours."

"Oh, I know it, I know it, Philip. Herbert promised me to meet you and tell you everything there is to be told. I should rather that you heard it from him."

"But he is not here."

"He has missed you. You will find him when you go back to the wharf. He promised me, and he will keep his promise."

("I wish I were as sure of that," muttered the man to himself.)

Then aloud he said through the telephone:

"To tell the truth, my dear, I was watching for you, and when I satisfied myself that you were not there, I fell into a sort of day-dream thinking of you. Everyone else had left the ship before I did, and it is quite probable that at this moment Herbert is searching the boat for me, or more likely standing guard over my baggage. He will know I must return to clear it through the Customs. I give you my word that I will receive him with all kindness and consideration, whatever has happened. And now haven't we said enough of Herbert? Tell me something about yourself. Did you miss me much while I was away?"

"Oh, Philip, you can never know how much I missed you. But I must not say that—"

"Why not, my dearest girl? I am delighted to hear you say it, for I can tell you I missed you every moment of the time I was away. I wanted to consult you about everything. Then there were so many incidents to tell you, and you three thousand miles away. I will never take another such trip without you, but all past regrets are swallowed up in the present delight of getting home again. You can't imagine what a thrill it gave me to see flat old Sandy Hook once more. I had no idea I was so patriotic. Thought I was a mere soulless business man. with an office on Broadway, and you can't expect much sentiment on Broadway, can you? But after all, there was no concealing from myself the fact that the foundation of all my delight was the ever-nearing prospect of seeing you again."

There was no response over the long-distance telephone, and after waiting a few moments, Philip spoke again.

"Can you hear me, Nellie?"

"Y—yes."

"Nellie, you are thinking of your brother and not of me."

"Philip, dear, I am thinking of both of you, hoping you will be friends. There is just one more thing I would like to say about Herbert, and that will be the last, for I fear you will become impatient with me, and no wonder, but you are patient, patient, patient, Philip. A successful man sometimes makes small allowance for one who is not successful. But achievement does not always follow merit."

"That is quite true, Nellie, still, after all, it sometimes does follow merit."

"Herbert has not been very prosperous in what he has tried to do, and his manner is against him. He seems sullen to those who do not know him very well, because he never has much to say for himself, but it is really diffidence and a lack of self-confidence. This makes me anxious that you should understand him and say an encouraging word to him now and then. Everything you touch seems to go so well that perhaps—"

"Now, Nellie, excuse me for breaking in on you, but that is a delusion which various other people labour under. There is no such thing as luck in business. At least, I don't believe there is. I was flung on the world at a very early age and had to sink or swim. I got very little help from anyone, and by-and-by I didn't need any help. You know the proverb about those who help themselves. I think Herbert would have done better if he had been assisted a good deal less. If he had known there was no one to run to when he failed, it seems to me he might not have had so much of what he doubtless calls ill-luck. This sounds harsh, but truth is often harsh, still for your sake, as I said before, I am more than willing to do all I can for him. Are you satisfied now, you sweet mediator between two stubborn men?"

"Yes, Philip, I am satisfied, if you will promise to say the kind word as well as do the kind deed. I never had any doubt about the deed, but I want it sanctified by sympathy—I—I wish you to think of him as my brother, and—and—see something in him of what you liked in me."

"Why, Nellie, of course, you dear girl. What a brutal tyrant I must have been to you after all, when you think you must plead with me like this. Good gracious, Nell, you frighten me. Have you been pondering on all my bad qualities ever since I went away?"

"Oh, no, no, Phil. Don't imagine such a thing. No one knows how good you are; no one appreciates you like your wife; always believe that, my own beloved husband. And now, Philip, let us talk more cheerfully. I fear you will think I am taking a very dismal strain with you, but I want you to be brave and happy whatever happens. Always remember that I shall be miserable if you are miserable."

"No fear of that, Nellie. My disposition is rather an optimistic one. I don't go half-way to meet trouble. Time enough to greet it when it comes, and to-day nothing could make me unhappy. The very sound of your voice thrills me with joy."

Once more there was a pause, and the receiver remained silent in his hand.

"You don't grudge me the hearing of it do you, Nellie? Well, I guess I had better go and see after my trunks, then I shall get to Pleasantville the sooner, and I can assure you the train will seem very slow that takes me out of New York."

"No, no, Phil. Don't go yet. I have so much to say to you. You have told me nothing of yourself. Has your trip done all you expected of it?"

"All and more. I came to London just in the nick of time. My visit there has proved a great stroke of fortune. I tell you what it is, Nellie, if the figure which I set five years ago as the limit of my ambition, as far as wealth is concerned, happened to coincide with the figure in my mind to-day, I have money enough to retire on. What do you think of that, my girl."

"That is splendid."

"What? Are you getting avaricious, Nellie? You never seemed to care much for wealth before."

"What I am thinking of is your success. That is what pleases me, and, Phil, it ought to please you."

"It does, of course. But I expected that you would say now I've made my pile I should retire, as I promised to do. I thought to have quite a discussion with you on that point, for it seems to me a man at my age ought not to turn loafer. Do you mean to say you advise me to go on?"

"Yes, for a while at least. I think you do not sufficiently appreciate all that great and continued success in business should mean to a man."

"Why, Nellie, you surprise me. From what you said a few minutes ago I surmised that you imagined I had too keen a conceit of

my own prosperity and, therefore, an over harshness in my attitude toward the inefficient."

"I am afraid I do not make my meaning very clear—"

"Oh, your meaning is clear enough, but you are taking such an
entirely new road, Nellie, that you don't seem to have got accustomed to it yet."

"What I am trying to set forth is this, Philip. If a man has but
one interest in life, and that interest goes wrong, it leaves him
stranded, and he is in danger of becoming a wreck. I think a man
should not concentrate his hopes too strongly on any one thing.
If a person has several outlets for his energy and ambition, then
if one disappoints him he may turn with renewed strength toward
the others."

"I'm sorry to say I don't at all agree with you. The man with
too many irons in the fire is reasonably certain to find most of
them go wrong. I have but two interests in life, my wife and my
business, and the former is the more important, for the latter
exists merely because she exists. You surely cannot find any fault
with that condition of things."

"Ah, Philip, but I do. The game of business should be a most
absorbing game. It alone should be enough to absorb a man's
whole attention."

"Certainly. It does with many men. You can't possibly mean
that I should pay more attention to my business and less to you?"

"That is exactly what I mean, Philip."

"Well, of all complaints a wife ever made to a husband since
the beginning of the world, that is the most extraordinary!"

"Oh, do not think I am complaining, Philip. I have never complained of you. I merely wish to impress on your mind the fact
that the world is full of opportunities for a capable man. I use
business only as an illustration. There are many other pursuits—
well, politics, for instance. Why should you have ignored politics
all your life?"

"Oh, politics! Nellie, you are a constant surprise to me. No decent man ever went into New York politics without regretting it."

"It shouldn't be so, and perhaps you may be privileged to inau-
gurate a change. You spoke of the thrill you felt on the first sight

of your own land when coming home to-day. Don't you think your land has a claim to part of your time?"

"Oh, technically, I suppose it has. Still the country is getting on right enough. You mustn't believe all you see in the papers. I don't doubt but the fellows who are running New York are doing the business quite as well as I would do it. Perhaps better. I vote now and then, when I don't forget to register. I guess that's about all the country can reasonably expect of a busy citizen. You wouldn't care to have me run for office, would you?"

"Why shouldn't you?"

"One reason is that I would be defeated; would be snowed under, unless I could fix it up with the bosses, and that would mean bribery in some shape or form. Nellie, I don't think we'll go in for politics."

"Is there anything that would interest you except business and—and—your wife?"

"Nellie, my very dearest girl, you are incomprehensible. The whole trend of this conversation is that I should think less of my wife and more of anything else. Now this is simply treason to your sex, especially in an age when most men are so absorbed in other things that they give but little thought to their homes. Besides, this new and most unexpected departure of yours is out of all touch with both the precept and the example of your past life. I don't pretend to understand it, but I tell you honestly that the greatest pleasure I shall ever have is the meeting with you after our first long separation. We won't talk any more about these new theories of yours, but I shall soon dissipate them when I get you in mv arms. So good-bye, Nellie, for an hour or two."

"Good-bye, Philip."

"And say, Nellie, tell them to send the fastest team of horses to meet me at the station, so that there will be no lost time. I'll get there by the first train I can catch, and will telegraph as soon as I know which one it will be."

"Good-bye, Philip, my dear, dear husband."

Radnor rang off the telephone, and hung up the receiver. He paid at the office the long charge made for the use of the instrument, then hurried toward the wharf where his unclaimed effects still lay.

"It is that young whelp of a brother," he said to himself angrily as he strode along; "he has done something this time which causes her to imagine I will think less of her. She always was a sensitive girl. Well, I'll straighten the matter out, if money can do it, as, of course, it can. Money will do anything in New York; thank Heaven."

All the incoming passengers had gone, and the great barn that covered the wharf was almost deserted. Already the unloading of the huge steamship had begun, and noisy, powerful cranes were swinging bulky wooden boxes ashore. A young man stood among the one heap of trunks and portmanteaus that remained in sight. There had been no trouble with the customs officer. He had chalked the unlocked pieces and had accepted the card that bore the address of the absent man who owned them.

A deep frown marked Radnor's brow as he recognised his brother-in-law standing among his trunks, but he smoothed away the wrinkles as he noticed Herbert's attitude of dejection, which recalled to his mind the words of his wife and his promise.

The elder greeted the younger with apparent cordiality.

"Hullo, Herbert," he said, holding out his hand, "I must have missed you. I was the last to leave the ship."

"I thought I recognised you on deck, Mr. Radnor, but when I searched the vessel for you, I could not find you."

"No; I went to the telephone office and called up Pleasantville."

"Then you did not get my cablegram in Liverpool?"

"No. What was it about?"

"After it was gone, I thought I should not have sent it, but that—it does not matter. Nellie died the day you left Liverpool. She asked me to meet you, and—and tell you before you heard of it from anyone else."

"Herbert, what nonsense is this you are talking?" said the elder man, sternly.

The other went on, unheeding the question, speaking with difficulty, as one who had learned an intricate lesson and was repeating it by rote.

"I was to tell you how much she had wished to live until you returned, but—"

The young man faltered; the emotion he was visibly struggling to suppress threatened to overmaster him.

"Then who—who is in Nellie's room?"

"No one. She asked me to leave everything there untouched until you came back. I was to lock it and give the key into your own hands. Here is the key."

THE HAUNTING OF SHUDDERHAM HALL
ROBERT BARR
The Idler Magazine, 1906

I am by way of being a journalist, and for many years have occupied a position on the staff of the "London Daily Herald," which, as everyone knows, is a newspaper of the older sort, supposed to be more respectable than enterprising. I have brought to the editor many startling stories, which have never been put into type, for the traditions of the journal are against all sensation, and it was at first rather provoking for me to see a vivid article that might have made a column and a half cut ruthlessly down, if used at all, to a few lines embodying a cold statement of colourless fact. Still, I was always well paid, and rarely overworked, so I made no protest, but soon got into an easy way of writing the kind of thing the proprietors wanted in a formal style that pleased them.

My occupation brings me into communication with all sorts and conditions of people, because one day I may be investigating a crime, and another day finds me a guest at a political country house. It was on one of the latter occasions that I became acquainted with Lady Betty Briscoe, the owner of Shudderham Hall and the broad lands surrounding it, in the county of Essex.

It will be within the memory of most people interested in such things that a number of years ago the Psychical Society became rather active in its investigations of the supernatural, inducing a number of distinguished men to visit certain houses reputed to be haunted and make private reports to the Society on whatever phenomena they encountered. I was younger and more credulous in those days than I am now, and I took a great interest in the proceedings which the Society had inaugurated. I became a member of that body, and thus, in semi-official capacity, took a hand in the search for ghosts, always hoping to meet some experience that would develop into an article, or perhaps gather enough material to produce a book. In this I was disappointed. Many a weary night I spent in remote and uncomfortable quarters, either with no result at all, or with an outcome that pointed plainly to fraud, detected in some instances, and in many others merely surmised. I came at last to the conclusion that wherever a house is said to be haunted, it is always to somebody's interest that the allegation should not be disproved. Often this person is the caretaker, who benefits by a good, comfortable, lazy berth, and does not wish it jeopardised through the incoming of a new tenant or owner. Be this as it may, I gave up my self-appointed, unprofitable task and resolved never to visit more of these houses, unless I could go unannounced. I must appear as a casual visitor, and not as an ostensible searcher into the under or upper world.

At the country house I have referred to my attention was drawn toward Lady Betty by her unceremonious leaving of the room while a narrator was in the middle of a ghost story. The talk had turned in that direction, and the lady, after listening for some time wearily, rose, shrugged her shapely shoulders, and, without a word, deserted us. The man who had been telling his experiences, seemed in no way perturbed by the implied slight on his powers of entertainment. He paused, smiled gently, and said—

"I had quite forgotten about Lady Betty's dislike of this subject."

Several persons, knowing nothing of the case, made eager inquiry simultaneously, and the man replied—

"The Briscoe family, time out of mind, has owned Shudderham Hall, a picturesque Tudor residence, alleged to be haunted. I don't know what the story is, and Lady Betty won't tell—indeed, it would take some courage to ask her. I don't suppose Lady Betty has any objection to ghosts except in their financial aspect. She will not live in The Hall, cannot let it, and must not sell it. The letting is said to be prevented by its evil reputation. I have never seen the place; but I was told it is rather out of repair, and a long distance from the nearest station, so the fault of its condition and situation is, perhaps unfairly, placed on the shoulders of the spooks. But, as I was going to tell you—" And he continued his own interrupted recital.

Lady Betty was a woman of forty or, perhaps, forty-five, with nothing old-maidish about her, her appearance being rather stout and matronly. She was good-natured, well-to-do, and very fond of motoring. I found her inclined to underrate her financial position, and to plead poverty, which in her case must have been largely comparative. The day after the ghost talk I put myself in Lady Betty's way, and we became acquainted. I nearly shipwrecked all my chances of future friendship with her by somewhat prematurely broaching the subject of the supernatural, for she at once turned away from me. But a journalist must be persistent if he is to succeed, and cannot afford to make too much of a seeming rebuff. I hastened to say that I quite agreed with her, and my object in mentioning the subject was that perhaps I might have an opportunity of effectually laying the alleged ghost of Shudderham Hall. This aroused her interest, and she turned and allowed me to proceed. I told her I was connected with the "Daily Herald," and suggested that, if an article were written about the historical old Hall, one might at the same time give a quietus to the ghost.

"I have hardly patience to talk on such a foolish subject," she said; "and would not, if the consequences to me were less serious. I have often thought of tearing down The Hall, and building with its materials a modern residence nearer the station. But nowadays property does not seem to belong to its owners, and what with falling rents and rising socialism I don't know what we landholders are coming to. If I touched the old Hall there would at once be an outcry that I was destroying something irreplaceable, which it isn't. As my ancestors built it, why shouldn't I destroy it if I wish to do so? Still, as I have no money with which to build a new house, there is little use in talking of pulling down the old one. It is this talk of ghosts that makes me lose my temper."

"Such talk is mostly irresponsible gossip," I hastened to assure her ladyship; "and, indeed, I am in a position to prove that, because for several years I spent much time investigating this subject, and never yet met anything that might be regarded as even a foundation for the stories told. Will you give me permission to visit Shudderham Hall?"

"Certainly. I shall write you a letter to the gardener, who will place at your disposal every facility for examining the place thoroughly."

I thanked her, and received the letter that afternoon, for, although I had not the slightest intention of presenting it to the gardener, I thought it best to hold such a document in case I was caught trespassing on the premises, and my right to be there questioned by some local person in authority. On reading the letter, however, I learned that Lady Betty's dislike of the subject of ghosts had kept her from mentioning them. The note merely requested the gardener to give me all the keys, together with any assistance I wished.

Shortly after this I was detailed to attend to a case in this same county of Essex which had begun to take a strange hold on the public imagination. A new reporter had been sent at first from our journal, but, as the extraordinary skein of circumstantial evidence began to unravel, it was seen that this might become an event of the first importance in criminal annals, so I was asked to take charge. I found the scene of the suspected crime a most lonely and forbidding spot. The farmhouse was ancient, but commonplace, and it was surrounded by a gloomy moat. The authorities were emptying this moat when I got there, with the intention of prosecuting a search in its slimy bed. I never was assigned a task I disliked so much. Day by day passed, but nothing was found bearing on the case. Yet I dared not leave, for at any moment a tragic discovery might be made. I went up to London every night and came down every morning, hiring a trap to carry me to and from the distant railway, but, seeing that this was likely to be a long job, I took my bicycle to the Essex station, and thus did not need to wait for the trap, as was sometimes the case.

The police found nothing in the moat itself, but they made the startling discovery that a trench had been dug which entered the moat, and had been filled up again, the surface of the filled trench having been thickly planted with shrubbery, evidently to conceal all traces of the trench—which it effectually did, until the digging of the side of the moat had disclosed the juncture. The authorities now determined to continue the excavating night and day, and I telegraphed to the "Herald" to send me a colleague to take on the night watch, suggesting the name of Rogers, if he were free. That evening Rogers came. He was wildly enthusiastic about the mystery, and thanked me for mentioning his name, which gratitude, considering what was ahead of him, seemed undeserved, for I was jaded and tired. The constant dig, dig, digging had got on my nerves. However, I said nothing to damp Rogers' ardour, but got on my bicycle and set off. I had determined not to take the train journey to London that evening, but to seek some cheerful country spot, if such was to be found, and stop all night at a likely-looking inn. I wanted a quiet night's rest, where the sound of spades would not mingle with my uneasy dreams. I rode through three villages, but the public houses in each seemed most unpromising. I stopped at one for a sandwich and glass of beer, but did not care to stay the night.

As night was coming on and no fourth village put in an appearance I began to get anxious about my lodging; so I got off my wheel at a wayside cottage to enquire my whereabouts, and learn what chances there were of my finding accommodation. The labourer who evidently lived there was leaning over the wooden fence smoking a short clay pipe. Numerous children played about him in the gathering dusk. In answer to my question, he slowly removed his pipe, and said he had no room for strangers, which fact hardly needed the stating when one looked at the children and estimated the size of the cottage.

"I don't know where there's room hereabout," he continued deliberately, "unless it's at Shudderham Hall, where there's a-plenty, but nobody wants it."

"Shudderham Hall?" I exclaimed, as a picture of the stout Lady Betty came before my mental vision. "Is that near here?"

He pointed across the fields towards what seemed to be a forest.

"If it was lighter you could see the chimleys atop o' them trees. Rare lot o' chimleys Shudderham Hall's got."

"How can I reach it?"

"The gate's about half a mile further on. There's big trees on each side of the road going up to it, so you can't miss it."

"They say the place is haunted, don't they?"

"I dunno."

"You don't believe there's ghosts there?"

"I dunno nothing about it. I look after my own business, and lets other folks look after theirs, and no ghost don't bother me."

"An excellent plan," said I. "Thank you very much, and good night."

I mounted my wheel, and, chancing the unlighted lamp (for the district seemed policemanless), made down the road. I did not intend to look up the gardener if I could help it. I had my suspicions of the gardener, and if I could enter the old house, and sleep there unmolested by ghosts or anything else, the chances were that stopping there another night with the gardener's cognisance, I might experience spiritual manifestations which would go far to confirm my surmise that their origin was human. This was the course I had hurriedly sketched out for myself during the brief ride in the dark from the labourer's cottage to The Hall gate.

The fine avenue of large trees so completely overarched the road from the gate to the house, and the foliage was so dense, that I felt as if I were entering a tunnel. The darkness of the highway was as nothing to this, so I dismounted from the bicycle and lit the lamp, although I was now on a thoroughfare where the law did not enjoin me to do so. It did not occur to me until afterwards that this illumination might attract attention. The road was rough and neglected, rain having furrowed it for months, and it had not been mended. I walked up to the mansion and found it was also a moated grange like the grim farmhouse I had left behind me. In the gloom I could not distinguish detail, except that of a very noble mullioned window, which extended from the ground to the roof, some of whose diamond panes caught a faint reflection of the light that still lingered in the sky. The avenue ended at the moat, and the black silhouette of this manorial pile, although completely surrounded by trees, stood nevertheless in an open space, extending, I should judge, to a couple of acres. The numerous clusters of twisted chimneys, outlined against an obscure sky,

gave a weird finish to the mass, which, with the faint phosphores-
cent-like glimmer on the huge window, was sufficiently uncanny
without them. I have since thought that perhaps the sickle of a
new moon might have given the scene a still more ghost-ridden
effect. An oppressive stillness surrounded the place; a stillness
that was accentuated rather than relieved by the occasional plop
of a fish or water-rat in the moat.

I wheeled my machine into an open outhouse, or shed, that
stood on the avenue side of the bridge, extinguished my lamp,
but took it off and put it into my pocket. I am a smoker, and was,
luckily, well provided with matches. I crossed the brick bridge,
and approached the dark house, and the more I diminished the
distance the less I liked my self-appointed task. If I had been sure
that one of the despised taverns I had passed early in the evening
was within reasonable distance I think I should have returned to
it. I had some thought of making shift in the outhouse with my
bicycle but that the heavy atmosphere and the lowering sky promised a rain storm before morning.

I tried to peer into the big window, striking a vesta and holding it to the pane, but I could see nothing. There was no opening,
so far as it was concerned. I groped cautiously along the front,
when suddenly my heart stopped, as a gruff voice said—

"What are you prowling about here for?"

The first action of my scattered senses, on hurriedly collecting
themselves, was to say to me, "There is the folly of lighting a lamp
and striking matches on such an expedition as yours"; their next
was to say aloud to the voice, "Are you the gardener?"

Although the man had startled me out of my wits, there came,
a moment later, a thankful feeling of relief that I had been caught,
especially as I had as much right there as he, and from the same
authority, as the document in my pocket would prove. If this man
was the producer of The Hall ghosts he would never again scare
me as badly as he had already done, should he march them on me
in battalions.

"I asked you a question, which you must answer before putting any of your own. Why are you here, and for whom are you
looking?"

"I suppose I am looking for you, although I haven't seen you yet. I am here by permission of Lady Betty Briscoe, the owner of this property, and I want supper and a night's lodging."

"If that is, the case—" He hesitated, and his voice was less harsh. "I saw your light among the trees. Then you put it out, and—well, your stealthy action misled me."

"It's all right. To tell the truth, I did not expect to meet anyone; and, if I could have found an entrance, I would have stopped the night and troubled no one."

"You did not expect supper in an empty house, did you?" The man's quite natural suspicions were by no means allayed, as was shown by his tone as well as his words. By this time I had lit my lamp, and I turned it full on him like a searchlight. I judged him to be twenty-five or twenty-seven years of age. He was dressed like a forester or game-keeper; I was not well enough versed in the differences of costume to determine his occupation. I thought he did not look like a gardener, although, by not denying the trade when I asked the question, I took his silence as a tacit admission. Whether it was the effect of the glare of the lamp or not, he wore a scowl the most forbidding I had ever seen on a human countenance, and I felt that he distrusted me more deeply than even the adverse circumstances of our meeting warranted. "What has this man to conceal?" was my thought, as I looked at him.

"You have, perhaps, a letter from her ladyship?"

"Yes, I have. Do you wish to see it now?"

"No. I will look at it in the house. I will lead the way, if you please."

We went round one comer of the mansion, to what I supposed was the servants' quarter, from one window of which a light shone, and this, despite the man's surly bearing, was a welcome sight, because I had had only a snack and a glass of bitter at one of the village inns on the way thither, and I felt the promptings of a healthy hunger. Since the encounter in the dark, one or two growls of distant thunder became audible away to the west.

"We will have a storm to-night," muttered my guide, as he opened the door.

I entered a sort of scullery paved with flagstones. A withered old woman was washing dishes at a sink, and did not look up as we came in. An inner door let us into what appeared to be a combined dining-room and living-room. A square uncovered table occupied the centre of the uncarpeted floor, and on the table rested an oil lamp. Seated at the table sewing was a young girl, with one of the most beautiful faces I ever saw. She rose to her feet on seeing a stranger, taken by surprise; and yet, from the lighting up of her lovely countenance, I thought that my visit was not unwelcome.

"My wife," said the custodian shortly to me. Then to her: "This gentleman comes from Lady Betty Briscoe. He wants supper and a room."

"I am sorry to be a trouble, and to come thus unannounced. I am not very hungry. I had a bite on the road. Anything will do. A bit of bread and cheese and a glass of ale, if you happen to have it; if not, water or milk. My tastes are exceedingly simple."

"Oh, it is not the least trouble," she said with enthusiasm, then checked herself, and glanced apprehensively at her husband, as if in fear of him, wondering if her response had been too cordial. Her husband's eyes were fixed upon her, and I guessed that they tried to convey some unspoken message to her, which she appeared to be too perturbed to comprehend, but stood motionless there, action arrested by the deepening frown on her husband's brow.

"There is bread and cheese and beer in the larder," he said at last.

"I will get them," she replied, in a trembling voice. His words seemed to dissolve the spell that temporarily bound her, and she disappeared hurriedly.

I jumped to the conclusion that the keeper was under no delusion regarding the nature of my visit, and that he had endeavoured to warn his wife not to be too loquacious. I also formed an opinion that she knew of the goings-on, disapproved of them, but was both helpless and frightened. My dislike for the man increased with every moment of our growing acquaintance, and this dislike was augmented by sympathy for a young girl doomed to live under such conditions in an environment so forbidding.

"I will look at the letter, if you please."

I took it from my inside pocket and handed it to him, thankful that it said nothing about ghosts, and yet certain that the night would not pass without manifestations of some kind which, the cautious thought came to me, I should be wise not to fathom too shrewdly. More and more did I come to the conclusion that the ghost-maker was not a man who would stick at trifles, if anyone was so unhappy as to cross his path. His next question clinched the matter, and I regretted a moment after I had given a heedless and too prompt answer.

"Does Lady Betty Briscoe know that you are here to-night?" he asked, after reading her short note.

"No, she doesn't. I could not fix a date for visiting The Hall when last I saw her. My calling to-night is purely accidental, and, as I told you, I did not wish to disturb anyone."

"Then no one knows you are here?" The question gave me pause. The man had spoken with what was almost eagerness for so cool a customer as he seemed to be.

"Oh, yes," I replied, nonchalantly, "the labourer at the cottage half a mile up the main road knows, for one, because he gave me the final directions that enabled me to reach The Hall."

He did not speak again, and did not return Lady Betty's letter, but placed it on a smaller table that stood against the wall, on which his wife had deposited her sewing when she left the room. Of course, I could not ask for its return, as it must be his authority for admitting a stranger should his action be questioned in the future. His wife came in with the food and drink, and placed them before me. It was not a sumptuous meal, but it was exactly what I had mentioned, and I could not complain if I did not particularly enjoy it. The ale was sour, the bread badly baked, and the cheese musty. I wondered if Lady Betty fared so badly when she visited her property. If so, it was no wonder she came seldom. I glanced across at the young wife who was standing in front of her husband.

"The tapestry room?" she murmured.

"No, the brown room downstairs," he replied. I fancied this answer disconcerted her, and that she was about to make some protest, but his intent gaze held her silent. Turning her head and meeting my eyes, she smiled uncertainly, and said, "I will prepare your room. I'm sure you must be tired after your journey," and with that she left us by another door that led to the main part of the house. I had finished my frugal meal, and the old woman came from the scullery and removed the dishes, leaving the keeper and myself alone together. Neither of us spoke, and it was at this point the disquieting idea came to me that it was not a ghost I had to fear so much as the host, and I regretted now that I had come entirely unarmed. I had carried a pistol on many other of my spook-hunting tours, and now that it lay in a drawer at home I feared I might have more need of it. I thought I would casually throw out an anchor to windward.

"As I told you, I came in a hurry, and am here rather by accident, so I find myself almost penniless. As I intend to leave very early to-morrow, and must buy my breakfast on the way, I should be much obliged if you would lend me a few shillings, which I will send back to you as soon as I reach town."

I could see by the partially-closed eyelids, and the cynical look which came to me from between them, that the man did not believe a word I had said—doubtless had discounted every statement I had made from the first.

"I have no money," he said, gruffly. "You did not expect to find money here?"

"I never gave the matter a thought till just now, when I remembered I might not see you in the morning."

He leaned forward, his right hand clutching his knee, his eyes now wide open, and almost sparkling in their fierce intensity.

"What *did* you expect to find here?"

"I expected to find an interesting old manor-house."

"Why?"

"Why? Because Lady Betty is very anxious to let it, and I thought I could be of some assistance to her in her object."

"I see." The man sat back in his chair again, and nothing more was said until his wife returned with a lighted candle in her hand. She spoke to me rather timidly: "Your room is quite ready, sir."

Her husband and I rose simultaneously, but he immediately sat down again, with some abruptness.

"Good night," I saluted him.

"Good-night," he grunted.

I followed the young woman down a very long passage which seemed to extend the whole length of the building. It was rather low, with beams overhead, and it had doors on either side at intervals. Except a few steps at the beginning, there was no stair visible, and my room proved to be on the ground-floor of the main building, and at the extreme end of the corridor. The door was open, and two candles were burning on the mantel-piece.

"I hope you will rest well," said my conductress kindly, more, I supposed, to make amends for the unsociableness of her husband than to give expression to a conventional sentiment.

"I shall be sure to," I replied, not at all so certain as I pretended; "and thank you very much."

"It is very quiet here."

"It must be."

"When did you see Lady Betty last?" she continued, fingering outside the door.

"It is some months since I saw her."

"I suppose she is on the Continent now. She is very fond of the Continent."

"That I do not know. It is quite likely."

"I wish she would come and live here. It would make such a difference with people about. It is very dull. No one at all to speak to."

The husband came so softly up the hall that he startled me almost as much as when I first met him. He took the candle from his wife's hand.

"This gentleman will not want breakfast to-morrow," he said, civilly enough. "He leaves very early in the morning, and so should get to sleep as soon as possible."

"Good night," said the young woman, in a voice scarcely audible. Her face had become deadly pale, and her lips were so dry that she had difficulty in pronouncing the two words.

"Good night, madam, and many thanks for your kindness."

The man said nothing. They went down the hall together, and I closed and bolted the door. "What an unmitigated brute he is," I said to myself, for he looked as if he would like to beat her if he dared.

I now examined the room very thoroughly, as is the invariable custom with ghost searchers. There was no fear of the door; the bolts were strong and sufficient to keep out any ordinary invader. The room was panelled in some wood lighter in colour than either mahogany or old oak, probably cherry, or perhaps cedar. It was furnished with a large canopied bed, a great arm chair and several ordinary chairs, all of ancient fashioning, and somewhat threadbare in their covering. There were two windows: one looking to the north, the other to the east, for this was a corner room. The windows of iron with lead and glass latticework, opened inward with some difficulty, and I was rather dismayed to see stout iron bars across the opening, which made a prison cell of the room. Closer examination, however, showed the obstructions to be less real than I had supposed. The bars were so rust-eaten at the ends, that one of them came out in my hands as I shook it; so there would be no difficulty in making my exit that way in the morning, the room, as I have said, being on the ground floor. Inside I could find no trace of trap-door, sliding panel or other mysterious feature. There were no alcoves or recesses in the square bedchamber, and the bare floor seemed solid enough. The storm still held off, and the room proved very hot and close; but I was compelled to close the window because of the numerous summer insects that came in, attracted by the lighted candles. The only sound was a mosquito or two that hummed against the ceiling, and for them I blamed the moat. I had come of late to cherish a great dislike of moats.

Sometime during the night I was partially awakened by either the vivid flash of lightning or the heavy clap of thunder that followed. I remember dimly the roar of a tropical rain, and more thunder, and then I dropped off to sleep again, and the next thing I knew it was daylight.

I sprang up, opened both windows and dressed. What a difference broad daylight makes in a man's feelings and thoughts. All tragedy, and terror, and doubt, and suspicion dissolved in the clear healthy light of this lovely morning, which the night's rain had freshened to a cool deliciousness indescribable. My watch told me it was only a little after four o'clock. No ghosts had disturbed my rest, and the actions and manner of my reluctant host, which had seemed so sinister the evening before, now took on their proper perspective, and I laughed aloud at the fanciful deductions I had drawn from them. Of course, he might have been, and probably was, the origin of the ghostly gossip which existed regarding the manor-house, and it amused me to think that very likely he had gone through the whole ceremony, moaning or shuffling his feet along the polished floors, or whatever else he did when there were visitors, while all the time I was so sound asleep that I heard nothing. I had slept so well that even the fierce thunder had not the power to thoroughly arouse me.

I slipped out of the window, after drawing the bolts from the door and leaving some money on the table to pay for the trouble I had caused. I paused on the bridge and looked down into the clear water in whose depths numerous fish darted. Even the moat was alluring in the morning light. Its sides towards the house were built of brick, which was almost entirely hidden by a curtain of long green fronds whose slender ends trailed in the water, and sometimes a little shiver ran along the drooping curtain, as a frightened waterfowl, unseen, swam swiftly along the wall, disturbed by my presence.

I fastened my lamp to its place and wheeled the bicycle down the avenue. I felt quite as hungry as if I had had no supper at all the night before, and so made record time along the highway, until I came to an early inn with its welcome ham and eggs and coffee. Some days later the gruesome discovery was made in the trench of the moat farm, and then I was free to return to London.

I was talking with my chief about the tragedy whose progress I had watched for so long, and casually mentioned the night I had spent at Shudderham Hall. He became interested in my ghost-searching experiences, and as he was a man who did not believe in anything much except the "Daily Herald," he asked me to write an article on my researches, which would go to show that haunted houses were all a delusion. When the proof of this article came to me I posted it to Lady Betty at her town house, marking with blue pencil the portion which dealt with Shudderham Hall. I had written nothing about her servants, but merely stated that

I had slept all night in the supposedly haunted room, and met no more ghosts than I would have encountered in the Hotel Cecil. By return I received Lady Betty's thanks, and an invitation to breakfast with her next day but one, at the continental hour of twelve o'clock.

Lady Betty was very gracious, and asked me to take a spin with her in her newest automobile, after breakfast. As my afternoon was free I accepted her offer, and we sat down to a dainty meal. She was very much pleased with what I had written, and expressed her satisfaction that it was to appear in so authoritative a newspaper as the "Daily Herald."

"When did you visit The Hall?" she asked.

I mentioned the date.

"You did not use my letter. The gardener was here yesterday, and I read to him what you had written, but he said he had seen nothing of you."

"I did not intend to use the letter, but circumstances forced my hand. I found him a surly beast, and didn't like him a bit."

"Oh, he is uncultivated and boorish, rather than surly. But his garden is well cultivated, if he isn't, and that's all I ask of him. He threw no obstacles in your way, then? If you arrived near nightfall, I'll warrant you couldn't induce him to accompany you to The Hall."

"It was at The Hall I found him, or, rather, he found me. It was pitch dark, with a storm coming on, and when he spoke, he nearly frightened me to death. Still, I don't blame him, for he caught me acting suspiciously, and it was your letter that saved me. I was sorry for his young and pretty wife. I should say she has a hard time of it with terror and loneliness."

"Why, what are you talking about? His wife is older than I am, yes, and stouter, and has nine children."

"In that case it was not the gardener I saw. I thought as much at the time. He seemed to be more like a gamekeeper, or a forester. The man I am talking about is the resident caretaker of Shudderham Hall."

Lady Betty stared at me a few moments across the table, then she said very quietly, "Please tell me what happened from beginning to end."

At first she seemed startled, and bent eagerly forward; but finally a shade of weariness came over her face, and she leaned back, becoming more and more displeased, until I faltered, and stopped.

"I see your ladyship does not believe me," I protested.

"Who told you the story?" she asked.

"What story?"

"The one you have just been relating with such circumstantiality of detail. All that happened a hundred and fifty years ago. But I should not have interrupted you. I am anxious to know how you will treat the culminating point of the tragedy. The Betty Briscoe of that day had sent a young London clerk to The Hall. He was to act as steward or secretary, or something of that sort. The forester was madly and unjustly jealous of his young wife. He strangled the stranger with a garter, and his wife with its fellow, then cut his own throat with his hunting-knife. The stain is still on the corridor floor near the door of the brown room. How did you intend to treat that incident?"

I pushed back my chair and rose to my feet.

"I have the honour to wish your ladyship good-bye," I said, with formality.

"Stop, stop," she cried. "You cannot leave the affair at this stage."

"The affair, madam, must be left at the point where you doubt my word."

"Tut, tut; sit down again," she cried, impetuously. "A young fellow like you should not be so sharp with an old creature like me. I wasn't doubting your word, but I thought you were playing a joke on me, and I didn't like it. Give me time to collect my thoughts before snapping my head off. I think, after all, it's merely a coincidence. I imagine you went astray in Essex, and that it was some other manor-house you slept in. Essex has plenty of such places. There has been no caretaker in The Hall within the memory of man. No one will stop for any wages I am able to pay."

"You forget that I gave the man your letter, which would have had no effect with a stranger. Also the chimneys of The Hall were pointed out to me by a labourer not half a mile from your gates."

"Yes, you're right. I did forget. Very well. We'll motor out there together. Please don't object. You promised to motor with me, and we may as well go there as elsewhere."

"I am quite ready, and more than willing."

Our first stop was at the cottage of the labourer who had directed me to The Hall. The man came out, cap in hand. He did not recognise me, but I instantly recognised him.

"Bring the keys of The Hall, Peter," commanded Lady Betty, and Peter slouched into the house again.

"Is *that* your gardener?" I enquired.

"Yes. It was to him I wrote the letter, and, if you remember, told you where to find him."

The verbal instructions had escaped my mind. When the man came out again carrying a bunch of keys, I spoke to him.

"Some weeks ago I cycled here and spoke to you. It was then so dark we could not see the chimneys of The Hall, but you pointed to the place. I enquired about a night's lodging, and you told me there was plenty of room at The Hall."

"Yes, I remember you now, sir. Lord love you, you never went there, did you? I thought you were just getting at me, when you said you would go there."

"That's all right. I simply wanted to know if you recollected our meeting."

We left the automobile at the gates, in the care of the chauffeur, while Lady Betty and I walked up the avenue to the house. I carried the bunch of keys, and led the way, not to the front, as she directed me, but to the door by which I had entered the night of my former visit.

"You must follow in my footsteps, Lady Betty," I said, and she made no objection. At last I found a key that fitted the scullery door, and we went in. The next door was also locked, and as I tried key after key, I said, "There should be inside a large square table in the centre of the floor, and a small side table. Also four wooden chairs. To the righthand is a cupboard with—"

My description was interrupted by the opening of the door, and we found the room furnished as I had foretold.

Lady Betty said nothing, but she picked up her own letter from the side table, and after glancing at it, crushed it in her hand. I led the way up the steps and down the long low-ceilinged corridor, opening the door of the brown room. The bed was exactly in the state it had been left by me, and the opening of the door allowed the gentle breeze to fling toward us the hinged window with a clattering bang that made Lady Betty jump.

"I could not fasten the window from the outside," I explained, "and that iron bar gave way in my hands the night before."

"Here are six shillings on the table," whispered Lady Betty. She had broken out a fan, and was fanning herself rapidly.

"Yes. I left the money there to pay—" I paused, not knowing how to designate the beneficiaries.

"Oh, Lord!" cried Lady Betty, collapsing rather than sinking into the arm chair.

Shudderham Hall may still be had at a very moderate rental.

THE IRTONWOOD GHOST
The Story of a Strange Haunting
ELINOR GLYN
Pearson's Magazine, 1911

I

Mrs. Charters arrived at Euston in plenty of time for the 2.30 train to Ileton. She was a woman who was well served, and her footman had already got her all that she required, and she retired with a paper to the farther side of the compartment.

"You need not wait, Thomas." she said. "There will probably be no one else getting in, and it is a corridor train."

So Thomas touched his hat and left.

Just before the guard gave the signal to start, a man—evidently a gentleman—opened the door of the carriage and entered.

He had been walking leisurely up and down the platform—and if she had known it, had observed her maid and footman, looked at her luggage, and ascertained her destination. It was the same as his own—Irtonwood Manor, that really charmingly romantic old place Ada Hardress and her obedient husband had just taken from the Walworths for a year.

"It is too exquisitely ghostly, pet!" she had written to Estelle Charters. "Creaking paneling, underground passages, haunted library, and a big cedarwood bedroom where the White Lady appears. There is no electric light, and a person with your sensibilities can be perfectly certain to receive a thrill! Come and spend Christmas with us!"

And Mrs. Charters had accepted—won by this alluring description—and was now, the day before Christmas Eve, on her way thither.

She was a tall, slender woman of twenty-eight or thirty, perhaps. She was not beautiful. but every single thing she put on seemed to enhance her grace. Rather plaintive and distinguished refinement appeared to be the note which first struck strangers about her.

That bore, Algernon Alexander Charters, had joined friends in another world some three years before this Christmas Eve, leaving his widow most comfortably provided for. Only an unpleasant jar had happened, not more than a week ago. The family lawyer had written to inform Estelle that there might be serious trouble ahead, and it might even eventualise in her loss of most of Algernon Alexander's money if a certain marriage certificate could not be found. The whole fortune was being claimed by a descendant of the great-great-grandfather, who contended that Algernon Alexander himself had enjoyed his ten or twelve thousand a year unlawfully.

It appeared that somewhere about 1795 the rich Alderman Charters' son, delighting to move in circles above him, had contracted a marriage secretly with the daughter of a decayed noble, who would have none of him!—and the lady, regretting her mistake too late, had denied all connection with him, and willingly relinquishing her son, whose existence she had concealed, and of whom she was ashamed, she had retired with her father to Italy, and there a year or two later had died, the wife of an Italian count!

The abandoned rich City husband had apparently taken the casual behaviour of the noble lady in a philosophical spirit, doting upon her son to whom, although he married again, and had a number of other children, he left the bulk of his great fortune.

These second family seemed to have been complacent people, and had accepted their fate. But now one of their descendants had come forward and claimed that, the will of John Charters expressly stating, "To my legitimate eldest son and his heirs," with no name given, the property should come to him as the lineal representative of the eldest son of the second family, there being no proof to be found anywhere of the first marriage with the Lady Marjory Wildacre.

Mrs. Charters thought of all these things as she sat in the train. Her attention had scarcely wandered from them even as she glanced up at the intruder in her carriage, but she did casually notice that he was a thin, dark man with something rather attractive-looking about him. And after a while she became conscious that his eyes were fixed upon her, and she felt compelled to look up.

They were too close together, the orbs that met hers, she decided, though their size and shape left nothing to be desired. She had a foolish shiver of foreboding and dislike as she turned away and let her mind revert to the ceaseless question of where on the face of the earth this certificate could be—and how were they to find it.

Presently the stranger leaned forward and said, in a most cultivated voice, which yet had a foreign accent somewhere lurking in the background:

"You are Mrs. Charters, I believe? We are both going to the same house. May I introduce myself, I am Ambrose Duval—I am afraid, not quite an Englishman!"

His smile was so pleasant, it made you forget the sinister impression left by his eyes.

Mrs. Charters was of the world and not easily disconcerted.

She bowed politely, and a conversation began, in the course of which it became apparent that Mr. Ambrose Duval (such a name, it reminds one of "Claude," she thought!) had met the Hardresses abroad, and had renewed his acquaintance lately, and was coming down now to this Christmas party.

Nothing could be more polished and smooth than his manner; it had that easy gliding from one subject to another, which makes so agreeable a conversationalist. He skimmed all sorts of interesting topics, and at last arrived at English architecture.

"Irtonwood is a very romantic old place, Mrs. Hardress tells me," he said. "A fine specimen of Tudor style, with additions of Jacobean. I am longing to study it. Do you know its history?"

"Not in the least," Estelle replied. "My friend, Ada Hardress, merely wrote I should be certain to see ghosts! I love the thought of them, although I have never been fortunate enough to encounter one, have you?" and she smiled her fascinating, elusive smile, that was half melancholy and half gay.

Sir George Seafield, who had already arrived at Irtonwood earlier in the day, thought Estelle Charters' smile the most divine thing in the world, but then he was in love—resentfully so at first, then resignedly, and now abjectly!

Ambrose Duval, on the contrary, mused: "She is no fool for all her gentleness, it is a capable mouth, perhaps her innocence about Irtonwood is all bluff, and she is bent upon the same errand as myself. I must lose no time."

By four o'clock, when they had reached Ileton, they had each taken stock of the other.

"He makes me creep down my back," was Mrs. Charters' comment, "although I do feel he is attractive."

Some more guests got out of another carriage, and there were greetings and chaff, and the whole party entered motors and were whirled to their destination.

Here all was holly and mistletoe and everything to make a real English Christmas. Huge log fires in every grate, and quantities of wax candles tried to make up for the want of electric light.

Nothing could have looked more like a story-book description of things as they were once in the good old days.

Ada Hardress gave her friend a most gushing welcome, and contrived that Sir George Seafield secured a chance for a tête-à-tête word in a suitable window-seat, as they drank tea.

"You were cruel to me," he said, looking devotedly at the lady of his heart with his keen blue eyes—"promising to be at the junction and never turning up by that train—I came down from Scotland on purpose, and thought I should have been allowed to take care of you from Crewe here."

"I can take care of myself," she protested softly, "and I found I wanted to shop this morning before I left."

"You think you are capable of looking after yourself always, under any circumstances, I suppose," he hazarded.

"But, of course.—when I feel I cannot, then I shall tell you," and she smiled.

"I pray fate to let the chance come sooner than you think!" he announced fervently.

But at this pious hope Mrs. Charters only looked sweetly disdainful, and changed the conversation to less personal things.

"You won't be a goose, darling, and snub Sir George to death, will you?" Ada Hardress begged, as she took her friend up the stairs. "You are so provoking with your aloof air, and now wanting to rest until dinner when he is dying to talk to you!"

But Mrs. Charters was unimpressed.

"I am really tired, Ada—and it does Englishmen good to be made to wait. I learned that in America," she said. "Algernon took me there when I wanted to go to Rome, but I never regretted it—I acquired so many hints from those clever women— Oh! what a heavenly place," she added, when they got to the Cedar chamber which had been allotted to her, "fancy it's not having been spoilt in these modern days!"

For it was all paneled and hung with faded orange silk in its three tall windows and capacious four post bed.

And presently, when Mrs. Charters was tucked up upon the rather hard sofa, preparing to have a siesta before dinner, she felt at peace with all the world. It was not long before she was sound asleep and here she had a strange dream.

She felt herself unaccountably moved and perturbed—she had a sensation of breathless, wailing tension, while she stood in some dark place, and suddenly it seemed as though only one spot in the blackness became illuminated, and then she saw an old escritoire. There was nothing else, no furniture, no room—nothing but this old writing bureau standing in space, and there, on it, lay unfolded a yellow parchment, upon which seemed to have fallen some drops of fresh blood!

Estelle woke with a sensation of supernatural excitement and fear. And then she reasoned with herself. Could anything have been more foolish! A dream with no incident, no personages, no action, to cause such a feeling! There was something uncanny about it though—what if the room were really haunted! She was not sure she liked it after all!

She got up quickly and rang for her maid, glad to have company and lights. But all the while she dressed, she saw nothing but the escritoire, the parchment, and the three drops of blood.

"You look pale and pathetic," Sir George Seafield told her, with tender anxiety in his voice, as they went in to dinner. "What has happened. I want to know?"

But it was not until about the first *entrée* that he could get her to unfold her dream.

Her other hand neighbour was the attractive half-foreigner who had come down in the train with her, and who had no intention of allowing her legitimate partner to monopolise the conversation. He listened attentively as she described minutely the strange incident to Sir George, bending forward so as not to lose a word, much to that gentleman's disgust.

"I hate the brute!" he thought. "Why cannot he attend to the woman he has taken in?"

"What a very strange dream!" Mr. Ambrose Duval said. "And where was the escritoire—you have no idea?"

"Not in the least," replied Estelle. "It was all in space—but why the blood?" And then a thought struck her. "Of course!" she exclaimed. "This is some vision sent to tell me where I am to find a most important document—how stupid of me never to have thought of it before!"

"A document?" both men asked; but while Sir George's eyes only expressed deep admiration for the lady herself, Mr. Ambrose Duval's had a concentrated eagerness to hear her words that was arresting.

"Why should this interest him so?" wondered Sir George, and it caused him to feel puzzled and irritated.

Mrs. Charters was no chatterer and not in the habit of imparting her private affairs to strangers, so she laughed and changed the conversation now to lighter things, dividing her time equally between the two men until the ladies rose to leave the room.

Sir George Seafield was incensed. Why had his good friend Ada Hardress asked this foreigner to Irtonwood? and why had she put him next to Estelle, the lady of his heart?

"I believe she is rather drawn towards the jackanapes," he thought angrily to himself, and with difficulty kept from sparring with him as they sat over the port.

"Ada, where did you meet Mr. Duval?" Mrs. Charters asked, as a group of women hung over the big drawing-room fire. "He seems an interesting creature."

"Doesn't he!" several of them chimed in.

"Mysterious and delightful," one affirmed.

"So good-looking," another announced.

"His eyes are too close together," old Miss Harcourt said in her sententious way. "I shan't play bridge with him."

"We met him in Hungary last summer," the hostess at last got in—"It seems absurd, but he was an hotel acquaintance, only he knew such a lot of people we did, he seemed like an old friend, and we saw him often, and he was always cheery and nice. He has relations in England that he has come to look up. I am so glad you find him attractive—I do myself! He has been too charming this last fortnight when we were up in town for Christmas shopping, he had just arrived from Paris and I have never had so delightful a companion, so I asked him down for Christmas. He said he would be lonely, and is so absorbed in the study of old houses."

Then someone began to play the piano and the group broke up, and soon the gentlemen joined them, and a general move to the big oak-paneled hall commenced, when the younger members started a valse, while the "fiddlers three," who had come down from London to entertain the Yuletide guests, played merrily.

Sir George Seafield was detained by his host for a second, and had the chagrin to see Mrs. Charters whirling in the arms of the foreigner! He shut his firm jaw with an ominous snap.

"I am dashed if I'll put up with it," he muttered, and went and claimed the next turn the moment the pair paused for breath.

"How cross you look to-night, Sir George!" Mrs. Charters said, as they danced, "My last partner was so agreeable and sympathetic!"

"I want to wring his neck," was all the answer she got. And then he added, as they stopped and wandered off to a distant sofa in the gallery, "I am sure he is up to no good, I'd watch the silver if I were Jack Hardress!"

"It is really remarkable to what depths of spite men will descend about one another," Estelle laughed as they sat down. "No woman would be so transparent, and all just because Mr. Duval is a foreigner and has good manners and does not show—moods!" And she leaned back provokingly among the cushions.

"You like him?" Sir George asked indignantly and then aggrievedly—"but anyone can see that!"

"If you are going to be unpleasant." Mrs. Charters said. "I shall leave you and dance with him again, he valses divinely."

Sir George's eyes blazed.

"If you do, I *will* wring his neck—I could easily," he blurted out.

"Absurd brute force!" and she smiled plaintively—"Englishmen are so crude."

"How you do tease me—Estelle—" Sir George said, and then stopped suddenly.

"Who told you you might call me that?" Mrs. Charters frowned. "A piece of impertinence!"—but here her voice faltered, for she saw that her companion was no longer listening to her, his eyes were fixed with an intense interest upon a picture which hung upon the wall opposite them—the portrait of a lady in late eighteenth-century dress, with the rather high waist, and flowing while draperies, while her hair fell in ruffled, unpowdered curls. It was not by any celebrated artist; but was a pleasing picture, and, as Estelle's eyes took it in, she knew why Sir George was so absorbed—for it bore a most wonderful likeness to herself!

"By Jove!" was all he said.

"It certainly might have been painted from me," she allowed. "Who can it be?"

But they could not find out. Their host, whom they questioned, did not know—he happened to be passing at that moment and joined them with his foreign guest. They had only taken the place from the Walworths for a year, he said, and the Walworths had bought it just as it stood from someone else. It had changed hands once or twice, and he could not remember now who were the original owners.

"It is supposed to be a portrait of the ghost, I believe," he told them. "Some old retainer informed Ada when we came. The White Lady who haunts the library and the Cedar chamber—"

"Where I sleep!" cried Estelle with a note of distress. "Oh! Jack. I believe I am half afraid!"

"I'll come and watch outside your door if you are," said Sir George. "Then you can call me if you feel frightened in the night and I will tackle any ghost for you—I should glory in the act!"

"I do not doubt it!" laughed the host and discreetly walked on.

But Mr. Ambrose Duval stayed behind, examining every turn of the brush in the picture with a critical eye.

Estelle had grown very quiet, Sir George noticed—she suddenly felt again that strange sense of excitement, a cold, unpleasant feeling of tension and dread; and she looked up into his face with an appealing pair of soft grey eyes.

"Let us go and dance again," she said. "I want to get warm once more—I feel cold."

And Sir George joyfully encircled her slender waist and held her close as they rejoined the dancers and whirled about.

"Who sleeps next to me?" Mrs. Charters asked, as a laughing group of women went up to bed about one in the morning—but she heard with secret dismay that the only other room in this quaint square wing was a sitting-room with a little oratory attached.

"You have always said you adored ghosts and weird things," Mrs. Hardress said, "or, dearest, I would, not have put you in the Cedar room."

"So I do—of course," returned Estelle rather half-heartedly. She was a proud woman and ashamed to show her fears.

Everything looked most bright and comfortable when she got to her room, and her devoted maid had waited up for her, and now put her to bed with every care. So, tired out with her dance, Estelle forgot her sense of uneasiness and soon sank to sleep between the slippery, fine sheets, while the dying fire made flickering lights in the vast room.

But in the grey dawn she awoke in mortal fright, for she had dreamed again of the dark space, the escritoire, the parchment, and the drops of fresh blood.

II

Next day was Christmas Eve, and much occupied with all sorts of bygone amusements, in which a Christmas tree for the children figured in the late afternoon. Everyone was particularly gay and cheerful, only Estelle Charters felt heavy as lead. Her dream haunted her. it had certainly some meaning; it was the second time she had experienced it, and the certificate, the loss of which might make such a difference to her, could quite well look like the parchment on the desk. But why there should be any connection with it and this house, of which she had never heard until her friends had taken it, she could not imagine. And if there were some strange thread in it all, why should the picture of the ghost be like herself? The money she could be deprived of had been Algernon's money, and had not come to her through her own family at all, so it would be more sensible and seemingly in sequence if the ghost looked like him or one of her sisters-in-law?

But she could not shake off the unaccountable depression she was filled with, and she tried to divert herself with Mr. Ambrose Duval's inspiriting conversation, to the rage of Sir George, who had left Scotland on purpose to be present at this party, and press his suit, feeling full of hope that she would show him some grace. But, for some reason, all had been at sixes and sevens between them, and this hateful foreigner appeared to be the cause.

Towards the end of the day, Sir George's temper had got the better of him, and he had finally gone off and talked to another woman in pique and disgust.

And so once more the night came, and Estelle was left alone in the Cedar room.

Now the conduct of the foreign guest had excited suspicion as well as fury in the breast of Sir George; and he had watched him unconsciously most of the day.

"The brute" had come to Irtonwood with some purpose—he now felt sure of that.

Such extreme interest in all the rooms and the furniture was overdone, if it were really an innocent fancy for old things. The library in particular seemed to have attracted him, and he even contrived to be shown the famous Cedar chamber, while he said most insinuating and admiring things to its present occupant. They had gone there, a company of four or five, after lunch, old Miss Harcourt among them, torn from her bridge.

"I would not sleep here for the world," she said. "I wonder how *you* can, Estelle. You must have nerves of iron and a conscience of snow-like purity—it makes me creep even in broad daylight."

"I am not afraid," affirmed Mrs. Charters, raising her head.

From there the group had returned to the library, and here Mr. Duval pointed to an old escritoire which stood in one window, used now as a writing table. Its surface seemed a good deal warped from the sunlight, which had come in upon it, probably for many years.

"This could be as the one you told us about in your dream," Mr. Duval said, furtively watching her face.

And Estelle recognised that it was, indeed, the same, with a sharp thrill. But she laughed a little nervously as she evaded a direct reply.

Mr. Duval was examining it closely, passing smooth, finely moving fingers over all its sides and top.

"There is probably some secret spring." he said. "It would be amusing if your dream came true, and it disclosed the parchment and the drops of blood."

But for some reason Estelle did not wish him to find it—if there were any spring. She would examine it herself another time, with Ada alone.

And Sir George, watching now intently, felt all sorts of queer ideas come into his head.

By the time they said good-night, the feeling that there was something going on underneath grew so strong that he determined not to undress or go to bed.

"He is going to have a try at opening that old bureau, I'd make any bet," he said to himself. "And I'll baulk him if I can and discover what is up."

So he pretended to be tired, and go on to his room when the other men moved to the smoking room, which was in a side wing, after the ladies had left, but in reality he waited until he thought the butler would have extinguished the lights in the library and the middle part of the house. Then he lit his candle and softly crept down, and stretched himself upon a sofa rather behind a screen, while the dying embers of the fire shed a mysterious glow all over the rest of the room.

And in the Cedar chamber, Estelle, tired out and rather saddened at the estrangement which she felt had grown up in the day, between herself and her hitherto ardent, would-be lover, got hastily into bed.

It was her own fault she knew; she had been most capricious, and talked far too much to the foreign man, whom she realised now she rather disliked underneath. She had been foolish and nervous and jumpy to-day and she felt quite ashamed of herself.

But in a very short time she grew sleepy, and all became a blank, until, with startling vividness, for the third time the dream returned and to it was added a dim figure, which seemed to beckon to her, and compel her to rise and follow from her warm soft bed.

It seemed that she crept across the room to a panel beside the fireplace, fascinated, but without fear, following the ghostly shape which, when it turned its face, looked so strangely like herself. And the panel glided back, disclosing a dark opening, and still she was impelled to enter its black depths, and all the while, as she felt herself descending a narrow stair, a dim iridescence seemed, like a nimbus, to encircle the head of that faint wraith which was leading her on. Whither?

Meanwhile, in the library, Sir George was almost dozing off to sleep on his sofa in the shadow of the screen. The clock had struck two, and the fire had burnt so very low that hardly a glow now illumined the room; but a broad shaft of moonlight came in from the top part of the window, to which the shutters did not reach. It was composed of small panes, with a coat of arms emblazoned in the centre, and the beams of the moon threw some weird shades upon the floor and upon the old escritoire, which happened to stand in its path of light.

Sir George thought to himself that he had, after all, perhaps been mistaken. The foreigner had probably gone to bed with the rest, and he, too, would turn in.

Then, just as his meditations reached thus far, he heard the faintest noise of the door opening, and someone, with stealthy footsteps, cautiously advanced up the room.

As he sprang to his feet he felt, rather than saw, that it was Ambrose Duval; he, himself, was securely hidden in the black shadow of the screen.

The man went softly to the shutter of the moonlit window, and, with quiet, nervous hands, undid its old-fashioned bolt, letting in a still broader shaft of light, which now allowed every detail of the old bureau to be seen. Then he came eagerly to its side, and Sir George held his breath and leaned forward, not to miss anything of what might be about to happen.

Mr. Duval seemed to be feeling the lid, which he opened with care, and then a search began for the secret spring. And once or twice, as he looked up as if for inspiration, his face seemed like a fiend's in the ashen light.

At last he appeared to have discovered something—a drawer flew open with a jerk, and he gave a sharp exclamation of pain. Some part of the steel spring had evidently wounded his hand. But his hesitation was only momentary; with frantic eagerness, he now drew forth a roll from the secret place.

It looked to Sir George like an old yellow parchment, and as Ambrose Duval bent to scrutinise it, with devilish satisfaction upon his face, there dropped from the cut on his hand some drops of blood.

The scene was the exact reproduction of Mrs. Charters' dream.

This was the moment, Sir George felt, for him to interfere; but before he could take more than a step, he was arrested by seeing the thief raise his head, and then start and grow livid and shaking with abject terror, as he gazed into a far corner, the parchment dropping from his nerveless fingers back on to the old desk.

And Sir George, following the direction of his eyes, also experienced a thrill which, even in him, was not unmixed with something akin to fear.

For both men could just distinguish, slowly and noiselessly advancing towards them out of the shadows, from a part of the room where there was no door, the tall, slender figure of a woman, in a rather short-waisted white garment, with ruffled curls of unpowdered hair.

She seemed to be ethereal and unreal; but when she got into the moonlight the likeness was unmistakable, the face was the same as the picture in the gallery, which the host had told them represented the Irtonwood Ghost.

The great grey eyes were wide and staring, like the eyes of a corpse, and the whole figure moved slowly with a gliding motion unlike life.

"My God! Is it Estelle?" George gasped to himself, as he waited the turn of events.

If it were his well-beloved, then she must be walking in her sleep. If the denizen of some other world, then something strange and awful might develop when she got to the escritoire.

In either case his best course would be to watch and be ready to spring. For he fully realised the securing of the parchment was to Ambrose Duval, for some reason, a matter of desperate need.

The figure advanced, growing more clear as it reached the goal; Duval was now crouching, an almost inert mass, some paces back, in mortal fright.

The lady—whoever or whatever she was—put out a transparent-looking hand in the moonlight, and, seizing the parchment, was gliding back again from whence she came; but Ambrose Duval gave the hiss of a snake as he saw the precious paper being taken from his grasp, and, with a half articulate cry of rage and terror, bounded forward.

But Sir George was quicker than he, and, ere he could reach the ghost, or woman, he found himself pinioned in the Englishman's strong arms.

Then the two men struggled, Ambrose Duval with mad fear in his breast at this new foe, and Sir George with cool determination to frustrate his opponent's ends.

As they tottered together, they both saw, with an indescribable thrill, the figure disappear, as it were before their eyes, into the darkness of the wall.

And they knew they were alone.

Was she a ghost, or real flesh and blood? That was a question which neither could decide.

But now that there was no more reason to protect Estelle—if it were she—Sir George let Mr. Duval go.

He was breathless from rage and fright, and he staggered to a chair.

"How dare you attack me like this!" he exclaimed furiously, drawing a revolver from his pocket and pointing it at his foe.

But Sir George, far more perturbed at the thought of what might have become of his lady love, took no notice of him. He walked over to the fire and poked up the dying embers, which threw up a last small flame, giving enough light for him to find his candlestick, which he had put down beside the sofa in the gloom, beyond the shaft of moonlight. Mr. Duval followed him, still livid from fear of the supernatural, and mad with rage at his failure and loss.

"You shall answer to me for this, now, with your life!" he snarled.

"In that case you will be hanged for murder," Sir George retorted, coolly. "You had better go quietly in the morning, before I denounce you as a thief."

"I am no thief!" Mr. Duval protested, violently. "How dare you attack a guest in our friend's house in this murderous fashion! It is I who can denounce you. You must give me satisfaction for this!"

"I shall do nothing of the kind," said Sir George. "I should not think of dueling with a thief. Just take my advice and go in the morning without a scandal, and prosecute your scheming tricks elsewhere. I have seen all you did, remember, and can describe it well!"

Then the two men glared at one another there in the old library, the one candle illuminating their angry faces, and the great shaft of moonlight lighting the rifled escritoire. And then Sir George calmed himself.

"You can take what course you please," he said. "I have a pistol, too," and he drew his small Derringer from the pocket where he had been holding it. "I am rather a good shot sometimes, so we may each hit the other, but there is no use in it, and rats like you are fond of life."

This reflection seemed to carry weight with Mr. Duval, unflattering as it was. For it is quite one thing to shoot at an unarmed man, and quite another to find him possessed of a pistol, too.

With what dignity he could, Mr. Duval now drew himself up, and prepared to leave the room.

"You have won this time." he said, between his teeth, "but some day I will level things up."

"I am quite indifferent about that," Sir George answered, hurriedly. "Get out now, and get away by the earliest train, I shall give you so much start. Now I have other and more important things to do. Go!"

And he almost drove Duval to the door and up to his room. Then, when he had seen him safely shut in, he paused to think what was the next thing to be done.

To awaken Jack Hardress and his wife, and ascertain if Estelle was safe in her Cedar chamber, seemed to be the best move. So, after some difficulty, he found his host's apartment, and knocked firmly at the door.

"Yes, what is it?" Jack Hardress called out, sleepily.

And Ada's frightened voice piped, "Oh! who is there?"

Then Sir George explained in as few words as he could, when his host and hostess, clothed in dressing-gowns, appeared in the passage, and they all three, carrying lights, set off for the Cedar room.

But here was deathly silence, no answer came to their knocks, nor could they enter— the door was locked from within.

A sickening icy hand clutched at Sir George's heart. What had happened? Some ill had befallen Estelle.

"If we both rush the door together we can break the lock, Jack," he said, desperately. "We must not delay an instant—now!"

And the two men hurled themselves against the stout panels; but, though they shivered, they held. Then, with the strength of despair, Sir George made a rush by himself, and the bolt gave, and he fell headlong into the room.

But, alas! Ada's two candles, which she held high, revealed no occupant. The bed had been slept in and left hastily, the clothes were turned back, but there was no sign of Estelle!

The three people looked at each other with blanched faces—what mystery was here? Sir George began hastily to examine the walls. It followed, his common-sense told him, if the door were locked from within, his beloved lady had left the apartment by some other means. The windows were out of the question; they were too high, and, besides, were closed and the orange curtains drawn. There must be some secret panel, and Estelle must have walked in her sleep—but how weird it all was! And he was filled with dread and foreboding as he fell each part of the wall.

"We must discover the entrance, Jack," he said. "I saw Mrs. Charters—or her ghost—with my own eyes in the library and she disappeared at the end of the room."

Now, with terrified eagerness, the three set to work, feeling and tapping each cedar panel, while Ada Hardress called continually: "Estelle! Estelle! Answer if you are there and can hear us!"

But only silence greeted them.

And, as the hopelessness of their task made itself fell, a sickening fear grew and grew in each of their hearts.

What if she had fallen down some deep secret place—some oubliette—and were dead? They might pull all the house down, and yet be too late.

At last Ada, almost weeping from grief and fright, subsided upon the sofa, while her husband and Sir George, rigid and grey with anxiety, faced each other, to decide what to do.

"Wake the servants and send for a mason and carpenter," Sir George said. "And, meanwhile, can't we get an axe and some tools? I will tear the woodwork down myself, when I have an implement."

Mrs. Hardress went off to wake the household, and send for the required men.

"And get a doctor, too," Sir George called, and when some tools were found by a frightened footman, and brought, he set to work with such a will that at last a steel bolt was discovered, and the paneling giving way by the fireplace, a very small, narrow door was disclosed in the stonework. The bolts in connection with it were stiff and rusted with age, and how a delicate woman could have moved them was a profound mystery.

The door gave way without much difficulty, and here, by the light of a lamp held high,

the very narrowest passage was revealed, which in three paces developed into a stair.

It was so extremely narrow that Sir George was obliged to force his broad shoulders through until he came to the descent. Suddenly, at a sharp turn, he could see the steps rising again on the opposite side, but there, in the space beneath, lay the figure of a woman in white.

With an exclamation of anguish, he saw that it was Estelle— but was she dead?

He handed the lamp to Jack Hardress, who was behind him. and in a second he was beside his love, and had raised her in his arms with difficulty in the confined space; and even in the excitement, he noticed that she still clutched in her hand the paper which seemed to have been the cause of all the tragic events of the night.

He detached it from her fingers, and saw that the blood drops had smeared her hand, as he put the paper in his pocket and lifted her in his arms to carry her back.

A bruise marked where her forehead had struck a projecting stone in the wall: perhaps she was only stunned, and not dead! This hope gave him the strength of a lion, and he clasped her close. But their exit was no easy task; the space had been narrow enough for one person here and there, and was impossible for a man cumbered with a woman in his arms.

Jack Hardress retreated before them, holding the lamp high, and when Sir George came to a turn that he could not pass, he was obliged to lay his precious burden down, and let Jack Hardress pull her through by the arms. Then he lifted her up again. And so, at last, all three were safe in the Cedar room, where a thrilled and excited group awaited them, including the doctor, who had now arrived.

The room was cleared of all but Ada, Sir George, and Estelle's maid, while the doctor bent over the inanimate form. And, at last, he looked up and announced, "No—she is not dead," and never were more grateful words sent up to heaven than Sir George's fervent, "Thank God!"

She was not dead then, his darling, and soon she might open her dear eyes and look into his own.

He could afford to wait in the passage now, as he told the good news to the rest of the alarmed guests.

And presently the doctor and Mrs. Hardress came out, and he heard that his beloved was conscious, and rapidly recovering.

"She must have walked in her sleep," the physician said, "and her head struck a stone, but it was the stifling air which made her faint, though, no doubt, she was stunned, too, by the blow; if you had been an hour later in finding her, I think she could not have lived."

So, after all, there were rejoicings on that Christmas morning, which seemed as though it was going to dawn so tragically; and in the excitement of it all no one thought then to remark upon Mr. Ambrose Duval's departure by the one and only early train.

His note of farewell to his hostess was a masterpiece, and caused Sir George to smile, as she handed it to him to read.

Late in the afternoon he was allowed to see his sweet lady in Ada's own sitting-room, alone, and in peace. She was lying on the sofa with a bandage round her forehead, and her small face looked ghastly pale against the blue silk cushions, but her eyes shone and she stretched out her hands, as he bent upon his knees to be near her.

"George—you were good to me!" she whispered. "And I can't take care of myself—" But she could not say any more, because he stooped and kissed her lips. And for some while they were too happy to talk of even a subject so interesting as her dream and the adventure it produced.

But at last they became sane enough to examine the parchment, which proved to be the certificate of marriage between John Charters, bachelor, and Marjorie Wildacre, spinster, celebrated at a little village in Leicestershire, in the year 1795.

So the Irtonwood Ghost had stood Estelle in good stead! For here was her fortune secured beyond any doubt.

But who, then, was Mr. Ambrose Duval? and what was his connection with the affair? and why did Estelle, herself, resemble the picture of the Irtonwood Ghost? These were questions which it would take time to answer.

"Though what does anything matter," exclaimed Sir George, after a while, "since I have enough for us both? And since you cannot take care of yourself, and are going to let me."

It was not before the happy pair returned from their honeymoon that all the mystery was unraveled. The lawyers had been busy investigating the while. It appeared that Lady Marjorie Wildacre had lived at Irtonwood, which was her old home, her father having sold it when they went to Italy.

She had had a daughter by her second husband, the Italian Count, who eventually married the great-grandfather of Estelle, thus carrying the likeness into her family.

And Estelle often loves to weave a romance round her dream, and imagine how, influenced by this far-back ancestress's unquiet spirit, she must have been drawn to go to the Irtonwood Christmas party and participate in the events which followed.

"You see, George, she probably loved the Italian Count," Estelle told her husband, "and wanted their descendant, by him, to benefit, too. That is why she directed me. But I cannot help being sorry for poor Mr. Duval."

"Loathsome foreigner!" was all Sir George said.

His real name was Charters, and he was the claimant to the fortune; but he chose to take his mother's name—she had been a Frenchwoman—the better to pursue his investigations unsuspected.

He had got hold of some letter, among the papers of his branch of the family, which referred to the certificate being at Irtonwood, and Lady Marjorie's residence there; and, hearing that his chance acquaintances, the Hardresses, had taken this place, he cultivated them in order to have access for his search, determining, when he found the certificate, he would destroy it, and then with certainty prosecute his claim.

But Fate takes care of things, and arranges what she thinks best. And even the thoroughly English Sir George Seafield is obliged to own that there are more things in heaven and earth than are dreamed of in our philosophy.

Also Available

Coachwhip Publications

CoachwhipBooks.com

LONELY HAUNTS

Also Available

Coachwhip Publications

CoachwhipBooks.com

A HOUSE A-HAUNT

CLASSIC STORIES OF HAUNTED HOUSES,
HORRIFIC ROOMS, AND OTHER GHASTLY ABODES

Also Available

Coachwhip Publications

CoachwhipBooks.com

Also Available

Coachwhip Publications

CoachwhipBooks.com

STRANGE
HAUNTS

STORIES BY
F. MARION CRAWFORD &
H. B. MARRIOTT WATSON

Also Available

Coachwhip Publications

CoachwhipBooks.com

UNCANNY

UNCANNY STORIES AND
MORE UNCANNY STORIES
FROM *THE NOVEL MAGAZINE*

Also Available

Coachwhip Publications

CoachwhipBooks.com

CATS OF SHADOW,
CLAWS OF DARKNESS

Stories of Were-Cats, Ghost Cats,
and Other Supernatural Felines

Also Available

Coachwhip Publications

CoachwhipBooks.com

Bestiarium Cryptozoologicum

Mystery Animals and Unknown Species in Classic Science Fiction and Fantasy

Also Available

Coachwhip Publications

CoachwhipBooks.com